THE FIFTH FORCE

SHERRY D. RAMSEY

Ramsey, Sherry D., 1963-, author

The Fifth Force / Sherry D. Ramsey

Email: sherrydramsey@gmail.com

Web: www.sherrydramsey.com

Cape Breton, Nova Scotia, Canada

The Fifth Force

Print ISBN: 978-1-990178-19-1
Ebook ISBN: 978-1-990178-20-7

Love science fiction, fantasy, urban fantasy, mysteries, and fun genre mashups? Sign up for the author's VIP monthly newsletter and receive a free eBook! Visit http://eepurl.com/bCUWPX or scan the QR code at the back of this book to find the join link. My newsletter brings you new releases, updates, book recommendations, freebies, great deals and giveaways, and other fun stuff, so don't miss out!

DEDICATION

This book is dedicated to everyone with at least one unfinished manuscript lurking in a drawer or on a drive. You know who you are.

PROLOGUE

In every world, there exists the possibility of magic. Or magick, majik, ma'jique…well, you get the idea. It is a latent energy waiting, embedded in the elements in the first milliseconds of explosion and cohesion that signal the world's star-driven birth. It abides quietly in the earth, the water, the atmosphere, the cells of every organism. Until something awakens it, or someone discovers it.

Sometimes this happens early in the planet's life, sometimes late. Sometimes it never happens at all.

And sometimes it happens at exactly the wrong time, in exactly the wrong way.

On a small, insignificant planet, much like Earth but known to its inhabitants as D'sharu, the sapient D'sharians have been evolving for approximately fifty million D'sharian years. Like much of the universe's intelligent life, it had begun, far back in the unimaginably distant reaches of time, as a thick, somewhat repellent sludge. In response to some unknowable event, the sludge moved. From there it was, on a galactic scale, a quick progression. Cells divide, limbs develop; crawl out of the water, swing in the trees for a brief million years; stand up straight, discover fire, stagger through some version of an Industrial Revolution, and there you are. The people of D'sharu, now two and a half billion strong and readying themselves to launch into a magnificent new era of manned spaceflight.

The people of D'sharu have never heard of magic.

The people of D'sharu have never imagined gods.

Things are about to get interesting.

A BAD DAY ON THE FARM

ULRIC

Ulric Grivetton was having a bad day, despite it being summer vacation. It was another bad day in a succession of bad days, beginning what seemed like months ago but was, in reality, only about a week. Although the yellow-white sun of D'sharu sailed high overhead and warmed the world in a benign and loving fashion, Ulric found it difficult to appreciate. He was, at the moment, dangling from the peak of a twenty-five-foot high barn roof by his fingernails and a thin, desperate scrap of hope.

That was enough to make it a very bad day indeed.

"Eiric!" Ulric shouted, feet scrabbling the clapboard in search of a toe-hold. "Tiny Enos! Poppy! Where the burned biscuits[1] is everyone?"

It was unsurprising that no one had heard the crash of the paint-can hitting the crumbling cobblestones, nor the skittering screech and clatter of the ladder following it. The friends had scattered across the grounds of this dilapidated farm, effecting what small repairs and odd jobs they could in return for the pittance Old Mean Melvin deigned to pay them. Although Ulric suspected Eiric and Poppy had slunk out behind the storage shed to mess around a little. And Tiny Enos, supposed to be painting the other side of the barn, was no doubt hunkered under the shade of the front porch eating an early lunch. Ulric hadn't seen Natelie for over an hour; based on past experience, she'd probably become

---

1. Since D'sharians have no gods, their swearing centers around sex, bodily functions, and interestingly, food. While food is far from taboo on D'sharu, destroying or wasting food is considered extremely bad form and gives rise to some unique language conventions.

immersed in an idea for a computer game, forgotten they were working, and wandered home to write code for it.

Ulric knew with a gut-clenching certainty that without assistance in the next thirty seconds or so, he would fall from his precarious perch. He almost screamed, but he was scared the vibration would hurry things along.

Many diverse elements contributed to what happened in the next few moments. The strident urgings of Ulric's terror had worked his anger and frustration to a fever pitch. Unknown to anyone, least of all Old Mean Melvin, the farm was situated fortuitously (or not, depending upon one's perspective) in a yawning puddle of highly concentrated and unsuspected latent magic. It had been hibernating here—sulking, honestly—for quite a long time.

And serendipitously[2], at that precise moment, the next nearest inhabited planet had just been blown into its constituent particles by the machinations of its aggressive, unrelenting, and warlike inhabitants. In response, the thaumic force of that world—known in colloquial terms as magic—had mere seconds ago fled the planet like the proverbial rat from a sinking ship, and was in search of a likely place to relocate. Accounting for the myriad cosmic phenomena affecting the magical force's trajectory between that planet and D'sharu, D'sharu's axial tilt and rate of rotation, and the interference of something no one could have predicted, the magic would make planetfall in exactly 1.227 seconds, right here on Old Mean Melvin's farm.

In all the time Old Mean Melvin had owned the farm, and before that his father, Old Mean Harry, and landowners stretching down the long past, the property had never been anything exceptional or noteworthy. It was a commonplace farm, with a big barn for the cows and sheep, a few outbuildings for pigs and storage, and long stretches of more-or-less rickety fence. The weathered farmhouse could only be called ramshackle, the drive up to it was pocked and rutted, and the chicken coop balanced on three precarious legs and a pile of mismatched bricks. It was worn

---

2. For Ulric, perhaps; certainly not for a not-insignificant number of other people (where the word "people" is used in its broadest interpretation).

to the point of decrepitude, but as far as anyone knew, nothing unusual had ever happened here. The latent magic had never, in any way, made its presence known.

Until now.

With no one in the vicinity to help him, and the strength in his numbing fingers exhausted, Ulric lost his grip on the barn roof and fell.

In that strange and mystical stretching of time in which the mind can think of a thousand things whilst the body is occupied with just one—in this case, falling twenty-five feet—Ulric's thoughts bounced like a hamster on a trampoline.

How unfair that he couldn't get a better summer job than doing unappreciated drudge work for Old Mean Melvin!

How insensitive of Eiric and Poppy to sneak off together behind his back, when it was only a week since his ex-girlfriend, the luscious Mattie Allegra, had ditched him!

How this was all Tiny Enos' fault, because he should have been holding the ladder, and although he had pleaded a need to use the facilities, Ulric knew his best friend was sneaking an early lunch under the porch.

And how right now, he would give anything to avoid the sickening crunch that awaited him on the paint-and-manure-streaked cobblestones in front of the barn.

At the edge of his peripheral vision, a swallow darted toward the open barn door. Ulric made a fervent, hopeless wish that he could fly.

The extraterrestrial magic made planetfall.

The latent magic in Old Mean Melvin's barnyard surged in response. Not a particularly welcoming response, if the latent magic were honest with itself, but forces of nature were hard to deny, especially out of the blue.

A pliant cushion of nothingness caught Ulric in mid-fall, buoyed him up like a wafted feather, and then dissipated in increments, setting him down feet-first on the worn cobblestones with scarcely a jar. In the centre of a spreading pool of spilled red paint, of course, but with supreme gentleness.

And he understood the exact scientific principles of what had happened.

The intersection of the flood of gamma waves emanating from his brain with the influx of thaumic energy had created a discrete field between himself and the ground, exciting subatomic particles into an initial density equal to his own mass, then immediately decreasing in proportional increments, allowing him to continue a slow drift toward the ground until he touched down. Simple.

Of course, ten seconds ago, he hadn't even known some of those words.

Ulric gulped one long, shuddering breath, then dashed to the back of the barn, shrieking for his friends and trailing sloppy red-paint footprints.

Ulric found Eiric and Poppy just where he expected; behind the storage shed, clothes in mild disarray. They startled as Ulric stumbled around the corner, then relaxed.

Then startled again as Ulric, mad-eyed, screamed, "I fell off the barn roof!"

"Ooh, Ulric," Poppy observed, making wide eyes as she smoothed her glossy blonde hair.

Eiric plucked a stem of long grass and tucked it into one side of his mouth. "You did not."

Ulric, swaying on unsteady legs, caught Eiric's words as a physical blow. He staggered back a step. "I *fell* off the *barn roof*. Didn't you hear me?"

"Yah." Eiric reclined back on his elbows, regarding his friend with open skepticism. "So how come you're not bleeding? Where's your broken arm? Your cracked skull? You never fell off anything. You just want us to come back to work."

Poppy giggled and straightened her t-shirt. The sunlight glinted off an expanse of glittery sequins that made it entirely inappropriate for odd jobs, but somehow Poppy made it work.

Ulric's eyes seemed ready and willing to leap out of his head. His face suffused with an apoplectic crimson and he lunged at Eiric with sudden, wild fury. He dropped to his hands and knees in front of his friend with a guttural snarl.

"I fell off the flarking[3] barn roof," he hissed in Eiric's startled face. "And *something caught me.*"

"Ooh." Wonder hushed Poppy's breathy voice. "Was it Old Mean Melvin?"

Ulric turned his head in slow motion to stare into Poppy's wide, cornflower-blue eyes. Her lips trembled, as if in anticipation of his answer.

Ulric giggled. He rolled over into the grass as his laughter grew to a shout, legs flailing and kicking with each guffaw. Red paint from his shoes daubed the grass like drops of blood. Eiric and Poppy edged away with uncertain smiles. Tiny Enos rounded the corner of the shed, no doubt roused by the maniacal laughter. He stopped short when he saw them. Tiny Enos was not easily shocked, but the sight of what looked like a lot of blood gave him pause.

"No!" Ulric shouted, gasping for breath. He climbed to his feet and stood, panting. "It wasn't Old Mean Melvin who caught me, you nitwit. Not him, and not Tiny Enos, and neither of you, and not a conveniently passing farm animal. *I* caught me. *I* did. And I could even tell you how, because I have all these new words in my head, see?" He knocked a finger against his temple for emphasis, leaving red paint smears. His eyes dilated again as he stared at his friends, a wide unnatural grimace stretched taut across his face like the grin of a death's head. His voice dropped to a ragged whisper.

"I just don't know what they mean!"

And Ulric collapsed, face down in the sweet-smelling grass this time, oblivious to the confusion and fear on the faces of his friends.

After a moment, Eiric nudged him cautiously with a ratty-sneakered toe. Ulric emitted a soft groan, but didn't open his eyes.

---

3. The reader may believe that this word has a similar counterpart in the English language, and they may be correct. Or it may have a more innocent connotation on D'sharu; the editor makes no comment either way.

"Not dead, anyhow," Tiny Enos muttered. "What the flark was he on about?"

Poppy sat back in the grass and burst into tears.

Eiric smoothed a hand over his shock of short, dark curls, then stuck his hands in his pockets and shifted from one foot to the other, staring down at their prone friend. "Ulric said he fell off the barn roof. And I said, no he didn't, 'cause he didn't even have a scratch. Then he said he caught himself with a bunch of words he doesn't know."

Tiny Enos waited for more, but that seemed to be the entire explanation. He pursed his lips and blew out a long sigh.

"Help me grab him, Eiric. We'll take him home. Poppy, go tell Old Meanie we'll be back tomorrow."

Poppy's blue eyes widened in terror.

"If he says anything about it, tell him Ulric got hurt and we hope he'll be okay if we get him home soon. Maybe we won't have to take him to the hospital. He'll be too worried to make a fuss."

Poppy opened her mouth, perhaps to argue, but Tiny Enos turned away, struggling the boneless Ulric upright with Eiric's help. "Move it, and I won't tell your ma you were grassin' with loverboy here."

Swiping the tears from her face, Poppy turned and scooted toward the house as Eiric's cheeks stained bright red. Tiny Enos pretended not to notice.

Behind the pig shed on the other side of the farm, a woman stood in knee-high weeds, staring in pleased surprise at her hands. To a casual observer, they might have looked like very ordinary hands, but since only moments before they'd been pale, translucent, and more or less ghostly, to the woman they were quite extraordinary. She patted her curling dark hair and stylish leather jacket, and yes, it was all completely materialized, right down to her khaki pants now dusted with yellow pollen. She'd felt it, of course; the surge of the planet's latent magic. It was her reason for being here, after all, searching to see where it hibernated. She'd followed, with meticulous research, a long and complicated matrix of clues to track it here, to this remote and dilapidated farm. But she'd never expected this. The arrival of the extraterrestrial magic—now that was a complete surprise. And the fact that being at the confluence of the two had resulted in her manifesting *in toto* on this planet was a bonus.

A pair of mud-speckled pigs grunted in the nearby pen, nosing along the fence for overlooked slop tidbits. The woman leaned over and scratched the nearest one's back, marvelling at the feel of coarse tufts of hair and warm skin. She did indeed seem to be fully in the world.

Experimentally, she made a few mental calculations and murmured a combination of arcane words. In a blink, she left the pigpen, transporting to the road at the end of the farm's long driveway. There, her abrupt arrival startled a pair of geese and five chickens meandering in search of seeds and bugs. Only a fading green shimmer marked the spot where she'd stood in the weeds and scritched the pigs.

A slow smile bloomed across the woman's face, but her dark eyes were calculating. "Well, well. Most interesting." She must contact her colleague and see if he was still stuck as a mere apparition. With even one of them entirely corporeal, so many new possibilities presented themselves.

And with another flash of green and a cascade of sparkling motes of light, she disappeared again.

A Bad Day at NCDSF

Gammy

Elsewhere in and around the capital city of Neemar, other important things were happening. On the northern outskirts of the city, far from Old Mean Melvin's farm, stood the North and Central D'sharian Space Facility. In the central chamber of mission control, mounted high above the myriad consoles, computers, and ragged-nerved flight technicians, a countdown clock ticked with tangible self-importance.

Tension filled the room, an almost visible entity humming through the usual ambiance of burnt coffee, stale doughnuts, sweat, and yesterday's lunch. Men and women hunched with eyes fixed on pulsing screens, punching a key here or muttering into a mouthpiece there. Printouts fluttered on clipboards and pens scratched final reminders on notepads.

A man stood at the back of the room, on a dais with a commanding view of everyone and everything else. His name was Argit, and he was a short, rather stout man, though well-muscled under his yellow polo shirt with the embroidered NCDSF logo on the chest. His coppery hair struggled in the cause of camouflaging his mottled scalp, but his pale blue eyes kept keen attention on the room. When Argit spoke, he didn't need the mouthpiece that hovered in front of his lips, because every word came out in a bark that circled mission control without breaking a sweat and then did it again just to prove it could.

But he didn't bark or even mutter unless the tiny woman beside him ordered it. She wore a polo shirt that matched Argit's, as did almost everyone in the room, but hers had three tiny gold stars stitched in gold thread above the logo. The fluorescent lights glinted off those gold threads just often enough that no one ever forgot they were there.

Many people, on first meeting her, were reminded of a wizened ferret peering out from under a grubby floor mop. If that unfortunate image brought a smile to their lips, these people never met her again. Everyone at NCDSF knew her as Gammy. Gammy *was* mission control. And all the years she had put in at NCDSF, all the work, the yelling, the backstabbing, the long hours, and the unflinching personal compromises, had led to this moment.

The first manned flight to Agarabous, D'sharu's largest moon.

"All systems are go," came the tinny voice of an astronaut over the room's loudspeakers. "Ready for final countdown, mission control. I say again, we are go for final countdown."

Argit looked down at Gammy and raised his eyebrows. She nodded once, her face a composed mask and lips set in an unemotional line. Only the glint in her small, dark eyes betrayed her excitement. Her hands, clasped behind her back, were also sweaty, but no one could see that.

"Final checks, everyone," Argit bellowed. Around the room, voices sounded off in unanimous confirmation.

At last they silenced, and Gammy nodded again.

"Commencing final countdown," Argit barked. "Ready for liftoff in ten...nine...eight...seven...six...five...four...three...two...one...*ignition*!"

Switches flipped, keys depressed, computers hummed, chambers opened, valves fluttered, chemicals mixed, fuels ignited, smoke billowed, and a roar of anticipation went up from a hundred throats in unison. The faint voice of an astronaut yelled, "Bye, Gammy!"

When the smoke cleared, the rocket had not moved. It stood like an accusing finger on the launch pad, wreathed in sad wisps of dissipating vapour. Forlorn red lights blinked across consoles. Technicians stared in horror.

An astronaut said, "Um...what the flark just happened?"

Gammy stood like a statue for a long, long, heart-stopping moment. In utter silence, faces set, everyone in mission control swivelled to look at her. They swivelled away again after a glance at her stony expression, fixing their gazes on screens or dropping them to the floor. Argit shifted uneasily, as if hoping he wouldn't wet himself.

Gammy, her lips pressed into such a thin line that they almost disappeared into a disgruntled wrinkle, turned and stalked without a word out of the room and into her office behind the dais. Mission control erupted in chaos as the door closed with an eloquent, too-quiet *click* behind her. A hundred voices and a hundred computers tuned to the burning question of *what went wrong*?

No one took much notice of the thin, worried-looking man who sat for a long time staring at his computer screen without really seeing it, then without fanfare or a word to anyone got up and left the control room, too. He didn't go after Gammy, though. He was headed in a different direction.

Inside her office and away from questioning eyes, Gammy drew the blinds, poured herself two generous fingers of Black Angus Knockdown and sat down at her desk to drink it. Half disappeared in the first gulp. Her eyes drifted over the framed photos crowding the desk; herself with technicians, academics, astronauts, and politicians. She could trace the passage of years in the relentless greying of her hair and gradual shrinking of her always-small frame. Everyone smiled in the photos, but some of those smiles had been hard won. She swivelled her chair away from the desk and faced the closed blinds instead. Her fingers tapped a heartbeat rhythm on the side of the glass.

Her whole life. That's what had been tied up in that launch, only her whole life. Her entire, ruthlessly engineered life since she'd been two years old and her mother had shown her a moon. Under a violet sky spangled with stars, her mother had sung "Sparkle Diamond Moon" to her daughter in her sweet, lilting voice. Gammy had reached up a pudgy hand to grab the shiny, beckoning thing down from the sky and her mother had trilled a twinkling laugh. "When you're grown, sweet one, perhaps it will be within your reach." That's what she'd said. Imagine. What a dangerous thing to say to an imaginative, intelligent, bull-headed, terrible-two-with-a-vengeance, I-can-do-anything little girl. *You can have the moon.*

Well, she almost had.

True, she would not get there herself. She'd reconciled herself to that fact thirty years ago, when it became clear that her mother's prediction didn't allow for the slow pace of technology. But if she owned this desk when the first manned mission got there, she could justifiably claim that the moon was hers. Not the Shadow Moon; that celestial sphere made only rare visible appearances, orbited further away, and kept itself more mysterious. But Agarabous was within reach, solid and waiting for Gammy's astronauts to set foot upon it.

The worst of it was not knowing what in the world had gone wrong. *No, that wasn't the worst of it,* she amended, sipping the second half of the Knockdown more slowly and savouring its bite. The worst was not knowing what had gone wrong because she hadn't been paying full attention when the launch failed. She'd been standing there, sure, but she'd been distracted. Distracted from the most important moment of her life. Distracted by the semi-transparent apparition of a lumpy-faced man with wild, shaggy hair who'd floated—floated!—a few feet away from her on the dais, nodding and winking at her while the launch suffered its spectacular failure. Since no one else had shown any reaction to him at all, it followed that no one but Gammy had seen him.

She shook her head and swallowed another gulp of Knockdown, relishing the burn at the back of her throat. She deserved pain for her failure. When she spoke aloud, her voice was harsh. "Well, it's a flarking rotten time to be going insane."

"Oh, no, dear lady, please do not doubt the competence of your formidable mental capacities."

The male voice, softened with mild distress, sounded from behind Gammy.

She swivelled her chair back around again, although not with any speed. There was no imaginable situation that Gammy could not face with steel-hard complacency. If she hadn't screamed when the launch failed, no disembodied voice would cause such a failure of nerve now.

It—or he—was back. The apparition from the control room bobbed just above the leather-covered chair facing Gammy's desk, limbs arranged in a comfortable sitting position. His thick mop of white hair—at least, she imagined it would be white if it were completely materialized—still started at all angles from his head. He wore an old-fashioned robe-style garment, with delicate embroidery embellishments around the neckline and sleeves. His semi-transparency made it difficult to discern further details. He had configured his lumpy facial features into an attempt at an understanding smile.

"And why not?" Gammy had a knack for putting any statement to the challenge, often to the discomfort of her conversational partners.

The apparition took up the gauntlet, ticking items off on translucent fingers. "Because while I am visible only to you, I am nonetheless quite real and will prove it in due course if you wish; because your mental abilities are vital to your people at this time; and because I give you my assurance that all is not lost, and if you want to believe *that*, then you must believe the rest of what I tell you."

The apparition might have wondered if Gammy heard him. She gave no outward reaction to his words, but inside they had shaken her. Oh, he was good. He was very good. He'd hit her in the soft spot in the first round, and she hadn't even seen it coming. *All is not lost.* The one thing she wanted desperately to believe was that her dream had not slipped from her grasp. That the mission was recoverable. If he could promise her that, she'd believe in him, flarking right she would, and she'd decimate anyone who argued otherwise.

Gammy was still Gammy, however, and it would take more than a lumpy-faced, smooth-tongued apparition to alter that fundamental reality. "And isn't that precisely what I would want a figment of my imagination to tell me?" she asked, eyebrows raised. She drained the last of the Knockdown and set the tumbler on the table.

"I rather think your imagination runs on different rails." The apparition glanced around the cluttered office with its framed night-sky photos and rocket prototype schematics.

Gammy sighed. "And the nature of this proof would be...?" She let the question hang in midair, as gravity-defiant as her visitor.

He waved a hand in a delicate gesture. "Your glass, you may notice, is no longer empty."

Gammy reclaimed the glass and raised it for a wary examination. Two inches of a rich burgundy liquid now swirled inside it. Gammy sniffed, sipped, and grimaced. "Wine," she stated, "and a vinegary one, at that. If you want to impress me, make it good Black Angus."

Another wave, and the liquid swirled and darkened. Gammy tasted again. The Knockdown was indistinguishable from what she'd poured from her own bottle. Lucky for the apparition. Gammy hated wine.

Gammy shrugged. "So you have a trick. Or you can make me think you have a trick. I don't suppose you could come up with something a little more, oh, convincing?" With slow deliberation, Gammy got up, crossed the room, and topped up her glass from the Black Angus bottle. She did not offer her guest any refreshments.

The apparition looked disgruntled but unwilling to be deterred. "Your assistant; what is his name?"

"You mean Argit? Big boy, lots of muscles?"

"He stood beside you earlier."

"That's Argit. He has even less imagination than I do, if you're thinking of getting him in on this. Just a word to the wise."

"What if I got him to walk through that door on, say, the count of ten? Would that be sufficient proof of my reality?"

Gammy considered. After what had happened with the launch, there wasn't a soul in the whole of the NCDSF who would walk into her office uninvited right now.

She shrugged. "All right. Ten, nine, eight—"

The apparition didn't even flinch at her rudeness in beginning the count without warning. In fact, he did nothing Gammy could see. But as her countdown finished, the door opened and Argit took two steps into the room. He stopped, his face masked in confusion that quickly melted into terror. He blinked and stepped back to leave again.

"Wait a minute, Argit."

He stopped, looking unhappy. His mouth opened as if he might try to apologize, but no sound emerged.

"Do you see anyone else in this room?" Gammy demanded. The apparition still hovered, suspended above the chair, in full view of both Gammy and the hapless Argit.

Argit may have thought it was a trick question, or perhaps he was simply a cautious man. He took a good, slow, thorough look around the room before he answered. "Besides you, Ma'am? No, Ma'am. You. And me. No-one else. Should I conduct a more thorough search?"

"No, thank you, Argit. That will do. You may go."

And he did, with relief and alacrity.

"So." Gammy tapped her fingernails on the side of her glass.

"So," echoed the apparition. "Shall I begin?"

Gammy raised the glass as an invitation for him to proceed.

The apparition nestled itself more comfortably into the seat, although it still made no contact with the chair. "My name is Corax. And I'd like to ask you two questions at the outset."

Gammy shrugged.

"Does the word 'magic' mean anything to you?"

Gammy shook her head. "Never heard of it."

"And what about the word…'god'?"

"Sorry, no. Is this going to take long?"

"What about 'deity'?"

"No."

"Omniscient creator?"

"No, and that's more than two questions." She pointed a gnarled finger at the apparition. "Let's get to the part where my moon mission makes it off the ground."

"We shall, dear lady, in good ti—" Corax broke off in mid-word, cocking his head as if he had heard something. "I fear we are about to be interrupted, but rest assured that I will return as soon as—"

And he winked out, leaving Gammy alone with her Black Angus Knockdown and a storm of emotions. While she'd always considered the drink to be better company than most people, the sudden departure of her conversational partner was galling. She spent ten seconds in successive flashes of anger, wonder, relief, and despair, and a further twenty on crisis planning.

Then she bellowed for Argit. He re-entered the room, trembling but looking relieved to be answering an actual summons this time, and she dictated a brisk string of orders. *That* would take the control room denizens through the rest of the day and half the night. She would get answers, and she didn't need the help of some see-through street hack to do it.

When Argit retreated again, Gammy fetched the bottle of Black Angus Knockdown and set it on her desk. She had a feeling she was going to need it.

A Good Day at the Nursing Home

Nerlim

At the same time as Ulric was not-falling at Old Mean Melvin's farm and Gammy's moon launch was failing at NCDSF, an elderly man lay on his deathbed in the nearby city of Williget. At least, it was supposed to be his deathbed; he'd claimed he was dying for months now, but he still looked chipper enough to the long-suffering nurse. She'd ignored the call buzzer from his room for as long as her conscience would allow, but then with a sigh she'd straightened the cap on her carefully tamed mop of red hair and popped her head into his room to see if he'd finished his lunch.

He hadn't. He sat up in bed, longish white hair combed back from his prominent forehead, a ratty green fisherman's sweater bundled over his pyjamas. The lunch tray reposed on the bed table before him, mostly untouched. The nurse tried to backpedal, but he'd seen her before she could slither back to the relative safety of the nurse's station. His berry-blue eyes, still bright as a bird's, fixed on her, and he crooked a finger to bring her further into the room. She took a reluctant step forward.

"What's this?" The question trailed into a long, querulous whine as the old man poked at the contents of the bowl. His aristocratic long nose appeared to quiver with dismay. Next to a styrofoam cup of stingy, weak-looking tea and a wrinkled orange, the suspect food looked, admittedly, like day-old oatmeal. An unappealing beige skin had formed over the top of the substance.

"Fresh, hot oatmeal," answered the nurse, whose name was Millie, in a less than convincing perky voice. "Come now, Mr. Pettibone, finish it up. It'll do you the world of good."

"Oatmeal for lunch?" the old man asked in a voice threaded with suspicion.

"Your special diet, remember?" the nurse chided him. "For your digestion. Oatmeal is a wonderful treat at any—"

"It's yesterday's oatmeal," the old man said, the words so quiet it should have been a warning.

"Oh, no, Mr. Pettibone, they just—"

"YESTERDAY'S OATMEAL!" he screamed. "I wouldn't eat it then, and I WON'T EAT IT NOW!" With startling strength and agility in his skinny arms, he flung the tray away with such force the *clang* reverberated off the far wall. The plastic bowl spun in slow revolutions on the floor with a *whop-whop-whop* sound until it settled with a shuddering clunk. Above it, a sticky grey mass clung to the pale blue wall, inching its forlorn way downward like an indecisive jellyfish.

The nurse's hazel eyes widened, and her face shuffled through a quick series of transformations. For a heartbeat, she looked as if she might cry; then as if she might surrender to the inevitability of cleaning up after unpredictable old cranks; at last her chin firmed and her eyebrows lowered. Even the sprinkling of freckles across her nose stood out in defiance against the offences of this frustrating patient. She planted her fists on her green-uniformed hips and shook her head at him.

"You're not going to break me, Nerlim Pettibone." She spoke in a low, even voice. "You think I can't take it, that eventually you'll leave me crumpled in a chair, sobbing, but that won't happen. I'm close to the end of my endurance, but I'm not there yet. Not. Yet." Her voice was so quiet, she might not have been speaking to him, but to herself. Perhaps she had ceased to care if the man heard her or not.

The old man laughed then, soft chuckles that evolved into a stutter of convulsive chortles. He coughed, making a fist with one hand and pounding his chest until the paroxysm passed.

"I've always wanted to do something like that," he gasped, fighting to regain control of his breathing. "Was it convincing?"

The nurse, still glaring at him, didn't answer.

"Well, I guess it was," the old man said with satisfaction. "Don't begrudge it, Missy. I don't have many pleasures left, you know."

"Millie." The nurse crossed her arms and made no move to clean up the contents of the upturned lunch tray.

"Eh?"

"Millie. My name's Millie, not Missy," she repeated with asperity. "And I should make you clean that up yourself, you old faker."

"Now, Missy—or Millie, rather. I'm not strong enough to take on housekeeping duties, am I?"

"You were strong enough to throw your tray."

"A momentary rally. I won't be around long enough to worry about—*gaaaackck!*"

The horrid, choking gurgle in the old man's throat made the nurse rock back an involuntary step. Her patient's posture was as alarming as the noise. He sat straight up in the bed, stiff as a corpse, eyes bulging, mouth hanging open, face pale and transfixed.

With a pang of guilty relief, Millie took a further step toward the door to fetch the doctor. This must be the end, hastened along by the man's radical emotional swings in the past few minutes. It must be said that she didn't hurry, but glanced at her watch. Time of death—

"What the flark was *that*?"

The nurse put a hand on the doorframe for support and turned back to her patient. She didn't bother to conceal the deep sigh of regret that welled up from the depths of her being. Mr. Pettibone had come out of whatever brief fit had seized him and sat shaking his head as if trying to clear his vision. But he was smiling.

"Did you feel it, Missy?"

The nurse shook her head wearily. "Millie."

"Only me. Only *me*. Then I know what it was. But it can't be. *It can't be!*" The old man gave a few vigorous kicks at the covers and swung his legs over the side of the bed. His wizened feet hung a few inches above his seldom-used slippers and he dropped into them.

"Now, Mr. P—" the nurse began, but he waved her into silence with a peremptory hand.

"No, Missy—er, Millie. Don't try to stop me. I checked myself into this place, and I can rotting well check myself out again. Seems I can't die just now." He rummaged in the tin box with drawers that served as a dresser, tossing clothes and sundry belongings onto the bed in a haphazard jumble.

"I know, I know, you're disappointed to see me go—at least this way," he continued, flashing her a gap-toothed grin. "But what I've waited for all my life just happened, and I can't settle down and die right now. Everything's changed. *Everything.* There's work to be done, and I might be the only man on D'sharu who can do it."

Millie blinked, trying to keep up. "You waited all your life to throw a bowl of oatmeal at the wall?"

"No, no. After the oatmeal. The—whatever it was. The thing you didn't feel."

Nurse Millie still stood near the door, bemused, trying to process the change that had swept her patient. He seemed invigorated, almost younger. The whining, sniping, tired and wrinkled old man had disappeared, leaving a purposeful, energized, excited and wrinkled old man in his place.

He pulled off the sweater and his pyjama shirt to reveal a sunken chest strewn with sparse grey hair, although his shoulders were straight. Turning to the clothes piled on the bed, he picked up a t-shirt, pulling it over his head. Then he paused and looked over at the nurse.

"You know, Missy, you could come with me. I'm off on a grand adventure, and I could use a sidekick—in particular, one with medical skills. Are you tired of this boring drudgery? These complaining patients? Want to see the world? That red hair suggests you might have some gumption."

"I'm off to call the doctor and tell her you've cracked your egg at last," Millie retorted. "I'll be surprised if you make it past the parking lot. And yes, I have gumption. I am *not* cleaning up that oatmeal." With an audible huff, the nurse turned and left.

The old man chuckled to himself as he pulled on his clothes and retrieved his shoes from the excuse for a closet. Easiest way to get rid of people—suggest they do something they wouldn't dream of doing. "Ah, Nerlim old boy, you've still got your sense of humour. It's good to appreciate living again."

In the sickly light reflecting off the pale blue walls of his hospital room, Nerlim Pettibone, disgraced physicist and expert—as much as there could be an expert on something that didn't exist—on what he called the fifth force, bundled his belongings into a worn brown knapsack. As an afterthought, he took the blanket and pillow from the bed and crammed them into a plastic bag marked "Patient Belongings." Sleeping arrangements for tonight would be uncertain unless he could call in some favours or get quick access to his funds. He glanced around the room for anything he might have left, then paused to peer out the window. Beyond the boundaries of the city, high in the sky, clouds swirled and eddied in odd shapes and colours. He wondered if he was the only one who noticed those anomalies, too. It was an all-too-familiar sensation, that there was something apparent to only him, and hidden from, or at least unnoticed by, others. Tonight, those roiling clouds would produce a brilliant sunset, banded pink and mauve and orange, behind the mountaintops. People would notice *that*. Notice it, but rarely question it.

Nerlim Pettibone noticed things. And also asked the questions.

He sighed and grinned. Somewhere out there, someone had just used—that thing for which he had no word. A power whose existence he had suspected all his life, but never identified. A knowledge that had ruined his life and reputation, but could lead to the ultimate unification of everything. An ability that could change the world. A fifth force. He knew it was there; felt it like a coiled knot of possibility in his gut. He had never been able to awaken or name it.

But someone—or something—had.

Now all he had to do was find them.

He surveyed the room, plucked the wrinkled orange off the floor, and slipped it into his pocket just in case. Then he left, scurrying down the corridors before Millie could return.

Not Feeling Like Myself

Ulric

Ulric woke in his bed, lying on his back, with the cat curled up on his neck and a pervasive ache in his body. The ache he understood—hadn't he fallen off the barn roof earlier? But the cat...*now, what was wrong with the cat—?*

He didn't have a cat.

Arms flailing, he scrambled upright in bed, knocking the cat away. He gasped as pain lanced his limbs. Oddly, the cat flew off about a foot distant, then fell back against his chest with a light thump. Ulric tried to leap to his feet, got tangled in the blankets, tripped, stumbled, thudded into his wooden dresser and came face-to-face with the apparition of a thoroughly pissed-looking, wizened old man.

In his mirror.

The cat was not a cat, but a long, thick, trailing white beard that cascaded from Ulric's chin to his navel. He regarded his reflection with wide-eyed horror.

"How flarking long was I asleep?" he whispered.

Heavy footsteps sounded on the stairs. Sweat bloomed across Ulric's brow and pricked his armpits as he gaped around his room in a panic, searching for something, anything, that would make sense. The familiar room looked the way it always did. His single bed with covers askew. The desk piled with notebooks and gadgets. One bookshelf, crammed with fantasy novels, gaming tomes, and a slew of new space adventures. The closet door, half-open to an untidy tumble of clothes and shoes that he and his mother clashed over every laundry day. Everything normal. Everything except him.

Side effects of untutored magic use may include nausea, vomiting, fainting spells, dental inversion, tsunamic saliva, sudden hair growth, ocular implosion, or incontinence. Side effects may be minimized or reversed via psychic copula with a subject well known to the practitioner and the subject's expectationary memory or presumptive data concerning the practitioner. Oral recitation of the phrase {auxniox vibralata pi disfraz} with strong inflection on the "pi" completes the incantation.

The source of the words was unclear; they played in his head in a low, rumbling monotone, like someone reading an instruction manual. He'd never heard half of them before, but he also, incomprehensibly, understood what they meant and their purpose—the same as he had with the cure for falling. If he followed the instructions and spoke those odd words, the beard would disappear. He'd look like himself again. And with luck, the chance of inverted teeth or imploding eyeballs would be averted. Ulric shuddered at the possibilities. His bladder was sending him urgent messages that he ignored with resolute determination. There was no time.

The door handle turned with a click and a squeal of complaint from dried-out hinges. Beyond the door, Ulric sensed a brain; a brain which contained an expectationary memory of himself, and he constructed a psychic copula with it. It was laughably easy. It was terrifying. He had to pee with such intensity he could taste it, but he managed by force of will to hold on. Good, no incontinence, at least.

In a low, trembling voice, he repeated the prescribed phrase. "*Auxniox vibralata pi disfraz,*" emphasizing the 'pi' as instructed.

Ulric checked the mirror, slapping his hands against his chest and cheeks. The beard was gone! He looked like himself again! His hands shook so hard against the front of his shirt he might have been trying to restart his heart—if it wasn't already thudding around in his ribcage like a captured bird. The result of fear, relief, or more side effects? He pressed his hands hard against his breastbone to quell their shaking and concentrated on long, deep inhales and exhales.

The door opened and Tiny Enos poked his head around. His relief at seeing Ulric on his feet was obvious. "Hey, lazy arse, glad to see you're awake. I brought you—"

But Ulric didn't seem to notice the glass Tiny Enos extended. Unfortunately, he had also moved too far away from the bed for it to break his fall when he fainted again.

Tiny Enos regarded Ulric in silence. Then he fetched a deep breath himself and puffed it out. "Getting flarking boring, this is," he remarked to the empty air. With a resigned shake of his head, he pulled a blanket off the bed, dragged it over Ulric, and sat down to wait.

Ulric awoke with the sickening sense that not enough time had passed since he'd fallen into unconsciousness. To be honest, unconsciousness was fast becoming his preferred state. Consciousness offered too many perplexing challenges, and wrestling with them frankly sucked lemons. The sound of Tiny Enos' voice confirmed his fear.

"So, do you plan to tell me about it, or go to sleep again? It's a rotting bore sitting here watching you snore."

Ulric sat up too fast, and the room wavered. His muscles wobbled with alarming liquidity, but Enos thrust a cup of some foul-smelling concoction under his nose.

"Faint again and I'll pour this down your throat. Don't think I won't."

"I'm all right," Ulric sputtered as his eyes watered. He pushed the cup away with one hand while making a surreptitious beard check with the other. Thankfully, his chin felt smooth and bare. He stifled a gag. "What's in that cup, anyway? The smell would wake the dead!"

"I told my Ma you had the flu; this is an old family recipe. She brewed it right up for me." Enos flashed an evil grin. "Worst thing I've ever tasted, and you don't want to try it."

"Enos," Ulric said in a thick, urgent tone, "how do I look?"

Tiny Enos cocked his head and regarded his friend with narrowed eyes. "You mean right now? 'Cause when I first came in, you looked like yourself. After you passed out, you sort of had a beard for a minute, but it disappeared again. Lucky it was me in here and not Eiric and Poppy, or you would have heard them screaming all the way out to Old Mean Melvin's farm. What's going on?"

Ulric turned to check the mirror. He was himself—almost. He looked older, as if he'd gained six months or a year. His skin had cleared up and his chest had filled out a little. Overall, Ulric liked the look. It was difficult, however, to like it much without understanding it even a little.

"Trouble is, I don't know," he muttered, more to himself than to Enos.

"Eiric said you fell off the barn roof, caught yourself with some strange words, and started acting crazy."

"That's...surprisingly accurate."

Enos snorted. "Sounds like maybe you went crazy first."

Ulric looked at his friend. "But you saw something weird when I was sleeping, right? So it's not just me. I need you to believe me."

"Well, I saw something," Enos allowed, sitting back on his heels and setting the cup of awful-smelling liquid on the dresser. "But you'll have to explain to me what that was."

And because Enos was a stolid, unimaginative, but loyal friend, and he had no one else to turn to anyway, Ulric did.

When he finished, Enos raised his eyebrows. "So you're saying you've developed some weird...powers or something; but you don't know what they are, what they do, or where they come from."

Ulric nodded. "Or why. There's something else, too."

"Go ahead. I'm past shocking."

"You see these new curtains Ma put up for me because of the moon launch?"

Both boys looked around at the curtains in question, a space-fever-inspired design of moons and stars on an undulating purple background. The comforter on the bed was the same design.

"Ya, so?"

Ulric hesitated. This was hard to talk about. In a rush he said, "So, I have this idea I'd like to take them down and make some kind of robe, or cape, out of them."

Enos made no comment, but lifted one bushy eyebrow.

"And maybe," Ulric added in a musing, dreamy voice, "a hat, too? A tall, pointy hat. That would go well with the robe."

"Anything else?"

Ulric was silent for a beat before he nodded. "I want a...a stick. Some kind of tall stick. With one pointy end and a...a glass ball or crystal or something on the other end. It sounds strange, but it feels right."

Tiny Enos considered the curtains before looking back at Ulric.

"I have a bad feeling about this, and I'm not good with sticks. But where's your Ma keep her sewing machine?"

An hour later, Ulric marvelled at the revelation that his friend, Tiny Enos, was an accomplished tailor. Together they had pulled down the curtains, hauled up his mother's sewing machine, and at Enos' direction, begun cutting and pinning. Following Enos' instructions, Ulric stood like a mannequin several times while Enos fussed over the fit or the cut, but he soon learned not to complain or to comment that this or that was "good enough."

"I can fix your clothes proper, or I can break your head," Tiny Enos growled at him around a mouthful of pins. "Your choice."

After that, Ulric said little unless Tiny Enos asked for his opinion. He watched with a growing mix of excitement and trepidation as, under Enos' deft fingers, the star-flecked robe and hat took shape. From time to time a small part of his brain wondered what in the name of spotted bananas[1] had happened to him, and what he would tell his mother about the curtains. But that voice grew steadily fainter as his brain filled with the rich stream of new words worming their way into his consciousness. He longed to try out one or two to see what would happen, but the echoes of those potential side effects stopped him. He should wait at least until Tiny Enos finished the sewing.

At one point, Ulric asked, "Where did you learn to do all this?"

Enos didn't look up from the zigzag finish he was applying with great care to the hem of one sleeve. "Ma. You remember she takes in sewing

---

1. Bananas offered a particularly diverse array of swears, as they could become progressively more dire as the fruit over-ripened. Thus "spotted bananas" could become the worse "black bananas" or the ultimate "rotten bananas," depending on the severity of the swear required.

from time to time. If she has too much on the go, she gets me to help her. Always has done. Sewed my first blind hem before I even started school," he said with a touch of pride.

Ulric shook his head. "And you never said?"

Enos quirked an eyebrow up at him. "And what would Charlie Fritter and his boys have to say about me sitting at a sewing machine? Imagine they'd have asked me to sew this button on, or fix the hole in those jeans?"

Ulric nodded. "S'pose you're right." Charlie Fritter's[2] gang had struck fear into the hearts of many kids tougher than Tiny Enos, who, for all his size, had no reputation as a brawler. *But now*, a little voice in Ulric's head suggested, *we could take a good strip off the likes of Charlie Fritter, no questions asked*. Before Ulric shushed the voice, it had outlined the means for this strip-removal in fine detail, and Ulric had to agree that it would be effective. Not something he'd ever *do*, of course. But certainly effective.

And even fun.

Ulric wasn't sure where that notion had come from, and he wasn't sure he liked it.

"I'm going to say they're done," Enos announced with unabashed satisfaction. "Here, try 'em on."

Shy in the moment without understanding why, Ulric turned his back to his friend and slipped the robe over his head. It settled around his body with a sensation of rightness so strong it constricted his chest and pulled at his gut, in much the same way the sight—the mere thought—of the delectable Mattie Allegra had once done. While Mattie had unnerved him, however, the robe seemed to elevate him, and set him down in a new place in the universe, a place where he was at home. He stared at himself in the mirror. Enos came up behind him and lowered the pointy hat onto Ulric's head. Something in his brain *pinged*.

Oh, yes. This felt right.

---

2. We all know a Charlie Fritter type, don't we?

"This is amazing." Ulric turned to view the outfit from all sides, even looking over his shoulder at the back. "You nailed it. Absolutely nailed it."

"Will you...er, have to wear 'em *all* the time?" Tiny Enos asked after a pause.

Ulric's first instinct was to say *yes, of course*, but then he imagined striding up to Old Mean Melvin's back door dressed like this, and he reconsidered. He couldn't very well scoff at Poppy's choice of work attire and then show up at the farm in this. "Probably not *all* the time," he said, although it was almost painful to admit it. "Just for, say, special occasions, or...or if I had to, um, meet someone important..." His voice trailed off because to be fair, he couldn't imagine who that important person might be or what the occasion might signify, but still...

"It's just good to have them here if I need them," he assured Enos.

Tiny Enos heaved a vast sigh. "Good then. So you'll be at work tomorrow? Because Old Mean Melvin's going to be mad as a wet owl if we don't show up. Falling off the barn roof will only go so far with him. And we still have to finish painting the barn."

Ulric nodded, his pointy hat bobbing gently. The notion of taking it off made him squirm inside, but Enos was right. Until he knew what all of this meant, he would have to go about life as usual to the best of his ability. That meant going to work, hanging out with his friends, and telling his mother about the curtains. *Something* about the curtains, anyway. They went to take the sewing machine back downstairs and he closed the door behind him. He'd put that part off a little longer.

Co-opted by a Dog

Wint

The thin, worried-looking man who left Mission Control after the dramatic launch failure still looked worried six hours later. In fact, his anxiety had blossomed so that he now looked even more worried than earlier. His name was Wint Astriminaud Usborne, which had concerned him for a time when he was sixteen, but he had, over time, come to terms with that. At this moment, staring out his kitchen window at the rising, taunting moon and trying to ignore the mystifying dog sitting behind him, he didn't understand a single thing that had happened to him since he'd left NCDSF.

That's what worried him.

He'd left the control room at NCDSF without a word to anyone, obeying an enigmatic, unfamiliar compulsion. The launch failure was enough to make any NCDSF employee worry, although Wint felt confident nothing about that disaster was his fault. It wasn't fear that spurred him to leave. Not even fear of Gammy and her reaction to the catastrophe, formidable as that might be.

No, Wint had left the control room and the NCDSF compound because he'd been gripped by a compulsion to *prepare*. Prepare for what? He didn't know where to find that answer. A low, bass thrumming in his brain, or his heart, or perhaps his liver, told him that something big was coming—might have already arrived—and his job was to *get ready*.

The problem[1] with nameless compulsions, of course, is their utter lack of clarity. Almost oblivious to where he was going, Wint left mission

---

1. Or at least, one of the problems

control and the blue-tinted ambient light from its dozens of computer screens. As if on autopilot, he bypassed the sprawling warehouse vastness of the Space Vehicle Production Facility and the now eerie and deserted Astronaut Training Labs. He exited the public-facing NCDSF lobby and strode out, squinting into glaring sunshine. With one hand up to shield his eyes, Wint stood next to his car in the NCDSF parking lot, wondering how he'd arrived there, then shrugged and got in. He drove straight past the gate guard without meeting her eyes. On his approach to the booth, Wint experienced an odd worry that the guard—Harriet, he thought her name was—might try to stop him from leaving, but she didn't even look up from her magazine as he drove past the gatehouse. An inexplicable thrill left Wint's hands sweaty on the steering wheel. He glimpsed his reflection in the rearview mirror as he checked for Harriet's reaction (there was none) and saw sweat beading the path of his receding hairline. His brown eyes, though, were feverish and bright. *He'd made it! He'd escaped!*

Wint shook his head, trying to clear it. Of course, he hadn't escaped; all he'd done was leave work early and no one had even noticed, so where did these strange thoughts originate? He fetched a deep breath, trying to calm his ratcheting heart and focus his babbling mind. *Home.* He'd go home and have a pleasant lie down before dinner, and everything would be back to normal by the time he woke up. He was simply overtired and stressed from the launch debacle.

Part of his mind—a part he tried hard to ignore—noticed that crooked rows of unmoving cars lined the sides of the road. In fact, many had stopped in the middle of the *lanes*, obstructing his path. This was strange, but Wint was busy focusing on how normal everything would be after his nap. He solved the problem by driving with slow caution around them. He ignored the black looks and occasional shaken fists cast in his direction from stranded drivers, and turned his radio up to drown out the shouts and expletives. These people also seemed quite upset with their cell phones, which apparently weren't working, either. On other streets, traffic flowed as usual. A part of his brain filed that information away to think about later. He glanced down at his own phone, but it glowed with silent encouragement back at him.

So, that had been his departure from NCDSF and his drive home. In the "weird things" department, there was no noticeable improvement when he arrived home. One of the neighbourhood dogs, a largish Whidden Shepherd with a black and silver coat and an unruly left ear, sprawled on his front porch as if waiting for him. The dog had looked Wint up and down with assessing, liquid brown eyes as Wint approached the house, unsure of this furry sentinel's intentions. The creature snorted in unmistakable canine disapproval.

"Good dog?" Wint suggested, attempting to edge past the creature in a non-threatening way. Wint had limited experience with dogs and other domesticated creatures, having owned only a succession of short-lived goldfish as a child, entered a brief partnership with a bad-tempered rabbit in middle school, and endured a love-hate relationship with a half-feral cat in his teen years.[2] If it were true that animals could sense human emotions, no doubt this dog understood how to manipulate Wint with ease. It eyed Wint in a way that made him extremely uncomfortable. The look seemed to say that if it was, indeed, a good dog, and that was in no way guaranteed, that was unrelated to Wint or his pathetic expectations.

Wint edged around the dog, giving it as wide a berth as possible on the narrow porch, and unlocked the door. He fumbled with his keys under the dog's unrelenting scrutiny. As the door swung open, the creature stood, slid through Wint's legs, and strolled into the house.

It was so unexpected that Wint stood frozen, his hand still on the doorknob and the key still in the lock. He pulled the key out and hurried inside, calling, "Hey! Hey, now, dog! Come back here!"

The dog ignored Wint with insulting disinterest, padding down the hallway and toward the kitchen at the back of the house as if its presence here was a matter of destiny.

Wint had the same unfortunate feeling.

---

2. Wint still bore a faint tracery of pale white scars on his forearms as testament to that particular co-dependency. The cat's name had been Mrs. Fury, which should tell you everything else you need to know about her.

The dog had settled itself on the mat at the back door, lowered its head, and gone to sleep. Wint stared at the interloper for a long moment and turned back to his original plan—now, more than ever, he needed that nap. He left the dog sleeping and climbed the stairs to his bedroom, closing and locking the door behind him. After a reflective pause, he shook his head and unlocked it with a defiant flourish. For cheese's sake, he told himself, there was no reason he should have to lock a door against a flarking dog. A doorknob was obstacle enough to a creature without opposable thumbs. He lay down on his bed in his clothes and, despite a fleeting concern that his mind wouldn't be able to settle, lapsed into sleep.

He woke to find the dog's brown eyes staring at him, mere inches from his face.

Wint jerked upright and bit back a yelp. "How the flark did you get in here?"

That was when the most worrisome thing of all happened. It made all the other worries pale by comparison, reducing them to mere trifles. Launch failures, strange compulsions, and pushy canines all paled in comparison.

"Sorry, mate, but would you get me some water?" the dog asked. "I can't reach the faucet, let alone a bowl."

A strangled scream left Wint's throat as he launched himself off the other side of the bed, forgetting that his bed snugged up against the wall on that side. His head bounced off the plaster with a resounding thud, sparks trailing across his vision like shooting stars. He lay stunned for a heartbeat, then scrambled for the bottom of the bed. En route, the quilt entangled him like the tentacles of a maddened octopus, and he toppled off the end, where his shoulder impacted the floor at an unfortunate angle. Pain lanced through it. The quilt slid off and covered his face, and Wint fought free of its enveloping folds, gasping for breath. When his vision was clear, the dog padded around to stare down at him with mournful eyes and a down-turned mouth.

Wint gasped and wheezed for a moment, trying to calm the wild palpitations of his heart. He forced a single word out through clenched teeth.

"What?"

The dog sighed and cocked its head at him, left ear flopping endearingly. "I said, could you get me some—"

"I heard what you said!" Wint yelled. "I want to know how you said it!"

The Whidden Shepherd huffed out a breath and muttered something that sounded like, *I might have known,* then added, "Well, to be fair, that's not what you asked."

Wint gaped up at the dog, clenching the quilt under his chin with white-knuckled hands. His mouth worked, but no further sounds emerged.

The dog sat down, emanating reluctant resignation. "Yes, all right; let's get it out of the way. I spoke. Yes, I'm a talking dog. Been that way for all of oh, four hours now. Completely unnatural; I get that. Difficult to realize, hard to accept, but here I am and there you have it. And I'm rather thirsty, as I've mentioned," he added pointedly.

Wint's gaping and white-knuckle clenching continued.

"I can't *explain* it, if that's what you're hoping for," the dog continued in exasperation. "This morning I'm happy chasing chickens and rousting a cat now and again. One moment I'm about to snap up an enticing scrap from the bin behind the grocery store, and then POW! I'm on the road with your language in my head, searching for the Technocrat Avatar or some such flarking thing." The dog pointed his nose up and shook out his fur before looking back down at Wint. "Supposed to act as his *mentor,* for bones' sake. What rubbish. What does that even mean?"

Wint found his mouth opening to sympathize with the dog's plight, but he shut it again. He took a few deep, soothing breaths. "And you're *here* because...?"

The dog blinked. "I'm not sure. Something told me to come here. I expect you're supposed to find this avatar person, too?"

It was a question for which Wint had no answer, so he asked another one. "What's your name?" It seemed only polite and Wint had always found that correct social form offered an anchor of stability in the storms of uncertain interactions.

The dog huffed out one more great sigh. "Knew you'd get around to asking that. Wish I could tell you it's something grand, like Makes-Cats-Beg-For-Mercy or Postman's-Terror. Even Guards-Like-A-Champion, now that would be livable. But no. People don't have a clue about naming dogs, do they?"

Never having owned a dog, only a cat named Mrs. Fury, Wint didn't feel qualified to speak to that.

"Sorry, you don't have to answer that; excuse my rhetorical musings. Name's Rex, of course, thanks to the failure of imagination of one particular human. Just Rex. Supposed to mean 'king' or some such thing. Whoopee. King of what? That's my question. Nice to meet you, Usborne. Now, about that water?"

In pain and at a loss for what else to do, Wint clambered to his feet and limped downstairs to get Rex a bowl of water. He did not ask how the dog had opened the bedroom door because, in all honesty, he preferred to remain ignorant. He also felt happier not knowing, at least for now, what or who a Technocrat Avatar was, why the dog was in his house, or how Rex had known his name. These questions clamoured in his brain, but as he pulled together some dinner for himself and the creature, he couldn't make himself ask Rex about any of those things. It took all of his available energy to live in the moment, because the recent procession of moments was quite the worst he'd ever experienced.

He knew that he should start packing in the morning, although the reason and the destination were unclear. Another thought he tried to push away, but it was more persistent.

Akin to everything else that had happened in the last few hours, it worried Wint. It worried him very much.

Intermezzo Uno

The Min

A sharp rapping sounded at the door of The Min's office.[1] The Min looked up from her desk. Surrounding her on every side, bookshelves towered up to and beyond the boundaries of vision—at least, the boundaries of normal vision. Someone with normal vision might also have remarked upon the existence of bookshelves that didn't seem to require walls, and ran along odd angles and axes. Gravity would have demanded the books fall off said bookshelves...if gravity held any real sway in this place. Gravity might make its demands elsewhere, but in this place, the books knew they could ignore it and maybe, in time, it would go away. Secure in that knowledge, the books nestled in quiet comfort on their shelves, ignoring the lack of anything comprehensible to hold them there.

The Min thought nothing of this flouting of gravity, since here, she made the rules. The rapping, though...that was an oddity, since the door was completely insubstantial and only there for show. She considered. The knocker must have a point to make—this was important. But the Convocation was set to meet in fifteen minutes, so whatever it was, it had better not take long.

"Come!"

---

1. It wasn't really an office as such, since the notion of an office presupposes the existence of other things, such as a building in which an office might reside, walls, a physical door upon which the putative rapping would have taken place. However, most of us are not trans-dimensional beings, so let's just call it an office and go from there.

Skete stumbled into The Min's office, gangling and breathless, red hair a mess of spikes and eyes wide. Skete always seemed to be breathless, and over the centuries she had known him, had never outgrown the gangling. Sometimes, The Min found the breathlessness annoying in the extreme. Running and walking were, for trans-dimensional beings such as themselves, entirely optional, and thus, so was breathlessness.

"New thaumic source...(*pant, pant*)...just opened up...(*gasp*). No active thaumic history...(*gasp*)...ever before...on the...(*pant, pant*)...entire planet."

"PRIVACY!" bellowed The Min. Her great hands quivered, sparks flashing at her fingertips and tiny bolts of blue lightning erupting in her hair. Skete hadn't even bothered to close the *semblance* of the door, just blurted out news like this when the whole Convocation could be eavesdropping. Did he want to start a riot? Did he want to start a *war*? She shook her head and lightning crackled. There was something wrong with the boy.

Four massive, marbled stone walls, anchored by coordinating ceiling and floor, materialized around Skete, The Min, the bookshelves and her desk with a noise like—well, like stone materializing. A heavy *whump!* or something similar. A chair appeared behind Skete and an invisible hand pushed him into it. It wasn't the most comfortable of chairs, but it was better than the marble floor.

"Report," The Min said, "and for Magic's sake, take a deep breath or two first."

Skete devoted a brief second to respiratory stabilization, then recited the facts with brisk precision. "Planet 2342β was decimated at 120:34:94 today; thaumic force departed at 120:34:80 and made planetfall at new destination at 120:36:42. New planet is 8435ώ." He lowered his voice to a dramatic whisper and stared into The Min's dazzling, lightning-shot eyes. "Thaumic force *latent* since planet formation."

"Until now."

Skete nodded. "Until now. Thaumic migration from 2342β activated it. Inhabitants call the planet D'sharu. Also, no cultural religious history in the planet's sentient population."

"Across the board?"

"None. When the Convocation gets wind of this, it'll be a free-for-all."

The Min was silent for a moment. "Or a riot. What were those times again? There's something—no, wait, never mind that for now. This could hit the fan any second. Well, we have a meeting of the Convocation in ten minutes—I'll move it up to right this instant and call for bids." She narrowed her eyes at Skete. "Did you tell anyone else before you staggered in here?"

"Absolutely not."

"All right then." The Min took up the great jewelled horn that hung at her side. It made a somewhat outrageous accessory for the trim dark business suit she wore today, but no member of the Convocation would dare to mention that. And what they said behind her back was less than insignificant. She fiddled with the horn's reed for a moment, then blew a blast that shattered the marble surround and sent loose pages flying in wild arcs from the safe embrace of their spines. The storm of pages whirled and eddied in the space, drifting like lazy, wind-tossed snowflakes. There would be no need to gather them up; they'd migrate back to their leather-bound homes in time. The horn's reverberating sound echoed up the towering bookshelves and off something in the unimaginably far distance, then returned to shatter the remaining bits of marble some more.

In normal circumstances, at the first hint of sound from the horn, the entire Convocation would materialize on the vast astral plains surrounding The Min's desk. The bookshelves would, by some trick of intra-dimensional accommodation, always leave room for everyone to fit. When She bade them come, they came. And they had to land somewhere. The Min was not oblivious to that fact. They came, or they faced the consequences.

When the bits of marble had ceased shattering and skittering around them in the shadow of the great shelves, the plain around the desk remained stark and empty. The Min and Skete exchanged a look. The Convocation had, for the first time since it had been established and convened (which was a mind-boggling length of time), failed to answer the summons.

The Min pondered, deciding how to handle this contempt. *If they're not showing up for bids, they're trying to bypass the process. What a mess. But by the Magic, not again. Not on my watch.* She turned to Skete. "We need to get them back here right now. If they won't answer the horn, they'd better come for the emergency call, or heads *will* roll."

Skete licked his lips and swallowed. "You can't let them have free rein. The planet doesn't deserve that. The people don't. If you have to be ruthless..." He let the thought trail off.

The Min hung the horn back on her belt and willed a keyboard into existence on her desk. She tapped out a few commands and hit *send*. She smiled with satisfaction. "If that doesn't get their attention, whatever happens next will be their own fault."

Behind Skete, a series of soft popping noises sounded as members of the Convocation began arriving in answer to The Min's concise and ominous text summons.

"All right, that's more like it." She looked back at Skete. "Now, before I deal with them, we'd better get some boots on the ground. Fancy a trip to D'sharu?"

Skete muttered a curse under his breath, but The Min ignored it. With an untamed and unclaimed thaumic force in play, she had bigger things to worry about than Skete being inconvenienced. Much, much bigger.

THE HAT IN THE CLOSET

HELINE

Heline Morrisanto took another sip of cold, bitter tea and grimaced. It had gone cold half an hour ago, but she was too busy writing to freshen her cup from the pot on the stove. Well, if she was honest, she wasn't writing anything, just sitting at her kitchen table and doodling, ready to capture the words the instant they arrived. If they ever did. As usual, the music had come into her head without accompanying lyrics. Heline chewed the end of her pencil with savage ferocity.

It wasn't fair; it just wasn't. This was a rollicking tune, the kind of song to which drunks always knew the wrong words and sang without restraint while they stumbled home; the kind of song burly men sang while their brows glistened with honest sweat and they put their backs into lumberjacking or stevedoring; the kind of song mothers sang while they jounced their giggling babies or danced them around the kitchen.

Only it had no words. Not even the wrong ones.

Heline sighed. It was as if her brain had a crack, big enough to let the music through, but too small for the words. She hated it. She'd hum a tune for days, until she thought she'd go mad, but the words never came.

And yet, she never stopped hoping. Heline dropped her pencil on the table and sat back, running her fingers through her hair and massaging her scalp. Maybe she could push the words around in her brain and they'd pop out like confetti from a burst balloon. It was a fanciful idea, but not likely to happen, and she smoothed her dark brown locks back into place with a sigh. Maybe if she got her hair cut shorter again? Heline shook her head at her own foolishness. It wasn't as simple as that. It wasn't her *hair*, for butter's sake. But the image of the words being stuck somewhere haunted her.

It reminded her of the secret room at the back of her cottage. Just a closet, big enough for her to walk into and close the door, turn on the lightbulb and gaze at the things arrayed on the floor-to-ceiling rows of shelves. Nothing ever came out of there, either. The closet's contents discombobulated her, but the compulsion to visit it caught her sometimes like an irrepressible sneeze.

Rot. And there it was again. Why had she started thinking about the closet? Now she'd have to look inside it. Half the objects on the shelves she'd made herself, some innate and inexplicable knowledge guiding her hands. The little soup pot she'd painted black, for instance, and embellished with a hanging handle. Why had she done it? And why black, for cheese's sake? Nothing in her cottage was black. Well, nothing outside that closet. Heline's cottage was cheery and feminine; pale yellow walls in the kitchen and dining area with rose-patterned curtains at the windows; colourful bright chintzes in the living room; pastels and ruffles in the bedroom.

The crystal sphere—well, nothing too odd about that, she supposed. Just a small, heavy glass ball big enough to cup in her hand, filled with pale, cloudy swirls of—something. Fog? A knickknack one could set on the coffee table, and no one would question it. Heline had found it in a jumble of odds and ends at a flea market and the sphere had spoken to her. Not literally, of course. But it felt right, as if it were already hers. She brought it home and set it on a shelf in the closet with an odd, uneasy sense of satisfaction. She'd taken care to lay the stick in front of it so it couldn't roll off and shatter.

Ah yes, the stick. She'd tripped over it down by the apple tree one summer afternoon. All right, at the time it seemed like it had jumped up and tripped her, but sticks weren't known for their indiscriminate jumping about and tripping people. About a foot long, with only a few gnarls and twists, stripped of its bark, but otherwise...just a stick. Why, then, the compulsion to polish it with furniture oil and paint that little gold fiddly bit on the end? Why did her fingers tingle when she looked at it on the dusty shelf? Annoying, all of it.

But not...the hat. The hat was not annoying. She had not made the hat, nor found it in the yard. The hat had been here, on the topmost shelf, when she'd inherited the house from an ancient aunt she'd met only rarely as a child. Heline had not been inclined to dislodge the hat when she'd moved in. The hat had an uncomfortable presence. She didn't like to think about it much. From it, she sensed a desire to come down from the shelf.

Which was, of course, ridiculous.

Still, Heline had never touched the hat.

She realized with a start that she'd been doodling all this while and had drawn the hat, or something resembling the hat. In her drawing, it stood straighter, no longer constrained by the closet's low ceiling. A graceful ebony point flopped over the edge of the brim, and for some reason she'd embellished it with a single, intelligent eye. It peered up from the page at her with an eerie presence. A shiver arced along Heline's spine and she scribbled dark pencil lines over the doodle, flushing as if she'd drawn something naughty by accident. The music floated with maddening persistence in her head, wordless and beseeching, like a lost twin missing its mate.

She crumpled the paper and went to check on the laundry. She'd take a brief glance into the closet on the way. No harm in that.

Heline's hand was on the closet door's handle when the doorbell rang. A flash of guilty relief shot through her. She hadn't wanted to look in the closet, with its black walls, black shelves, black inscrutable somethings, and the vexing black hat seeming to peer down at her from the top shelf. It was only that recurring, persistent urge that had brought her here, and she was just as pleased to put it off. Heline turned on her heel and scurried down the hall to the front door.

When she opened that door, though, she rather wished that she'd opened the closet after all, and stepped inside, pulled the door shut behind her and not answered the doorbell at all. Because there on her step, grinning and twisting a curl of sea-green hair around her finger, was Eleanor.

Her little sister Eleanor, the recurrent runaway.

"Heline, are you not even going to ask me to come in?" Eleanor asked, pouting. "You haven't seen me in months!"

"Do Mom and Dad know you're here?" Heline heard herself respond in the high, prissy voice Eleanor always seemed to provoke. Heline hated that voice, but Eleanor always triggered it.

Eleanor sighed, dropped the curl, picked up a battered suitcase covered in assorted band and city stickers, and brushed past Heline into the cottage. The guitar case slung over Eleanor's left shoulder passed within an inch of Heline's nose, but the younger girl didn't seem to notice. She dropped the suitcase in the hall and stalked into the living room without looking back or bothering to remove her chunky boots.

There was little point in continuing to hold the door open, so Heline sighed and shut it, allowed herself one skyward eye roll, and followed her sister.

Still not answering Heline's question, Eleanor unslung the guitar case with care, settled it on the sofa and plopped down next to it. She slipped out of her black denim jacket, dropped it onto the floor, and tucked her legs up, smoothing her red and black checkered skirt with deliberate care.

Heline perched on the sofa on the other side of the guitar case. From the riot of patches and logos adorning the back of her sister's jacket, an embroidered skull patch with a rose between its teeth grinned up at Heline. She quashed a grimace even while she found the image oddly compelling. She fixed her eyes on her sister.

"Of course they don't know." Eleanor answered Heline's query at last with an exasperated sigh. "It's called *running away* because you don't keep the people you're running away from informed of your whereabouts."

Heline drew a deep breath and let it filter out between pursed lips. She managed with an effort to pin on a smile. "Okay, let's start again. How are you, Eleanor? And what brings you by?"

Eleanor smiled at her sister. She had a beautiful smile, pearl-white teeth contrasting with glowing olive skin, and she used this to her advantage. The skill was far too well-developed for a seventeen-year-old. "That's so much better!" she squealed, and jumped up again, scurrying to Heline's end of the sofa and wrapping her sister in an enormous hug. Heline returned it after a startled pause.

When Eleanor pulled back, she said, "Well, I left the band and I'm broke; how's that for starters?"

"Not great," Heline said through a fixed smile, "but it's good that you're being honest."

Eleanor waved a dismissive hand. Four fingers held at least six rings, great clunky things with skulls and disembodied eyes and huge fake jewels. That might explain the network of holes and tears in her black tights. Her fingernail polish alternated between red, black and green, varying by finger. "I can get another gig anytime I want, but I'm ready for a break. So, why not visit dear Heline? We could have such fun catching up!"

And Heline has a nice warm house and plenty to eat, and she won't turn me away or charge me board because I'm family and she's a sucker. And the sad part was, it was true.

"How did you know I'd be here?"

Eleanor cocked a pierced eyebrow. "Um, you live here."

"But most days I wouldn't be home from work yet."

Eleanor shrugged. "Then I would have waited on the front porch until you got home. No big deal. Are you on vacation or something?"

"Yes, all week," Heline admitted, even more annoyed. She loved her job with the humane society, but everyone needed a break sometimes, even from the best job. And now she wouldn't have the time to herself. She buried the resentment because that's what a good sister would do. It wasn't like she'd had any proper plans, anyway.

"Will you at least let me call Mom and Dad and tell them you're here?"

Eleanor frowned. "Are you crazy? They'll be banging on the door before you hang up the phone. No. Non-negotiable. I forbid it." She crossed her arms over her chest and glared at her older sister.

The image of all those black, inscrutable things in the closet rose in Heline's mind and she imagined herself striding down the hallway, throwing open the door, picking up...something...the stick, perhaps? And—

What? Heline couldn't visualize what she might do with the stick. But it would be something that Eleanor was not expecting, and wouldn't like very much, and it would *show her*.

Heline swallowed and blinked. She loved her little sister. She would never hurt her. Not for real. Eleanor was just so flarking annoying sometimes. She stood up, brushing invisible dust from her clothes. "Well, I won't call them tonight. That's all I can promise for now. You're welcome to stay for supper, although what we'll be having—"

The doorbell rang again. Heline sighed and went to answer it.

Jans stood on the step, beaming as usual when she opened the door. He'd styled his sandy hair in a sleek wave and his clothes oozed casual chic. His arms bundled brown paper shopping bags bristling with long, elegant and mysterious foods.

"And so! Supper is served to your door! I am preparing the feast for you tonight, is it not?" He leaned through the forest of packages to kiss Heline on the cheek and she stepped aside to let him in. He strode straight past the living room doorway without even glancing inside, so he didn't see Eleanor or seem to notice her suitcase in the hall.

Somewhere in her heart, in that one hidden place where no one can fool themselves no matter how many nights they lie awake trying, Heline sighed. Just the tiniest sigh—not a huff, you understand, and nothing even akin to a groan. Just a sigh; a sigh that said she wasn't in the mood for Jans and his cheerful, exuberant courtship rituals tonight. She already had enough on her plate with Eleanor and that song and the recurrent pull of the closet—she pushed the notion of the closet away with desperate determination. Jans was...he was...

Whenever that sort of disloyal thought wriggled up to the surface of her mind, Heline's instinct was to bury it again before she could get a good look at it. Jans was perfect; he really was. He had a good job as manager of a local amusement park, and a cheerful disposition. His job suited him because he liked to have fun. He was out of the ordinary, his imperfect command of her language endearing, his kindness and generosity boundless, his demeanour gentlemanly. She believed his affection for her was genuine.

[he's boring]

Heline jumped, spinning in the tiny entryway. Someone had spoken—but it hadn't been Eleanor's voice. Muffled thumps from the kitchen assured her that Jans was occupied with unloading the shopping bags.

[b o r—i n g]

The whispered word was drawn out in a sing-song cadence this time, like a child's taunt. Heline put a hand to her chest. Her heart fluttered like the chickadee that had once flown in her kitchen window, trapped and frantic until Heline gathered it in a towel and released it outside. She returned to the living room and looked in. Eleanor had pulled her guitar from its case and tinkered with the tuning, half-reclined with her feet up on the sofa as she plinked and strummed. At least her boots were off.

"Did you say something?"

Eleanor looked up. "Nope. Who was that guy? Boyfriend?"

Heline bristled but calmed herself. It was an innocent enough question. "Yes. His name is Jans. He's cooking supper."

"Can he cook? Or does he only think he can?"

"Well, yeah, he's a great cook. You lucked out, coming by tonight. I'd better tell him you're here. I don't think he noticed you on his way through."

She took a couple of steps down the hallway and pulled up short before her unthinking feet could take her all the way to the closet.

"Jans?"

He poked his head out of the kitchen doorway, wiping his hands on a tea towel. "Ja?"

"My sister's here, too. She might stay with me for a while. So there'll be three of us for supper."

He grinned. "Excellence! I am yearn to meet the so-nice sister of my sweet Heline. You go, sit. Put up feet and visit with sister. Supper I will take care of, *yako*?"

It had been delightful and cute, the first time they realized that "okay" in her language had a close counterpart in the "yako" of his. In recent weeks, however, she found the word jarring, like the repeated raucous call of a crow outside the window at dawn every morning for a month.

Heline pasted on an answering smile that masked clenched teeth and nodded. Jans disappeared into the kitchen, whistling a cheerful tune.

[yako, yako! what a wonderful word. yako, yako, yako!]

All right. That voice did not belong to Eleanor. And not Jans. And there was no one else here. Heline looked herself in the eye in the hall mirror. The eye looked back at her, unblinking. She looked the same as she always did. No twitches, no shakes, no psychotic grimaces. *I am not going crazy,* she told herself. *Something strange is going on, and I am going to find out what it is.* Her right hand twitched, felt empty, and goosebumps prickled her scalp. Where was her hat?

I wasn't wearing a hat.

With a last glance back toward the living room, Heline let her unerring footsteps take her toward the closet. It was the logical place to go. The rest of the cottage was, always had been, a cozy, normal place. The closet, not so much. She glanced back over her shoulder. Jans had never seen inside the closet, and she didn't want him to. And she didn't want Eleanor following her. That would lead to no end of unwelcome questions.

Opening the door took most of her courage, but she pulled it toward her with a jerk, and when nothing and no one jumped out at her, she slipped inside and eased the door closed. The only option for light was a single bulb with a long string to switch it on, and Heline pulled it. As the bulb struggled to life she gazed around; the contents of the closet looked...different. Some items on the shelves appeared almost fuzzy, their edges and shapes less distinct than before. The fog in the crystal sphere shimmered and glowed, lit from an inner source Heline couldn't fathom. She reached a hesitant hand toward the sphere but snatched it back, still empty, when the voice spoke again.

[they've been infused with thaumic force. at last.]

The voice was louder now, and Heline didn't bother looking behind her. She didn't stop to wonder what the words 'thaumic force' meant. She almost forgot about Jans and Eleanor. With an abrupt sense of inevitability that allowed her a measure of nonchalance, she let her eyes travel up, up to the topmost shelf, up and straight into the imaginary eye of that flarking hat.

Which was, by dint of some awkward maneuvering, standing almost straight up, only the last hand-width of its tip now bent down toward her. In a weird echo of her doodle, it regarded her with an eye that was amber, bloodshot, and not even a little imaginary any longer.

[it's about time. now will you for majick's sake get me down off this bloody shelf? i'm not a snake, you know]

There are times and situations where there is only one proper course of action, and there's no sense in lallygagging about, debating ideas and delaying the inevitable. Heline didn't hesitate.

She screamed, and the light winked out.

THE FIFTH FORCE

NERLIM

Nerlim Pettibone spent the morning of the day after magic arrived on D'sharu calling in every favour he'd accumulated over his considerable lifetime. He even contrived to sneak in a few that, truth be told, he'd already claimed years before. But since most of the folks who owed him those favours were at least his age, their memories were imperfect.

The day before, he'd convinced a cab driver to take him to the nearest cash machine after he left the nursing home. The cab driver, suspicious of an escape in progress, hesitated to accept him as a fare. Luckily, Nerlim kept one fifty-wern[1] bill hidden in his slipper at the nursing home, enough to convince the driver that being an accessory to the escape would at least be lucrative. With bills from the cash machine secure in his pocket, Nerlim caught a bus to the nearby city of Neemar. A quick nap on the bus revived him and he'd bought some new clothes, rented a room in a decent hotel, and upgraded his old cell phone before falling into a fitful sleep. When he woke, he set up a makeshift desk at the room's single table, ordered breakfast, and started making calls.

So now, only a day after he'd lain in his hospital bed and felt his body, mind, and spirit shaken, he found himself installed in a vacant office at a weather station on the outskirts of Neemar. He had access to all their information and a telephone all to himself. Considering that he had little

---

1. The wern being, of course, the currency of this part of D'sharu. Fifty wern would get you a nice dinner and a bottle of halfway decent wine at a good restaurant in Neemar, or two bottles of Black Angus Knockdown. The editor has no idea which choice the cab driver made, but will take bets on the Knockdown.

idea where to look or what to look for, the unusual cloud formations glimpsed from the nursing home window seemed as good a place as any to start. And his presence in this office indicated progress.

He poked his head out of the office and smiled at the man working in a cubicle nearby. "Harold, would you find me all the satellite weather photos for the last, say, twenty-four hours? I'd appreciate it."

Harold nodded with only minor reluctance. A youngish man with an oldish face, sparse sandy hair and large glasses, Harold had the look of someone who, in another time and place, might have kept important secrets safe. Nerlim suspected there were few important secrets at the weather office; still, one should never assume. Nerlim and Harold had been strangers before today; Harold's uncle owed Nerlim the favour. How the uncle had recruited Harold's help, Nerlim neither knew nor cared. Harold was in the right place at the right time, and as long as Nerlim kept his requests reasonable and his demeanour deferential, Harold seemed inclined with only minimal reluctance to help him out.

With the sheaf of weather maps in hand, Nerlim closed the office door and eased down on creaky knees to spread them on the threadbare beige carpet. All held time stamps from the past twenty-four hours, but he eliminated any marked more than two hours after he left the hospital. That left sixteen images.

The event had most likely occurred in this hemisphere—a leap of logic, but most people on the other side of the world would have been asleep at the relevant time, and he just hoped his target wasn't some raving insomniac on the overcontinent of Styre.

So once he removed the images taken over other continents, six remained. Well, seven, but the last was almost completely black, a dud. Nerlim eased back on his heels and tsk-tsked over the photos, rubbing his chin as he considered them. Not the clearest, for all they'd come from the much-lauded SORIT-3 satellite, supposed to be quite advanced from its predecessors 1 and 2 (since Nerlim had worked on the first SORIT, he admitted that he might be biased).

However. Nerlim ran a hand through his slightly too-long white hair. They constituted all he had to work with, so he gave them close attention. The one from yesterday morning showed little of interest.

High, thin clouds swirled across the northern half of the continent, leaving much of the planet's surface open to view. Nothing seemed unusual. The next, from later in the morning, appeared much the same.

And so it went, each picture a grainy black-and-white image of the planet's surface, more or less obscured by cloud, more or less all the same. At last, he had only the dud. Nerlim tossed it on top of the others with a sigh and the glossy paper slid and spun like the clouds in the images. The featureless photo reminded him of his life.

Nerlim Pettibone had spent much of his long life being dogged by the nagging certainty that something important eluded him. In a heroic effort to discover that something, he'd applied himself to broad study—physics, chemistry, mathematics, meteorology, psychology, astronomy (with a foray into astrology thrown in for good measure), history, folklore, and gourmet cooking. (This last had been a matter of desperation combined with the realization that he was always hungry, having skimped on satisfying his gastronomic needs during a lifetime spent trying to satisfy the hunger in his mind.)

He found no answers (although in time he ate much better). He did, however, form several theories—theories for which he had no solid scientific proof, but satisfactory enough to keep him from going stark, raving mad. To wit:

1) In addition to the four recognized fundamental forces (gravity, the weak force, electromagnetism, and the strong force), there exists a fifth force (*nf*) which we are unable at present to detect, measure, define, predict, or utilize.

2) The fifth force (*nf*) may exist in a latent state, so that its effects on the other measurable forces are nil or negligible.

3) If the fifth force (*nf*) becomes a patent force, it has the potential to counteract or interact with the effects of all the other forces.

4) It remains uncertain what eventuality or eventualities may result in the fifth force *(nf)* becoming patent.

Of course, Nerlim never published these theories, nor the six hundred and forty-seven pages of mathematical forumlae and ten thousand pages of a dissertation manuscript which supported them. Because in the end,

Nerlim was arguing for the existence of something entirely hypothetical and unsupported by even a thread of evidence.

Except that he *knew* it existed.[2]

Kneeling on the floor of the borrowed office had triggered an ache in his arthritic knees, and Nerlim reached to gather the scattered satellite photos. As his shadow fell across the topmost one, the one he'd characterized as a dud, a somewhat less black, somewhat less shadowed shape appeared on the paper. He halted his reach as if someone had pressed a pause button, staring at the image now revealed by the right viewing angle. The shape had been there before, but it required the proper light—or lack thereof—to be revealed. Nerlim squinted; shook his head. He took off his glasses and polished them on the hem of his shirt, then looked again. Surely not. He must be seeing things.

It looked like a face. A shadowy, fuzzy, barely discernible face, traced in the undulating edges of cloud formations.

A face he recognized.

In the course of his long career, Nerlim had, on various occasions and in diverse capacities, visited the North and Central D'sharian Space Facility. He walked the buildings, he consulted on projects, he understood the business. He knew Gammy.

Nerlim had known Gammy for a long, long time, on various occasions and in diverse capacities.

But why would a shadowy image of Gammy's wizened, ferrety face appear in a ruined weather satellite photo of D'sharu?

Nerlim glanced at the time stamp, which he hadn't bothered to look at before. The same time, or very close to it, as he'd experienced—the event. He almost doubted his luck. He'd found something, and on the first try.

If only he had a hint of a clue what it meant.

---

2. Which didn't do anybody, especially Nerlim, any good at all, although he happened to be one hundred percent correct.

Nerlim did some fast talking to himself in the taxi en route to NCDSF. He had to convince himself, and retain the conviction, that the logical next step would be talking to Gammy. Nerlim didn't want to talk to Gammy. He didn't enjoy talking to Gammy.

He had once been in love with Gammy.

Because of course, Gammy had not always looked like a wizened ferret peering out from under a floor mop. Gammy (then known as Gameldina) had once been young and vibrant and quite attractive to Nerlim. Nerlim, too, had been young and, in the eyes of many young women, (including Gameldina,) quite handsome in an academic way. Two mutually attracted, intelligent people who shared many common interests; it might have been a wonderful match.

But while Nerlim fell quite in love with Gammy, and Gammy appeared to be quite fond of him in return, Gammy's first and strongest love belonged to the moon. And so that was that. Unfortunately, she'd told Nerlim so in no uncertain terms, never having been one to understand the concept of letting a person down easy. There had been "words," and while fate forced them to interact in professional capacities over the years, those words continued to hover about their heads like malignant wasps, darting in to inflict a new sting whenever the opportunity arose.

A colleague once observed that they bickered like rival cats fighting over last night's leftovers.

So no, Nerlim did not want to talk to Gammy, in particular after yesterday's failed launch and how she'd be feeling about *that*. But what choice did he have? The indistinct but unmistakable image on the weather satellite photo formed his only clue to whatever had happened on D'sharu. And for that, he wanted—he *needed*—answers.

So, Gammy.

Nerlim's once and continuing stature in the scientific community at least meant instant entrance to NCDSF. Identity confirmed, hastily produced visitor's pass obtained, and the entire complex lay open to him. He navigated the confusing corridors with the alacrity of a well-trained lab rat.

Until he reached mission control and the doorway to Gammy's office, and came face to face with a man he knew well.

Argit, Gammy's assistant, accomplice, and sometime protector, stood before the door like a mountain, unyielding and insufferably polite.

"Good to see you, Mr. Pettibone, and may I say you're looking well. But she's not to be disturbed."

Nerlim fought to maintain his patience. "But she doesn't know I'm here. She'll see me."

"You could be right, sir," Argit acknowledged, his manner quiet and deferential. His loyalty to Gammy knew no bounds, but Nerlim was also a respected figure at NCDSF. "But I can't disturb her to ask, right? Because she told me not to disturb her. And I'm not going to. Because I'll get in more trouble for disturbing her than I will for saying no to you. Pretty simple, when you think about it. Right?"

Nerlim studied Argit for a moment. He'd always cultivated an amiable relationship with Gammy's right-hand man. Now Nerlim sensed a hint of desperation in his defiance. An unwarranted sheen of sweat on his brow in this climate-controlled space. A new, recurring twitch, just below his right ear. Nerlim pitched his voice low, confiding.

"Has anything...strange...happened since the launch failure, Argit? Not counting that, I mean."

Argit swallowed. "She...she never went home last night, sir."

Nerlim regarded him. "That's not unusual for her, though, is it? Anything else?"

Argit's eyes darted left and right like penned rabbits. He shook his head a little, but he didn't answer.

"I understand, you can't say. But if there was something, Argit, it may be related to my reason for being here. I may have information of interest to Gammy, if you get my meaning. Great interest." Nerlim infused his voice with a fine melange of understanding and intimacy. He'd seen enough spy movies to get it just right. He'd lived enough situations like this to get it right.

Argit looked like he'd rather be anywhere else right now, except perhaps inside Gammy's office. The tic under his ear leapt like a pulse.

Nerlim laid a wrinkled hand on Argit's shoulder and leaned closer. "I'll tell you what, Argit. You just step aside and let me in, and you won't have disturbed Gammy in the least. I'll be the one doing all the disturbing, and I'll take the blame. If there is any blame. But if I'm right, Gammy will be so glad to hear what I have to tell her that there won't be any trouble at all."

To give him his due, Argit didn't nod or speak. In fact, he made no sign that he and Nerlim had agreed to anything, or that he'd even heard Nerlim's proposition. Except that he stepped aside, just the smallest step, just enough for Nerlim to slip past, open the door, and pass through. And he held in his massive sigh of relief until the door closed behind Nerlim.

Gammy looked up the instant the door opened, of course, but she said nothing until it had closed again. Then she spoke only one word, narrowing her eyes as she did.

"You."

"Me," Nerlim acknowledged, crossing to her desk without waiting to be invited. He noted with interest the empty Black Angus Knockdown bottle on the desk and the fact that Gammy looked exhausted. Her clothes puckered with wrinkles, no doubt a testament to spending the night in her office. Her rich brown skin held a sallow tone, and lines of exhaustion and worry bracketed her eyes. Even her mop of grey curls seemed to sag. He steeled himself, knowing he should take advantage of her unpreparedness at seeing him. He had to come in on the offensive or she'd crush him, tired or not. From the large manila envelope under his arm, he slid a glossy dark photo and placed it without fanfare on the desk in front of Gammy.

Gammy glanced at it.

She squinted and looked again.

She picked it up, held it up to the light, held it down in the shadows, and then laid it back on the desk. She folded her hands and looked straight at him. "You gave up pretty easily forty years ago, Nerlim Pettibone."

It was not the attack he expected. He faltered for a moment, then regrouped. "You didn't offer me much hope of success. Now, what's your face doing on a satellite weather photo taken above the surface of this planet mid-afternoon yesterday, Gameldina?"

"Is that what it is? It's a poor likeness. You might have made it seem just a little more important, the whole *being in love with me* thing."

Nerlim blew out a sigh, left his chair, and crossed to the cabinet on the other side of the office, retrieving a new, full bottle of Knockdown from its depths. With slow and careful deliberation, he opened it and poured himself a finger in a clean glass. "Maybe in the grand scheme of things it wasn't—or maybe I didn't understand it myself, then. What's got your boy Argit so jumpy today? Not just the launch failure. It's more than that."

At the unguarded look that flashed for a moment in her eyes, he regretted that salvo. Too fresh a wound. Their rules of engagement should have kept him from mentioning the launch failure first.

Before she could snap back at him, he hurried on, "I think it's all related, Gameldina; the launch, and something that happened to me yesterday, and whatever else is going on. Cards on the table?" Not an apology, but as close as either of them ever came to one. He held up the bottle and raised his eyebrows in a question.

She held out her glass, and he took it without a word and half-filled it for her, even though he wasn't sure he should. The empty bottle on the desk made it a decent bet that he shouldn't. But this was important, for the love of cheese.

When he handed the glass back to her, she took a contemplative sip. "Please, *please* don't tell me you think this is a Nameless Fifth Force issue."

He pursed his lips and nodded with slow intensity. She stared at him for a long moment, closed her eyes, then knocked back the rest of the Black Angus in her glass. Picked up the photo from her desk and squinted at it again.

"Well, flark. It always is, with you. And this *is* me, isn't it? You'd better sit down and tell me all about it."

THE PIG THAT LIVES NOT

WINT

Wint Usborne was still worried. Wint lived with a low hum of worry, like a persistent and anxious colony of bees, in the back of his brain at the best of times. Thus, some low-level anxiety wasn't unusual. However, he had now achieved a greater level of worry than he'd been functioning with yesterday, if that was possible.

His night had been restless, as he tried to convince his brain to leave the unanswerable questions for the morning, not worry about the talking dog snoring with soft huffs in the spare bedroom, and just go to sleep. It had seemed only polite to offer that room to the dog, and he'd accepted with thanks. Wint had debated whether to invite the dog to use the bed; what were the social protocols for interacting with talking animals? He knew of none. So, in the end, he simply offered the room. There were more important things to contemplate than dog hairs on a comforter.

They'd eaten dinner together in the kitchen in relative silence; the dog didn't appear inclined to volunteer more information and Wint wasn't ready to ask for any. Wint had let Rex outside without a word afterward. Rex had gone out, also without mentioning the reasons, and had whuffed discreetly at the door to come back in. Wint wasn't sure why he let the dog stay, but the last thing he wanted right now was to get into an argument with a talking dog. That kind of thing required a man to be at the very top of his game. Wint was not at the top of his game. He wasn't even in the top ten percent of his game. To be honest, he wasn't even sure what the game was.

Wint must have slept at last, however, because the morning sun slanted in his window at the usual angle and woke him with soft fingers of light playing over his face. In that blissful state of half-waking, it might have been any other morning, and Wint's thoughts drifted in lazy whorls over the workday ahead. Then Wint opened his eyes to see the dog standing next to the bed, liquid gaze fixed on him. Wint tried to smother his startlement, because he'd fallen asleep clutching the hope that yesterday was the product of a nightmare. The dog's placid presence knifed that hope right in the back.

"Sorry to bother you, mate, but that back door latch—" The dog shrugged, which was interesting to watch. "I can't manage it."

"No bother, I can let you out," Wint said in what he hoped was an affable tone.

"Some doorknobs I can manage, but without thumbs, well…"

"Of course."

Wint fixed breakfast and showered, and then the dog came back inside, and Wint, still following his nameless compulsion, climbed the stairs to his room to pack. Which all seemed weirdly reasonable, except that Wint had no inkling of *what* he was supposed to pack. No one had told him where he was going, or why. He sat on the side of the bed and attempted calm consideration of the problem, but considering the problem made him anything but calm. Restless, he clattered down the stairs again. Rex had settled on the living room rug with his head resting on his front paws, making the wordless point that he wasn't even attempting to get up on any of the furniture.

"I'm supposed to pack," Wint told him, sitting in the armchair facing the dog.

"Makes sense."

"Yes, well, actually it doesn't, because I don't know what I'm supposed to pack for or where I'm going. Any insights about that?"

The dog sat up, taking a moment for a good scratch behind one ear before he answered. "Not precisely. I might have your language, but I've only ever been a dog, so I'm not all that up on people stuff, if you take my meaning. Probably…some clothes? Most humans I've observed seem attached to them. And some food?"

"But you do know where we're going, right?"

"I'm looking for the Technocrat Avatar," Rex said. "And I presume you are, too. So, somewhere with a lot of...technology?"

"I work at NCDSF, which has a lot of technology," Wint mused. He leaned back in the chair and crossed his arms. "But I had a compulsion to *leave* there, and it's not far enough away that I'd need to pack anything special to go back."

The dog shook his head. "No, seems like packing indicates a longer journey. I guess I can't help you, mate. I expect I'll understand how to get there once we're underway. Dogs have powerful instincts, you know?"

"Yes, well, I'm not sure how that applies to going places you've never been to or even heard of," Wint muttered, a hint of testiness creeping into his voice despite his best efforts to maintain equanimity.

"Well, you'd never met a talking dog until yesterday, either, so there's that," Rex countered with a philosophical tone. "Maybe you need to follow your own instincts. Open a bag and see what you think of putting in it. They might be the right things."

Thanks for what may be the stupidest piece of advice I've ever received, Wint wanted to say, but he bit back the words and stopped after "Thanks." He left the dog and went to the spare bedroom, noting that although the bed showed signs of being slept upon, only a few stray dark hairs adhered to the cream-coloured comforter. He pulled an overnight bag out of the closet and carried it into his room. Then, almost ritualistically, he laid it open on the bed and closed his eyes, trying to allow room for his instincts to manifest themselves. *If I even have any.* He'd seen no evidence of their existence before this.

Okay, no instincts. Maybe he'd just pack for a long weekend out of town. Trying not to overthink it, he put things into the bag. Three sets of underwear and socks. A pair of jeans, two t-shirts, and a long-sleeved shirt he wore to work sometimes under his yellow NCDSF polo. Toothpaste, brush, razor and shaving cream. The book from his nightstand, a biography of a famous astrophysicist. He'd wear his comfortable walking shoes, and the time of year made other footwear gratuitous.

He carried the overnight bag downstairs and set it on the kitchen table. The dog watched him pass the living room without comment. In the kitchen, Wint made ham and cheese sandwiches and packed them into a cooler bag with several apples, three bottles of water, and a handful of granola bars. He looked around the kitchen. Everything he'd added to the bag made perfect sense for a brief jaunt to an unknown destination, but it didn't feel finished. *Instincts*, the dog had said. Wint went to the pantry and pulled out a dusty bottle of Mericel wine that had been there for at least five years. He wiped a considerable layer of dust from the bottle and put it in the overnight bag, nestling it into the clothing for safety. Yes. He gave the wine a crisp nod and added a corkscrew. That felt right.

He looked around. Pulling open the utensil drawer again, he rummaged around until he found a sterling silver teaspoon his mother had given him. He put that in, too. This was getting easier. He considered the dog's mention of technology. From a little-used shelf in the coat closet, he took an old ham radio setup and made room for that in the suitcase as well, folding his clothes into smaller squares to free up the space.

The dog ambled into the kitchen. "Smelled like you were making food," he observed with a hopeful glance around the counter and table.

"Some sandwiches to take with us to—wherever," Wint said. "They're ready now."

"I knew it. Dogs have profound olfactory senses," Rex said. "Of course, I expect most people aren't aware of that. So, is there any food for right now?"

Sighing, Wint opened a can of tuna and dumped it into the bowl he'd set on the floor next to the refrigerator for Rex. The dog chewed with gusto while Wint waited for inspiration about what else to take, but nothing came to him. The tuna finished, Rex padded over and put his front feet on the seat of a chair, craning to look into the packed suitcase. As the Whidden Shepherd was a large breed, this was no significant challenge. He sniffed the teaspoon, the wine, and the topmost of Wint's folded clothes with delicate interest. Then his attention focused on the ham radio.

"What's that box?"

"An old ham radio that belonged to my dad. Don't ask me why I put it in there." Wint shrugged. "I was trying to follow your advice about instincts."

The dog backed away from the table, his bright brown eyes fixed on Wint. Even his floppy ear was pricked forward. "Ham? Radio? Those two words don't go together. Ham is to eat; radio is to listen. Even a dog who just learned to talk knows that."

"That's just what it's called." Wint twirled one of the radio dials, a hint of defensiveness creeping into his tone. "Something to do with the word 'amateurs' 'way back when it got started. It's a hobby. People from all over the world use them to communicate with each other. It's a technology, and it seemed right."

Rex's stare increased to a frightening intensity. His liquid eyes had opened so wide Wint saw the reflective membrane behind the irises. The dog's tail stiffened and the fur on his hackles bristled. "But that's what it's called? Ham. Radio?"

"That's what it's called. For cheese's sake, I'll take it out if it's freaking you out this much." Even for a talking dog, Rex was having a weird reaction to the thing.

"'*The pig that lives not, yet speaks with many mouths.*' Do you think you could call it that?"

"What the—? No, I could not call it that! I suppose *you* could, if you wanted to say something completely cryptic and deranged." Wint stared at the dog. Rex's eyes had become enormous pools, his entire demeanour more expressive than Wint would have thought possible from a dog. Unfortunately, he didn't recognize dog expressions. "What's wrong with you?"

The dog shook his head, and let the shudder continue down his back for a good whole-body shake before he answered. "You're him! By all the Bones, you're him." Rex sounded both wondering and disappointed.

"I'm who?"

"You're the Technocrat Avatar, of course," said the dog, lowering his haunches to sit. "Although you're not at all what I expected, I have to admit. Still, you've got the talking dead pig, and that's the sign as far as I know. The pig radio does work, I suppose?"

"*Ham* radio, and yes, it works, and it has nothing to do with pigs. And I'm not the techno-whatever. I'm a launch controller at NCDSF. Or at least I was. I expect I've been fired by now," he added in a gloomy tone.

"What I don't understand," Rex said, tilting his head to the side in that way dogs have when they're considering something unusual, "is why you don't have more answers about all this, if you're the Technocrat Avatar. I thought you'd have more information."

"Well, I guess that must mean *I'm not him!*" Wint snapped. "And furthermore, I'm done. This is stupid, and I'm tired, and I'm not playing along any more." He turned on his heel and left the kitchen without another word.

He was back ten seconds later, and took the sandwiches and the water bottles out of the suitcase and put them in the fridge, because he wasn't about to waste perfectly good food even if the world had been upended. The dog said nothing, for which Wint was grateful. Then he left the kitchen again, returned to his room, closed *and locked* the door, and threw himself on the bed. He had no plan for what he would do next, but he had a moment of profound regret that he'd left the bottle of wine downstairs.

Lunch Date

Nerlim

Nerlim Pettibone was enjoying a late lunch with Gameldina Gannand. It was almost unbelievable, after all these years, that they were sitting here having a civil conversation, and had been doing so for over two hours. Their previous record for civility had been closer to two minutes.

Sometimes two words.

They were in a cozy little neighbourhood restaurant called *The Sugar Goat,* only a short walk from NCDSF. The decor was mundane and not ashamed: a mix of tables and booths, squares of tempered glass covering bright tablecloths, and potted ferns lurking in the corners. A hand-lettered menu in colourful chalks hung above the counter, offering a wide variety of lunch items, but the current offerings comprised cold sandwiches and tortilla chips with salsa and sour cream. This was, as the bewildered waitress explained, because most of the kitchen appliances (like many devices across D'sharu) had stopped working without explanation or responded with cantankerous randomness. Rather to his surprise, Nerlim found he didn't care about the cold sandwiches, because he was far more interested in the ongoing conversation than in what he was eating. His gourmet sensibilities were, so to speak, on the back burner for now. Anyway, it was a flark of a lot better than what he'd been served at the nursing home. He thought of that last bowl of grey porridge and repressed a shudder.

Nerlim and Gammy were no longer drinking Black Angus Knockdown, which was for the best.

They had switched to a twenty-year-old fortified wine, which was not.

"But *if* the fifth force exists, Nerlim," Gammy said, for what might have been the fourth time, "why haven't we discovered it before this? We have astronomers, we have planetary geologists, we have physhi—physicisss—other scientists who have studied everything about our world for centuries. Why haven't we found it?" She punctuated each of the last five words with a rap of her knuckles on the glass-covered tabletop.

Gammy's watery brown eyes had become ever more watery as the lunch wore on and the alcohol flowed. The liquid gaze she fixed on Nerlim now made him worry he might be in danger of drowning. He marshalled his patience.

"I've explained that. I think it's a *latent* force, Gameldina. It's been inactive, dormant—sleeping, if you will—all this time. Now whatever has happened has activated it; woken it up. And now that it's active, it's interfering with the known forces. They've de-stabilized. It's why the launch didn't work." He held up his half-eaten egg salad and watercress sandwich on whole wheat bread. "It's why appliances aren't working. Why there are cars stranded everywhere. The fifth force interferes with how things work."[1]

Gammy shook her head doggedly and wagged a stalk of celery[2] at him. "But it's not comprehensive. It's random. Appliances are working *in some places*. Cars are running *in some places*. Where they aren't, they might start up again at any moment. And where they are, they might stop. How can you explain that? There aren't any exceptions to the effects of the other known forces. How could this one work differently?"

---

1. Nerlim was perfectly correct in this theory, although he hadn't yet narrowed it down to a specific clash with technology. Given what he had to work with, though, kudos to him for getting this far.

2. The combination of celery (or celery-adjacent plants) with fancy drinks is a universal phenomenon. Drop into any planet with both fancy drinks and celery, and it's guaranteed that someone will have invented a drink that requires a stick of celery. No one understands why this is so, not even The Min.

Nerlim shrugged, mouth full of egg salad. "How should I know?" he asked as he chewed. "It's not like I've ever been able to study the thing. All I know is that it exists."

"Oh, you *know* that, do you?" Gammy tossed back the last of her wine and dropped the celery into the empty glass. She'd polished off her ham-on-rye while Nerlim explained his theories—the first time. "The way you always knew it? You could just *feel* it?" She waggled her fingers in a woo-woo gesture, and the mockery in her tone threatened to snap the tenuous thread of civility.

"Gameldina, can you explain your connection to the moon?" Nerlim asked quietly, leaning across the table toward her. His longish nose twitched, and his blue eyes were intent on hers.

She shifted in her chair, caught off guard. Frowning, she asked, "What do you mean?"

"The moon. You told me once that your connection to it led you down every pathway you took in your life; it coloured the way you approached everything else; it guided you to the choices that would lead where you wanted to arrive. Can you explain to me what that connection feels like? What it is?"

She didn't meet his eyes, and spent a few moments fiddling with her dish, her wineglass, the silverware. "No," she said at last, looking up to meet his gaze with a touch of defiance swimming in her watery eyes. "I can't explain it. It's just there."

Nerlim sat back in his chair. He made as if to clasp his hands behind his head, but a crackling protest from one shoulder made him change his mind and he crossed his arms over his chest instead. "Well, that's how it is for me with the fifth force."

"But I can see the moon," she argued. She plucked the celery back out of her glass and waved it around like a pointer. "Everyone can see it. It's a real thing. There's nothing mysterious or uncanny about it."

"So just because I'm the only one who can sense the fifth force—or at least the only one you've met—you think it can't be real?"

Gammy blew out a breath and deflated. "Chicken on a stick. I suppose that doesn't sound fair," she admitted. In a display of optimism, she tipped the wine bottle upside-down over her glass, but only a few paltry drops sputtered out. "However, please keep in mind that I'm quite drunk right now."

For a moment, her face went pensive, and she seemed about to say something more. But then she blinked, and her face relaxed, and he understood that whatever it was, she'd changed her mind.

"We still haven't talked about the photo," he reminded her.

"If you ask me, it's a fake," she snapped. A heartbeat later, she burst out laughing. "Oh, your face! It was priceless!"

Nerlim attempted to muster his dignity as her hoots of laughter settled into chuckles. "Gameldina, you're drunk."

"Well, didn't I just tell you that? Look, that photo is the only thing that got me to listen to you today. I can't discount it. It's too—well, it's too something." She shook her head, as if grappling with an idea she couldn't articulate. She pointed a finger at him, and despite all the wine, it was steady. "But figuring out what it means—that's more than I can do. I think it's more than you can do, too. We have to find some help on that one, Nerlie. And it's been a very long day for me, even if it is only the middle of the afternoon. I need sleep, and a headache pill. Anything else will have to wait until tomorrow."

He felt the chill touch of disappointment like an icy finger on the back of his neck, but she was right. That they were even talking was a huge step forward; that she'd admit the possibility of a fifth force was a leap beyond that; her acceptance of the notion that they would work on this together was a bounding spring across a crevasse that took a good long run-up just to attempt. It was time to accept her cooperation with gratitude. He'd get Gameldina into a cab, if he could find a functioning one, and see that she got home safe. Then he'd go back to his hotel and study the weather photo some more. He had a few acquaintances he might reach out to for help; some ideas he was percolating. He blinked at the empty bottles ranged around the table. Or he might just follow Gammy's lead and take a nap. He wasn't running on much sleep, either.

He wished she wouldn't call him Nerlie, though. He'd always hated that.

Finding the Words

Heline

Heline, smothered by the enveloping darkness of the closet, didn't stop screaming until Jans opened the door. She twisted and fell into his arms as it opened, because she'd backed up against it in her terror.

"What is?" he demanded.

Heline tried to take a deep breath, but his arms crushed her to him. He smelled very male. His heart pounded under her ear, his own body trembling as much as hers was with the adrenaline rush. He was ready and willing to protect her. It was a sweet gesture. Her panic melted as if the enveloping presence of those flexed muscles had vacuumed it out of her.

Over Jans' shoulder, she glimpsed Eleanor in the hallway, her elfin face twisted into a scowl. She'd planted her hands on her hips in an aggressive stance.

"What's going on? Heline, is this guy bothering you? I've taken a lot of self-defence classes, you know, and if you need help, I can take care of it." She said *take care of it* in such a menacing tone that Heline was absolutely convinced she meant it.

It was so ridiculous that Heline almost laughed. "Of course not. I told you, he's my boyfriend," she said. She tried to push away from him, overwhelmed by the urgent need to get them away from the closet and close the door before they could see anything. "Jans, this is Eleanor. Eleanor, Jans."

"Nice to meeting you, Eleanor, sister of Heline." Jans glanced back at Eleanor with a perfunctory smile. "But is not nothing, Heline. Is something bad scaring you, to make the banshee screams come from your so pretty lips." He transferred her over to his right arm in a smooth motion, without diminishing his support. "Do you think you see a *miske*, a mouse? Is it a spiderling?"

Jans peered into and around the closet in a way that made Heline's throat constrict. It was just that he was *looking* at everything, she thought wildly. As grateful as she had been for him a moment ago, now she wanted him to *go*. And yet he seemed to take no real notice of the unusual items on the shelves or find them in any way remarkable as he searched for the source of her fright.

Coming up behind them, Eleanor rested a hand on Heline's back and stood on tiptoe to peer into the closet past her. Heline turned at the touch and saw her sister's eyes go wide as she glimpsed the closet's odd contents. She read her sister's thought in her face: this was not what she would expect to find in Heline's welcoming and cozy cottage.

"Yes," Heline gasped past the invisible hand of fear squeezing her neck, "that's it—it was a spider. It—startled me. I'm fine now, Jans." She slipped in front of him, putting her hands on Jans' chest and pushing, but he didn't step back.

Instead, he brushed past her, stepping inside the closet, and set to his self-appointed task of spider-hunting. "Then we will to find this spider and—" He closed a fist in a descriptive crushing gesture, then pulled the string for the light. It flickered on, weakly. Jans picked up the little black-painted soup pot, looked under and inside it. "He is hiding, yes, this spiderling?"

Just don't touch the hat. Heline glanced up at it, looming in the half-shadows of the upper shelf, but the eye had disappeared...or closed. Her heartbeat ramped up again, and she battled the urge to body-check Jans out of the closet. "It's okay, Jans, forget it. It's yako. The spider's gone." *Don't touch the hat.*

Jans lifted a black cardboard box, moved aside a bundle of dried herbs. "Still, I look for him," he said with maddening patience. "So no more he will be scaring my Heline." His eyes travelled up the shelves.

"What's that?" Eleanor asked, pointing to the crystal sphere.

Heline was horrified to see tiny red, blue, and green bolts of energy crackling inside the globe. That was new. Sweat pricked her forehead as she tried to turn her body to block Eleanor's view. "Nothing. It's just a—nightlight." She tried a casual laugh, but to her own ears it sounded more like a weird cackle.

"Is not a very good one. More light would be helping," Jans muttered. "Why everything is being so black? And this needs new lightbulb."

The words screamed in her mind now. They pierced her brain like an icepick headache. *Don't touch the hat. Not the hat!* She looked up again, and the flarking thing had the audacity to *wink* at her. In desperation she grabbed Jans' arm, tugging him toward the door.

"I don't care about the spider, Jans. Just go—go and finish supper, okay? Yako? Yako, Jans?" She hated the pleading note in her voice. *Don't touch the hat!*

She might have been a spider herself, for all the effect her efforts had.

Heline watched in horror as, in seeming slow motion, Jans reached up and plucked the black, pointed hat down from its shelf at the highest point of the closet. Dust feathered down on them like the innards of a burst pillow, drifting and swirling in a pale cloud against the black backdrop of the closet. Jans blew more dust from the hat with great puffs, like the belches of a steam-engine.

This is a nightmare. Heline's pulse pounded in her temples and her heart raced like an adrenaline-frenzied squirrel. She wondered if she might just die. Jans straightened the point of the hat and peered inside.

"No spiders," he proclaimed. "But what is this? It is not looking something you would wear? But then again, anything Heline can make look good." And with a final swipe at the dust, he playfully fitted it over her head, tilting it at a jaunty angle.

He considered her, grinning. "No, as they are saying, it is not being you. And since the spiderling is gone, I am back to the kitchen!" He strode off, brushing his hands together and whistling.

Heline stood rooted to the spot as if her feet had truly become embedded into the wooden floor, another scream stuck far, far back in her throat. It seemed to hang there, suspended in the moment as if it would never break free. And if it never broke free, neither would she. The touch of the hat on her head had sent an electrifying shock coursing through her body, from the top of her head to the tips of her pink-polished toenails. Not pain. Something far beyond pain or fear or understanding.

She had the words.

She had the words *to the songs.*

She had the words to ALL the songs.

And she had to write them down.

When the scream escaped, it had shrunk to a squeak. Heline pushed past a startled Eleanor and sprinted after Jans, still wearing the hat.

Corax Returns

Gammy

Gammy woke with a crick in her spine, a mouth that tasted like someone had been storing old socks in it, and a tender left elbow. Something hard and sharp dug into her back between her shoulder blades. These complaints were nothing, however, compared to the pain that assaulted her senses when she attempted to open her eyes. An icepick headache had nothing on the sensation of having one's eyes removed *from the inside*.

"Nggunngghhh," she grunted, and slammed them shut. Too fast; big mistake. She grunted again.

Had she been mugged? Hit by a truck? Left for dead in an alleyway? To the best of her recollection, however, alleyways did not tend to be furnished with leather-covered sofas, which her other senses suggested she reclined upon. The smell—not reminiscent of alleyways, either, although she didn't frequent such spots. She expected an alleyway scent would be more about spilled beer, garbage, and old urine. No, this place smelled like her office at NCDSF: the homey aromas of well-worn carpet and stacks of papers and cheap wood, and underneath that a nuanced layer of oil and metal and ozone that came from the launch pads and permeated every building in the complex.

With extreme caution, Gammy let one eye flutter open. *Careful, careful; no sudden moves this time.* She frowned and concentrated on bringing into focus one blurry thing in front of her. It resolved into a glass, beaded with condensation. The glass held a full complement of liquid, and not, she noted with gratitude, Black Angus Knockdown. She raised a slow hand—the left one, because her elbow twanged a mild protest of pain. She grasped, lifted, and guided the glass to her lips and drank. Water. Cold and sweet and perfectly non-alcoholic. She closed her eye again.

"Sorry I couldn't get you all the way home."

The voice thumped in her head like a train passing through it, rattling the furniture of her thoughts. She wondered with annoyance why Nerlim Pettibone would shout at her. They'd gotten on fine yesterday.

"Shhhhh," she managed, although even that soft susurration hurt her ears. So to be fair, perhaps Nerlim wasn't shouting.

"I couldn't find a cab running out to your place," he continued, softening his voice. "All the vehicles in this part of the city have stopped working again. I got you this far, and we were fortunate to find Argit still here. He let me in and said he was going home for supper. Sorry about your elbow, too. You banged it on the door frame getting out of the cab, so it might be sore. Now, try to swallow these, and I'll come back later to check on you. Argit left me a key."

Something small and hard and round was pressed up to her lips, and she opened her mouth like an obedient baby bird. Headache tablets, she assumed, unless Nerlim had plans to poison her. At this point, that might be a welcome relief. She swallowed more water and the medication, and felt the soft warmth of a blanket being drawn up around her shoulders and tucked into place with care. Nerlim's footsteps retreated across the threadbare carpet.

Gammy slept again before the door closed behind him.

An unknowable length of time passed before she woke next, with the impression that someone had just spoken her name. She opened her eyes, feeling grateful that it involved much less effort and pain this time, and expected to see Nerlim's worried face. She planned to let him have it for letting her drink so much. Why, it had been years and years since she'd let a man get her drunk, she thought with righteous indignation. Since then she'd been able to manage quite well on her own, thank you very much. And if she recalled correctly, that last time, she'd been drinking with Nerlim, too...

She sat up, a slow, careful movement, but Nerlim wasn't there. Instead, she saw the same lumpy-faced apparition whom she had encountered twice now. He hovered near the sofa, wringing his semi-transparent hands in evident dismay and looking down at her. He still wore the same embroidered robe—too eccentric for good taste, in Gammy's opinion—and his hair spiked with the same wild abandon. *Chicken on a dirty stick*, Gammy mentally swore. If she'd known, she'd have pretended to keep sleeping. Oh well.

"Are you going to stay long enough to be any use to me this time?" Gammy barked at him. She winced, twitching one eye against the consequence of speaking too loud—the twinge of her not-quite-cured headache. But without Nerlim here to get what was coming to him, then the next available target would have to do.

"It is good to see you recovered, dear lady." The translucent individual bobbed in the air in agitation. "I was concerned."

Gammy sat up. The apparition retreated a couple of feet back from the sofa. "What's your name again?"

"Er, Corax. Are you sure you're well?"

Gammy gave him a withering stare. Gammy's withering stare was a thing of legend. Staffers at NCDSF lived in fear of it; astronauts shifted in discomfort if it found them; plants might literally shrink and pale in its path. The translucent figure did not react to it, which annoyed Gammy even further. She stood and crossed to her desk, smoothing the wrinkles out of her clothes with absent motions as she walked. She kept a few spare clothing items in the closet, but she'd wait to change until after this—person—left. Gammy sat, rotating her chair with slow precision until she faced him. In the tone of voice one might use for interrogating a misbehaving child, she said, "When we spoke earlier, you were about to explain some things to me. For instance, how my launch is going to happen now?"

Corax floated over to the armchair facing Gammy's desk and seated himself—or appeared to sit—in it. He made a visible attempt to belay his agitation and speak with calm dignity, clasping his hands in his lap. "I believe we can help each other. This is a time of significant change for your world. That also means it is a time of great opportunity."

Gammy sighed and suppressed an eye roll. She much preferred people to cut to the chase in their conversations with her. She had little tolerance for circumlocution, although she held a grudging respect for anyone who knew the word. "Right. Significant change, yadda yadda yadda, I can get my launch back on track. What's the opportunity for you?"

Corax's gaze darted around the perimeter of Gammy's face in what she considered a shifty fashion. He looked at the closed window blinds over the sofa, the credenza where Gammy kept the Black Angus Knockdown, the myriad press photos on the walls. He didn't seem to share Gammy's preference for directness. When he returned his attention to her he said, "You told me you didn't recognize the word 'god' when I asked you about it before."

"That's right. Never heard of it."

He steepled his insubstantial fingers and tapped them against his translucent lips. "How do D'sharians think the world came into being?"

Gammy stared at the apparition from under her grey mop fringe of hair. Not only was he solidity-challenged, he was also, apparently, mad. "Everyone knows how a world comes into being," she said in a measured tone, now speaking as if to a flighty child who hadn't been paying attention the first time they had been told something very important. "A nearby star went supernova, and after the explosion, the debris flattened into a protoplanetary disk—"

Corax held up an insubstantial hand. "Thank you, dear lady. I know what follows from that. Do all D'sharians ascribe to this belief?"

She raised an eyebrow at him. "With the exception of some who missed out on that lesson in school or are dissociated from reality due to mental health issues, I'd expect so. Seeing that it's not so much a belief as established scientific fact."

"There are no competing theories of creation by other beings, spirits, supernatural forces, or the like?"

Gammy sat back and crossed her arms over her chest. "In a word, no. That would be ridiculous."

"And you're sure everyone thinks this way?"

"Asked and answered. Are you going somewhere with this?"

Corax pursed his lips. "So it's true. Interesting," he said, speaking more to himself than to Gammy. "Very interesting. I shall have to consider how best to proceed, but I must move without delay—"

Gammy reached out a hand and snapped her fingers in front of his insubstantial face. "That's what I'm trying to get you to do. Move without delay *in this conversation*. Let's get back on track here. You're going to tell me—"

A knock sounded at Gammy's door, hesitant and soft. Corax startled and disappeared with a soft popping sound, leaving the chair—well, still empty, but in some way slightly more empty than it had been the instant before.

Gammy swore with lurid originality and aimed a petulant kick at the leg of her desk. Would the thing ever stay in one place long enough to finish a conversation? Would she ever find out if this hallucination was real, and if so, what he might do for her?

She wanted the launch back, and she wanted it now.

The door opened and Nerlim's head poked in. His long nose twitched, betraying his nerves.

Well, Gammy told herself, *next available target*. She took a deep breath and prepared to let him have it.

"I think I know what happened with the launch," he said before she could start, holding up one placatory hand. "And I might have figured out what the cloud picture means. Hear me out? Or should I come back later?" He stood poised on the knife edge of Gammy's anger, ready to retreat out the door if a stabbing, either verbal or literal, seemed imminent.

With a sheer effort of will, Gammy deflated her anger and let it go. She couldn't risk refusing any information, since she didn't know what bits she needed to get the launch back on track. "Come on in," she said in a voice weary with resignation. "But it had better be good."

At the Junkyard

Ulric

Ulric and Tiny Enos had not had a good day at Old Mean Melvin's. They'd been supposed to work only half the day, since they'd stayed late one night earlier in the week, but he refused to let them leave until the entire barn was painted, and that took until almost suppertime. Old Mean Melvin seemed determined to live up to his name, or maybe he was lobbying to have it changed to Old Bastard Melvin. Eiric, Poppy, and Natelie hadn't shown up at all, which had contributed to the length of their day. Ulric planned to have some choice words for them later. He certainly had no shortage of words these days.

"Might as well come and have supper at my house," he said to Enos as they trudged home through the sparse streets of the city's outskirts. The outlying farms, like Old Mean Melvin's, gave way to more dense residential areas, but their route traced the edge where farms, warehouses, and light industrial buildings intermingled. Cars here seemed (at least today) to have succumbed to whatever weirdness had seized the world, because abandoned vehicles littered the streets. One would have thought this would lead to more people walking, but the foot traffic on the sidewalks was sparse. Maybe most people's response to the strangeness was to stay home.

Despite his invitation to Enos, all Ulric wanted to do was go home alone and try on his robe and hat in the privacy of his room. But Enos was the friend standing by him during a tough time, and he needed to acknowledge it. Past, best-forgotten experience told him that Tiny Enos' mother would not win any competitions for the world's best cook, no matter how good she was at sewing.

"Okay." Enos accepted the invitation with a shrug. He looked at Ulric sideways. "Got any weird new words in your head?"

Ulric flushed, ready to blurt out a defensive retort, but he realized Enos was not teasing him. His eyes were clear and interested, and it seemed like an honest question. "Well, since you're asking, yes, I do. And I wish I understood what they mean."

"What's it like?"

Ulric shrugged. "Strange. It's a bit like when you're doing something and you feel like you did it before. Like I somehow knew these words existed, but I never paid attention to them. But there's more, too. It's like there's a power in them, a potential to do stuff...if I can figure out how."

"Stuff like not getting killed when you fell off the roof?"

"Yeah. I think that was a fluke, though."

Enos kicked an empty can ahead of them as they walked, its tinny protestations echoing in the deserted street. "How can you find out what they mean? I guess if it wasn't school vacation, you could ask Mr. Coddlington, but I don't guess he'd be much help." Enos chuckled.

Ulric smiled in return. Mr. Coddlington was a good enough teacher; he tried his best, but even normal words like "spaghetti" gave him a hard time depending on the day. Since he consistently mixed up words like "bought" and "brought," it was doubtful he'd be able to help Ulric with something like "inter-dimensionally subsequent vectors."

"I dunno; maybe look them up in a dictionary or something?"

"Yeah, maybe." Enos didn't sound too hopeful about any dictionary on D'sharu being comprehensive enough to contain these particular words. "What if you...tried to use them?"

Ulric stopped walking and stared at his friend. "Don't you think that sounds kind of dangerous?"

His friend also stopped and turned back to meet his gaze. The much-abused can rolled ahead and dropped unheeded into the ditch. "Oh, it might be. But you've gotta be curious."

Ulric was more than curious. He'd fought the urge all day to say a few of those unusual words and see what happened. Only fear—of what atrocities Old Mean Melvin would perpetrate on them if something went wrong, and of the terrifying list of "side effects" reciting itself in his brain—kept him silent.

"The thing is, some terrible things could happen to me if I mess around with this stuff without knowing what I'm doing. I didn't tell you this part before." He recounted the catalogue of dire warnings.

"Flark," Enos said in a hushed, reverent voice. "That is nasty."

"Tell me about it."

"Keep walking, come on." The two friends continued in silence for a moment, and then Enos mused, "They might have been trying to scare you. Like, because they're worried you might be too powerful. That's the way it would be in a book, or a movie."

"Who's 'they'?"

Enos shrugged. "There's always a 'they,' isn't there?"[1]

"Maybe so, yeah. But the thing is...something kind of bad *did* happen after I stopped myself from falling."

Enos stopped again and put his fists on his hips. "How am I supposed to help you with this if you hold stuff back from me? What happened?"

"Remember? I grew a beard," Ulric mumbled. He kept walking, making Enos catch up to him.

"That was real? I thought it was like, a mirage or something. I only saw it for a second."

"Yeah, when you saw it. But that was the second time. It was real. A long, white, old grandpa's beard."

"Well wow, a beard sounds super dangerous," Enos said with a smirk. "Did you cut yourself shaving it off?"

"No, that wasn't the bad part. I had to—"

Enos glanced over at his friend when Ulric broke off. Ulric stared straight ahead, his lips pressed together in a grim line.

"What? You had to what?"

"Nothing. Never mind."

"Look, I didn't mean—"

"I said it's nothing."

---

1. There is, in fact, always a "they," but for the most part they remain shadowy beings, never fully seen in the light. Also, if you're part of a "they," you probably don't know it.

Enos stopped walking again, while Ulric strode ahead even faster now. "Which means it's definitely something," Enos muttered. He crossed his arms and waited to see if Ulric would look back. Ulric must have realized Tiny Enos wasn't following because his shoulders slumped and he slowed, finally turning back to his friend.

"Are you coming?"

Enos shook his head. "Tell me what you were going to say. What did you have to do?"

Ulric still had the face of a donkey who's been asked to do one more thing instead of going home to a nice warm barn and some tasty feed like he'd been promised. He said nothing.

Enos sighed and walked up to rejoin him. "I can't help you if you don't tell me everything. Just say it. I'm not scared of this stuff. Not so far, anyway."

Ulric dropped his eyes to the sidewalk. "I know. It's just—I didn't realize, and I was scared. I didn't have any other ideas."

"For crusty cheese's sake, Ulric, what did you do?"

Ulric muttered something too low for Enos to catch.

"What? I swear if you don't tell me, I'll go tell your ma about the curtains."

"I sort of—read your mind." The words came out in a rush.

Enos' face twisted into a disbelieving grimace. "You read my mind? When was this? And how did I not realize you were doing it?"

"I don't know. I only peeked in at one particular spot, so I guess you didn't notice." Ulric put his back against the graffiti-splashed side of the warehouse crouching next to the sidewalk and slid down until he sat on the pavement. "When you were bringing me the drink. I'd just discovered the beard, and I was desperate to get rid of it before anyone saw. The voice in my head said if I formed a psychic copula with—"

"Whoa, a what?" Enos sat beside Ulric.

"Like, a mental connection. If I made one with someone who knew how I was *supposed* to look, their image would help me put myself back." He blew out a sigh. "Or at least, that's the best way I can explain it."

Enos took a moment to digest this. "All right, so you looked in my mind for a picture of you. Doesn't sound so bad, since I didn't feel it."

Ulric turned to face him. "But that's the point! You weren't even aware. I could have poked around in your head and found all kinds of things, things you wouldn't *want* me to find. What if I could do it to anyone? I don't want to. I don't want that kind of power. That's how you get supervillains like PainLord or the Vermilion Viper," he added, naming two of the most famous evil-doers in a comics series the boys both read. "And you're my friend. I especially don't want to do creepy stuff to you."

"Fair enough," Enos said after a further moment of contemplation. "But with the beard, I'm just helping you fix something. I didn't give you permission that first time, but of course I would have if you'd asked."

Ulric nodded. "I guess."

"So if you need a quick look inside my brain to keep yourself from being hurt, it's fine with me. You don't need to ask permission, and don't beat yourself up about it. Besides," he said with a grin, accompanying his words with a light punch to Ulric's shoulder, "you're too much of a chickenshit to be a supervillain."

Ulric punched him back. "So funny, I forgot to laugh. Come on, let's get going."

The two stood and dusted off, turning towards home again. "Yeah, but go back to what we were saying. I still think it's worth experimenting a little to see what you can do. Especially if you've got some guaranteed protection." Enos tapped a finger against his temple.

Ulric squinted. "It might not be guaranteed. For some of those side effects, I wouldn't be in any shape to fix them by looking in your brain. Remember, exploding teeth. Imploding *eyes.*"

"Right." Enos shuddered. After a minute, though, he mused, "But I expect it's only if you do something super intense and spectacular. We're just talking about a little minor experimentation. They must expect you to try things. Who wouldn't?"

"There's 'they' again," Ulric complained, but he was giving the idea real consideration. Catching himself from that fall must have been pretty serious...magic, as the voice in his head had called it. He wanted to know what else he might do. But to find out, he'd have to test it a little. "You think I should?"

Tiny Enos nodded. "What's the good of something if you can't use it?"

"All right. Come on." Ulric turned down an alleyway before he changed his mind. It led to the back of a junkyard, and a fence low enough to climb over without too much effort. Crowbar McLaughlin didn't care if kids sneaked into the junkyard from time to time, as long as they didn't steal much. It was a junkyard, after all. What were they going to hurt?

They clambered over the fence and stood in a small clearing, an island awash on all sides with the discards of society. Junk grew and flourished in organic piles; microwave ovens balanced atop a precarious three-legged table, overgrown with twining loops of black-coated cable. Here a one-wheeled lawn seeder held a partial set of dishes; there a hairless baby doll with a terrifying permanent wink peered over the rim of a battered bucket, which sat on a sagging mattress. The whole place was a jungle of detritus. The perfect place to experiment.

Enos hauled a small, three-legged stool out from under a mildewed chair cushion. The stool's seat was cracked, and it looked like several generations of dogs, or perhaps beavers, had cut their teeth on the legs. "Here," he said, setting it down in front of Ulric. "Experiment on this."

Faced with such a direct test, Ulric quailed. "And do what?"

"Come on, there must be something," Enos insisted. "You made yourself fly—or at least float. Try that."

"Er," Ulric said, unsure how to begin. He wished with unspoken desperation for his robe and hat. They lent him such confidence, made him more sure of himself. He closed his eyes and tried to imagine he was wearing them. It helped—a little. Now, he told himself, concentrate. What had happened when he'd saved himself from falling?

He had created a discrete field between himself and the ground, exciting subatomic particles into an initial density equalling his own mass and proceeding to decrease it in proportional increments, which allowed him to float toward the ground until he touched down like a proverbial feather.

Ulric picked up the stool, hefting it to estimate its weight. He set it down and walked a ring around it, noting the precise points at which its well-gnawed legs touched the sandy, weed-dotted ground. This completed, he stepped back and stared with single-minded intensity at the stool. If he could tap into what the voice in his head called "magic" or thaumic energy, he might create a similar field between the stool and the ground, and increase the density of the field in increments to make it—

The stool shuddered as if experiencing a sudden chill, then with agonizing hesitation, rose into the air. It wobbled, but hovered a full two inches above the sandy ground. Ulric glanced at Tiny Enos and grinned, then turned his attention back to the stool.

With only a faint cautionary wisp of smoke to indicate anything wrong, the stool pulsed once in a way that wood, at least in this universe, was not intended to do. Without further warning, it exploded into a blizzard of splinters. They sprayed out like toothpick shrapnel, humming like bees, peppering and piercing anything in their path in all directions. Unfortunately, two of those directions were occupied by Ulric and Tiny Enos.

It flarking *hurt*.

INTERMEZZO DUE

THE MIN

Life on D'sharu was...challenging.

Machine and electronics reliability was sporadic and whimsical. Travel became next to impossible as airlines grounded all flights rather than risk having them tumble, electronics gone dead and useless, from the sky. (Someone noticed, sometime later, that there had not been a single airplane crash as a result of whatever had happened. No explanation ever surfaced, and other news soon overshadowed the phenomenon. The people of D'sharu, as a whole, accepted a good thing and got on with life. They never once suspected the background interventions of a shadowy figure such as The Min working to prevent the worst catastrophes. But The Min neither expected nor wanted recognition for such things.)

Even if one did not want to travel, even if one wanted nothing more than to stay cozy at home and eat a toasted bagel with some hot tea, there might be complications. Heaters and furnaces functioned, or not, with a will of their own. The kettle might turn off halfway to the boil and not switch on again until one had given up and drunk a large glass of unpleasant, lukewarm milk from the intermittently working refrigerator instead. The toaster was every bit as temperamental. Let's not even speak of the stove. And good luck watching television or listening to the radio; you might get to the end of a program, or be left hanging in the middle when the picture or the sound winked out without even a warning flicker.

Calls deluged repairmen of all descriptions to fix items that might be working again by the time they arrived, tools in hand. Or they might labour for hours over an item in apparently perfect working order, only to admit defeat moments before the thing came back on of its own accord.[1]

Region by region, the entire planet seemed to pulse—functioning, not functioning—everything, everywhere, in fact everyone, because a people so dependent on their machines didn't pivot overnight to work as efficiently without them. A distinct air of uncertainty hovered over every aspect of life as D'sharians wondered whether to find new ways to do things or wait a moment to see if the old way might work out after all.

However, no one can live in that kind of uncertainty for any great length of time. Not comfortably. Not without the possibility of going mad. The Min understood this, and followed it all with a mix of interest and trepidation. What transpired in these first few days would be critical, and set the course for what would come later. And while most of the Convocation had answered her second summons, several had not. That worried her. It meant they thought they had an actual chance to exert influence down there. That they would risk everything for power, and bet against the limitations set out by the Convocation itself.

She didn't like it.

A considerable number of people on D'sharu were also thinking things, and some even doing things, that they had never considered before. A lot of these things involved pointy hats, staves, small bottles and pots containing odd ingredients and the recitation of hitherto unknown words. Most of the time, these magic forays resulted in unremarkable results; no one knew what they were doing, after all. Small successes could be explained away as natural phenomena or coincidence, or conveniently ignored as being somebody else's problem. Unsettling times, both for the people actively involved, and for anyone who observed them. The Min, of course, recognized it as the awakened thaumic force flexing its influence and waging a tug-of-war with

---

1. In fact, in the weeks following the awakening of magic on D'sharu, all repair-related fields suffered a record out-migration of workers. It became too maddening to continue. Few ever knew what had precipitated the abrupt left turn in their career paths.

technology, something she'd witnessed many times before on other worlds.

Not quite the same, though. Some anomaly niggled at the back of her mind, although she couldn't identify it. It bore watching. But D'sharu was not the only world where burgeoning magic and trans-dimensionals playing at being gods and all the attendant problems needed oversight. The Min couldn't spend all her time watching one planet.

Thus, she was distracted when another knock came on her virtual door. Her attention was focused far from D'sharu, on a planet where a cosmic event had activated the latent magical abilities of the world's sentient, amoeba-like creatures. Great hilarity ensued as they experimented with the concept of limbs and other appendages in various numbers and configurations.[2] It took her a moment to compose herself when the knock came, feeling somewhat disgruntled when she looked up to see the source of the disruption.

Her mood did not improve when the caller turned out to be Xya. The Min heaved an inward sigh. She wouldn't be required to start the conversation. Xya would take care of that.

She breezed into The Min's office as if she owned it. It required a certain *je ne sais quoi* to do this in an office routinely defying several fundamental physical laws. Xya seemed to consider such details beneath her notice.

A tall, blonde woman, curvy but athletic, Xya had dressed today in a purple frock coat with intricate embroidery, open-throated white blouse, dark trousers, and knee-high black boots. Her pale hair fell in soft waves past her shoulders, and she fixed The Min with eyes the colour of overripe blueberries.

"You sent Skete to D'sharu," Xya noted, not bothering with greetings or salutations. Her blonde hair wavered around her face as if blown by a caressing breeze, although of course there were no breezes here in The Min's office-slash-library. Xya expertly accessorized even her environmental effects, leaving nothing to chance.

---

2. They eventually successfully magicked themselves into a prosperous, thriving, bipedal civilization, which would go on to form a galactic empire. But that's another story.

The Min held up a careworn hand. "Now wait, I sent him to watch, that's all."

Xya responded by holding up a finger, which became accusing when she levelled it to point at The Min. "You sent him to the Technocrat Avatar."

"I sent him to *watch* the Avatar. There's a difference."

Xya put her hands on her hips. The gesture made her look threatening in the most feminine and dangerous way possible.

"And who have you sent to 'watch' the boy? Or any of the others?" Xya demanded.

"The boy has friends. He'll have a much easier time. And the others aren't as vital. They'll find their own way."

Xya pursed her lips and shook her head. Her blonde hair responded with alacrity, floating around her head in a shiny, undulating halo as if suspended in water. "Most of the boy's friends don't matter, and at the moment, he's in some trouble. He'll bear closer attention, or he might attract undue influence from those rogue Convocation members. Not everyone is willing to abide by the rules, obviously. Don't forget what happened at 98475φ."

The Min gave a mental shudder, although she concealed her discomfort from Xya. Visions of that planet of madness swirled in the back of her mind, elbowing their rude way to the forefront. Trees walking and talking and trashing the place. People deformed and disfigured with horrible afflictions just for the sake of experimentation that before long degenerated into all-out war. Sentient monsters whose beastly instincts had been enhanced and intensified through magical means. Animated objects with nascent sentience of their own and no moral or ethical codes for guidance—not that those codes had been much help to the people who had them. She shut her mind to the images, but they never faded completely. No, she wouldn't soon forget that fiasco.[3]

---

3. The fate of 98475φ was not, to be clear, The Min's fault. But it was a testament to the potential disasters that awaited when trans-dimensional beings with no conscience flouted the rules. She was not about to let that happen on her watch.

Xya continued to press her point. "The fate of this planet's future is at stake here, and you know it. The boy deserves support, too. Unless you're taking sides, which a High Administrator is not supposed to do?" She crossed her arms in a belligerent accusation.

The Min might have bristled at such an insulting suggestion, but instead, she said in a weary voice, "And I suppose you think *you* should be the one to go and 'watch' him?" She could envision the eruption of a huge kerfuffle as this little drama unfolded. She'd sent Skete as an observer, but the Avatar had turned out to be the hapless sort who needed more guidance than she'd expected. And The Min did not take sides or interfere...much. Granted, Xya had been the first to come to her, but others might argue seniority or experience or favours to support the notion that they should have been chosen to go. She sighed. She'd hoped Skete's presence might slip by unnoticed, but she'd miscalculated. And although Xya might not have been The Min's first choice, she had certain qualities to suggest her for the task.

"As a matter of fact, I do." Xya ventured a smile, calculated to demonstrate her allegiance to The Min in all of this.

"You'll have to accept some restrictions, same as Skete," The Min warned her. "There's enough unauthorized activity going on down there, and I don't want to make it worse."

"Let's hear them," Xya said.

"But Xya—"

"What?"

The Min frowned. "There's something...not quite right about this. It's more than rogue members of the Convocation jockeying for position. That's par for the course, even if I might wish otherwise. There's a feeling on that planet that I don't like. Something's amiss."

"I promise to keep my eyes open."

"And report anything...odd...back to me at once?" The Min didn't like Xya's overconfidence, but she could trust her. To a point.

"Agreed."

"Have a seat, then." The Min conjured a chair and set it behind the blonde woman. On appearing, it might have bumped the backs of Xya's knees with more force than necessary, but judging distance was tricky with all that distracting hair blowing around.

Xya sat down with a thump, looking surprised only for a moment as she landed on the well-cushioned seat of the chair. Then the calculating look returned to her eyes and she narrowed them at The Min.

"Here's the deal." The Min leaned forward and rested her elbows on the desk. Silently, she thought, I hope *that poor boy is up to this*.

Just Bad Timing

Nerlim

Nerlim entered Gammy's shadowed office with hesitant steps and an abundance of caution. The lights were off and the blinds closed, and it felt like he was breaching the inner sanctum of an ancient temple. He'd blurted out some words to forestall the hurricane brewing in her face, but now he wondered if that had been advisable. She wouldn't appreciate his ideas, and she might discount them out of hand. And judging by the dull pounding in his own temples and her preference for a darkened room, she probably still had a headache, too. He tried to make no noise or sudden moves as he crossed the threadbare carpet to the big armchair and sat down. The fabric held an almost eerie chill at odds with the comfortable temperature of the office. He shivered.

She eyed him with an expectant, gimlet stare.

"How are you feeling now?" he ventured with a tentative smile.

"I'm fine." Her voice was brusque, as if they hadn't spent the afternoon eating and drinking together. "What do you have to tell me?"

Nerlim flinched. Perhaps he shouldn't have alluded to her earlier frailty by inquiring after her feelings. "Well, here's the satellite weather photo." He removed it from the leather satchel, still stuffed with all his meagre belongings. "I took it to a friend of mine who does cryptography work. Didn't tell him where it came from. Instead I asked him to look for hidden messages."

"And?" Gammy's voice dripped with skepticism. She raised an eyebrow, a feat Nerlim had always wished to master.

"He suggested it might be a way to draw attention to a particular geographical location," Nerlim said. "By calculating a direction in which certain, ah, features of the photo seem to point, or the area below the superimposed image, that sort of thing."

Gammy shook her head, white curls rustling. "But we're not looking for anything in a particular geographical area, are we?"

"Well, since you mention it, yes, I am," Nerlim confessed. When the silence got too uncomfortable, he said in a rush, "When the—I'm going to call it the anomaly—happened, I felt something. It told me something had changed. I was still in the hospital. But the fifth force was—awake? Active?" Nerlim spread his hands in a helpless gesture. "Something."

"Mm-hmmm."

"But I didn't know *where*, or even how, to find out. So when my friend said it might point to a geographical spot—"

"You believe the image might lead you to that mysterious 'something,'" Gammy finished.

There was a dangerous quality in her voice, but Nerlim nodded. "Or someone."

"And what conclusions have you reached regarding the launch failure?" she asked in a tone that said even before hearing these conclusions, she expected them to be complete and utter rubbish.

Nerlim licked his lips. "I think the launch coincided with the activation of the fifth force on D'sharu. Remember, I theorized that the fifth force would have the potential to interfere with other things—other natural forces and even physical laws. The launch happened at the wrong time, and that interference caused it to fail."

"And you think this, why?"

"Because I checked the scheduled launch time. It fai—was supposed to happen at the moment of the anomaly, and I wasn't even in Neemar when the anomaly hit me. I was in Williget. It's the same time that's stamped on the weather satellite photo. The same time—to the minute—that other things like phones, cars, and appliances stopped working altogether or went on the fritz. I checked, and people took note of it. There are records. It's all tied together, Gameldina, it has to be. That's too much coincidence."

She sat back in her chair and let her hands rest on the arms. Nerlim noticed with alarm that her knuckles had gone white, fingers gripping the arms of the chair with a peculiar intensity.

"You're telling me," she began, but stopped. Although her gaze met his, he didn't think she saw him at all. In a low and deliberate voice, she tried again. "You're telling me, Nerlim, that this launch, that I've worked toward all my life, schemed and planned and begged to achieve, failed at the very last second because of *bad timing*?"

"Oh! Well, er, yes. I'll admit it—well, it sucks." Nerlim shifted in his chair, uneasy. This wasn't going as he'd expected, and he hadn't arrived with high expectations.

"So," he said, infusing his voice with manufactured cheerfulness, "I want to go to the spot the photo seems to indicate and have a look around. It seems to be a large farm on the southwest edge of the city. There may be nothing to find, but I have to look. Do you want to come with me?"

After another long moment that stretched into a place of exquisite unease, Gammy emerged from her trance and blinked. "No." She shook her head. "No, I don't believe I will. There's so much I have to do here—" She broke off and shook her head again. "Tell me what you find, would you?"

"Uh, sure." Nerlim was surprised, and a little disappointed. For all her abrasiveness, it was...nice, after all these years, to be with Gameldina again. He'd allowed himself to imagine them setting off together to investigate the mystery; intrepid partners on a mad adventure. Nerlim sighed. Nothing had changed, he supposed. Her commitment to the moon remained absolute, and no words of his would change that.

She didn't add anything else, so he got up to go, slinging his satchel over his shoulder. "Okay. I'll tell you if I find anything."

She nodded, eyes on some papers on her desk. Unable to think of anything else to say, Nerlim left.

It came as a surprise that the weather photo of Gammy's face pointed to a farm on the outskirts of the city. He'd half expected to find another scientist at the other end of this puzzle; one whose investigations and experiments had succeeded where Nerlim's failed. Someone with a clearer understanding of the fifth force and its secrets. Someone who, like Nerlim, had a natural attunement to the energy; seeking it, perhaps searching for answers about it all their life, much as he had. Of course, that was more of a hope than an expectation; the photo might lead him anywhere, to anyone. Young, old, any gender...or to no one at all. A farm was no less likely to be involved than anything else.

He'd taken a cab partway but the cabbie pulled to the curb before they reached the farm.

"Word is, cars aren't working past the end of this street today," she said, turning to explain to her fare why the drive was being cut short. "You'll have to walk from here, sorry. Don't want to get too close and have a breakdown."

Nerlim assured her it was understandable, paid the discounted fee, and exited the cab to continue the remainder of the trek on foot. It might be for the best, he told himself. Exploring the general area first seemed preferable to arriving unannounced on someone's doorstep. If he had the lay of the land, he might have more and better questions to ask. He strolled along the edge of a residential area, where the houses thinned out and gave way to small businesses and then, warehouses. Graffiti splashed the walls in colourful outbursts, but other pedestrians and even vehicles were sparse. It was the dinner hour lull, probably exacerbated by the interference with working machines.

He was hurrying past an alleyway, nearing the street that would wind out of the city to the farm, when he heard a noise. Or rather, his brain corrected, he *felt* a noise. It thumped against his chest and reverberated through his brain. It was a *whump* that came from the inside, leaving him doubled over, clutching his stomach. It smashed into him like a punch in the gut from an oversized hand; a hand encased in a boxing glove carved out of wood.

The sensation also had an odd familiarity, he realized as he leaned against a building, gasping to regain his breath. It reminded him of...the anomaly. The fifth force. A wooden boxing glove was milder than that initial lightning bolt to his brain, but it reverberated across his synapses in the same way.

Once he could breathe and stand straight again, Nerlim made a stumbling run up the alley. A wire fence guarded the end, not very high, but still a daunting obstacle for a man of a certain age. Through the fence, he glimpsed a junkyard collection of castoffs and rubbish. In a small clearing in the forest of junk lay two young men, still teenagers. They appeared to be unconscious, which seemed fortunate for them since they were both also viciously peppered with what looked like oversized porcupine quills. Blood oozed from dozens of puncture wounds where the quills had penetrated.

A slight depression shimmered in the sandy ground near them. Wisps of smoke rose from the shallow crater and drifted away in the breeze.

Nerlim gazed at the scene, wondering how to help, but the decision was made for him. A woman materialized near the boys and stood looking down at them, hands resting on her curvaceous hips, blonde hair shining as she shook her head.

She tsk-tsked and muttered, "Good thing I talked the old biddy into letting me come."

The faint words trickled to Nerlim's ears. Luckily, listening was a passive activity, because he stood rooted to the ground. Running wasn't an option, even if a pack of rabid weasels faced him down in the alley. Where had she come from? How was this possible? His brain tried to assure him that she must have come around the corner of a pile of junk, walked into the scene without him noticing. He'd been focused on the boys, after all. But his eyes disagreed. She hadn't been there, and then she was. It was as simple as that.

Another anomaly. More fifth force. The tender muscles in his abdomen confirmed that. Mind racing, he could only gape, mesmerized, at the woman.

It wasn't only that she was beautiful. In Nerlim's considerable lifetime, he'd seen his share of beautiful women. She was *otherworldly.* He hadn't understood the meaning of that word until now. Her corn-silk hair danced on the breeze as if it had a life of its own. Her clothes suggested another time and place; a waistcoat of lavender cotton speckled with tiny white dots, sleek black trousers, a long violet brocade coat thrown over it all with a studied nonchalance. She was tall for a woman, looming over the boys as she gazed at their unmoving forms.

And of course, he had seen her materialize in the junkyard out of thin air. That alone should be enough to mesmerize a person. His brain dithered between trying to speak and trying to hide, so the unsatisfactory compromise was to stand with his mouth hanging open, like a doomed rabbit in the glare of onrushing headlights.

"Are you going to help, or just stand there?" the woman demanded, not looking at Nerlim. There was no doubt in his mind, however, that she had spoken to him.

"Gaaa…" Nerlim said.

"You can make it over; the fence isn't that high." She knelt next to one of the unconscious youths and began doing something, but her body was blocking Nerlim's view.

His brain said, *of course I can climb the fence if she needs help.* Too quickly to think better of it, he cajoled his old limbs and joints into doing work they hadn't attempted for years, if not decades. He went at it with a game spirit, if an unconvinced body, scrambling over to stand, panting and wheezing, on the other side. Now that he stood inside it, the details of the junkyard came into focus; piles of random detritus teetered at precarious angles on all sides. Abandoned appliances, empty paint cans, abject furniture, scraps of wood and metal, worn tires; everything jumbled together with complete disregard for organization.

"Start pulling the splinters out," the mysterious woman instructed without looking up from her work. "They won't feel a thing—not yet. I'm Xya, by the way." She pronounced it *Ziya.*

"Nerlim," he croaked as he knelt beside the larger of the two boys. He was startled at how much…wood, it looked like…had embedded itself in the boy's face, chest, and arms. He shuddered. It must have hurt something terrible. The boy was fortunate that none seemed to have struck his eyes.

"If we work fast, Nerlim, I'll be able to have them fixed up before they wake. We have to get most of the splinters out by hand first.

Concentrate on the largest pieces." She worked with deft fingers on the other boy, pulling splinters out in threes and fours. The slivers of wood came away bloody and left raw welts on the skin, but she didn't seem disconcerted, even when her fingers stained crimson. Nerlim wondered how she planned to "fix" the boys up when he saw no evidence of medical supplies in the vicinity, but at this point, his brain wasn't equipped to ask questions. His task was pulling splinters, and he did it.

It seemed to take forever, and his hands were soon bloody. Nerlim marvelled that no one else had stumbled across them by now, demanding an explanation for their presence in the junkyard. Asking what had happened to the boys. Shouting things like *I'm calling the police*, and *don't dare move*. But no one came. Nerlim and Xya worked on the two youths in an almost surreal state of detachment, as if they had separated from the rest of the world. The chaos of the junkyard enclosed them in a little bubble of unreality.

After some indeterminate length of time, Xya said, "All right, that should be enough. What's left can't contain much residual magic, although the Fates know he must have poured an incredible amount of arcane energy into the thing. He needs a mentor, and soon."

Nerlim didn't understand the context of this strange speech, nor half the words in it, so he straightened up from the boy and nodded. Xya spoke again, this time in an unfamiliar language. Nerlim felt it prudent to back away, nudging into a stack of old car parts that rattled an ominous warning. He hastily steadied them. The woman waved her hands over the boys in a graceful, convoluted dance that reminded Nerlim a little of a belly dancer he'd seen during one of his youthful travels around D'sharu.

Nerlim's own belly squirmed, and something like a shadow of that earlier *whump* passed through him. Another fist punched him in the gut, but this time it was smaller and lighter, with no boxing glove involved. He winced but kept his eyes on the boys.

Nothing happened.

Until with a weird ripple, like heat haze rising from softened asphalt, the boy's faces *healed*. Their skin smoothed and morphed into something clear and unblemished. Bloody lesions and cuts disappeared as if a healing cloth had wiped across them, washing away the wounds and imperfections. Any pre-existing acne had also gone, along with all evidence of their injuries. Rips and tears in their clothing neatly closed and bloodstains faded, and Nerlim had to assume the wounds beneath the clothing disappeared, too.

Erased. Just like that.

The junkyard and its miscellany of detritus swam around Nerlim most alarmingly. He put out a hand to steady himself, but his trembling fingers found only air. The nearest stack of junk lay inches beyond his reach. He swiped at the air again, but the air remained as stubbornly unsupportive as ever. Nerlim had time to feel his knees go watery before dark spots peppered his vision, and the junkyard, its refuse, and the others occupying it shrank to a tiny pinpoint of light that flickered out.

So did Nerlim's consciousness.

Xya and the Old Man

Ulric

Ulric woke with an ache in his back and an incessant pounding in his head. All of his exposed skin tingled, the way it did after he rinsed off that weird peppermint-smelling acne treatment his mother made him use. He wasn't convinced it improved matters, only made him smell like a peppermint stick for the rest of the day.

The stool. A fuzzy, dreamlike memory coalesced in his mind, of staring at the decrepit wooden thing, recalling the words that had filled his head when he'd fallen off the barn roof. Trying to twist his mind somehow to apply the power of those words to the stool. He frowned, and his face tingled harder. After that, things had gotten loud and extremely painful—he patted his chest with cautious fingers, remembering the piercing sting of a million flying slivers of wood impacting his body. He expected to find barbs and blood, but he encountered only his intact and unmarred clothing.

Ulric turned, fighting dread, to search for Tiny Enos. His friend lay not three feet away, looking healthy, if asleep. Between them shimmered the spot where the stool had been, its former existence now marked only by a small crater and a scorched blast mark. Inexplicably, a blonde woman in a fancy purple coat knelt nearby, hovering over an unconscious old man. Ulric blinked. These people had not been there when he'd exploded the stool. She was slapping the old man's cheeks, which seemed unfair since the old guy couldn't fight back.

"Hey—" Ulric croaked, and the woman snapped her head around to regard him. His eyes went wide and all the saliva evaporated from his mouth—he couldn't force another word out. She was the most beautiful woman he'd ever seen. In that instant, Ulric forgot Mattie Allegra.

"Ah, feeling better?" the vision in purple asked with a smile. "Rather unfortunate attempt, that. But we'll soon help things under control. I'm Xya."

"Er...Ulric," he managed. He glanced at Tiny Enos. "Is he all right?"

"Oh, yes, no worries," the woman assured him, her blonde hair slithering prettily over one shoulder. "He was caught in the blast as well—ah, there we go."

Enos twitched and struggled to raise up on his elbows, although his eyes remained closed.

"And who's that?" Ulric nodded at the elderly man Xya had been slapping.

"He said his name was Nerlim." She picked up Nerlim's hand and chafed his wrist in a businesslike way. "Although he did rather mumble it. I expect he'll help us out once he's back on his feet."

Ulric wondered if she knew he'd seen her slapping the old guy earlier. And who did she mean by "us"?

Tiny Enos opened his eyes and blinked, focused on Ulric, and scuttled crab-wise away from him, flicking dirt in all directions and raising tiny puffs of junkyard dust. He backed into a half-dismantled stove, dislodging a metal banker's lamp that fell inside with a clang. Enos didn't flinch at the sound, keeping his eyes fixed on Ulric. "Don't ever...do that again...when I'm around, okay?" he said in short bursts, as if he had to keep replenishing the store of oxygen in his lungs.

"Sorry. Um, Enos, this is Xya. She must have helped us, because we should be rather badly hurt, and we're not." His friend seemed so shaken, Ulric felt compelled to take control of the situation. "And the old guy's name is Nerlim."

"Erk," was all Enos managed when he looked at Xya.

Nerlim opened his eyes, but lay still. He stared up at Xya, clutching at the hand she'd been using to chafe his wrist. "You used it," he bleated. "Somehow...you used the fifth force. I saw. I...*felt* it."

Xya nodded, a complacent, knowing smile lifting the corners of her mouth. "You're a sensile, I expect. No magical abilities yourself, but sensitive to the arcane back draft. Comes in handy sometimes, knowing when magic's being used, trust me." She stood and brushed dirt from the knees of her pants. It fell away with an apologetic air, without leaving a trace or smudge on the fabric. "Other times it can be a pain, but what can you do?"

Nerlim scrambled to his feet like a man half his age...well, three-quarters, at least. His hands twitched as if he wanted to grab Xya by the lapels and shake her, but he seemed to decide that he hadn't quite taken leave of his senses to that extent. He balled his hands into fists instead. His face, pale when he lay on the ground, suffused with a dull red colour that looked even less healthy. "Tell me about it! The fifth force! I've waited my whole life—"

She shushed him with the wave of a lavender-manicured finger. "All in good time, my friend. I suggest we get these young men home to rest, and tomorrow we'll all sit down and have a pleasant chat, shall we? I think we've all had enough excitement for one day." Her words were the epitome of politeness, but Ulric heard the ring of steel that lay beneath them. There would be no arguing with this woman. Her "suggestions" would be followed. Or else.

But he quailed at the idea of being delivered to his house by this troupe and trying to explain it all to his mother. He hadn't even talked to her about the curtains yet.

"Tiny Enos and I can get ourselves home," he assured Xya. "We can walk. My, er, mother isn't expecting company, and—"

"Oh, she won't even know we're there. I'll pop in with you and pop out again."

And without waiting for further discussion, she raised both hands in a complex gesture and spoke in a language Ulric couldn't comprehend—at first. Then it was as if a two-language translation dictionary opened inside his head, flipping pages back and forth to make sense of what she was saying.

Obtain first sequential target (x,y,z/q) position from Thaumaturge Avatar memory cache. Parse vector differentiation between current (x,y,z/q) position and desired (x,y,z/q) position. Utilize thaumic force at power 4.89343 to—

"Wait!" the man named Nerlim shouted, trembling all over. "What are you—"

"The discomfort should be minor," the woman assured him.

—transport targets to first desired (x,y,z/q)—

"Oof." Nerlim huffed as if someone had punched him in the stomach. He bent over, clutching at his midsection with both arms.

Ulric couldn't concentrate on the translation any longer as he saw the others shimmer like heat mirages and fade out before his eyes. His vision blurred around the edges and he felt weightless, like when he'd fallen off the roof—but this time he wasn't the one doing it. Someone else—Xya—was using the power on him, and his mind rebelled against that. He'd known this woman for only a few minutes. Beautiful or not, could he trust her?

With mounting desperation, he struggled against the strange energy that sought to engulf him. He snatched with mental fingers at the vision of the cluttered, chaotic junkyard, trying to ground himself in it. His mind flailed, scrabbling for the strange new power in his brain; he found a shred of it tucked into a corner and threw it around himself. The forces surrounding him cut off as if severed by a knife. The ground materialized with reassuring solidity underneath his feet, and he stumbled a step, blinking to clear his vision of the cloudy mist. Words scrolled through his mind and he read them in a mad, wild torrent, willing them to help him.

Like the sun cutting through early morning fog, his vision sharpened, and his surroundings lurched into focus. He was still in the junkyard.

The others, however, were gone. Only a fading green glow and a cascade of dissolving sparkles marked where they had been.

Ulric did not see the other three materialize in his room. He didn't see Nerlim stagger, still half-bent over, and Xya take his arm to steady him. He didn't see the old man's puzzled expression as he took in the posters on Ulric's walls (ranging from space and rockets to girls and rock bands), the curtainless windows, and the star-dotted robe and hat reposing on Ulric's desk chair.

He didn't know Enos took one glance around and asked, "Where's Ulric?"

He might have caught an echo, on some ethereal channel, of Xya saying "Oh, crap," before she sat Nerlim on the end of Ulric's bed and raised her hands in the intricate gesture that would transport her back to the junkyard. He might have, but in fact, he was too distracted to notice.

The distraction was the thing that, the instant the others disappeared, swooped down out of the sky on ragged wings, screaming as it dove to attack.

For a moment, everything was hooked beak and bedraggled, oily, horrid-smelling feathers and raking claws. Ulric passed from gentle uncertainty about the wisdom of fighting off Xya's transportation magic to sincere regret that he'd done so.

He snatched up a hefty discarded wooden table leg and made a few desperate but unsuccessful swipes at the creature. His immediate goal was to beat it back so those claws would not connect with his flesh. Being able to fly, it avoided his efforts with nimble negligence. Ulric dodged away from the creature's beak and tried to jam himself under a three-legged antique desk. Unfortunately, the desk was propped on a battered oil barrel as a makeshift fourth leg, so there wasn't as much room underneath it as one might have hoped. The thing screeched and dove at him again, driving its horrid smell before it with the great beats of its raggedy wings. Ulric gagged, eyes watering, and squirmed further under the desk, but it was futile; the ancient desk already provided all the cover possible. He closed his eyes, instinct pushing him to reach for his strange new abilities, but the memory of the stool gave him pause. Did he really want to explode this disgusting thing all over himself?

A faint pop sounded nearby, audible only because the nameless thing had returned to the sky, pumping greasy, ragged wings to gain momentum for another dive-bomb.

"Oh, no, you don't," said a voice that Ulric was inordinately pleased to hear again. The words preceded an angry, ear-torturing screech that cut off with a gurgle. A handful of greasy feathers fluttered to the ground in front of Ulric's erstwhile hiding place.

Xya hadn't sounded happy.

Ulric crawled out from under the desk with care and stood up, brushing the dirt from his jeans self-consciously. The dirt did not depart from them as elegantly as it had let go of Xya's pants. "Where did you go?" he asked, risking a glance up at the sky. The creature had disappeared.

Xya stood staring at him, hands on her hips. Her face was a study in contained exasperation. "If you'd come along, you'd already know that, wouldn't you?"

Ulric's stomach clenched, and he took a half-step back, bumping into the rickety desk. He folded his arms across his chest. "Well, you didn't warn me or anything. I didn't understand what was happening. We've only just met. Can't blame a fellow for being careful."

She regarded him for a long moment, her eyes narrowed and her blonde hair performing exciting undulations in the breeze. She sighed. "I suppose you're right. It was a mistake to move so fast. I wanted to get you home quickly and safely, but I should have explained better."

Ulric nodded, relaxing with relief. He did not want to antagonize this woman, but he had to stand up for himself. "All right. So where are Enos and that old guy?"

She shrugged. "I left them in your room. Where did that creature come from?"

"It blasted out of the sky the instant you were gone. It was kind of familiar, now that I think about it—"

"You wouldn't normally see one here, you mean?" Xya asked, her voice sharpening.

"No. That thing was definitely not normal. And terrifying. Still, I'm sure I've seen something like it—"

"It wasn't pretty; I can agree with that. Let's go," Xya said, "before any more of them show up. We can talk more about it when we get you home safe."

This time Ulric didn't fight the energy. Xya had saved his life—twice, now, maybe. And his brain worried at the possibility his mother had noticed Enos and the old man materializing out of nowhere.

They appeared inside Ulric's room with that same soft popping sound he'd noticed when Xya returned to the junkyard. Nerlim sat on the end of the unmade bed, and Tiny Enos sprawled on the floor with his back against Ulric's desk. Nerlim's gaze was fixed on the robe and hat, a thoughtful look on his face.

"Has my mother come up?" Ulric asked as soon as his vision cleared. He put a hand on his desk to steady himself.

Enos chuckled. "You think we'd be sitting here if she had? No, the house is quiet. I didn't check, but she might be out."

Ulric heaved a relieved sigh. "Okay, I have time to figure something out." He crossed to the bookshelf snugged up against one wall and hauled down a thick hardcover book. The spine read, "Creature Concordance v. 2.5," and below that in smaller letters, "For use with the Dungeonography Hero Gaming System."

Xya frowned. "What's that?"

"A book. If I'm right, there's a picture of that creature in here, the one that attacked me. It was familiar to me, but not from real life. I think it was in here."

"Attacked you? What attacked you? When?" Enos demanded.

Ulric answered in an absent voice, flipping pages as he spoke. "After you left—it flew down—didn't get me though..." Monsters and strange creatures of all sizes and descriptions filled the pages he thumbed past, all replete with full-colour illustrations and tables of statistics, many of which he had long ago committed to memory. "There," he said, pointing a triumphant finger. "This is it!"

Tiny Enos and Nerlim crowded close to peer at the page he held open.

"A harpy?" Tiny Enos asked in disbelief. "You were attacked by a harpy at the junkyard?"

"Yeah. It was just like this, only its feathers were even grosser. And the book doesn't tell you how awful they smell."

"Gosh," Enos said with excitement. "They've got, like, eighty life points! And three action attacks!"

Ulric gave him a quelling stare.

"Uh, yeah, right, this was real life," Enos muttered. "Sorry about that."

Xya had not bothered to peruse the book, her lovely brow furrowed in thought. "I was hoping we'd have more time," she said in an abstracted tone.

Ulric looked up from the book at her. "More time for what? Look, a lot of weird things are happening. Can you tell us what they mean?"

"The boy is right," Nerlim said. "Someone owes us some explanations."

Xya nodded, considering. "That's one reason I'm here. But it will have to wait until tomorrow. I have to make a report and do some research first. I can't give you answers I don't have myself. So, I'm going to take you and you—" nodding to Enos and Nerlim, "—home, and we'll meet up tomorrow and figure out what to do. Clear some space on your schedules. This is going to take a while—and we might not have much time."

The Words and the Music

Heline

In the aftermath of her epiphany in the closet, Heline was only dimly aware Eleanor had followed her out to the kitchen, and Jans darted concerned, wordless glances at her as he continued to make supper. The delicious aromas of roasted garlic and caramelized onions suffused the room, but Heline took no notice. Eleanor pulled out one of the kitchen chairs and plunked down next to her sister, peering at the words scrawled on the paper. Heline resisted the urge to curl a protective arm around the notepad. She was most concerned with getting the words down before they disappeared.

Eleanor sat for a moment, saying nothing. Then, "What the flark, Heline?"

"They're songs." Heline didn't even glance up to chastise her younger sister for swearing.

"They look like poems."

"Well, they're not."

Another pause. "So where's the music?"

Heline sighed, but still didn't take her eyes from her notebook. "In my head. I get the music, but never the words, and now I have the words and I have to get them down on paper."

"Do you write the music down, too?"

Heline shook her head. "I can't write music. But I can hum it. And now, I think I'll be able to sing them."

Eleanor said, "I can write music, you know." She pulled out her phone and thumbed the screen a few times. "I can compose it right on here. Hum something for me."

"Let me finish this, would you?" Heline snapped. "It might not last."

"Fine." Eleanor pocketed the phone. "Nice hat, by the way," she said with a sneer.

[wow, catty] the Hat said.[1]

Eleanor didn't appear to have heard.

"You're telling me," Heline muttered, and kept writing.

Eleanor left the room with a flounce, heading back to her magazine.

Heline took a brief break from writing when her hand cramped up and Jans sulked and rattled dishes because the supper was getting cold. To cheer him up, and because she was honestly starving, she went and fetched Eleanor, who had fallen asleep on the sofa. When Heline touched her shoulder, she woke at once and seemed to have forgotten their earlier spat.

Eleanor spent the meal telling them, at length, about the last band she'd played with and why she'd left them. The lead singer had turned out to be a jerk, which wasn't surprising to Heline because Eleanor always seemed to get entangled with jerks. Further, the band's manager had been embezzling their money, which was more surprising, mainly because it amounted to about five hundred dollars and didn't seem worth the risk.

Jans listened with polite interest, although he wouldn't meet Heline's eyes and contributed little to the conversation. Heline made sure she ate the meal he'd prepared with great relish (which wasn't difficult, because it was delicious and she was, as noted, starving). Jans had tossed the garlic, onion, and herbed cheese compote into a succulent pasta and served it with fresh rolls and a tossed green salad bright with colourful vegetable chunks. He'd brought wine and offered, with a broad wink, to pour a small glass for Eleanor, but she'd declined in favour of a strange-smelling tea she'd brought with her. Heline ate well, although she hummed in distracted snatches between bites.

---

1. It is interesting to note that on every inhabited world, there is at least one language containing this word, and all mean precisely the same thing.

She ate with the Hat on. The idea that the words might disappear again if she removed it filled her with terror. She made a silent vow that she would not take it off until she had written everything possible. She'd begun thinking of the Hat with a capital letter, like a name, which was a bit weird. But it talked to her, after all, so shouldn't she offer it the respect of a name?

Earlier, Jans had looked at her askance after Eleanor had gone off in her huff. "I am only make the joking when I try the hat on you," he offered, flipping the contents of the frying pan with expert ease.

Heline shushed him with a hand. "I know, it's okay. *Yako*. Just let me finish this…"

"It is not the hat for wearing in the house—"

"I *know*, Jans, but does it matter? Now please, I need quiet while I work out this rhyme…"

It had gone on like this for a while, all his attempts at conversation rebuffed while she sat at the kitchen table, wearing the tall black pointy Hat and scribbling with mad abandon in her journal.

The meal gave her wrist a welcome rest, but she refused to leave the writing for long. After supper she wrote some more, filling pages in her notebook while Jans and Eleanor washed up the dishes and filled the empty air with various conversational gambits. He told Eleanor all about life in his homeland, and if she wasn't interested, at least she didn't say so. It occurred to Heline fleetingly that there weren't many men who would be so stoic in the face of her odd behaviour, but her mind flitted off to find the perfect rhyme for "poorer" and she forgot about him again. The Hat, she thought, must have opened its eye from time to time (no doubt keeping itself hidden from Jans and Eleanor), because she felt it tilt forward as if reading her words. Although she couldn't see it, she had the absurd and discomfiting notion it might be smiling. Heline half-wondered what would happen if Jans or Eleanor turned around and noticed it, but somehow she thought the Hat would not let that happen.

She answered Eleanor's "Goodnight!" with a rote "have a good night," and didn't notice when Jans left her alone in the kitchen to fall asleep on the sofa.

No Harm in a Short Drive

Wint

At about the same time Heline finished her supper and returned to writing, Wint Usborne woke up. He didn't realize he'd fallen asleep until a scratching at the bedroom door woke him. He lay still for a moment, disoriented and wondering how an animal could have gotten inside the house. And what kind of animal was it? Racoon? Badger? Skunk? How would he get it out?

With a start, he remembered. It was a dog, and he, Wint, had opened the door to it himself. *Flark.*

"Flark," he swore, before adding in a louder voice, "All right, all right, I'm coming. Don't scratch the wood!"

The scratching stopped. The room had dimmed as the sun began its descent toward the horizon and dusk waited to creep in. How long had he been asleep? Wint glanced at his phone and saw a stream of notifications from his colleagues and supervisor at NCDSF, but decided to ignore them. He'd wasted an entire day, missed work, and accomplished nothing but a nap. While refreshing and appreciated, it didn't further his situation in any meaningful way.

Blowing out a heavy sigh, Wint clambered off the bed and opened the door. Rex sat in the hallway, head cocked. "Thinking of eating again soon? Also, I need to go out. But, you know, doorknobs." He held out a paw as evidence of its incompatibility with doorknob utilization.[1]

---

1. Wint could have mentioned that the dog had managed a doorknob once, but it seemed petty to start a conversation with that. He never did confirm how the dog had done it, but considering the revelations later, it made enough sense to let it go.

Without a word, Wint nodded and trudged down the stairs to let the dog out into the back garden. He stood in the middle of the kitchen, wearing clothes wrinkled from his impromptu nap and a blank expression. Staring out the window, seeing nothing, he considered the consequences if he didn't let the dog in again. Would it eventually give up, and go away to bother someone else? Wint shook his head. It did not seem like an easily discouraged creature. And right now, it represented his only fragile hope of figuring out what was happening to his life.

"I was thinking," the dog said in a conversational tone, when Wint opened the door and it padded back into the kitchen, "we could go for a drive. Not far, of course. To see if I get a feeling for our eventual destination. Not that we'd go there right now," he added, perhaps seeing a hint of mulishness spark in Wint's eyes. "This is only an exploration, to see what pops up. I mean, the more you know, the better you'll be able to make decisions. And it might be good for you to get out of the house for a bit."

"That sounds far too logical and reasonable to be coming from a dog," Wint said.

"I take offense at that remark," Rex said, drawing himself up to his full height, his back rigid and the fur on his neck ruffling. Even his floppy ear stood taller with indignation. "Dogs are intelligent and social creatures, I'll have you know."

"Didn't you tell me that before this happened, you were quite happy running around after chickens and cats?"

"We're also playful and curious," the dog said in defence of his kind. "And I didn't say I spent every waking *moment* on cats and chickens."

"Oh, whatever," Wint said, feeling the fight drain out of him. Arguing with a dog was too much work. "I guess there's no harm in going for a short drive. But I'm *not* taking my suitcase, because we *are* coming back here afterward. No thinking you're going to trick me into going on some adventure."

Rex raised a paw and extended it as if to shake. "Honest to bones," he affirmed. "Shake on it, pal."

Wondering if he was the first person ever to be told to "shake" by a dog,[2] Wint held the paw for a reluctant beat and released it.

"We could take those sandwiches you put in the fridge in case we get hungry," Rex suggested. "They'd make a fine supper."

Wint rolled his eyes but fetched the sandwiches from the refrigerator, snagged a light jacket and his car keys from the hall, and held the door open for the dog. They stood for a moment on the step, each in their own way appreciating the cool freshness of the early dusk air. Wint opened the back door of his compact car for the dog and he leapt in. By the time Wint opened the driver's door, the dog had already climbed into the front passenger seat and settled there. Wint opened his mouth to protest, snapped it shut again, and tossed the sandwiches into the back seat before climbing in himself.

He turned the key in the ignition and as the engine sputtered to life asked, "All right, where to?"

"Could you open my window a bit?"

Counting silently to ten and gritting his teeth, Wint did so. Rex put his head out and snuffed in several deep gulps of air. "Nope, still not sure. Why don't you just start driving, and I'll chime in when I get a vibe."

This is going to be flarking great. Wint put the car in gear and backed out of the driveway too fast, failing to notice a skinny figure on a scooter who had turned in the driveway at that moment.

It was Skete, but of course, Wint didn't know that.

Fortunately, Wint did not hit Skete with the car. It would have been impossible anyway, as The Min would have grumbled and fiddled a bit with time and space to let Skete come out of the encounter unscathed. To Wint, it seemed a lucky miss.

Lucky or not, it pissed him off. He rolled the window down, furious.

---

2. In point of fact, he was, at least on D'sharu.

"Watch what you're doing! I almost ran you over!" It was a sign of Wint's mounting frustration with life that he raised his voice to a total stranger.

"Sorry! My name's Skete, and I couldn't help noticing that you seem to have one of the few working cars around here. Does that mean you're headed for the Dingle?"

"What? No." Wint had no idea where he was headed and had only ever heard a vague mention of something called the Dingle.

Rex leaned across Wint to speak to Skete. "We might be. Are you?"

"I might be," Skete echoed. "I think I'm supposed to meet someone there. Can I get a ride?"

"Sorry, no." Wint tried to regain control of the situation, even while his mind grappled with the fact that this Skete person seemed unfazed at being addressed by a talking dog.

"I'm sure we can get you closer, even if we don't end up going there ourselves," the dog in question said in an *everybody's-our-friend* tone. "Put your scooter in the hatch and climb in."

Skete moved around to the hatch with alacrity. Glaring at the dog, Wint pulled the lever to open it.

"What are you doing?" Wint hissed as Rex settled back in his seat. "We don't know this guy! And I'm not going to the Dingle, wherever that is."

"He's here for a reason," the dog hissed back. "I'm sure of it. Instinct, remember?"

Wint muttered something that Rex could do with his instinct, but he hadn't counted on Rex's keen canine hearing. It is unknown how badly things might have deteriorated from there if Skete hadn't climbed into the back seat at that moment.

So Rex let it go, one ear askew as he stared at Wint. "Are you going to drive, or what?"

"Thanks for asking," Wint ground out as he jammed the car into gear again.

"Hey, sandwiches," Skete said from the back seat, sounding enthused. "Mind if I have one? I skipped lunch."

"Help yourself." Rex gave a gracious wave of one paw, ignoring the black glance Wint shot his way.

"If you folks are headed for the Dingle," Skete said between mouthfuls of ham and cheese on whole wheat bread, "Are you going there to meet the Technocrat Avatar? If you don't mind my asking, because that's why I'm going there."

The car lurched as Wint twitched at the words *Technocrat Avatar* and his foot punched the gas pedal. He tried to regain his composure as Rex chuckled. It was an interesting sound, a chuckle from a dog, somewhere between a growl and a cough but with an unmistakable overtone of amusement.

"You can count that as mission accomplished, then, because I'll introduce you. Skete, meet the Technocrat Avatar, your driver, Wint Usborne. And I'm Rex."

After some sounds of choking on ham and cheese sandwich and sputtering recovery, Skete said, "Get flarked! Really? Where's the talking pig? Don't tell me you're it?"

Wint drove on in ferocious silence, taking turns at random through the deserted streets. His face twisted in a grim smile at Skete's question, though.

Rex let out an involuntary bark. "Do I look like a pig? No? Then I'm not it, am I? By the cat's claws, you people are even thicker than I thought when I could only understand half of what you were saying."

"My apologies. I got hung up on the talking animal bit, I guess. Is it true he's the Technocrat Avatar, though?"

"Yes, he—"

"No, I'm not." The words were hard to make out through Wint's clenched teeth.

"Yes, you are, sorry." Rex turned to look back at Skete. "He's having a bit of trouble coming to terms with it. The pig turns out to be a box with knobs on it. It's back at his house, but I've seen it. 'Ham radio', he says it's called. Sounds like someone was playing games with the prophecy. I expected a real pig as well, but there you are. Bit of a disappointment, right, ham you can't even eat? Toss one of those sandwiches this way, would you, Skete?"

Wint pulled over to the side of the road, not gently. His random driving had taken them through the centre of Neemar, and, had he but known it, set them on the route that would in time lead them out of the city toward the Dingle. All things considered, it was better he was unaware of this. They had stopped near the river that flowed through the city, the Glassy Beck, and if Wint had opened his window, his frazzled nerves might have been calmed by the soothing hum of rippling water. Unfortunately, he did not choose that moment to open his window. He took the keys out of the ignition, ignored Rex, and turned to talk to Skete.

"Do you think you could tell me, in rational terms, who this Technocrat Avatar is, what he or she is supposed to do, and why you are going to meet him or her? And possibly where and what the Dingle is? And where this ridiculous 'prophecy' comes from? I'm afraid I've developed a terrible headache talking to the dog, and he hasn't been the most cooperative."

"Hey, I'm trying my best here," Rex protested, but his mouth was full of sandwich, so it sounded more like *hah, I'b chrying by besh ear.*

"Mind if I have another sandwich?" Skete asked.

"Will it stop you from answering my questions?"

"I don't see why it would."

"Then by all means, go ahead."

With a happy sigh, Skete dug into the bag, chattering all the while.

"Well, I don't have a lot of details. The Technocrat Avatar's supposed to explain it all, but if that's you, and you're in the dark, I guess we're in trouble, aren't we?" he said in a voice that seemed far too cheerful. "Anyway, I was in my boss's office yesterday afternoon when I heard a voice in my head telling me that D'sharu was about to change, and that the Technocrat Avatar would need my help, and that it was my destiny to meet up with him as soon as possible. So I set out to do that." Skete's voice trailed away, and he stopped chewing for a moment.[3]

"At least, that's how I remember it now," Skete went on, continuing to play dumb. "It all seems a little foggy and unlikely, I admit, doing

---

3. All of this was, of course, the absolute truth, although couched in terms Wint could understand. Skete considered himself a consummate actor, and enjoyed having a chance to practice his skills.

things without knowing why I did them. I followed my instincts, packing a few things and getting on the road. And your house seemed like…I don't know. A good first stop."

Wint felt a shiver caress his back, remembering the semi-daze in which he'd left NCDSF. The way he'd accepted the dog's arrival. The compunction to pack for a journey. It was all too familiar.[4] "And the Dingle?"

"Now that, I do know. It's an old lookout tower or something on the outskirts of the city; not sure what it was used for, but it's up there almost on top of the mountain."

Wint thought for a moment. "You mean at the old barracks?"

"Might be." Skete shrugged. "Looks sort of like an old castle, I hear. A lot of kids like to hike and explore up there."

"But why is it called—no, never mind. What about the 'prophecy'?"

Skete considered, head tilted back to look out the car's sunroof. "In my limited experience," he said finally, "prophecies are weird. They're intended to help people figure things out, but over time the fashion has trended towards the cryptic."

"This one is in style, then," Wint muttered. "Where did it come from?"

Skete took another bite of sandwich. "Sometimes they appear in people's minds out of the blue," he said. "To guide them. Like this one guided me and Rex to find you."

"That's the most preposterous thing I've ever heard," Wint said, giving up. "Okay. Any other information about this Technocrat Avatar?"

"Well, I have an inkling there's an altercation—I hesitate to say battle, that sounds too dramatic—coming, and I'll be on the Technocrat Avatar's side—your side—and other people, of course. And another group will be on the other side. But that's about it. Like I said, it's foggy."

Wint sat back in his seat and drummed his fingers on the steering wheel. "So, see, it can't be me. I never have altercations."

---

4. Quite as Skete intended.

"Well, I'm tired of talking about it." The dog stretched his jaws wide in a massive yawn, pink tongue curling elegantly. "So, how about this: we drive toward the Dingle and I'll see if it feels right, but go back to your place tonight and re-think everything in the morning? Skete can bunk on the couch if he needs a place to stay. One step at a time, right? What do you say?"

"While you sleep in the spare bedroom again?" Wint asked with raised eyebrows.

"Well, to be fair, I was there first."

"I don't mind the couch," Skete said. "That would be awesome. I don't mind if Rex here has dibs on the bed."

So now Wint had two unwanted guests, but at least no hard decisions were being demanded of him tonight. Returning home and retreating to bed sounded manageable. "Okay, fine. Maybe tomorrow I can drive you two to this Dingle," he said with some relief. "And then I expect I'll turn around and go home."

"Whatever you say, Usborne," the dog said. "Whatever you say."

What the Flark is Magic

Gammy

Gammy woke the next morning and spent a considerable time lying in her bed before she moved to get up. Life had devolved into a jumble of confusion, and she needed a few minutes to hammer it into some sensible shape. Gammy did not like confusion; it stood in the way of accomplishment. She began by reviewing the events of the previous evening.

She'd spent a short time yesterday dealing with guilt because she hadn't gone with Nerlim Pettibone to find out what meaning, if any, her face on that satellite photo held. Part of her had wanted to go along with him. Deep in her soul, in the place she never revealed and avoided peering into herself whenever possible, she regretted not marrying him all those long years ago. His reappearance in her life was making her feel…strange. Perhaps—younger? Gammy didn't consider herself old, but Nerlim and his enthusiasm, even for ideas beyond her understanding, illuminated colours in her world that had long been absent.

But. Everything always came back to the launch. People depended on her to get it back on track, to make it happen. She depended on *herself* to do that. And there was only one person—was he a person? was he, indeed, real?—who might lend her the necessary assistance, if his claims were true. And despite his oddities, he seemed connected to something powerful she didn't understand.

The oddly transparent being, Corax.

She needed a chance to talk to him without constant interruptions, and so after Nerlim had left her office, and even though many people would stay on at NCDSF and work through the night, Gammy decided she'd go home. With any luck, the frustrating creature would find her there, where they might converse in peace. Before she left, she called Argit at his desk in the outer office.

He answered on the first ring, and Gammy found it soothing to picture him on the other end of the call. His flat face conveying mild interest, every hair slicked into place. Clothes plain and well-pressed. Nothing about Argit ever gave cause for perturbation, a look he sought with assiduous determination. No doubt working for Gammy had taught him much about control.

"Report," Gammy said without preamble.

As she expected, he delivered a concise and accurate report, telling Gammy everything that had transpired when she'd been out for lunch with Nerlim and during the time she'd been indisposed afterward. He rattled off every step undertaken in the launch failure investigation and the schedule of tasks continuing through the night and into the next day. After a while, Gammy was only half-listening, because the results were negligible. The investigation hadn't yet uncovered anything useful or concrete, which pointed to the probability that Nerlim's theory was correct. The chances of discovering any straightforward scientific answers seemed low.

When he was finished, she said, "Acceptable. I'm going home, and I'll be in sometime tomorrow. I'm not sure when just yet. Keep everyone on track, Argit."

He didn't ask unnecessary questions, saying merely that he would see her tomorrow. She couldn't see him, and he never saluted her, but that was the thing about Argit; one always *felt* that he had saluted. They ended the call.

Gammy had attempted to get a cab home, but nothing that ran on batteries and gasoline was moving in this part of the city. She started walking but hailed a passing rickshaw after about ten minutes. It was remarkable how little businesses sprang up to fill gaps whenever there was an opportunity.[1] Two days ago, walking was her only alternative way

---

1. Messenger services, street vendors, and crank-flashlight manufacturers were doing a booming business.

to get home in the absence of cars or buses, but here was another pleasant option. Relatively pleasant, at least, as the jouncing left something to be desired.

Once home, she'd eaten something tasteless and stayed awake long into the night, attempting to read and waiting for Corax. When he failed to appear, she'd eventually given up, falling into bed and instant sleep. Now, this morning, with a clear head, she might consider the situation from an objective viewpoint. She lay for a few moments appreciating the play of light through the leaves and the way it dappled across her quilt, letting her mind poke into the current issues as it would. The problem was, she decided, that she still didn't know enough about this Corax—who or what he was, and what he was offering. She had to talk to him.

First things first, though—she needed a long, hot shower. Gammy wondered fleetingly as she turned her face up to the steaming water if Corax might take it into his head to appear at an inopportune time, but then she shrugged. If he showed up now, let him wait in the living room.

But he didn't appear. Gammy reasoned that he turned up when it was convenient for him, not for her, and so she dressed and had breakfast. She tried the television but found only snow, then read another chapter in her current book. When she'd read the same line for the third time, she tossed the book on the floor. "Blackened bananas!" she muttered. "I can't concentrate on anything!" She looked around the room, with its accumulated lifetime's worth of awards, well-worn furniture, overflowing bookshelves, and space-related memorabilia. Had it all driven her mad, leaving her sitting here waiting for a mysterious apparition to manifest itself?

She glared at a photo of herself with a long-gone politician who'd tried to hitch his own star to her space program. *Well, if I'm mad, why not take it a step further?*

"Corax!" she called into the empty air of the living room. "If you've got something to say to me, then for flark's sake would you come and say it!"

"Of course, dear lady." He greeted her in a mild voice, materializing just above a tapestried chair across the coffee table. "I didn't wish to interrupt."

"The only thing you would have been interrupting was my waiting for you to show up," Gammy snapped. She blew out an irritated breath. "Anyway, let's try to get somewhere with this conversation before we're interrupted again."

"Certainly," Corax said, settling himself more comfortably above the chair. There was room to pass a decent-sized book between his translucent form and the cushion.

It was unnerving. Gammy fought an urge to put her hands on his shoulders and push him down into the seat. She wasn't sure it would work, so she tried to concentrate on his face instead.

"Now, what I would like, is to exert a certain amount of...influence in your world."

Gammy raised one eyebrow. "What kind of influence?"

Corax shrugged. "Now that your world has an active thaumic force—"

"Thaumic force?"

"Yes. The reason your rocket launch failed. The reason machines are not working. A new fundamental force has been activated on D'sharu, and it is interfering with the other forces."

If Corax's eyes hadn't been on her, Gammy knew her mouth would have hung open. *Nerlim had been right.* The flarking old genius had been one hundred percent right, about the fifth force, the problems with technology, about everything. Admitting it sparked annoyance but also an absurd pride.

"So, this force," she mused, "it's always been here, but dormant?"

Corax nodded. "It's a little more complicated, but that's close enough."

"Even when it was dormant, would it have...affected some people?"

"In a mild way, perhaps. Sometimes, even when a thaumic force is, as you say, dormant, there are elements of it that may come close to manifesting. People with extreme sensitivity to it, or an affinity for it, might notice. They might sense it as something pervasive, but missing.

They might carry out certain acts, hoping to find it. But it would all be vague and nebulous, even to them. There wouldn't even be a word for it in any D'sharian language."

"So, what's it called?" This mysterious fifth force might explain a lot of odd behaviour she'd witnessed over the years.

Corax frowned. "Hmm...I suppose in your language you might call it 'Magic.'"

"Magic." Gammy rolled the word around on her tongue, tasting it. It sounded interesting, almost like something good to eat. But fattening, she thought. Definitely not something good for you. Too rich and decadent to have all the time. "What is it called in other languages?"

"Magick, majick, m'agjikk, ma'zheek, maijik—" It seemed like Corax would keep going, so Gammy held up a hand to forestall the list.

"Okay, I get it," she said. "What does it do?"

"What does it *do*?" Corax looked bemused. "It does...everything. Or rather, one can do anything with it."

Gammy stared at him with a look that would have made Argit quail on a good day. "And what does that mean? Could you make even a half-hearted attempt to be a little less cryptic?"

"It's a natural force that can be wielded—moulded to one's will," Corax said, ignoring Gammy's barbs. "The skill of utilizing that force—which can be accomplished by various methods—is a natural talent for some, and a learned ability for others."

"So it's like...learning to draw?"

Corax chuckled. "Almost entirely *unlike* learning to draw, my dear lady. But perhaps the analogy is close enough for our purposes."

"Can you use it?" Gammy demanded, stung by his laughter.

"I can."

"Then show me."

He looked discomfited. "In my current form, that is impossible beyond some minor tricks. I assure you, I am an expert with magic in normal circumstances. I was able to exert some small influence over your assistant, if you recall, and I filled your empty glass, but more complex demonstrations are out of reach while I am in this form."

"And you're stuck in this form?" His story sounded less and less compelling. Gammy wondered if she'd have been further ahead going with Nerlim.

"And that is what you can help me with," Corax said. "If I can exert enough influence here on your planet, then I can become corporeal. Once in more substantial form, I will be able to wield magic here, and thus help you get your rocket off the ground and to your unexplored moon."

"But this force would interfere with a rocket launch. You've just said that already happened."

Corax waved an airy hand. "Not a problem when an experienced practitioner is in control. One must learn to exert dominance over the warring forces."

"Show the magic who's boss?"

He smiled, although it looked pained. "Something like that."

Gammy sighed and rolled her eyes. At last, here was the crux of the matter. "So you want influence, control, and power. There's a story I've never heard before. And what is it you want me to do?"

Corax leaned toward her, floating further and more alarmingly away from his chair seat. "Help me convince your people that I am a god. Do that, and the moon will be yours."

The intensity of the semi-transparent Corax's stare made Gammy squirm. He'd floated much too close in his eagerness. She swiped at him and was surprised that he ducked back, perhaps unwilling to have her hand make contact with his insubstantial form. Would it pass right through? She filed that away for future reference.

"What is this 'god' thing, anyway?" she asked, frowning. "You asked me before if I'd ever heard of the word, and I told you no."

Corax sat back and folded his hands. "It's an interesting concept, and one that manifests itself in many ways. But in essence it means a Supreme Being, perhaps according to some particular conception, or presiding over other beings or affairs, or perhaps supreme in influence over a particular attribute or range of ideas." He coughed. "To some, the Supreme Being is the creator of the universe, but of course we already know that wouldn't apply here—"

Gammy interrupted him. "Let me get this straight. You want me to help convince people you're some kind of Supreme Being?"

A ripple of something like discomfort slid across his face. "Er, well, yes. Your word holds a surprising amount of influence, you know."

She ignored the empty flattery. "And are you?"

"Am I what?"

"A Supreme Being."

Corax drew himself up. "I should have thought that would be obvious," he said, gesturing to his incorporeal form.

"Humph. Supreme in what way? Specifically?"

"Oh. Well, perhaps in wisdom?"

"No offense, but you haven't impressed me as particularly wise."

Corax bristled. "We haven't talked all that much."

Gammy shrugged. "Still, I'd have to believe it before I could sell it."

"Fully manifested, I'm a consummate expert at wielding the thaumic force—magic. With that, I could do wonderful things for your people. That's how I would manifest my supremacy. The people of D'sharu would be amazed. They'd *want* to worship me."

"That's still open for debate. But you can't wield it now, at any rate?"

"No. Not at the moment, but as I said—"

The other thing he'd just said made landfall in her brain. "Wait, you want people to *worship* you?"

Corax squirmed in his non-seat. "Yes, well, that's what being a god is all about, when it comes down to it. They worship, that gives me power, I substantiate, and then I can subjug—I mean, use the thaumic force to repay the people for the worshipping. By doing good things for them. It's a fair exchange. An elegant cycle. Everybody wins."

Gammy shook her head, frowning. "I still don't see what you get out of it, except being responsible to repay a lot of people for what they've done for you. I know what it's like to owe people favours, and believe me, it's no day at the beach."

Corax rubbed a nebulous hand over his nebulous brow, as if he were getting a headache. "Shouldn't you just worry about how I can help *you*? Help me, and you'll get your moon launch! It's a simple transaction!"

Gammy sighed. Oddly, she wished Nerlim were here. She wanted that launch, more than anything else, but this way seemed...fraught. With confusion at best, and peril at worst. These notions of Supreme Beings and transactional worship didn't sit right with her at all. "I'll consider it. Come and see me later, or maybe tomorrow, in my office."

"Time is vital," Corax pressed, floating forward in his chair again. "Every day that passes—"

"Not now." Gammy gave him a look. Men more substantial than Corax had faltered in the face of that look, and Gammy didn't expect it would fail her now.

She was right. Corax pressed his lips together as if to contain some ill-advised words, gave a brief nod, and vanished.

Gammy went to the bathroom to wash down some more headache tablets. She wondered where Nerlim was, and tried the number he'd given her, but heard only dead air. She tossed the phone on the sofa in frustration. At this moment, she wanted his advice rather badly.

THE ONE THE MAGIC HAS CHOSEN

ULRIC

"What if I don't want to fight this Technocrat Avatar?" Ulric asked Xya. "He might not even be a bad guy."

They sat at the kitchen table in Ulric's house; Ulric, Tiny Enos, Nerlim and Xya. Ulric's mother had left for work an hour ago, and Ulric and Tiny Enos had decided this meeting was more important than going out to Old Mean Melvin's farm today. Let Eiric, Poppy, and Natelie take up the slack, as Ulric and Enos did yesterday. Xya had arrived with Nerlim just after Tiny Enos got there. Ulric didn't ask how she'd known it was a good time to come.

Making a good cup of tea was bred in the bone in Ulric's family—you didn't grow up in this house without learning that skill. A steaming mug sat before each of them on the table, and they sipped as they talked. Ulric had also produced a package of cookies from the cupboard, because tea was one thing, but baking belonged to a different level of hospitality. The Creature Concordance lay on the counter, along with the robe and hat. He didn't dwell on the reasons, but Ulric had felt the need to have them nearby. The kitchen in Ulric's house was a cozy room, with cherry red checkered curtains in the windows and a flowered rug on the floor in front of the sink. The residual scents of hundreds of cookies baked in the oven imbued the walls with a homey ambiance. Pots gleamed on a rack above the stove and greenery spilled from plants on the windowsills. Ulric thought its soothing atmosphere might ease a discussion he expected to be challenging.

"I know, but nice guy or not, he'll try to subjugate the magic," Xya said patiently. She held her mug with both hands wrapped around it as if for warmth. "It's his job. The magic has chosen you as its champion. It's your job as the Thaumaturge Avatar to protect it."

"Sorry, the what?" Nerlim interjected.

Xya sighed. "All right, here's the condensed version of what happens in these situations. When magic essence or thaumic energy is displaced from a planet—"

"And that's what happened here?" Nerlim asked.

She nodded. "It can land on any planet where magic is not already active. This avoids an overload or clash that could be very destructive."

"So this 'magic essence'—or what I've been calling the fifth force—wasn't native to D'sharu, but is sort of...an immigrant?"

"You could think of it that way. Now, on a planet with developed technology—"

"But if there was no fifth force here before, what have I been feeling or sensing all my life?"

"Sometimes magic essence is present on a planet, but not manifested. You may have been sensing echoes of it, even though it was dormant or latent." A hint of exasperation edged Xya's voice.

"Sorry, I'm a scientist. I want to understand this," Nerlim said, not sounding very apologetic. "I always suspected something like this existed, so this is important."

"Even though I'm not a scientist, I want to understand it, too," Ulric said. "Especially since I seem to be involved without my consent."

Tiny Enos raised his mug of tea as if in a toast. "Agreed."

Xya looked toward the ceiling as if trying to compose herself. "Fine. So, magic here, latent. Magic somewhere else, active. Active magic comes here because there's space for it."

"Got it so far," Nerlim said. "Does that do anything to the dormant force that was already here?"

"This might go faster if you'd stop interrupting me."

"Okay, okay, but I want time for questions later."

"That will depend on a lot of things that are beyond my control." Xya took a calming sip of tea. "Now, since there's active technology on the planet beyond a primitive level, the magic isn't going to find itself altogether...welcome. So the magic chooses a champion—in this case, you, Ulric. And the technology will do the same."

Nerlim held up a hand. "Hold up. You're talking about 'magic' and 'technology' as if they're—*beings* of some kind. Like they have consciousness, and will."

"My computer seems to have a will of its own sometimes," Tiny Enos offered. "So does my phone."

Xya nibbled her bottom lip as she considered. "Perhaps not a being so much as a...spirit? A manifestation? I suppose we're running up against the limitations of your language since these concepts haven't come up before."

Nerlim sighed. "I'd like to understand this better, but I guess that comes later. Carry on, then."

"All right. So there will be a Thaumaturge Avatar and a Technocrat Avatar, and whichever one defeats the other will determine whether magic or technology becomes ascendant on the planet. It's quite simple."

"And we can't have both because...what?" Ulric had the oddest sensation there was a lot more Xya wasn't telling them, but he was unsure if he should force the issue.

Xya pointed at Nerlim. "He knows why."

Ulric turned to the old man and raised his eyebrows. Nerlim nodded in a contemplative way.

"It's because the forces can't co-exist in peace. They interfere with each other, so if they're both present, neither one of them works very well. And that's not good for the inhabitants of the planet."

"Or the planet itself," Xya agreed. "An imbalance in the worldweft is never good."

Nerlim opened his mouth as if he were about to ask what that meant, then closed it again, perhaps wisely.

Ulric sighed. "Okay, but I don't know if I can do it. I don't seem to have much control over what happens when I try to use this magic stuff. Why would it choose me, anyway?"

"The magic is ineffable," Xya said, "but like your intermittent technology, it's not infallible while both forces are active. But I'm wondering if you might find it easier with a dencrypter."

Tiny Enos rolled his eyes. "What's that you were saying about unfamiliar words?" he asked Ulric.

"Shhh. What's a dencrypter?"

"A...magic enabler," Xya explained. "The dencrypter creates support for your spells—"

"What's a spell?"

Xya fetched a deep breath and blew it out. One could almost see numbers appear above her glossy head as she counted to ten in silence.

"It's a...a blueprint, or maybe a formula, that helps you focus the magic energy and direct it in the way you want."

"Like when I caught myself from falling. So I can create my own spells?"

"I don't know. Why don't you try it?" Xya asked, and sipped her tea. Ulric thought she might be using the teacup to hide a smile.

Ignoring that, he turned his mind to the problem. How would he go about creating one of these formulas? He understood Xya's reference to a formula because of the way words and explanations had unfurled in his head the few times he *had* accessed this new ability. But in those instances, it had been more instinctual than anything else. And he'd been in, or felt he'd been in, grave danger. When he'd tried to do it at will, in the junkyard, the results had been more or less disastrous.

Sitting here at the kitchen table with Xya and the others, he couldn't summon a single thought that might be useful in controlling or focusing magic, instead of making something explode in an uncontrolled *boom*. The words and thoughts associated with it in his mind were slippery, like he was trying to catch hold of a live fish. He met Xya's faintly mocking eyes. She'd anticipated that.

"That's why you need a dencrypter. With practice and education, you won't need a dencrypter any more," she assured him. "But just starting out, they're useful."

"So where do we find a dencrypter?" Tiny Enos asked. "Or could one of us be one?" He gestured between Nerlim and himself.

Ulric suspected that either he'd always underestimated Enos, or Enos allowed himself to be underestimated on purpose. His friend had been invaluable over the past few days.

"Neither of you, no," Xya said, after giving them a considering examination. "Although as I mentioned, I believe Nerlim is a sensile. He can sense when magic is being used, and manipulate it to some extent."

"That's what I sensed in the nursing home? The magic arriving, or Ulric using it?"

Xya nodded. "I believe so. And it's why you heard echoes for so long."

"Could that help us find this dencrypter, then?"

"I rather think that he or she will find us," Xya said. "We won't worry about that just yet. Ulric, if they arrive sometime when I'm not present, you may need to explain to them what's going on, and make them comfortable."

"Explain?" Ulric squeaked. "I don't understand what's going on myself!"

Xya shrugged. "You don't have to make them understand, you just have to tell them what to do, and how to help. They'll just be happy there's someone in charge."

Tiny Enos sniggered. "Ulric is in charge? We're all in trouble, then."

Ulric glared at him.

"Just joking." Enos looked at Xya. "Why aren't you in charge? You seem to understand what's going on and everything. You can do magic on your own. Why is Ulric involved at all?"

Xya looked down at her teacup as if the questions made her uncomfortable. She exuded such confidence, was so in control that it was odd to see her discomfited. Her hair slid across her back with an agitated *swish*. "I'm not from your world, and my magic is different. It's limited here. I'm only here as a helper, and I won't be staying. And Ulric is the one the magic has chosen."

"How'd you know to come here, then?" Tiny Enos's curiosity had fuelled more than one adventure for him and his friends over the years, and once he latched on to something, he was as tenacious as a dog with a bone.

She looked even more uncomfortable at that. "I—should't talk about that. I was sent to help. That's all I can say."

Of course, that only opened the door to more questions, and Enos opened his mouth to ask one. But Ulric flashed him a look that said, *don't push it.* Xya's words from a moment ago rang in his ears. *The one the magic had chosen.* He didn't want to be chosen, and he had no idea why he had been.

He needed a little while to mull that over.

Intermezzo Tre

The Min

Three days in, and the people of D'sharu adjusted with surprising alacrity to the addition of the fifth force to the makeup of their world. Individuals continued to discover abilities heretofore unknown, although most were minor and innocuous. People displayed a remarkable ability to adjust to the intermittent functioning of items they would have thought they couldn't live without, and to develop workarounds.

The Min, observing D'sharu whenever a break opened up in her already-crowded schedule, was impressed. Of course, there was still the advent of magical creatures to come. Sometimes that marked the furthest edge of what people could accept without cracking. It would bear close attention.

Now, when to call the Convocation again? Private messages had pinged in from almost every missing member, making lame excuses for not answering her call the last time. Too many of the same lame excuses to be a coincidence. She'd wager every one of them had nipped down to the planet D'sharu, checking out the situation to see if interference might be worth it. Most of them would be circumspect and not do anything too egregious. They knew better than to risk The Min's full wrath.

However, no word, not even a lame excuse, arrived from Corax or two other members of the Convocation, Alsina and Sedrict. Corax was a regular agitator for a chance at a foothold world, and it would be like him to play fast and loose with the rules. He suffered from an inflated opinion of his own abilities. She wouldn't be surprised if he tried to stick a finger in the D'sharian pie. Alsina and Sedrict kept their aspirations quiet, but they were unabashed schemers. She simply didn't know what scheme might be brewing now. Skete and Xya were on the planet to keep a lid on perturbations over the new magic, and that kept them busy. The Min had a nagging suspicion further machinations churned beyond her notice.

She ran a hand over her dark hair, and it shimmered as if set with stars. The problem with a loose affiliation of magical beings like the Convocation was that it only worked while those involved agreed to the rules. The Min wielded great power, yes; she'd been administering the Convocation for a long time by any standard, and enjoyed her reputation as a straight arrow. She's accumulated enough resources and allies to enforce rulings she made against anyone who broke the Accords.

Still, the situation on D'sharu worried her.

The thaumic force itself made nary a peep. Magic, as a rule, threw itself with enthusiasm into the mix of natural energies on a new world, stirring things up with vigour. This one seemed to be lying low. Granted, it had been through a traumatic experience with the destruction of its old world—and nobody liked the upheaval of moving. Perhaps it worried about the reaction of the world's latent magic to this uninvited interloper and chose to keep a low profile.

And speaking of the world, she hadn't gleaned any idea of how D'sharu felt about the whole situation, or if it noticed the arrival of the new thaumic force at all. The planet's silence made her wonder if perhaps it slept through the whole thing.

The Min sighed. She'd learned through painful experience that the quiet ones required the closest attention.

WILL TO LIVE

HELINE

It was well after midnight when, eyes and brain burning, hand cramped, Heline had taken off the Hat and gone to bed. The Hat's influence was such that she briefly considered sleeping in it, but she resisted the idea. The Hat hadn't liked that.

[i would have been quite comfortable to sleep in, by the way] it said in a baleful voice from the bedpost where she'd hung it.

"Thanks, but no thanks," she'd replied. To tell the truth, she'd had a frightening moment when she'd taken it off and the words had disappeared from her head. She slapped it back on and they'd materialized again, though, so she relaxed. *I can put it back on anytime,* she reminded herself as she slipped between the sheets. She hadn't wanted to wake Jans from his slumber on the sofa downstairs, so she covered him up with a blanket before seeking her own bed. With luck, he wouldn't be too angry with her in the morning.

[bor—]

"Stop it!" she hissed at the Hat. "Or I'll put you back in the closet."

[sure you will] the Hat retorted, a sneer evident in its voice. But it quieted.

The words of the last song she'd written replayed themselves in Heline's head as she tried to drift off to sleep. It was a good one, she thought. Fantastic.[1] About a toxic ex-boyfriend, and the younger girls loved that stuff. She'd titled it, "Will to Live".

> *Misery; clouds make me ill*
> *Misery; tears defeat my purpose*
> *Misery; rain impales my soul*
> *I may die*
> *Is it rainy days that make me feel this way?*
> *With the green rays of misery pounding on my brain?*
> *Or am I lost in a tale of sadness, adrift far from home*
> *I didn't ask for this. I didn't ask for this.*
> *(Chorus)*
> *Fred broke my will to live*
> *Fred broke my will to live*
> *Thought I'd get better, but then*
> *Fred broke my will to live*

Not everything she'd written was this bleak, of course, but this marked the pinnacle of the day's achievements. She'd type it up tomorrow and maybe even show it to Eleanor. Unless she wrote something new and better in the morning. Yes, she might try a few new ones and choose the best of the bunch. A tingle of trepidation ran across the back of her neck. The idea of showing them to Eleanor unnerved her. Eleanor understood music; Eleanor lived music. And she didn't mince words.

What if they weren't as good as she thought? But no, surely she'd know that.

Heline rolled over, suffering a twinge of guilt at having brushed aside her younger sister's offer of help. Eleanor had been right; words needed music, and even if Heline could hum the tune, she couldn't send a piece of paper and a recorded *hum* to an agent or producer. Heline had always

---

1. It was not, in fact, fantastic. It was awful, but Heline was so thrilled to be writing words, any words, that it quite clouded her judgment for a time. The important thing is that she got better, with time and practice. Which is a good lesson for us all.

respected Eleanor's talents as a musician. It might be something they could bond over. They hadn't had much in common for a long time.

That settled, Heline's mind wandered down other paths before she dozed off. She might get some of those other things out of the closet tomorrow...why had she left everything in there for so long anyway?...

The smell of bacon frying woke her. Her panicked mind yelled *house fire!* but then she remembered Jans, and Eleanor, and the night before, and the Hat and the words. She was seized by a desire to clap the Hat on her head but fought it down. It could wait until Jans left. Already last night's guilt had returned, making her cringe at the way she'd ignored him. And she must make more of an effort with Eleanor today, too. She dressed in a hurry, fixed her hair, and dusted on some makeup. It would be a good day, and she'd put everything right.

"Goodness of the morning," Jans greeted her with solemn good cheer when she appeared in the kitchen. He was indeed frying bacon, and scrambled eggs waited on the warming plate, orange juice glistened in glasses, and coffee perked with enthusiasm. He wore an apron bearing the words, "Kissing the Cook." She wondered where he'd found that, and if it was intended as a joke or not.

"This smells wonderful," she said, sitting down at a table setting and taking a sip of orange juice. "Is Eleanor awake yet?"

"She is not appear in the kitchen yet. Do you thinking she will like breakfast?"

"She might sleep late after travelling yesterday. We'll save some for her."

Jans nodded and scooped perfect crispy bacon out of the pan and brought it over to the table, along with fluffy mounds of butter-yellow eggs. He portioned each out among the three plates, covered one, and set it in the fridge. Then he sat down across from her and frowned.

"I am wondering if we have trouble," he said. "Last night—"

She shook her head and laid a hand on one of his. "I'm sorry, Jans. I wasn't myself last night, and it was rude of me to ignore you. Can you forgive me and forget about it?"

He spooned up some eggs with his free hand and chewed them with a thoughtful air. "Not that only—the closet, and the hat—with hat on, no, you were not my Heline. You were—someone else. A different Heline. Not sure that I was so much liking her."

Guilt strummed Heline's heart like a guitar. "Would you like to see what I wrote?" she asked on impulse. "I was writing songs."

He brightened. "*Yako*, I would liking that very much. Jans is musical, did you know? Play kalimba in my old country." At her blank look, he explained, "Is something like a piano, only much small." He mimed holding a tiny box in two hands and made plucking motions with his thumbs.

"Really? No, you didn't tell me that. I get these ideas for songs in my head all the time, but this was the first time I had any of the words to go with them."

She retrieved her notebook and set it down for him to read as they ate, and tucked into an exceptional breakfast. The eggs were light and flavoured with green onion and a hint of cayenne, and the bacon was crisp but not brittle, cooked to the moment of perfection. There was nothing boring about Jans' skills in the kitchen. She didn't look up again until she'd emptied her plate. When she did, Jans's face had paled, his expression fixed on his plate and almost...haunted? He wouldn't meet her eyes, pushing the last crumbs of breakfast around on his plate.

"Jans? What's wrong?"

"No—nothings is the matter," he stammered. "Is only—I am late for the park. Must go. Inspection of new ride is happening." He glanced at his watch with exaggerated concern, then began collecting dishes and utensils. Heline gulped the last of her orange juice before he snatched her glass and added it to the stack.

"Oh...okay. Did you like the songs?" she asked as he pushed away from the table and stood up.

Now the pallor fled before a bright flush that stained his cheeks and forehead. "I think—they must be good. Only Jans's reading of your language maybe is not so wonderful. Needs more practicing." He ferried the dishes to the sink and turned back to her.

"I can finish cleaning up," she said. "You cooked, after all."

"That would be preferable, because I am late, as I have been mentioned already. When I am better understanding, I will again read the songs, *yako*?" The words came out in a rush as he shuffled backwards, aiming for the door.

"Well, sure, I guess so." Heline gave a mental shrug. She supposed it was his turn to act weird. From his perspective, she'd had her turn last night. "Thanks for breakfast; it was delicious! I'll talk to you later."

He seemed to remember himself and rushed back to the table, pecked her on the cheek, turned and was gone. Bemused, Heline picked up the notebook and began thumbing through, re-reading one here and there. Oh yes, this was good stuff. She decided that her second favourite next to "Will to Live" was a country-style ballad she'd titled "Meeting Her."

I met her on the highway, dead all over
I still recall that creepy smile she wore
She was drinkin' something fizzy and illegal
And she told me I was just a crashing bore
I promised her I'd love her dog forever
She told me that Black Angus made her high
But who'd have thought she'd leave me for my best friend
She freaked out on the lawn and screamed goodbye
Meeting her was everything
Meeting her was life
Losing her was everything
She never was my wife
I saw her in a jail cell that September
I still recall that miniskirt she wore
She was talkin' something trashy with the warden
And I knew what hurtin' country songs were for
I sprung her, and she said all was forgiven
She told me that our love would never die
But who'd have thought she'd sky dive with another

I never had the chance to say goodbye

Heline was certain that between those two songs, her dreams must be close to coming true.[2]

[stick with me, baby, and we'll do great things] said the Hat. Heline startled, tried to pretend she hadn't (even in the empty kitchen), and decided to ignore the fact that although the Hat remained upstairs in her bedroom, she'd heard it down here at the kitchen table.

She blew out a deep sigh, smiled, and refilled her coffee cup. Maybe dealing with a talking Hat was a small price to pay for the release of finding the words. She'd put it on again once she finished this coffee. Put it on and write some more. Next, get all that cool stuff out of her closet. Eleanor might like to help her redecorate, and they could talk about collaborating on the songs.

"You want to put all this stuff out around your house?" Eleanor's voice held a dubious note as they stood under the single light bulb and surveyed the contents of the small closet.

"Well, why not?" Heline asked, hating the way her voice squeaked, high and defensive. "I like it. It's all kind of..."

"Goth?" Eleanor supplied.

"No," Heline snapped. She wasn't sure what *goth* meant, but it didn't sound right. "Not goth. Just kind of...cool, and...powerful."

Eleanor shrugged. "Well, it's your house. Whatever." She picked up a few items from the shelves and took them out to the living room.

Heline sighed. Some of the fun had gone out of this idea, but she was determined to carry on, anyway. She'd always had the perception of being under her younger sister's thumb, somehow, which didn't make sense. *She* was the older sister, the responsible one. Eleanor made irrational decisions and didn't care about other people's opinions of her—and it made her maddeningly *free*. Heline sighed. If she made

---

2. However, they were still quite distant, as already noted.

an irrational decision, she only felt irresponsible. And somehow, that became Eleanor's fault.

But she wouldn't let Eleanor's difficult personality spoil this for her. Heline picked up an old-fashioned broom and a jar of murky liquid studded with odd lumps, then hesitated and put the jar back with a little shudder. Perhaps not everything needed to be liberated from the closet.

Together, they moved through the house and changed and rearranged, and Eleanor didn't impose her will on Heline's ideas *too* much. In the end, Heline stood back and surveyed the results with a satisfied eye. So much more black now, soothing and numinous and brimming with an exciting feminine mystique she'd never been able to achieve before. Or even known that she'd wanted, for that matter.

But now it looked great. The little black soup-pot sat on the stove. The stick leaned beside the door, its smooth polished wood enticing her to pick it up and—what? Her brain tripped on the question, a mental stumble. Go for a walk, she supposed. It was long enough to make a lovely walking stick. They'd replaced the white-and-yellow checked kitchen curtains with some lengths of filmy black fabric Heline had picked up in bulk six months ago.

The Hat remained in her bedroom. Intermittent mental nudges pushed Heline to fetch it, to put it on, but they warred with a strange compulsion to see how long she could resist. In odd moments—just now and again—she wondered if the Hat had too much influence over her. It must not be necessary to wear it unless she was writing lyrics, after all.

Eleanor came into the kitchen. "Oh, you've changed!"

Heline had exchanged her jeans and t-shirt for her one black dress, the one reserved for office parties and funerals. Why didn't she have more black items in her closet? She'd have to go shopping soon to remedy that. She gave a little twirl in the middle of the kitchen. "Do you like it?"

Eleanor gave her an unreadable look, but smiled. "Yes, it's very nice. Are we going to talk about the music now?"

"Yes. Yes, let's do that." Although Jans's strange reaction earlier made Heline even more nervous to show Eleanor her songs, it would be great if her sister could write out the music. The idea of her songs being complete sent a frisson of excitement tripping down her spine. She fetched her notebook from the table and followed Eleanor into the living room, where her sister had left her guitar.

"So how do you want to do this?" Eleanor asked, poking at the strings and fiddling with the tuning pegs as she spoke. "Do you want to hum a song for me, or try to sing it now that you have some lyrics?"

Stricken with a sudden shyness, Heline said, "What if I hum it first? Would that work? So you have the general tune. And once we have a start, you can read the lyrics and we can develop it more. I don't know how songwriting works for other people," she admitted in a rush as heat suffused her face.

Eleanor didn't seem to notice, though, engrossed with her guitar. "Sure, that should work fine. There's no one 'right' way to write songs—or anything else, I imagine."

"This one is called, 'Will to Live.'" Heline hummed the tune that had rolled around in her brain for so long, wordless and incomplete.

"Okay, okay, go slower," Eleanor instructed in a good-humoured tone. She'd pulled out a small, battered notebook of her own and worked back and forth between it and the guitar, plucking notes, strumming chords, and jotting down notations in pencil.

When they had a good working start, Eleanor asked to read the lyrics.

[i'm not sure this is such a good idea] The words appeared without warning in Heline's head.

"What?" Heline sputtered aloud, startled by the intrusion.

"Can I see the lyrics now?" Eleanor repeated, a faint line of puzzlement creasing her brow.

"Oh, no, not you," Heline said, flustered, which only made Eleanor look more confused.

[i don't know if she's ready. if she can be trusted] the Hat went on.

"Excuse me a minute," Heline said to Eleanor, and fled upstairs to confront the Hat. It sat on the bed where she'd left it, the eye visible now, still amber and somewhat pink around the edges, but not as bloodshot as it had been before. It stared back at her, but not with any malevolence. The Hat seemed to be...enjoying itself.

"You waited long enough to tell me not to show Eleanor," she hissed at it. "What did you think we were doing all this time?"

[i don't pay attention to everything you're doing. i have other things to worry about]

Heline threw her hands up in frustration. "You're a hat! What else are you so busy with?"

[cute. you think I'm only here to help you write songs, but it's far more than that]

"Well, you were in my closet for ages, and you've never seemed particularly busy with anything before now," Heline countered, putting her hands on her hips.

[to be fair, the hat was in the closet for ages; i was not]

Heline continued with her argument, not stopping to question that odd statement. "And you haven't done anything else when I've put you on."

Engrossed in her argument with the Hat, Heline hadn't heard Eleanor follow her upstairs. She almost jumped out of her skin when her sister demanded from the doorway, "Heline, who the flark are you talking to?"

THIS IS A LOT TO TAKE IN

GAMMY

It took Gammy a good part of the morning to get in touch with Nerlim. She hadn't had to worry about it before now, because he just kept showing up, but now, when she was desperate to talk to him, his phone was unresponsive. Of course, it was her fault, because she'd refused to go with him. Because the launch was more important to her. And so he'd gone off without her. She had no one but herself to blame, but she wasn't admitting it yet.

Besides, after talking to Corax, she had information that would help them. Corax had confirmed what Nerlim had thought about the fifth force all along, so that was a good thing. That validation would please Nerlim, even if it came from a semi-transparent apparition. An apparition who, she had to admit, might still be a figment of her imagination, a translucent symptom of an imminent mental breakdown. Was Corax's sudden appearance a symptom of launch failure stress? But she'd seen him at the moment of failure, and there was some evidence he was real. Like the way he'd seemed to summon Argit from outside her office, and the trick he'd done with the Black Angus Knockdown. For now, she would proceed on the assumption, however improbable, that he was real.

Which made her even more anxious to tell Nerlim about Corax's 'god' talk and see what Nerlim thought of it. Gammy found it confusing and somewhat distressing. She didn't see the point of it, either from Corax's point of view or the people's. What would anyone get out of such a notion? The thaumic force, as he'd called it, was already present on the planet, and he'd said some people would have a natural talent for using it and others might be able to learn. He'd told her one could do anything with it—'bend it to one's will'—so where was the necessity or usefulness in having this 'god' person mucking about in the background?

It worried her. She didn't understand it, and Gammy didn't like not understanding things. And Nerlim was the only person she could talk to about it.

So when his cell phone remained stubbornly unresponsive, she'd found the number he'd called her from at the weather office and reached his friend there (who turned out not to be a friend so much as someone who owed a favour to a friend). He was no help because Nerlim hadn't left him another number. Then she'd traced him back to the nursing home in Williget, but they wouldn't share any personal information, and when she became as insistent as only Gammy could be, they admitted he'd had no cell phone number on file with them, anyway. Finally, she'd called Argit on the off chance Nerlim had mentioned where he might be staying.

"No, he didn't tell me that," Argit said in an apologetic voice. "But he gave me his cell phone number. Would that help?"

Gammy closed her eyes and counted to ten. "Argit, I have his cell number. I've been calling it. But he must be in a temporary dead zone."

"He must have moved out of it, or it shifted, because I spoke to him on it not five minutes ago."

Gammy could have kicked something. If she'd simply kept trying— "Thank you, Argit. I'll try again."

She hung up and called it right away, wondering why Nerlim had been speaking to Argit. She should have asked, but strictly speaking, it wasn't her business. This time it rang, although there was no answer. She left a brusque message on the voicemail: "Nerlim. Call me." After she hung up, she regretted being so abrupt. Also, she should have apologized for not going with him. Then she hated herself for wishing that.

This was a significant problem she had with Nerlim, and it had always been there. He made her feel—without ever saying anything about it—like she was a much nicer person than the front she presented to the world would suggest. And that it would take less effort to simply let her sunnier self shine through. That triggered guilt when she didn't do it, and all of it made her annoyed with both herself and him. The worst part was, he didn't have to say anything to prompt these feelings. His simple presence brought on the whole thing. It was one reason she'd always told herself she shouldn't marry him.

And it was one reason, on those thankfully rare middle-of-the-night sessions of soul-searching to which all sentient beings are prone, she knew she should have.

Nerlim called back while she was pouring up a third cup of coffee. He didn't sound at all put out about her refusal to go with him yesterday, or her lack of an apology. "I got your message."

"Good. Where are you?"

"Ah. It's a little hard to explain. I'm still in the city, though."

"Okay. I have some news. About...you know." She was reluctant to mention the fifth force by name over the phone. As if someone might be listening.

"About the fifth force?" Obviously, Nerlim did not share her concerns. He did, however, lower his voice, which now sounded muffled, as if he'd put a hand around the receiver to hide what he was saying. "I've found out more, too! And some other people who understand about it! You won't believe the things I have to tell you!"

"I might," she said dryly, but he didn't respond. "Look, can we get together? I need to talk to you."

"Hang on a second." His voice grew fainter as he spoke to someone else in the background. It sounded like he asked, "Are you sure you don't want help to explain to your mother?" but she must have misheard. They were long past the age of worrying about their friends' mothers, for the simple fact most of them had passed on long ago.

"Can you meet me at The Sugar Goat again?" Nerlim asked, his voice still low as he turned his attention back to her. "Even if their power's out, they have good sandwiches. But later. Suppertime? I have some things to do first."

"Yes, I can meet you. Are you in trouble?"

Nerlim seemed to choke back a laugh. "Either we're all in trouble, or it's the best time of our lives. Which one is still up in the air."

"Okay, if you're going to go all cryptic on me, I'm hanging up," Gammy said. "I'll be at the restaurant at six o'clock."

"See you then," Nerlim said, and broke the connection.

Gammy stared at the receiver for a moment before she ended the call. Nerlim had sounded almost—giddy? She didn't understand what was going on with him, but she was pretty certain she wasn't going to like it.

Listen to the Radio

Wint

Wint Usborne had decided that he didn't enjoy waking up anymore. He'd always considered himself a "morning person," or at least someone with the potential to be a morning person with the help of a decent breakfast and an infusion of strong coffee. Now, however, as he once again lay in his bed and watched the morning light filter in through his window, he felt quite done with mornings. Yes, mornings, from now on, could flark right off.

He remembered his two unwanted houseguests with a silent groan. Were they awake? Would he have to cook them breakfast? At least the dog hadn't scratched at the bedroom door yet; with any luck, he'd bother that Skete person to let him out and leave Wint alone. Skete had babbled on the drive home about the fifth natural force now in play on D'sharu with other four forces (he'd gone on to list them; gravity, electromagnetism, the strong force, and the weak force, as if Wint didn't know about *those*) but Wint had tuned out after that. It was all too much to take in.

Wint rolled over to face away from the window and its annoying cheery light. When was the last time he'd been this miserable? It was, on reflection, quite possible he'd never been this miserable. It was even possible that he'd never imagined he *could* be this miserable. And his life up until this point had been rather serious to start with, not what anyone would describe as a juggernaut of fun.

Sadly, or perhaps fortunately, he did not know that within the next few minutes, things would get even worse.

He heard the dim murmur of voices. At first he assumed it must be Rex and Skete, but one was a woman's voice. Wint frowned. If this was another person arriving on his doorstep to further complicate matters... He put his pillow over his head and burrowed into the sheets like a tortoise, and the voices faded. *Maybe if I stay here, they'll all go away. If I can't hear them, eventually they'll have to stop talking to me, right?*

His mind refused to be convinced of this, however, because the now-familiar compunction to pack some belongings and set out on a journey was like a voice inside his head. It never stopped urging him on, and he didn't know how to burrow away from that one.

At last, he tossed the pillow aside and sat up. There were more voices now, but when he focused on them, he realized they were not in the house. Outside, for certain, so that was something. Wint rolled out of bed and crossed to the window, pulling aside the curtain to peer out.

He gaped.

He widened his eyes and gaped some more.

His jaw developed an ache from gaping, so he closed his mouth and contented himself with staring.

The yard was full of people.

They were all strangers, and they appeared to have made themselves quite at home. Sleeping bags and rumpled blankets scattered across the lawn, dotted here and there with small tents. The roadside was packed with parked cars, as was his driveway, and a few had even driven up onto the edge of the grass to squeeze in. Several of the invaders slept with apparent unconcern that they were in someone's yard, while a few sat scrolling on their phones or conversing in amiable tones. Three people moved through the smooth flow of a yoga practice.

A faint tearing noise made Wint startle, and he saw that he'd gripped the curtain with such force he'd put his fingers through the fabric. A slight woman with short dark hair and a red t-shirt that read *G33K G1RL* in sharp white lettering glanced up at the window, saw him, and smiled and waved. Wint hurled himself back from the window and slammed into the wall next to it, clutching the tortured curtain to his chest. Under his clenched fist, his heart beat out a frantic tattoo. Who were all these people? Where had they come from?

And what could they want in his yard?

"That tears it," he muttered through gritted teeth. He dropped the curtain and rushed downstairs in his pyjamas, determined to get more than cryptic platitudes from the dog and this Skete person. It had all been fine—well, not fine, but almost manageable, he amended, remembering the failed launch—until they'd showed up. They owed him.

They owed him *big time*.

He found them in the kitchen, Skete watching a pot of coffee perk with industrious sounds while the kettle also boiled. The young blond man turned to greet Wint with a goofy smile as he burst into the room.

"Hey, good morning! I wasn't sure if you were a coffee man or a tea drinker, so I started—"

"Who are all those people?" Wint demanded, pointing a rigid finger at the end of an equally rigid arm toward the front of the house.

"Well, I haven't met them personally—"

"Where did they come from?"

"Now, hang on, Usborne," the dog started in a placating voice. Wint glared at him.

Skete tried a cautious smile. "Haven't a clue, mate, but—"

"What are they doing here?"

"I expect, like me, they're looking for the—"

"Don't say it!" Wint gritted out between his teeth. He waggled a menacing finger at Skete. "If you even begin to utter the words Techno-whatever I'll—I'll—" he floundered, at a loss to come up with a single threat that might perturb these two maniacs in the least. In a flash of brilliance, it came to him. "I'll smash the ham radio," he hissed.

"You wouldn't," the dog said, his words backed by a growl.

"Don't try me. I want answers, and I want them now."

The dog sat down and looked as unconcerned as only a dog could.[1] "We've given you answers. It's not our fault if they're not the ones you want."

Wint felt as if the top of his head was about to come off. "But who *are* these people? I don't know them. What do they want?"

---

1. Which was not even close to how unconcerned a *cat* could look, of course, but there were no cats in the vicinity for comparison.

Skete didn't answer Wint. He asked the dog, "Do you know which he likes? Coffee or tea? He needs something."

Rex cocked his head. "If I recall correctly, he had coffee yesterday."

With a nod, Skete filled a mug with the steamy, dark brew and set it on the table. He pulled cream from the fridge and sugar from a cupboard and put them next to it. With an encouraging smile, he gestured Wint toward it like he was coaxing a feral cat to let itself be caught.

"It will make you feel better, and we'll talk."

With poor grace and a faint scowl, Wint added cream and sugar to the coffee and sat down at the table, wrapping his hands around the mug as if he were cold. Although he'd been awake mere moments, weariness crashed over him like a wave.

"How'd you know where the sugar was?" he asked Skete.

"I determined which cupboard I would be least likely to put it in," Skete said, "and I checked there. When you're looking for something in someone else's kitchen, it works every time."[2]

"That's good information," said the dog, as if he browsed strange kitchens all the time.

Wint took a tentative sip of his coffee. It was excellent, robust but not bitter. He refused to let it cheer him up yet. "So," he said again. "All those people. You say they want the Techno-whoever. You believe that's me, even though I don't see how that's possible. I still want to know why they're here."

Skete sat down across the table from Wint with his own coffee. "They're here to help you."

"Help me what?"

"Win the battle," Skete said with ultimate patience. "Or the altercation, if you like that word better," he amended at the look on Wint's face. "They're people who love technology, and wouldn't want to see it supplanted by some other paradigm."

"Well, neither would I—I suppose," Wint said. There had been times in his life when he hadn't much liked technology, like when his electric

---

2. This was possibly the most insightful observation about life that Skete had ever made.

razor had gone berserk and scraped an inch-wide swath of skin from one side of his neck. Or when the girl he liked had decided she preferred a guy from the computer club instead of Wint, who was in the science club. But on the whole, technology had treated him well. It had provided him with a career, with a goal, a dream to belong to something important. He didn't want it subjugated by this fifth force. "But I don't want to fight anyone over it. So it makes no sense for me to be the person you all say I am."

"But you've been feeling...something," Skete suggested.

"That's right," Rex said. "Why did you leave your work the way you did? Why did you pack up that bag with your teaspoon and your pig radio? What are you doing if you're *not* the Technocrat Avatar?"

It was the question Wint had been asking himself almost constantly since he'd left mission control at NCDSF, and it was unsettling to hear it echo from the dog's mouth. He had convinced himself that he'd gone, or was going, insane; the surprise was that it could happen with such speed. Wint stalled for time by sipping his coffee to cover furious thought.

The moment the launch had failed, the voices in his head had appeared. It was as quick as a finger snap; one moment, he'd never even considered the possibility of hearing voices, and the next, there they were. He'd always understood that folks who "heard voices" might turn dangerous, since they seemed to want to obey those voices. And one never knew with voices, whether they would advise nude dancing in the park or taking a sledgehammer to the next-door neighbour. This was different. Wint didn't want to listen to the voices.

When one told him to get up and leave mission control, at first he hadn't realized that it was *inside* his head. He thought it was Argit or Sams, or even Gammy, although it hadn't sounded like any of them. He was outside the door when he realized the difference, and by that time, he was stuck. If he went back in, everybody would ask why he'd left. He couldn't very well say, "Oh, didn't one of you tell me to go out?" No, that would sound ridiculous. He wasn't a good enough liar to make up anything else. So he kept walking.

The voices were still talking, anyway. They told him to go home and pack. Wint tried to resist. But he found that voices inside one's head are exceptionally difficult to ignore. Perhaps this is not surprising. There's no drowning them out with loud music, or sticking fingers in one's ears. They're there no matter what. So it seemed the easiest course of action, for now at least, to go along with them.

He wondered if this was what the sledgehammer people felt like, too.

And then events had continued to sweep him along. The dog—what could he do about the dog? A normal dog, now, he might have dealt with that. Ordered it out of the house, or dragged it out by the scruff of the neck. He might even have called the animal control people as a last resort. But a dog that *argued* with you? How did a person deal with that? Then this Skete person, arriving out of the blue in his driveway. The dog taking charge, inviting him along and chatting as if they were all on some glorious adventure together. Wint didn't want adventures or altercations. He didn't want talking dogs or pig radios or cranial voices or strange people in his house or his yard.

But he had to trust that there was some reason behind it all. Because if there wasn't, he was, well, flarked.

So he had no other answer for Rex and Skete but a muttered, "I don't know."

"Here," the dog said, in the most kindly tone he'd displayed thus far, "why don't you go upstairs and get dressed, and then you can go out, wander around and say a casual hello to people. Nothing elaborate, nothing strenuous. I'm sure they'll all be glad to see you; you can take a quick turn around the yard, shake a few hands, toss a few smiles around, and come back inside."

Skete nodded. "Dog's got a good idea. Sounds like a plan to me. One step at a time, right, mate?"

So Wint finished his coffee and trudged upstairs, dressing as if he were going to work, although it felt wrong to don his yellow NCDSF polo shirt. He opted for a plain black long-sleeve instead. When he returned to the kitchen, Skete and Rex were not there; he looked out the window and saw that were outside, moving through the crowd. Skete was greeting people, but Wint assumed Rex kept his mouth shut since no one screamed or ran. More and more people had turned to watch the house. Some appeared to have been waiting for him to emerge for quite some time. The expressions on other faces ranged from curious to excited to wonder-struck, and he wondered if perhaps they were looking past his house to something beyond it, like a double rainbow or an alien spacecraft. He crossed to the front door and looked out. More faces, sporting similar expressions, greeted him there.

Wint returned to the relative safety of the kitchen, his heart pounding. He leaned back against the counter, out of view of the windows, and closed his eyes. Should he sprint for his car and drive away, hoping the sea of faces would part to let him through? He suspected, somehow, that it wouldn't be that easy.

"No, it wouldn't," came a voice from across the room. It crackled with an odd static.

Wint jumped so violently that he knocked his empty coffee mug into the sink with a clatter that threatened to send his heart in the other direction—a sudden stop. He stood with both hands clutching his chest, gasping and swearing.

"Sorry about that. If you'd be so kind as to get me out of here so I can see better..."

Panting, still pressing his hands to his heart, Wint opened his eyes with trepidation to see who had entered the kitchen. The voice hadn't sounded like either Rex or Skete.

He was alone.

This was far worse than the internal voices. Although, come to think of it, this voice had reminded him of one of those.

"I'm here, in the suitcase," the voice crackled again. "Remember? You put me in here yesterday."

Wint licked his lips. He'd never suspected that losing his faculties would be so difficult or unnerving. He'd always imagined that it might be a rather happy, carefree state, where everything made sense, only differently than it did for other people. This was not like that at all. This was a nightmare of stress.

With halting steps, he approached the suitcase, where he'd pushed it up against the wall out of the way last night. He eased open the lid with a deep breath and a feeling of *what-the-flark*.

It was empty.

Well, no, that wasn't true. There were things in it, but they were the things he'd put there himself. Messier now, and minus the water bottles and the sandwiches Skete and the dog had polished off. There were his clothes, the book, the bottle of wine, the teaspoon, the ham radio—

"Well, are you going to assist me, or stand there and stare at me? It's more than a little rude." Lights flickered on the radio's dial face as the words emerged, as if it were winking at him.

With trembling hands, Wint lifted the radio out and placed it on the kitchen table. He would have much preferred to run screaming from the house, but the press of people outside forestalled that.

"That's better."

Skete opened the back door. "Are you coming out to speak to them? They're getting anxious."

"Would you come inside for a minute first? And get the dog, too?" Wint marvelled at how calm his voice sounded.

When they returned, Wint said with a patience that surprised him, "Now it seems the radio is talking to me, too."

Skete frowned. "The radio is talking?" He glanced at the dog with what could only be called a speculative look.

The dog perked his ears forward and sniffed at the radio's dangling cord.

"Hey, watch it," said the Radio.

"Sorry. Instinct, you know?"

"Interesting." Skete leaned in to inspect the radio—but not close enough to invade its personal space.

"Interesting? All you have to say is *interesting*?" Wint's astonishment drove his voice up an octave. He looked at Skete, as if seeing him as a real person for the first time. "Who *are* you?"

Skete shrugged again. "I'm just someone who's here to help. We're all going on instinct and nerves right now, wouldn't you say?"

And voices in our heads and instructions from inanimate objects, Wint thought. He didn't say that, though. The radio hadn't said anything since Skete and Rex had come in, and Wint wondered if he'd imagined that part.

He sighed. "You still know a lot more than I do, so let's call you two my advisors. In that case, what should I do now?"

"Listen to the radio," the Radio said, lights dancing and flickering in an eerie cadence as it spoke. "And make that three advisors."

NERLIM AT THE LIBRARY

NERLIM

Nerlim had left Ulric's house with his head spinning, unsure where to go or what to do next. He'd told Gammy he had things to do, but that was, at best, a half-truth. Nerlim *felt* like he had things to do; he was not, however, sure what they were. And he needed time to think about what he'd learned from Xya before he talked to Gammy again. Gammy would ask questions, and when Gammy asked questions, it was best for all concerned if one could offer answers.

As he strolled along the sidewalk, little butterflies of excitement caroused in Nerlim's stomach because, despite everything, *he'd been right*. The fifth force existed, this thing called magic, and it seemed to make no sense and he still didn't understand what it did, but by cheese, *he had been right*. Most of his research had been wrong, of course; his dissertation was worthless and his many mathematical proofs inapplicable to an energy that was, if he understood Xya correctly, sentient. *Sentient energy.* He stopped walking and thought about that, barely noticing the woman pushing a stroller who almost ran into him and muttered "banana-brained idiot" as she wheeled around him. Sentient energy that could, furthermore, be harnessed and used by everyday people to achieve extraordinary things.

Nerlim shook his head and started walking again. He had the urge to call Gammy back and move up their meeting time so he could talk this through with someone, but he wanted to understand more, to be on solid footing before they spoke again. It never paid to cut corners with Gameldina; she wouldn't let you get away with anything. So he would need answers to her questions—and his own—that were logical and based on solid information. And the most pressing question in his mind right now was whether there had been others like him, or like Ulric, who had suspected or experienced the existence of this *magic*. Had he never found them because he didn't know the proper name for the fifth force? Was he alone only because of faulty search parameters?[1]

And so, almost by accident, it seemed, his footsteps led him toward the Neemar Public Reference Centre. It occurred to him that there might be more technical sources to peruse at the university library, but that was clear across town and he wasn't in the mood to walk that far, and the buses in this area were experiencing one of the irregular but ever-more-frequent "downtimes." He'd start with the Ref Centre, anyway.

The Neemar Public Reference Centre was an imposing structure, engineered to resemble a stack of books, each floor of the building being a "book" set askew from the ones above and below it. Many a construction crew had called curses down upon the heads of the architects responsible for this visually appealing but logistically nightmarish approach to housing accumulated knowledge. It sat in a well-groomed park, with mature shade trees and well-tended flower gardens, dotted with quiet benches and secluded nooks where one might disappear into the borrowed volumes one had just checked out inside. Nerlim paused on the front steps and tilted his head back to stare up at the tower of "books," the windows inset in their spines glinting in the sunlight. On which floor might he find a book containing the word "magic?" Was it possible that such a thing existed? A shiver of excitement edged its way down his spine.

Then his stomach squirmed, and his chest contracted, but it wasn't from excitement. This sensation was more familiar now, and he understood what it meant. It signalled that somewhere nearby, someone was using the fifth force. Someone was using magic.

Nerlim whirled around, half-expecting to see Xya or Ulric or someone else invoking the fifth force. Everyone on the street at

---

1. Faulty search parameters have been responsible for more failures of research and personal philosophy than almost anything else.

that moment, however, looked normal. No one paused in what they were doing—walking, jogging, chatting on their phones, herding children—or gave him a second glance. Something caught the corner of his eye—a shadow of movement flickering among the trees to his left—but although he peered in that direction, squinting in the sunlight and shading his eyes with a hand, he saw no more of it. He stood a few more long moments on the steps, studying the area around the Reference Centre, then shrugged and went inside.

The interior of the Reference Centre was just as impressive as the exterior, and Nerlim stopped inside the foyer to appreciate it. He hadn't visited the building in quite a while, since his various researches had been carried out in more scientific and specialized libraries. This one, though, reflected a love of knowledge and reading that made him happy for a moment. The inlaid wood floors, patterned with intricate designs and polished to a warm, glowing shine, formed subtle paths that guided the visitor around the various sections of the building. Comfortable chairs in red, orange, and brown leather offered places to study, browse, or peruse books, some nestled up to inviting desktops, and some tucked away in secluded nooks. What the building's exterior didn't reveal was that the central core of the building ignored the idea of "floors" and opened in a vast vaulted cylinder all the way to the roof, where stained glass panels refracted rainbows of colour around and through the space. Gleaming black railings ringed the open area on every floor and white globe lights illuminated the building with the perfect level of cozy light for browsing or researching. And everywhere one looked, there were books. Books of every size and every description; books old and new; books on every topic under the yellow D'sharian sun.

And one or more of those books might hold the word "magic," Nerlim thought, rubbing his hands together at the very idea.

Technology on D'sharu having reached a certain level of sophistication and infiltrated even this shrine to the printed word, there were computers available for searching the library's vast collection. Nerlim headed straight for one, because while paper card catalogues held a certain charm, they were exasperating if you didn't have a title or author to start with. He opened the computer's search function and typed in the word *magic* with a certain amount of relief.

It returned no results. Nerlim sighed, but the outcome wasn't unexpected. He might have the spelling wrong, after all, or the topic could have been so obscure that an author might not have used the word in the title. He pulled up a nearby chair and settled in to do some serious exploration of alternate spellings, phrasings, and descriptions of this thing he called the fifth force and Xya had called magic.

Two hours, three cups of coffee, and a stale, disappointing muffin from the library café later, he found something. Nerlim had brought to bear all his research skills in those two hours, and scrolled through so many entries and references that his eyes were bleary and his back beginning a nagging complaint. He'd spelled "magic" every way he could conceive and skimmed countless scientific dissertations in almost every field of study. Now he sat back and stared at the screen, trying to arch his shoulders the opposite way against the chair back to relieve the ache in his protesting bones. What he'd found was not even a book in the Reference Centre; he'd expanded his search into the far-reaching and mysterious realms of inter-library databases and, at last, found something promising in the university library's antiquarian collection. The book was not in circulation, so he'd have to travel out there after all if he wanted to access it. The title alone, *Echoes of Potentiality*, wouldn't have caught his notice, but the brief description of the book in the database read, *An exploration of the theory that an obscure energy once existed on D'sharu, then vanished from the world leaving few, if any, traces behind. Little remains that would qualify even as myth, but the author herein presents arguments for the forgotten existence of this elusive lost power.*

Nerlim checked the publication date and was startled to see that it dated back over a hundred years. The author's name was Chetlin Tweddle, but Nerlim had never heard of them. He pursed his lips and rubbed them with the back of his hand. He hadn't found the word "magic." The book might be so much quackery—likely was, as a matter of fact—but he was compelled to check. Not that he didn't trust Xya—at least to some extent—but he had a feeling that she would tell them only what she thought they needed to know, and he didn't know that he trusted her judgment on that point. Everything she'd told them about these Avatars, and primal forces butting heads, and the future of life and technology and magic on D'sharu, sounded to Nerlim like something one should understand as fully as possible. Although Xya hadn't mentioned it, it sounded like something that came at a *cost*. Because if Nerlim Pettibone had learned anything over the course of a long life, it was that power wasn't free, natural laws didn't allow for argument, and there was no such thing as a free breakfast.

If there was a cost to the fifth force, Nerlim wanted to know what it was, and who would be expected to pick up the tab.

Half an hour later, he was at the Neemar & Environs Conservatory of Higher Universal Education, fondly known by its pronounceable acronym of NECHUE. Admittedly, it sounded somewhat like a sneeze, but the university would not deign to change its historic moniker for such a paltry consideration. Nerlim had left the Reference Centre and begun the long walk to the university with grudging footsteps, but as fortune would have it, he soon entered an area where vehicles were operating correctly and caught a cab.

Now he stood at the desk of the NECHUE library, trying to explain to the Head Librarian why he should be granted access to the library's treasured antiquarian collection. And although Nerlim Pettibone was no stranger to the university and had taken part in several high-level, well-funded research projects on these very hallowed academic grounds, that fact held little sway with the formidable personage of Petronilla Alva deCleverly, M.R.L.S.[2]

Petra deCleverly stood behind the polished wood bastion of her desk, fists planted on her hips as she assessed Nerlim over the tops of her standard-issue librarian's half-rim glasses. Her thick ginger hair had been

---

2. Mistress of Research and Library Services, First Class. This was, interestingly, one of the most respected academic achievements in D'sharian society, and one of the things the people of D'sharu got exactly right: revering librarians.

pulled into a loose knot atop her head, but tendrils had escaped over the course of a long day in the library, falling to frame her narrow face. She regarded Nerlim with skeptical hazel eyes and skewered him with a question.

"You've filled out the paperwork for accessing the antiquarian collection?"

"Oh! Well, er, no," Nerlim admitted with what he hoped was an ingratiating smile. "But I'm happy to do so now if you have the forms."

"The rare books aren't available for just anyone to go in and paw over," the intimidating deCleverly continued in a scathing reprimand. "The special collection is *special*. We take great care to keep it intact and safe."

Nerlim nodded and smiled. "I understand that, of course. But if you'll check my credentials with the university, you'll see—"

"We must schedule visits so that you can be accompanied into the collection room by a staff member who will remain there during your visit and monitor your interactions with the assets," the librarian continued, talking over him in a severe tone. "They don't happen on the spur of the moment, even for someone with *credentials*." The way she said the word suggested a high level of suspicion that Nerlim possessed any.

"There's only one specific book I'm interested in, and I don't need to take up much of anyone's time. I'm a personal friend of the Chancellor; perhaps if we called him—"

"The Chancellor," Ms. deCleverly snapped with an edge of ice in her voice, "is away on university business at present."

Nerlim realized that mentioning the Chancellor had been a mistake. Petra deCleverly was not impressed by name-dropping. But he *had* to see that book. He tried another tack.

"If you would be so kind as to retrieve the book for me, I could look at it right here for a few moments," he suggested, patting the smooth wood of the librarian's desk. "It would never be out of your sight."

At the way the librarian's eyes rounded and her eyebrows rose, Nerlim knew he'd made another misstep.

"We do not remove the antiquarian collection from the Collections room," she said in a voice now so icy that frozen crystals seemed to shimmer in the air around her head. "It is environment-controlled, and we're having enough trouble with the recent power interruptions—" She broke off and shook her head as if further explanations could not be endured. "I'm sorry, but that won't work. I can have someone bring you the forms, Mr. Pettibone, and you can fill them out here."

With a sigh, Nerlim agreed, but inside he seethed. To be this close to more information about the fifth force, only to be thwarted by an over-protective librarian! It wasn't as if Nerlim didn't know how to treat a book with care, even one as old as this one. With an air of glum resignation, he took a seat on a low, orange-upholstered sofa off to one side of the circulation desk, and a moment later another librarian—one of Ms. deCleverly's minions, Nerlim thought—brought him a clipboard, a pen, and a triplicate form to complete.

It took him fifteen minutes, during which time he had more than one occasion to snort, scowl, and shake his head at the ridiculous number and breadth of questions asked. "Surprised they don't want my blood type," he muttered, but the form stopped just short of that. When he returned it to the librarian who'd supplied the form, she took it with a bright smile and inquired when he would like to see the book.

"As soon as possible," he gritted out, trying to fake a smile. "I have time now if it's an option."

She looked surprised, then raised her eyebrows. "Well, I'll see if we can accommodate you now. Just take a seat while I check the schedule."

Nerlim wondered if they'd just let him see the book to get rid of him if he created enough of a fuss, but dismissed that idea. Petronilla deCleverly wouldn't be bested by shenanigans of that sort. Restraining his mutterings to keep them under his breath, he took the indicated seat and settled in to wait.

It took an hour.

Nerlim was fuming so hard smoke almost wisped out of his ears when deCleverly returned with a junior library assistant in tow.

Without preamble, the librarian said, "Mr. Pettibone, this is Alwi. He's very familiar with our antiquarian books. He'll take you back to the collection and stay with you while you peruse the book."

Alwi was perhaps twenty-five, with deep brown skin and shrewd eyes. He gave Nerlim an assessing smile but said in a pleasant tone, "If you'll come with me, sir?"

Nerlim tamped down his irritation and followed the man through a door behind the circulation desk and down a short, dim hallway. The walls had, at a date in the distant past, been painted a yellow that had now faded almost to a creamy grey. There was nothing to indicate that this hallway led anywhere anyone would want to go. At the end, another door waited; a heavy-looking oak door, bound with iron strips and adorned with a sign that read *Authorized Entry Only*.

"I see the antiquarian collection is well-guarded," Nerlim observed.

"We're very serious about security," the young man assured him, pulling a heavy iron key from his pocket. He fitted it into the lock and turned, the clicks of the tumblers so ponderous they echoed in the hallway. Then he swung the door open and motioned for Nerlim to proceed inside.

The room beyond the door had nothing of the neglected air of the hallway. Cool but not cold air greeted Nerlim, evidence of the careful environmental regulation deCleverly had mentioned. The lighting was adequate but soft, with no harsh fluorescents, illuminating rows of neat, orderly stacks marching lengthwise down the room.

And as soon as he stepped inside, Nerlim felt it. The same gut-punch he'd experienced in the nursing home, and again at the junkyard. He gasped. The presence of the fifth force...magic. This was different, though—not the sudden pulse of a discrete action, but a pervasive, constant thrum of background energy. Nerlim glanced at Alwi, but the librarian was entering notes in a leather-bound logbook on a table near the door. He gave no sign of having noticed anything unusual. Did that mean he was oblivious to the magical force? Or that he was used to it?

"Your phone likely won't work in here, so you'll have to use pencil and paper if you want to take notes," he said. "We've found that some technology isn't reliable in this room. Fortunately, the lights and environmental controls seem to be okay."

Nerlim was surprised, since the rest of the library had normal function; lights and heat and computers. "Is that part of the—er, strange things that have been happening the past few days?"

Alwi shook his head. "No, this is a long-standing issue. I assume it's something to do with the security and environmental controls in this room. I've never learned the full details."

Ha, Nerlim thought. He would bet it had nothing to do with anything the library was doing. It was the book's presence, disrupting technology the way magic had been disrupting technology everywhere on the planet since its arrival here just a few short days ago. But that realization brought with it a flood of questions.

Xya had said that active magic was new on D'sharu, activated only days ago. This book that seemed to talk about magic, however, was at least a hundred years old, and Alwi had just said that the disruptions caused by its presence here were long-standing. These two bits of information contradicted each other. Xya seemed to know what she was talking about, but could she be wrong? And if she were wrong, what did that mean?

"Mr. Pettibone?" Alwi prompted, and Nerlim broke out of his reverie.

"Thank you. I'll try not to take up too much of your time." He started off in the direction of the magical pull that tugged at his gut, where the book must be.

"I can show you where—oh, you already know?" The librarian sounded puzzled.

"Oh, er—lucky guess!" Nerlim threw a chuckle and his best slightly-dotty-old-man look over his shoulder, hoping to deflect any further questions. How *could* he explain being able to sense the exact location of the book he was looking for?

Well, he couldn't. So, without another word, Nerlim continued toward the enigmatic book.

You're a Dencrypter

Heline

Heline spun around, startled by Eleanor's voice. She barked a high, half-hysterical involuntary giggle and said, "Oh, no one! Just chattering to myself. I thought I left some of the other lyrics up here, but I must have been mistaken."

She moved to block Eleanor's view of the Hat on the bed, hoping her sister hadn't seen that baleful, red-rimmed eye peering out of the thick folds. She didn't dare glance back to see if it was still open.

Eleanor leaned on the doorframe, arms crossed, regarding Heline with narrowed eyes and open suspicion. "You said you already had everything in your notebook. And it didn't sound like you were talking to yourself. It sounded like you were annoyed."

"Well, I was, but only with myself for being a silly cheesehead about those lyrics," Heline insisted with bright intensity. "Come on, let's go down to the kitchen and make some coffee and then I'll show you."

Eleanor gave her a skeptical look. "There's something else going on, Heline. You had the lyrics in front of you. Are you nervous about showing them to me?"

Heline snatched at this explanation with relief and a nervous laugh. "Yes, yes, I suppose that's it. You know me too well, Eleanor."

Her sister shrugged. "Hey, I get it. It's not easy to share your work. I get nervous sometimes when I'm going to play a new song for someone."

"Thanks. That's good to know."

Eleanor allowed herself to be herded back down the stairs with obvious reluctance, but she let the matter drop. She returned to the living room and Heline bustled around the kitchen making coffee, wondering if the Hat would have anything more to say, but it stayed silent. When the coffee was ready, Heline took two steaming mugs back to the living room. Eleanor had been working on the melody for "Will to Live" and played a section for Heline as she entered the room.

She looked up with raised eyebrows. "Sounds pretty good, I think."

Heline nodded and smiled. "Just like it sounds in my head!" She passed Eleanor a coffee and her notebook and settled herself with the other mug. Her heart had upped its pace, ticking like an overstimulated metronome, but she took a deep breath and tried to focus on the warmth of the coffee mug in her hands. "Okay, give me your opinion. And be honest. You know a lot more about music than I do."

Eleanor set her guitar aside and accepted both items, sipping the coffee first and then looking at the notebook page. She read it through once, eyes skimming the page, then returned to the top for a more careful read. A tiny frown line appeared between her brows and she pursed her lips. She took a sip of coffee and scanned the lyrics again. Heline thought she might scream from the building tension.

Eleanor looked up and met her eyes. She squinted at her sister as if trying to see her better. "Heline," she said, "this is pretty terrible."

Heline swallowed against a throat pulled tight, as if a drawstring had been tugged up. "Wha-what?"

Eleanor shook her head. "These lyrics are awful." She held up a hand. "I'm not saying we can't fix them, or at least improve them. I get the mood you were going for, and there are a few lines—or words, anyway—that are decent. But overall? Well, they suck. Do you have any more?"

Heline's heart had changed from a metronome to a bass drum and she had to swallow a few times before forcing any words out. "What's wrong with them?" she gasped in a thin voice that didn't sound like hers.

Eleanor tilted her head at the notebook page, considering. "Well, the imagery is all over the place, for one thing, and the length of some of the lines doesn't scan with the melody as you've been humming it. The lyrics aren't...cohesive, I suppose you could say. The words come across as discordant, unpolished—but not in a way that feels intentional. And the name Fred—" Eleanor broke off, her mouth twisting to one side as she squinted one eye at the page. "No, it's not at all the right sort of name for this song."

"There are lots of men named Fred," Heline protested with staunch certainty. It was the first retort that popped into her head. She wouldn't entertain the possibility—the devastating possibility—that Eleanor might be right about everything else.

"Well, yeah, but that doesn't mean they belong in a heartbreak song." Eleanor tapped her pencil in a thoughtful rhythm against her lips as she continued to assess the words on the page.

"Why not?"

Eleanor blew out a sigh. "It's just—it doesn't have the right tone, somehow. The vibe is all wrong, unless you were going for something ironic. I guess it's hard to explain."

"Well, can you explain 'not cohesive'? Or 'discordant'? I guess I can figure out 'unpolished' for myself."

Eleanor glanced up at Heline and blinked, seemingly struck by her sister's tone. "Cheese and rice, Heline, are you all right? You're not upset by what I said, are you?" When Heline didn't answer, Eleanor sat back on the sofa and folded her arms. "I thought you were looking for constructive criticism?"

"You call that constructive? 'These are awful' is constructive to you?"

Eleanor looked abashed. "Well, okay, I shouldn't have said 'awful'. But they need a lot of work. I'm not saying we can't fix them."

"You mean *you* can fix them? Apparently, *I* can only write things that suck." Even Heline was surprised at the thread of venom in her voice.

"Hey, *you* asked *me* for my opinion, remember?" Eleanor reminded her in a scathing tone. "And you specified that I should be honest."

"Well, I guess I thought honesty would be a little less brutal."

"Well, I guess *I* thought you wanted actual help, not just someone to pat you on the head and say you're wonderful *as usual*." Eleanor set her coffee cup down on the table with extreme precision and stood up.

"What's that supposed to—" Heline started, but Eleanor walked out of the room without another word or glance in her direction. A moment later, the front door closed with a quiet, aggressive click.

[that went well] said the hat.

Once it became clear Eleanor wasn't coming back right away, Heline climbed up to her room. She hated fighting with her sister and already regretted their tiff. She knew, although they didn't talk about it, that Eleanor harboured a deep resentment for her that had stretched over most of their lives. Although she'd never asked for such a role, Heline was the "good" sister who did well in school and never caused their parents any trouble or worry. Eleanor was the rebel, and although she claimed to stand by the choices she made, she still seemed angry at Heline an awful lot of the time. And Heline recognized this fight was on her—she'd been too sensitive after asking Eleanor for her help.

Heline sighed and moved the Hat gingerly from the bed to the top of the dresser. What if she put it back in the closet and took a nap? She'd been up much of the night, and dealing with Eleanor's mercurial moods could be exhausting. She needed a nap, and she wouldn't be able to sleep with the Hat watching her.

[i can hear what you're thinking about me, you know]

Heline bristled and glanced at it. The eye had opened again. "I'll thank you to stay out of my head unless you're invited in. Just because I've finally figured out what you're good for—or claim to be good for—"

[what's that supposed to mean?]

"Well, you helped me write lyrics, but they're apparently awful."

[i don't see how that's on me]

Heline ignored that. "At any rate, you're less helpful than you first appeared—"

[ha. you don't know the half of it]

Between Eleanor and the Hat, Heline was out of patience. She glared at the hat, fists on her hips. "Well, here's a suggestion—explain a little better, and then I might."

[you're a dencrypter. but you were blocked because magic was dormant. my arrival opened the path for your dencryptic channel, but—]

Heline narrowed her eyes at the Hat. "But what?"

For the first time, the Hat seemed uncomfortable. [well, i had to get myself, and this hat, out of the closet. so maybe i kept it blocked until you got me out of there]

Heline's glare intensified to the force of the sun. "So you used me."

[just a little] the Hat admitted. [but it was a fair trade. you got what you wanted. and now i believe your sister is something, too. a dencryptic fulcrum, possibly. she made some excellent suggestions down there]

"I'm not thinking about my sister at the moment, so let's not bring her into this." Heline shook her head and picked up the full laundry basket she'd set in here earlier. Dropping it on the bed, she began pulling clothes out and folding them with angry precision. She snapped t-shirts and balled matching socks into tight wads, her lips pressed into a tight line as she worked. Heline suspected the Hat was playing with her, trying to provoke her, and yet she was intrigued. She wanted to understand what all this meant, and right now, the Hat was her only source of more information. That meant she'd have to play along to some extent.

Heline remembered what it had said a moment ago about hearing her thoughts and bit her lip. If that was true, it had overheard those ruminations, too. Well, too late now. "All right, so what's a dencrypter?"

The Hat waggled its tip. [you support the use of magic by bringing your talent to bear—in this case, singing. you regulate thaumic force and provide a foundation for spells that shape it]

"Thaumic force? Spells?" Heline folded a light sweater along crisp lines and added it to the growing pile. " And what's magic? Are you sure you're not just inventing words? Because you're making no sense."

Although lacking in lungs, the Hat gave the impression of heaving a tremendous sigh. [look, until a short time ago i was...somewhere else entirely. i'm a refugee finding my way in a new world, literally, and not everything works the same here. all i ask is if i help you, you help me. i'm trying, but i don't have all the answers]

Heline snorted as she folded a pair of underwear, turning her back so the Hat wouldn't get a good look at them. She wasn't ready to relent just yet. "You don't seem to have any of the answers, or at least no sensible ones."

The Hat gave the impression of a shrug. It was getting quite adept at these impressions. [a dencrypter creates support for spells—a formula, or a recipe, perhaps—for controlling and manipulating a special kind of force in the world]

"Oh, I see. My songs create things called 'spells' that will allow me to control a force I've never heard of, is that it? Everything's so much clearer now, thanks."

[your songs *support* the spells. enable them. but they aren't for you to use] the Hat said, ignoring her sarcasm. [your part in magic is to help someone else]

"And that someone would be who? Eleanor, I suppose?" She was tired of this game now, and she snapped the wrinkles out of a cotton skirt so close to the hat's 'face' that dust blew off its brim in a tiny swirl. She crossed to the closet to hang it up.

[no, i don't think so. someone called the thaumaturge avatar. i don't know who he is. or it could be a she. or a they. it might be anyone, to be honest]

Heline stacked the last folded piece of laundry on the bed. She didn't trust the Hat as far as she could throw it (not that she'd ever throw it, of course, since it was her only reliable way of finding the words even if they *were* crappy, and she wasn't about to give that up) but it seemed to have some information she didn't. Of course, it seemed much of that information came in words she didn't understand. It was...worrisome, and also annoying. The Hat could be making the whole thing up to camouflage its failings as a lyric muse. Or she might be the punch line in some cosmic joke she didn't understand.

More worrisome right now, though, was the tune in her head that was crying out for words to go with it. She wondered if Eleanor would take it as an acceptable peace offering if Heline suggested they work on the lyrics as they came to her, but right now, she didn't even know when her sister would be back. She *would* return, Heline felt certain, because she'd left the house without her guitar. It wasn't within the realm of possibility that Heline could make Eleanor angry enough to abandon that.

It might take a while, though.

Still, a nap was out of the question, with this music roiling in her brain. With a resigned sigh, she plunked the Hat on her head and pulled a receipt from a pile on her dresser. The back made a nice, blank canvas. She found a pen and transcribed the words that had, when the Hat touched her head, swirled into her mind as if someone had opened a faucet.

A world in flux can never rest easy
Forces align, forces cross swords
Two seek ascension through gathering clouds
Ring the troubled world in shadow and light
Falsename or truename, there can be only one
Minds may meld and hearts may search
Eyes may see for the very first time
Words in the wind, creatures in the wood
Choosing their sides, doing the needful
Cherish the dark teaspoon
Fear the dark teaspoon
Lonely the Dingle, marking time on the hill

When Heline finished and read it over, she tried to see it, not through her own eyes, but more objectively, perhaps through Eleanor's. When she set aside her natural desire to like what she'd written, she realized this one differed from the previous songs. It had no discernible theme. In fact, it made no sense. The words carried a weird sense of foreboding that raised goosebumps along her arms, but what they signified, she had no guess. Much of it seemed like pure gibberish and she thought, with a pang, that Eleanor would agree.

And yet it seemed like the most important thing she'd written so far.

[the songs...they're for the magic, remember] The Hat broke in to her thoughts, its tone almost kind. [they don't have to meet any other standards, so be careful how you judge them]

Heline considered that for a few moments as she ran her gaze over the cryptic lines again. *But I want them to be good,* she decided with a stubborn intensity. *Won't they do better magic or whatever if they're esthetically good*? She folded the receipt, then slipped it into her pocket. And tried to ignore the uneasy sensation that she was into something way over her head.

Parked and Idling

Ulric

After Xya had told them all she seemed willing or able to share, she and Nerlim had departed Ulric's house and Ulric found himself reluctant to be alone. He offered to walk home with Tiny Enos, who, being Tiny Enos, probably understood why Ulric offered and accepted without hesitation.

On the way to Enos's house, they talked about everything except the things Xya had told them and the events of the past few days. For that, Ulric was grateful—he needed a reminder that "normal" life still existed beyond all the recent craziness. When Tiny Enos invited him inside to play their favourite video game, *Bladecraze*, Ulric agreed at once, happy to escape into worlds of imaginary challenges instead of thinking about real-world ones. They laughed and snacked, and for a little while, Ulric forgot about weird forces and strange women and incomprehensible words in his head. When Tiny Enos had to do some chores for his mother, though, Ulric found himself standing on the sidewalk outside Enos' house, hands in pockets, unsure what to do next. He didn't want to go home, which echoed with weirdness Ulric was reluctant to return to yet. Ditto for Old Mean Melvin's farm, and the thought of answering awkward questions from his other friends. So he started an aimless meander in the general direction of home, but found his feet steering toward the park.

Ulric had never been a particular nature-lover, but the park's cool, green depths called to him this morning. It had rained overnight, and a hint of petrichor still scented the air. At the park's entrance, beds of some fluffy pink-and-white flowers he couldn't name added a soft fragrance to the breeze and dusted the trail with petals. He stepped through the gates, feet crunching on the gravelled path. Ulric pulled a deep, refreshing breath and sighed it out. The park seemed to fold him into a woodsy embrace, and his mind eased again.

When he rounded the first bend in the path, that ease fled, chased away by a very different emotion. An elegant ironwork bench had been tucked into a leafy alcove, and a girl perched on it. Curls of sea-green hair framed a face etched with sadness as her downcast eyes studied the tips of her chunky boots. She wore a short denim jacket well-decorated with patches and logos, a short red and black chequered skirt, and tights which looked like they'd been punched full of holes with haphazard deliberation. She looked up at the sound of his footsteps and rearranged her face to look bored, with a hint of challenge in her eyes.

The girl was attractive in a dangerous and intriguing way that was outside Ulric's previous experience. Any last vestiges of regret for the lost Mattie Allegra fled.

"Uh—hi," Ulric said with a polite hand wave, or at least that's what he meant to say. It came out more like a cross between a wheeze and a gasp. He felt like his brain had been disconnected from all other parts of his body. His feet continued to walk toward her.

"Yeah, hi, whatever." The girl looked up into the surrounding trees as if leaves and the possibility of seeing a squirrel were far more interesting than Ulric could ever dream of being.

"Nice, er, day," he managed. He'd taken back control of his feet and stopped them before they walked him too close to her personal space. He also succeeded in shoving his hands in his pockets in what he hoped was a nonchalant way.

"Actually, it's been a slice of burnt toast slathered in steaming crap for some of us," she said, not bothering to return her gaze to him. "So."

Stung, Ulric felt a slow burn creep up the back of his neck, and he almost turned and walked away. A week ago, he would have done just that. Then he remembered how sad the girl had looked in that first glimpse he'd had of her unguarded face. Instead of walking away, he nodded in sympathy.

"That sucks. Mine hasn't been what I'd call bad, but it's been super weird. I came here to sort of...I don't know, get away from it, I guess." He glanced up and around at the trees. "There's no actual getting away from it, but being here feels like an improvement."

Ulric paused, waiting for the rejection that *would* send him walking away. If this girl didn't want company, he wouldn't argue. *At least I tried,* he was already telling himself.

Instead, though, she said, "I get that. It is nice in here. I wish I hadn't walked out without my guitar."

"You play guitar? That's cool."

She shrugged. "I play in bands, until people turn out to be jerks or I get bored. I'm in between gigs at the moment."

Ulric did *not* say, *I do odd jobs on a farm near here,* because that could in no way compare to playing in a band with jerks or anyone else. But he wanted the girl to keep talking, because she had a wonderful voice.

"I have an old guitar someone gave me, but I can't play it; I only play around with it. Always seemed too—"

He broke off, not wanting to say *difficult* because that sounded lame.

But she must have known what he meant, because she said, "It comes easier for some people. A good teacher makes all the difference."

He nodded and blurted, "Did you ever have something happen to you that was so weird you couldn't get your head around it, but all the evidence pointed to it being true?"

Ulric could have kicked his stupid, stupid brain. There was nothing left for her to do but give him a pitying look, get up, and walk away. He would totally get it if she did.

To his surprise, though, she didn't. She turned her gaze back to him, a slight frown tensing her forehead, and regarded him with narrowed eyes.

"Like, because you were drunk or high or something?"

Ulric almost stepped back. "Uh, no! Nothing like that. I don't even—no! I was having a pretty normal day until things got weird."

She looked at him for a long moment, then slid to the right side of the bench, making room for him without another word. He took tentative steps forward and sat down.

"I was having a pretty normal visit with my sister yesterday, until things got weird. Not so much for me, but for her. So maybe something's going around." She looked at him and flashed a smile, quick and bright, before her face turned serious again. "I'm Eleanor."

"Ulric. Nice to meet you."

She drummed her fingertips on the bench seat on either side of her thighs. "As part of the weird stuff, I had a fight with my sister earlier and left her place without taking my guitar, which sucks, because playing it makes things better. I don't know what to do with my hands when I don't have it."

"Did she...kick you out?" Ulric asked, not wanting to pry too much, but genuinely concerned. "Were you staying with her?" Having no siblings of his own, Ulric wasn't always sure how these relationships might be expected to work.

Eleanor barked a short laugh. "Cheese and rice, no! Heline would never do that. She's the perfect one in the family. Well, until now, at least. No, I'm sure it'll all be fine when I go back. She might still be prickly, but she'd never kick me out. I'm not homeless or anything."

"Okay, that's good."

After a moment of silence in which Ulric wondered what to say next, she asked, "So, what weird thing happened to you?"

It was a fair question; she'd told him a little of her story, after all. Although his weirdness seemed to be on a whole other level of weirdness. Like, weirdness squared. He realized she expected an answer and blurted, "Ah—well, I sort of...I had a minor accident, but I didn't get hurt, and then...I found out some stuff—about myself. Stuff I could do, except I don't know how. And—and—it's just weird," he finished. It sounded as lame as fries without ketchup, he knew, but he was not about to say that he'd gained special abilities with a thing called magic and people said he was the Thaumaturge Avatar. No, thank you. Ulric had always battled awkwardness around most girls, but even he knew that was not information to share in a first conversation.

"Hey, you don't want to go into details, that's cool," Eleanor said, shrugging again. "My sister found this weird hat in her closet, and when she put it on, it made her write bizarre—and bad—song lyrics."

Ulric's mouth fell open, but he had no words queued up and ready to come out. "Wow," he managed at last. "That is definitely weird."

"Tell me about it. I think I caught her talking to the thing when she thought no one was around. She asked me if they were any good—the lyrics—and she told me to be honest. And when I told her they sucked, she got mad." Eleanor threw her hands up in utter exasperation. "Like, what was I supposed to say?"

"Er—"

"I mean, I told her I'd help her fix them and write out the music," Eleanor went on. "It wasn't like I was going to walk away after telling her that."

"No, no, of course not."

"It was just so bad, I mean—" She turned an intense stare on him. "Do *you* think Fred is a good name for a guy in a romantic song?"

Unsure how he was supposed to answer that, and not having paid much particular attention to romantic songs in the past, Ulric hedged.

"I guess—maybe not? Depending on the song?"

"No, it's not," Eleanor said in a voice that left no room for argument. "Not for this song."

"Well, it's...it's good you were honest with her, I think. She asked for that, after all. Does she have—er, a history of any kind of mental, you know, issues?"

But when he glanced over at her, Eleanor was staring past him, into the trees. "What's that?"

Ulric turned to look over his shoulder in the direction Eleanor was facing. At first he saw nothing unusual, but his gaze caught a small shadow that flitted from one trunk to another. He blinked. "A bird?"

"I don't think so. It didn't move like a bird," Eleanor said, squinting. "More like a moth or a butterfly."

"So...a moth or a butterfly?"

"It's too big for a—there's another one!"

Ulric saw it, too, higher up, moving between two other trees. It moved with the fluttering flight of a butterfly, although it seemed more the size of a small bird. After his encounter with the harpy the day before, however, flying creatures the size of small birds didn't trigger a lot of anxiety. He turned back with a smile. "I guess I'm too much of a city boy—"

"Watch out!"

Eleanor had been half turned to peer into the trees behind them, with one arm over the back of the bench, but now she ducked her head below her elbow. Something small and dark, no longer fluttering but swooping in a quick, scything arc, flew past Eleanor's head. Wisps of her green air danced in the breeze created by its flight. Ulric ducked too, throwing his hands over his head. He heard a deceptively soft whir as another one passed, not the placid buzzing of a bee, but more like fabric whipped by a stiff wind.

When the sound faded, Ulric raised his head for a cautious glance around. Next to him, Eleanor did the same.

"What the flark—" she began, but was cut off when another darting shape dive-bombed her.

Ulric glimpsed this one as it sped past, and found confirmation that it was neither a butterfly nor a bird.

Because neither of those had a mouth full of razor-sharp teeth.

Ulric and Eleanor almost fell off the bench in their effort to get closer to the ground and away from the dive-bombing creatures. Eleanor rolled under the bench and Ulric scuttled underneath the spreading branches of a shrub next to it. Neither option offered much better cover.

"What do we do?" Eleanor breathed. "What are those things?"

"I don't know." Ulric closed his eyes and concentrated, trying to grasp a strand of fifth force energy anywhere around him. He didn't want to explode the metal bench with Eleanor huddled under it, but maybe there was something else he could do with the energy if he could harness even a smidgen.

"Uff," he gasped, as if someone or something had punched him in the stomach. The problem wasn't a lack of magical energy, it was too much of it—strands and pulses rippling everywhere around them. Dark tendrils like puppet strings leapt and danced in the vicinity, making Ulric think they represented the attacking creatures. But they felt...slippery, oily, like something he couldn't get his mind to latch on to. He stretched his mind further, sensing something else nearby, not dark but flashing the bright colours of a rainbow—

"Ulric! The bench!" Eleanor yelped.

Ulric felt her grab at his shirtsleeve and he opened his eyes to see the metal bench trembling over Eleanor, bright spots of super-heated alloy glowing here and there along its length. It had risen a few inches up from the gravel and hung shuddering in the air. Ulric grasped Eleanor's hand and pulled her out from under it, at the same moment releasing the energy strands he'd been clutching in a mental fist. The bench thumped to the ground, the glow fading from the metal, but now Eleanor had no cover and the winged attackers swooped toward them again.

"Under here," Ulric hissed, and tried to pull Eleanor under the shrub as well, but it was asking too much of a small shrub that had up until a few moments ago been innocently minding its own arboreal business. There simply wasn't room.

The ground trembled beneath them, and Eleanor swore under her breath.

"What now, for rot's sake? Come on," Ulric muttered. He twisted around to see what was coming, even as he swung a fist over his head and into the flight path of the onrushing creature. When its threatening mouth was a foot from his face, he connected with it and sent it spinning in a wild arc out of sight over the top of the shrub. The impact was like hitting a rubber ball covered with feathers. A few dark bits of fluff floated to the ground in its wake.

Eleanor whistled her appreciation and said, "Let me try one." As the next attacker whistled toward them, she clenched a fist and pulled it back, swinging it with perfect precision into the flight path. She connected with the side of the creature's body and it hurtled sideways to crash into the gnarled trunk of a nearby tree. It bounced off into a thick shrub and disappeared from view.

Eleanor shook her hand as if she'd punched someone in the face. "Those things are solid," she said, "but that felt awesome."

Although the minor victory had been a momentary distraction, the rumble in the ground intensified, reminding Ulric that something else was happening. He risked sitting up to survey the surroundings.

And saw it.

At first, he thought it was a black horse, trotting at a brisk pace up the path toward them. Its hooves striking the ground generated the rumble he'd noticed, and he was struck by the size of the thing. This was no show horse or racing mount. This was draft horse size, muscles rippling as the ears atop its massive head swivelled toward Ulric and Eleanor. Dark eyes fixed on him with a liquid stare.

Then the sunlight caught it and Ulric saw the horn. A spiral protrusion of bone-white stuck out like a poised weapon from the animal's forehead. The light glinted along its length. Nostrils flared in a velvety muzzle as it snorted. The creature lowered its head and leapt forward, hooves drumming the earth as its pace increased.

A voice in Ulric's head, the same one that always seemed to have something to say when magic or the fifth force became involved, whispered the word *unicorn* to him. A strange word, but he assumed that's what this was. It made sense, of course, because *uni* meant *one* and there was that single conical horn, which when you put the words together could make *corn*—[1]

"Oh, shiitake mushrooms," Eleanor breathed as the thing bore down on them. She clutched at Ulric's hand, the touch of her fear-chilled fingers knocking all nonsensical etymological musings from his head.

He scrambled to his feet, pulling her up with him. In a paralyzed moment, they watched as one of the flying creatures dive-bombed the unicorn. Without breaking stride, it swung its horn toward the thing, twisting its head to the side at the last minute to reveal bared, dazzling white teeth, and snapped the winged attacker out of the air. With an audible crunch, it bit the flyer in half, one wing and the tail tumbling to the ground in a spray of dark ichor.

---

1. One might think a creature such as a unicorn would have been imagined in the Dungeonography game of which Ulric and Tiny Enos were so fond, but it had not. There are some creatures so magical they can choose *not* to be imagined until it suits them.

"Cheese and rice," Eleanor said, her voice admiring.

"Flarking *run*," Ulric breathed, and they turned their backs on the grisly attack and fled down the path deeper into the park.

Intermezzo Quattro

The Min

The Min regarded Skete's image in a small duck pond. Sometimes when The Min was very stressed, she created this little garden in the middle of a courtyard, and populated it with birds and the occasional rabbit. The Min liked rabbits. They were peaceful creatures, found with only slight variations on most inhabited worlds. She'd once begun compiling a list of all the different names they were called, but gave up when the numbers approached four digits.

Today, however, the rabbits were not working. It was amazing, the number of rabbits it would take to counteract the stress level produced by interacting with even just a few members of the Convocation.

She'd been strolling in the garden, trying to calm her nerves. The three uncommunicative Convocation members remained silent, and she had to presume they were down on the planet D'sharu, stirring up trouble. It hadn't been much of a surprise when Skete contacted her, and the duck pond was the closest surface she could use to receive his image. The Min liked at least a semblance of eye contact when dealing with her subordinates.

Skete looked more than a little stressed himself when his face wavered into view on the not-quite-placid water of the pond. "This guy is driving me crazy," he said, running a hand through his already messy blond hair.

"What's wrong?"

Skete shook his head. "He doesn't want to cooperate, for one thing. He doesn't have a clue what's going on or why it's important; he doesn't believe he could have any special abilities; he doesn't like the dog—"

The Min narrowed her eyes. "Dog? What dog?"

Skete stopped short in his tirade. Behind him, The Min could see a towel rack festooned with damp towels and the corner of a shower curtain patterned with sedate polygons. She assumed he'd initiated contact with her through a mirror, where he'd now see her image. "The talking dog—he showed up at Usborne's house even before I did. I thought you must have sent him, too. You didn't?"

"I sent *you*," The Min said with a hint of testiness.

"Then who sent the dog?"

The Min moved her eyes away from Skete's image in the still water of the duck pond, letting her gaze drift over the soothing green of the grass and a pair of adorable fawn-brown rabbits whose lazy hops had just brought them into view. "I don't know," she said in a contemplative voice, tapping one index finger against her lips. "That is a very interesting question." After a few moments of silent contemplating and tapping, she shook herself out of her thoughts. "Well, monitor the situation. And go easy on Usborne. Talking dogs can be trying. Be glad it wasn't a cat."

"I know, I know. But I can't even get him to understand the importance of confrontation between him and the Thaumaturge Avatar. He just keeps saying he wants to go back to his job."

"You can get him through this period of denial. I have faith in you."

"He almost lost it when the Radio started talking to him."

"Hmm, a talking radio, as well. Interesting choice. It's the manifestation of technology?"

Skete flung his hands wide, his expression exasperated. "I guess? It hasn't said that in so many words. It said it's one of Usborne's advisors, but it's been pretty close-mouthed apart from that."

"Well, it's a lot for Usborne to take in. What about the Thaumaturge Avatar? Have you heard from Xya yet?"

"Not yet, but I expect she's found them by now. They aren't making any noise of their own yet, though. No rallying cry for the new magic regime or anything like that."

"Perhaps Xya's having as much trouble as you are," The Min suggested with a hint of a smile.

"Yeah, that would be something. Goodness knows what Usborne will do when the Creatures show up. I don't know that he has the mental wherewithal to handle it. Try to hide in here, I don't doubt." Skete glanced around the tiny confines of the bathroom.

"You might as well warn him about them. It sounds like he might do well with a bit of a heads-up."

"I think I will. Found the others yet?"

The Min pursed her lips and shook her head. "I don't doubt the three of them are down there, although I don't know if they're near you. None of them have shown up to side with the Technocrat Avatar?"

"Not directly. I wondered at first if the dog might be one of them, but I've changed my mind. It's too—perfectly doglike. No Convocation member could keep their personality in check for so long."

"Will he be ready for a confrontation? The Avatar, I mean, not the dog."

Skete shrugged. "I have no idea, honestly. I suppose it depends on how soon it comes. The Radio is agitating for it to be sooner rather than later, but Usborne is resistant. He's not rushing into anything."

"I suspect the magic will be just as eager. Well, keep me informed."

"Wait! Don't you have any advice about working with Usborne?" Skete's voice was edged with desperation.

The Min shook her head. "Sorry, I don't. I didn't realize it would be this difficult an assignment, but I'm certain you're up to the task. Just keep nudging him in the right direction." She thought a moment, then added, "If that doesn't work, tell him the planet will face destruction if he doesn't come through. That should work."

In the pond image, Skete's eyes widened. "Is that true?"

The Min shrugged. "Unlikely. But tell him anyway. It might help him focus."

When her call with Skete ended, The Min stared into the pond, unmoving, for a considerable time. She was having Thoughts. And those Thoughts were leading to Suspicions.

And those Suspicions were making her very uncomfortable.

The presence of the unaccountable dog was one thing, and disobedient and uncommunicative Convocation members another. But neither of those was the first thing that had given her pause. No, that had been, in fact, something Skete had told her the first time he'd come to her office to tell her that a thaumic force had escaped from a decimated planet and relocated to D'sharu. Her conversation with him had brought back the memory. There was something that had caught her attention, but she'd let it slip past in her haste to gather the Convocation so proper procedures could be followed. She'd been too slow anyway, and they'd all gone down to the planet to try their luck, texting her their sad excuses for being absent from the last meeting. There was no indication that any of them had succeeded in getting any attention from the locals or the new thaumic force, and she'd sensed most of them returning empty-handed to the upper realms. With a few notable exceptions.

Let's not get distracted again, she told herself, and shook her head. The Min stood, and with an irritated flick of her hand, the garden, the courtyard, the duck pond, and the rabbits dissipated into the ether. Her office, with its myriad bookshelves, shimmered back into being around her. She pointed a finger at her desk, and a holographic image appeared above it, wavered, then steadied. The image played back a tousled Skete from two days prior, arriving in her office with his breathless announcement. The Min frowned, concentrating on his words as they emerged from the recording. The reproduction was quite lifelike.

"Planet 2342β was decimated at 120:34:94 today; thaumic force departed at 120:34:80 and made planetfall at new destination at 120:36:42. New planet is 8435ὡ."

Also known as D'sharu to the locals. A world without previous knowledge of a thaumic force, or gods of any description. A world, rather unlikely, where neither magic nor gods had ever been imagined. A world ripe for the picking, honestly. But it hadn't, as far as she knew, been picked. Even with all the Convocation down there trying to perform "miracles" and get attention from potential worshippers.

And a pause. A delay. Just two segments, but still. A brief but too-long time between the destruction of Planet 2342β, and the arrival of the thaumic force on the new planet. It was a minor discrepancy, but in conjunction with the other oddities, it might be meaningful. The Min leaned back in her chair and closed her eyes, letting her fingertips tap out a meandering dance on the desktop. She could think of one...two...three potential explanations for that pause.

One: a natural phenomenon had created an obstacle in the path of the thaumic force, causing it to slow in its juggernaut toward a new home. Something like an extra-dense patch of dark matter, or a nebula concealing something unusual in its depths, or even a faint brush with the gravitational pull of a distant black hole might have caused it. She could check on the existence of something like that in the force's path.

Two: a faltering in the thaumic force itself. Perhaps there had been more than one planet it might have chosen, and it dithered over that choice. Again, she could check for the existence of such planets on the force's route and, if it became necessary, even travel to the planet and interrogate the incarnation of the force to find out whether that had, indeed, been the case. She didn't care for the idea of contacting the force in person—it might seem too much like interference—but she could do it if she had to.

Three: interference from another entity. The Min opened her eyes as she considered this possibility and stared across the plane that sprawled, vast and endless, outside her office. She liked this possibility the least, because it would mean the involvement of some unknown entity, or one of the Exiles. And that second option should not be possible.

But if it was possible, it cast a different light on things. A light that sent long, dark shadows shivering over the world of D'sharu. A light The Min didn't like at all.

A short time later, The Min called another meeting of the Convocation. She took down the summoning horn, put it to her lips and blew hard, one long blast that would reverberate from one end of the astral realm to the other. Not that she thought any of them were further away than D'sharu, but she wanted to be sure she got everyone's attention. She followed up the blast with an announcement, in her best serious announcement voice. It was deep and sonorous and next to impossible to ignore. "The Convocation is recalled under Article Ten of the Regulations. Any member who does not attend its summons without a valid excuse will be subject to expulsion from the Convocation and revocation of all attendant powers."

The Min sat back in her chair and waited. It wouldn't be long. An Article Ten recall should be enough to rattle any chains that needed rattling.

Sure enough, within seconds they were popping in, some of them looking peeved, certainly, but responding to the call. The book-lined walls expanded and shifted to accommodate them, only the odd dislodged page fluttering through the quiet air like a lost butterfly. Given time, they'd find their way back to the proper books.

Although some members were slow to arrive—almost slow enough to be insulting—most of the Convocation made an appearance this time. The Min sat at her desk, also enlarged to present an appropriate air of authority. Fingers steepled, she leaned back in her chair and surveyed the lot. Some of them had the decency to look shamefaced for their earlier transgressions. Three faces were still absent (besides Skete and Xya, who would know they didn't have to make an appearance). The diehards. The troublemakers. Corax, Sedrict, and Alsina.

"So most of you have come back," she said in a too-casual voice. "Do tell me where you've been. I thought it was such a coincidence that you'd *all* choose the same moment to take a vacation."

"Haha. Hilarious," said a tall, thin man, so tall and thin that you'd expect him to disappear if he turned sideways. He would, and he enjoyed the look on people's faces when he did. His name was Drix. "What's going on with that planet, D'sharu?"

"Yes, what's happening down there?" echoed a tall man with a long beard. Judging by the clusters of iridescent bubbles clinging to random spots on his beard, he'd been in the middle of a bath when the summons came, and he wasn't happy to have been disturbed.

"Oh, is that where you've been?" The Min feigned surprise. "All the way to D'sharu and back?"

"Pfft, it wasn't worth the time or the effort," complained a stout woman with flaming red hair. Upon closer inspection, one realized they were, in fact, actual flames, but she didn't seem to mind.[1] "Magic's not working properly down there, and we want to know why! What did you do?"

The Min shook her head. "I didn't do a thing. At least, nothing that would interfere with anyone's ability to control the thaumic force. Even I don't wield that kind of power."

"Then who did?" lisped another man, a little rotund figure in a toga. Anyone hearing him might wonder how he contrived to lisp a sentence containing no "s" sounds whatsoever, but somehow he did. In his right hand, he gripped a brown paper bag moulded to the obvious shape of a bottle. He wavered a little left and right as he stared at The Min with bloodshot eyes.

"There's more happening on that world than you might think," The Min mused. "At first, I'll admit it seemed like just another instance of a displaced thaumic force crash-landing and activating a dormant force as a consequence."

"If that was the case, it should have been a free-for-all," said the first, thin man. "In reality, I couldn't even magic a coin out of someone's pocket."

"I couldn't ignite a measly sacrificial fire," added the flame-haired woman, an undercurrent of indignation threading through her voice. The Min recalled her name: Ignacjianna.

"Do you have anyone on the ground?" asked a woman who'd been quiet until now. Her long auburn hair was adorned with crow's feathers. "I notice some faces missing from this meeting."

The Min nodded. "I put Skete on the ground first as a precaution. And then Xya came to me and presented a case for sending her as well. She made a good point, so I approved her to assist on the planet. They're guiding the Avatars."

"And what powers do they have?" demanded the thin man.

---

1. They didn't burn, only gave a very convincing appearance of burning.

"Whatever they do or don't have is out of my control," The Min said. "They went as they were, with no special boons from me, but I've had reports from both of them that magic use is happening. No matter what obstructions you may have encountered yourselves, whatever is happening with the thaumic force on the planet is being allowed or disallowed by something I don't control."

Mutters arose from the crowd. Whatever their personal opinions of The Min's decisions or actions, it was obvious they considered nothing ought to be out of her control. And they weren't pleased that something had blocked their own access to the force.

"That doesn't make any sense. It's not supposed to work that way."

The Min spread her hands out on her desk. "I can't say I understand it myself," she admitted. "The planet itself may have something to do with it. But I suspect that something—or someone—had bigger plans for D'sharu than turning it into a playground for bored trans-dimensional beings."

The assemblage looked around at each other. After a pause, the little fat man said, "But beshides you—and ush—who elsh is there?" It was an excellent question, more cogent than might be expected considering his obvious state of intoxication, but it was never wise to underestimate him.

The Min folded her hands and set them on the desk. "That I don't know for certain. But I'm forced to consider the possibility of interference from an unknown quantity, or an Exile."

As she'd expected, the Convocation erupted in gasps of alarm and noises of dismay.

"That's not possible!"

"Which of them is it?"

"How could one get free?"

And more in the same vein. The Min let them go for a moment, then raised a hand for quiet until the clamour died down. She waited until silence reigned again.

"I don't have those answers yet, and I'm more than a little worried about them myself. So if the rest of you will stop mucking about on the planet, I can concentrate on finding out what's happening."

"But, Exiles?" asked the woman with the flaming hair. "That would be bad."

"Indeed, it would," The Min agreed.

"Why do you think it's a possibility?"

The Min sighed. "There's something more important I want you all to think about. I don't know what it means yet, but it has me…concerned."

She had their attention now. Anything that made The Min concerned wasn't good. "Allow me to illustrate." With a wave of her hand, she called into existence a huge three-dimensional model of the known universe. Then she allowed the viewpoint to zoom in on the sector in question. She created a glowing pointer that picked out a planet in the sector and hung above it, twinkling to keep their attention.

"This," she said, "is Planet 2342β. Or it was. That planet was decimated at 120:34:94 a few days ago. The thaumic force, aware of the danger, departed at 120:34:80. It made planetfall at 8435ώ , which we now know as D'sharu, at 120:36:42." The original planet disappeared, and the glowing arrow swung in a long, slow, vertiginous arc to a new destination.

The Min looked out over the crowd of faces gazing at the model. It was obvious they were waiting for the next bit of the story. No one seemed to have noticed anything strange.

One by one, awareness grew that she was looking at them. The silence grew, became uncomfortable, and stretched, trying to ease the discomfort. Finally, it fled.

"And?" asked a short, stout person of indeterminate gender with garlands of fresh flowers in their hair and around their neck.

"Two segments," The Min answered. "That's how long it took the thaumic force to get from the original planet to D'sharu. Two segments."

"That's…unusually long?" a young man suggested, not sounding at all sure of himself.

The Min closed her eyes for a moment. No one paid attention to anything these days. If she weren't here, observing… "Yes, it's unusually long. There's a pause there. An unexplained pause. And watch," she added. The pointer skipped back along the path it had just followed, highlighting three planets as it went. "The thaumic force could have made planetfall at any of these first," The Min explained. "In fact, it should stop at the next closest one. Instead, it skipped them and continued on to D'sharu."

No one said anything for a moment.

Then someone near the back asked, "Why?"

The Min nodded. "Exactly."

ECHOES OF POTENTIALITY

NERLIM

Nerlim Pettibone didn't look back to see if the librarian, Alwi, followed him down the narrow aisle between bookshelves in the environmentally controlled antiquarian book room. Of course he would, since he was tasked with making sure Nerlim didn't do anything...untoward...with the precious books collected here. Nerlim didn't mind. In fact, he needed the librarian to ensure Nerlim found the proper book and didn't waste his time wandering around the stacks searching for it.

At least, Nerlim expected to need the man's help. As he drew closer to the singular copy of Echoes of Potentiality, however, the tome's location became very obvious. Even though it looked little different from any other book on the shelves, to Nerlim's magic sense it was sending up fireworks, banging a gong, and waving a flag labelled "HERE I AM!". He could have picked it off the shelf blindfolded. He could have found it if it were the proverbial needle in the proverbial haystack.

It was chock-full of fifth force magic, and Nerlim sensed every atom of that. It wasn't painful, like the gut-punch of magic being used nearby, but a humming, thrumming energy that pulsed like a heavy bass line at a rock concert.

Rather than react to it, however, he made the wise choice to hesitate and let Alwi edge past him and pluck the book from its home on the shelf. In the librarian's hands, the volume was unassuming, bound in dark green leather from which threads of stitching hung in worn strands. The title had been stamped in gold lettering on the front cover, and the author's name, Chetlin Tweddle, sat in quiet satisfaction on the spine.

Oh, Chetlin Tweddle, Nerlim thought, *who were you? And what did you know about my fifth force—magic?*

"Here we are," Alwi said in a pleasant, jolly-the-old-man-along tone. "There's a reading table at the back of the room if you'd like to look at it there."

"Of course, that would be perfect."

Get me out of here, said the Book.

Nerlim blinked, thinking the young librarian had spoken. "Excuse me?"

"Yes?" Alwi said over his shoulder, still leading Nerlim toward the back of the room.

"I—I thought you said something," Nerlim said.

I did, said the Book, leaving Nerlim to cover his startle of realization that the voice had made itself known only in his mind.

"No, I didn't," Alwi assured him.

Nerlim squeezed his eyes shut, as if the voice were something he could physically force out of sight. Of course, that was the wrong sensory approach, but to be fair, Nerlim had never encountered a talking book before.

"Is—is there a chair with this reading table?" Nerlim asked in a thready voice. At that moment his legs, head, and bladder felt quite frail and uncertain about meeting their various responsibilities.

"Yes, there is. Are you all right?" Alwi slowed his steps to look back at his charge, concern written with a heavy hand on his face. No doubt he was imagining all possible and devastating repercussions of having an old man take ill in a room full of priceless books.

Buck up, old man, I'm counting on you to steal me out of this detention centre, the Book told Nerlim.

"I'm fine," Nerlim managed. "Just tired from waiting, I guess. Stiff after sitting for so long. It will pass."

"So you don't twant to sit?" Alwi asked in a puzzled tone as they arrived at the promised desk and chair combination. He set the Book down on the table with reverent care and pulled two white gloves from a discreet cardboard box. He handed them to Nerlim.

Nerlim held up his hands. "No, that's not what I meant. I'll sit," he assured Alwi as he took the gloves and slipped them on. Alwi pulled out the chair as if he were a waiter seating Nerlim at Neemar's finest eating establishment. Nerlim sat.

"Just be gentle with it," Alwi instructed. "Pages in these old volumes are fragile. If you need to sneeze, cough, or—anything—please be sure to turn your head away from the book."

Not like I can catch your cooties, the Book huffed. *Look, sensile, you need to get me out of here before I lose the last of my sanity. I've been in this prison cell for decades.*

Nerlim blinked again. That word—sensile. That's what Xya had called him. It meant he could sense the use of magic, but the Book wasn't *using* magic, was it?

You hold magic as long as I have, pal, you don't need to use *it. You are* it.

"Perhaps I would like something to write with," Nerlim said to Alwi, wondering with desperation how long he could keep up the charade of acting like a magical book wasn't carrying on a telepathic conversation with him. "Do you have a pen and some paper?"

Alwi regarded him with a stern face. "No pens in the Collection room," he said. "One might explode ink everywhere or someone might drop one on the page of a book. But I can fetch you paper and a *pencil*," he offered with unnecessary emphasis.

"That would be perfect," Nerlim said.

"One moment, then." Alwi disappeared down another row of books.

Alone at last, said the Book. *I can't even count how many times I've tried to talk to that guy, but he never hears me.*

"Lucky him," Nerlim hissed in a furious whisper, leaning close to the Book. "I can't decide if this is happening, or if all this fifth force stuff has melted my brain, like Gameldina always claimed it would."

Oh, it's real, the Book retorted. *And I can hear you, if you direct your thoughts to me. No need to whisper or put your mouth that close. Yoiks! Back up a bit, would you? Warm and moist exhalations are not good for my parchment.*

Nerlim sat back in the chair, both insulted and assaulted. He hadn't *asked* for this freakish tome to talk to him.

Although to be fair, he had come hoping it would have information for him.

I assume you can pick up on this, then, he thought at the Book, keeping his distance but staring at the wrinkles in its green leather binding.

Loud and clear, neighbour. Fast learner, huh? I like that.

I also assume you have knowledge and information about the fifth force, or magic, or whatever you call the energy that allows you to communicate this way?

Knowledge and information, said the Book, *I got in spades. You want it, the slow way, or the fast way?*

What do you mean? Nerlim asked with apprehension.

Pfft, the Book sighed. *I mean, do you want to read me, or do you want me to tell you? You'll get a lot more information if I tell you, by the way.*

"Here you go," Alwi said, appearing behind Nerlim's chair on silent librarian feet.

Nerlim stifled a yelp and managed not to fall out of his chair. With a puzzled frown, the librarian offered him the pencil and a small notebook.

"I'll just tidy up while you're perusing," Alwi said, trying and failing to disguise the consternation with which he now regarded Nerlim. "We close in an hour."

"That will be fine," Nerlim managed, and Alwi left him alone. To the Book, Nerlim thought, *I guess you'll have to tell me. I can't read you in an hour, that's for sure.*

This way will be more fun, anyway, the Book told him. *So you promise to get me out of here, right?*

Nerlim chewed his lower lip. *That might be easier said than done. You've been here long enough to know security is pretty tight.*

The Book appeared to mull this over for a few moments, as it went still and silent. *Okay, but if you can't get me out today, will you promise to come back with someone who can?*

Sure, of course, Nerlim said, although he wasn't sure who that person might be. The boy, Ulric, perhaps, or maybe Xya. He'd have to consider it.

I'll be super annoyed if you don't, the Book assured him, a stern note replacing its earlier joviality. *I might even devise a way to take...revenge.*

Nerlim was sure the Book put as much quiet threat into the word as possible, drawing out the syllables. But he couldn't imagine what a locked-up book might do to him. He shoved that thought aside before the Book picked up on it. *I get it,* he told the Book. *Now, what can you tell me about the fifth force?*

Well, magic has been around on D'sharu for a long time, the Book said, *but in a dormant state.*

But if it was dormant, how did Chetlin Tweddle find out enough about it to write a book about—

Hey! the Book interrupted him. *Am I telling this story, or are you asking questions?*

Nerlim sighed. *Continue, please.*

This dormant state suffered a brief interruption about a century ago, which is when my author, Chetlin Tweddle, wrote me. The Book sounded far too self-satisfied at this. *Following this short period of activation, the magic reverted to its dormant state.*

Why?

My author believed that there was undue influence exerted to activate the magic—what you call the fifth force, a rather silly name if you ask me, but anyway—this influence was unnatural and untimely, and so the effect had to be reversed. All traces of magical residue and aftereffects were erased from the planet, and the planet itself magicked to forget the brief lapse.

Nerlim frowned at the Book. *Not* all *traces, obviously.*

Obviously, the Book said with smug satisfaction.

But whose responsibility would that be—activating the force and then turning it back off? And why has it been activated again now?

The Book shook its metaphorical head. *That was unknown to my author and remains unknown to me. Powerful forces or beings, they would have had to be.*

Nerlim stifled a groan. Every new thing he learned generated new questions. *So how do you have—magic?* he asked. *Did your author have access to it while it was active?*

No. He was aware of it—a sensile, like you, I believe, although he did not have that nomenclature. But because he wrote about it, the truth of it somehow became manifested through me. You must understand, a lot of this stuff is pretty vague in terms of what's written on my pages. You wouldn't get all this just by reading *me. I've had lots of time to reflect on it all, and now with magic active again, well, things are even clearer and—*

Yes, Nerlim interrupted, even though the Book wouldn't like it. *So tell me what you can about what's happening now.*

Okay, this is where things get interesting, the Book gushed. *New magic arrived on the planet—*

Whoa, wait—new magic? How is that possible? Where does magic come from? Nerlim was floundering now, trying to keep up with and make sense of what the Book was telling him.

Magic is always inherently possible on a world, so it must have come from somewhere else. I don't know where, the Book told him. *My theory is that a new magic force arrived from somewhere, another world, and sparked the old, innate planetary magic back to life when it landed. It's unclear to me if they're getting along, these two magical forces, or if they're butting heads and rolling toward some big magical showdown, but there's a* lot *of magical energy roiling around on D'sharu these days, I can tell you that. I can feel it in my bindings. And it's not...happy.*

Nerlim nodded. The Book had that part right, anyway, in Nerlim's limited understanding. But his mind raced. Why hadn't Xya mentioned anything about D'sharu having magic before? Did she not know? Or was she keeping things from them for her own purposes?

I sense another external conflict in play as well, the Book continued. *As if magic is competing with something—*

Technology, I'd guess, Nerlim said. *Technological stuff isn't stable, like something's interfering with it.*

That would make sense—

"How are you getting along?" asked a voice behind Nerlim, and he startled again at the sound of a voice in his ears instead of one only inside his head.

"Oh! Great!"

There was a pause. "Okay, but," Alwi said at last, puzzlement clear in his voice, "You haven't even opened it yet?"

"Um...er, yes, I have, of course! I only just closed it again for a moment to make a few notes. So as not to expose the pages to too much light or air," Nerlim babbled.

Alwi stared at the open notebook he'd fetched for Nerlim, which remained accusingly blank.

Nerlim was saved from having to explain this by the unexpected recurrence of the gut-twisting, chest-clenching awareness that he now recognized as the harbinger of magic use. He'd been okay when conversing with the Book, because it hummed with a continual, low-level magic resonance that coursed like river water over his senses but didn't pummel them. This, though, was different. This sudden punch meant the deliberate and nearby use of the fifth force. Nerlim doubled over in his chair, gasping for a couple of hitching breaths before he regained his composure. When he looked up, he was unsurprised at the appearance of a tall, dark-haired woman next to the small reading desk.

Contrariwise, Alwi was surprised indeed. His voice came out in a much higher pitch than before. "Where did you come from? You're not authorized to be in here!"

The woman's expression passed from worried to annoyed and settled on a kind of frustrated resignation. Her eyes were a steely blue with flecks of violet—Nerlim was close enough to her to see the details—and she raised a hand to pat her close-curled tresses. They looked like the bobby pin curls Nerlim's younger sister used to twist her hair into every night before bed.

"I'm sorry for this inconvenience," she said in a voice like wind sighing through trees. "But it's vital that I find out what's in this book." She reached a hand toward the Book, which squealed in protest.

Hang on there, lady, I don't know you and I don't—

But neither the woman nor Alwi gave any sign of hearing it.

You're still talking to me, Nerlim hissed at the Book.

The woman, who, now that Nerlim had time to take her in, looked formidable enough to take Alwi down if it came to fisticuffs over the book, glanced with narrowed eyes at Nerlim. Her hand paused in its trajectory toward the book. "Hmm. A sensile, are you? Well, that's interesting. Sorry if my arrival caused you any discomfort. Have you chosen a side yet?"

The woman's lips looked as if they spent a lot of time pursed in disapproval or consternation, but she spoke in an almost kind tone to Nerlim.

It was Alwi who answered her, though. "This is more than an inconvenience! You are not supposed to be here unaccompanied. How did you even get in? No, no, never mind," he corrected himself. "You don't have to tell me. Someone else can sort that out. What I need to do is—"

He was reaching for the Book as he spoke, with the obvious intention of whisking it away to some safe place, out of the clutches of this upstart woman who clearly did not understand how Special Collections worked. The woman's attention snapped away from Nerlim and back to the book, though, and she made an odd twisting motion with her hand. Nerlim felt an echoing twist in his belly and clutched at it. Alwi froze with his hand hovering mere inches over the Book.

As Nerlim looked up at him, the librarian's eyes went wide. He twitched, as if trying to move but finding himself unable to manage it. With a half-smile, the woman scooped the Book off the desk and into her arms. Alwi squawked in incoherent rage.

Unhand me, villainess! The Book demanded, but the woman remained unmoved as ever. *Sensile, aren't you going to do anything?*

Nerlim shrugged. *What do you want me to do? All she has to do is use a smidgen more magic, and I'll be on the floor in pain. There's no way she'll let me take you back.*

The woman, oblivious to or ignoring this discussion, opened the Book at a random page and ran her gaze down it. A faint frown line appeared between her generous brows, and she licked a finger to turn a page. Alwi looked as if the veins in his neck and forehead would burst at the affront. Which would not be salutary for the rest of the precious books in the vicinity, Nerlim thought.

"Who are you?" Nerlim asked the woman to distract Alwi and give his blood pressure a chance to settle.

She smiled, a genuine smile, for the first time. She looked quite pleasant when she did that. "I'm someone who's going to help sort out all the magic problems messing up this world at the moment. And I need to borrow this book in case it can help me do that."

I'm not helping you with anything, bitch, the Book muttered, although Nerlim was at a loss to imagine how it would stop itself from being read. No doubt it was a knee-jerk reaction to the damp-finger-page-turning treatment, which was understandable even if the Book lacked knees.

"Rest assured, gentlemen," the woman told Alwi and Nerlim, ignoring the Book if she could, indeed, hear it, "that I will take good care of this tome. I might even return it when the time is right."

"Might? Might?" Alwi spluttered, looking apoplectic but still unable to move more than his lips. Nerlim had a moment of genuine worry for the young man. But then Alwi relaxed. "You won't get five steps outside that door without someone stopping you," he told her.

"I'm sure you're quite right, and although they wouldn't succeed, it would be easier to avoid any unpleasant encounters," the woman said. "So I might skip using the door at all." And with no fanfare or flourish, she and the Book faded from sight, as if they'd been made of fog and a brisk breeze had blown in. Only a pale green flash and a glitter like falling sparks marked her departure.

Alwi's power of movement returned in a lurch, and he sprawled across the reading table. He stretched out a hand to the space the woman had occupied, waving his fingers through it as if he expected to encounter her.

He did not. Alwi turned wide, confused eyes to Nerlim. "Did you see that?" he asked. "What just happened?"

Nerlim sat back in the chair and shook his head, trying to recover from the punch he'd felt when the woman disappeared. "Magic," he said, "And if you don't know what that means, I'm afraid that despite my best efforts, I'm not the one to explain it to you."

Not Another One

Gammy

There were hours to go before Gammy was scheduled to meet Nerlim at The Sugar Goat, and she wasn't having the best afternoon. She might have gone to NCDSF, but the idea, for once, held little attraction for her. Others were working around the clock on the mystery of the launch failure and how to rectify the problem, and all she would be able to do was glare at them. Sad experience had taught her that the glare produced faster results only in very specific circumstances. No; better, for once, to stay away.

But what to do instead? She spent half an hour on a desultory cleaning of her house, but since she had a man who came in once a week to clean for her and did a much more thorough job than she could, it seemed pointless. Gammy was keenly aware that a cabinet in the kitchen held an unopened bottle of Black Angus Knockdown, but she steeled herself to leave it alone. She needed all her wits about her, and after her recent over-indulgence, the thought of the liquor made her feel queasy and green around the gills. Best to leave that bottle where it was.

In desperation, Gammy took a walk around the block, but even the bright sunshine didn't lift her mood. There were too many people, too much noise (because vehicles in the area were working today), and it was too warm. Returning home, she flung herself down in her comfortably worn easy chair and switched on the television. Five minutes later, she turned it off and hurled the remote across the room. It hit the wall with a satisfying crash, but the battery compartment door flew off, and two batteries bounced and rolled to a stop under the sofa.

Gammy swore. Gammy's swears were colourful and inventive, particularly when she was alone. Or thought she was alone.

"Frustrating times, I'm sure," someone said in a mild and sympathetic voice from the living room doorway.

Gammy was too angry and resentful to be startled, even though she didn't recognize the voice as Corax's and he was the only "acquaintance" who was likely or able to materialize out of nowhere. She turned her head casually to survey the intruder and said, "What would you know about it?"

It wasn't Corax, although this visitor was just as translucent. The intruder flashed her a grin. He was tall, perhaps six feet, and had taken up a casual stance, leaning against the doorframe with arms crossed as he regarded her. He wore a tailored suit that might have been blue if there'd been enough of it to hold colour, and his hair slicked back from his forehead in a sleek, if improbable, wave. His well-shod feet hovered two inches above the carpet. Both hands bore heavy-looking rings as he tapped his fingers on his arms. "Maybe not as much as you; maybe more."

Gammy rolled her eyes. "Cheese and rice, not another one," she observed in a voice dripping with sarcasm, and hauled herself out of her chair to retrieve the television remote.

She watched him in her peripheral vision, though, and she thought his grin flickered in an instant of doubt. Good. Keep him on guard. Then the grin redoubled.

"You don't seem startled by my appearance, so I'm guessing one of my...er, colleagues may have already been speaking with you," the apparition said. "May I come in?"

"Little late to be asking." Gammy grunted as she scooped up the remote and the battery compartment cover. "But sure. Make yourself at home."

The man moved into the room and Gammy bent, ignoring the protests from her lower back, to peer under the sofa. "Get those out of there for me, would you?" she asked, just as the man lowered himself to "sit" in a chair.

"Excuse me?" he hovered over the seat, gripped by uncertainty.

"The batteries. Fetch them out from under the sofa," Gammy explained as if speaking to a small child. "I'd do it, but I'd rather not make unnecessary demands on my knees."

The man glanced down at his corporeally challenged form. "I'm not sure I—"

"Oh, come on, now. You don't have to touch them. You must be able to use some woo-woo jackfoolery to scuttle them out where I can reach them easier." Gammy waved her fingers in the air and rolled her eyes as she said *woo-woo jackfoolery*.

"I don't—" the man tried again, but Gammy cut him off without mercy.

"Look, Corax did some mind trickery on my assistant, *and* he changed a glass of vinegary wine into decent Black Angus Knockdown. If you can't fish a couple of batteries out from under a sofa, I'm not sure why you're here."

"Ah, Corax," the man said in a knowing voice. "I'm not surprised."

Then he closed his eyes and gestured toward the sofa with one outstretched hand.

Gammy peered under the edge of the sofa. No batteries presented themselves to be retrieved. "Try again?"

The man's lips flattened into a line and he clenched his other fist, gesturing again. This time, the batteries rolled just into sight, and Gammy reached down and scooped them up. The man let out a stifled groan.

"Appreciate it," Gammy said as she slotted the batteries back into the remote. "So I suppose you want to be one of these god-thingys, too. I have to tell you, Corax seemed a little smoother at using this force everyone's so het up about."

The man seemed to bite back a retort, and instead said in a pleasant voice, "My name is Sedrict. I'm very pleased to meet you."

"The pleasure's all yours, I'm sure." Gammy returned to her own chair and gave a *come-on* gesture with her fingers. "All right, give me the spiel."

"Well," Sedrict said, crossing his legs, clasping his hands and hooking them around one knee. "To begin with, I'm not here on my own behalf.

Corax may be out for himself, but I represent a much more significant being."

Gammy raised an eyebrow. "Who couldn't be bothered coming to speak to me himself? I might be insulted already."

"Oh, no, it's not that at all," Sedrict hurried to clarify. "He is unable to appear on this planet at present. If he could appeal to you himself, I'm certain he would."

"Is this going to take long?" Gammy asked. She looked at the clock above the window. "I do have other things to do today."

Sedrict pressed on in the face of Gammy's attitude. "This being is well-placed to assist you in attaining your heart's desire—a successful mission to your moon."

"Great, someone else spying on me," Gammy said with a sniff. "I suppose I'm expected to be grateful, but perhaps you've never been spied on. You might be surprised to learn that it doesn't facilitate a grateful state of mind."

"Corax has likely asked you to use your influence to help him gain the same," Sedrict continued, switching with practiced smoothness to another tack. "However, what I'm requesting on behalf of my colleague is far less onerous. It would require very little action on your part."

"I can't wait to hear about it," Gammy drawled.

Sedrict swallowed, his semi-translucent throat bobbing. "All we—I—require is access to your place of work, and the temporary use of some of the equipment there."

Gammy stiffened, her bored demeanour evaporating. Her eyes narrowed and her words were clipped. "My place of work?"

Sedrict continued, oblivious to the subtle warning signs. "Yes, the institution known as the North and Central D'sharian—"

"I know where I work, thanks. What in the name of cheese and rice do you want there?"

Sedrict looked a bit startled, since Gammy's words had been delivered in a low growl.

"Nothing would be harmed or compromised, I assure you," he hurried to clarify. "It's very simple. I want to send a message to the colleague I mentioned. He's very...er, distant from here."

"Send a message? You want to use my state-of-the-art space exploration facility to call a friend?" Incredulity edged Gammy's words.

"This colleague of mine is, as I said, a significant being. In fact, the only person—I emphasize, the only one—who can assist you in getting your space launch active again," Sedrict said. "Corax has probably promised you the same thing, but he cannot deliver on that promise."

"Don't like Corax, do you?"

"It's not—that isn't—I have no personal disagreement with Corax," Sedrict spluttered. "But he's—well, between you and me, he's a bit of a poser. Likes to talk big but doesn't follow through. You know the type."

Gammy frowned, because she did know the type. She'd met an uncountable quantity of them in the course of her career. And to be honest, that's how Corax had struck her. But she didn't like being told this, as if she wasn't capable of forming such assessments on her own.

"Who's this colleague of yours? Mr. Significant Being. Why isn't he here, mucking about for himself like the rest of you?"

"Well, that's why I want to message him," Sedrict said, reverting to his previous cheerful tone. "To tell him to come and see the amazing opportunities—to help people here."

Gammy heard it, the slight hitch in the man's voice; the tell that he was holding something back, not telling her the whole truth.

"So he doesn't know about this whole fifth force debacle," Gammy said. "You want to tell him to come and get in on the *opportunity*. What if he's not even interested?"

"Oh, he knows about it. He just needs—you could think of it as directions to get here."

Gammy directed a level gaze at him, one eyebrow cocked. "This significant being who's the only one who can get my launch working can't find an entire planet on his own? Yeah, he sounds formidable."

"It's not like that! He's in a difficult situation and he needs just a small bit of assistance to get...out of it." Sedrict looked flustered, as if this interview had not gone as expected. Gammy liked that.

"So now you're using my instruments to send help, not just a message." Gammy snorted. "What kind of help? Instructions to break out of prison?"

Somehow, Sedrict's translucent form went even paler for the space of a heartbeat, and Gammy hid a smile. So her casual joke had struck a nerve. Wasn't that interesting? Had this Sedrict person had the effrontery to come here on behalf of a *criminal,* soliciting her help? She was almost impressed at the gall that took.

Almost.

Gammy settled back in her chair and crossed her arms. Now she was going to enjoy this. "So, what's your offer? Corax has promised to get my rocket ship working. You say your absent colleague can do the same, but I expect you want to raise the ante."

"Raise the—" Sedrict looked confused for a moment, as if he didn't understand the term, then brightened. "Oh, of course. You want a better offer."

"Might as well get what I can, seeing as I'm so in demand," Gammy agreed with a predatory grin.

"Well, the moon mission is only a start, of course. I'm sure my colleague would be able to offer wealth, power, all the usual things—"

"But you've said this colleague doesn't want to become a god, like Corax. I understand from him that's what is needed to master or control this fifth force. This magic. So how will all these things be accomplished?"

Sedrict shook his head. "Corax might want to become a god, but that's not necessary to control magic. Anyone can do it with the right—"

He broke off and Gammy jumped on his words. "Anyone?" Nerlim's words came back to her from their phone call earlier. Somewhere, he'd also found other people who knew about the fifth force. She might not need these apparitions at all.

"Well, not *anyone*—" His eyes jumped around the room like a frog looking for a way out of a pot of hot water.

"But you said anyone. And if anyone can do it, why do I need any of you lot?"

"Anyone already attuned to magic," the apparition said with reluctance and an edge of petulance. "You still need one of us if you want your moon mission back."

Gammy stood from her chair. "I'm not convinced of that. Not yet. Now get the hell out of here and leave me alone. I have thinking to do."

Perhaps Sedrict had already, in this one brief interaction with Gammy, recognized that there was no arguing with that particular tone of voice. He left.

Gammy swore again, but this time, she was smiling.

NOT EVEN TRYING

WINT

An hour after the Radio had spoken to Wint, the others were still trying to convince him to go out and address the crowd in his yard. Wint had gone to his room to "take a break" and the others had agreed to allow him some time to think and adjust to the idea of sentient electronics. It seemed fair. But after an hour, Skete had persuaded him to come back down to the kitchen.

"I still don't see why I would go out and talk to those people. They don't know me, and I don't know them." Wint peered out the window at his still-occupied lawn.

"Because I told you to, and because you have to," the Radio answered.

Wint looked at Skete and Rex for help. Rex continued studiously licking himself. Skete spread his hands and shrugged. "That seems a bit authoritarian, Radio. Wint should do it to be friendly—to meet his followers."

"You keep saying you want me to 'address my loyal followers,'" Wint said. "But I don't have any loyal followers! I barely have any close friends!"

"Then who do you think all those people outside *are*?" the Radio asked, a bit of static in its voice.

"I just thought they were...waiting for something."

"They are. They're waiting for you. The Technocrat Avatar."

"And what should I talk to them about?"

Skete looked at Rex, who looked up from his ablutions at Wint. "About how technology is going to subjugate magic but also make use of it when you're in control, and rule the world and make everything better."

"Oh, of course. Because I know all about this *magic*. What kind of word is that, anyway? It sounds super sketchy to me. And ruling the world. Ruling the world?" Wint's voice had risen and now seemed about to crack. "I don't want to rule the world! I don't even want to run mission control. I don't even want to be head of the Neighbourhood Watch!" He thrust his face down toward the Radio on the kitchen table. "I don't even belong to the coffee club at work!"

"STOP COMPLAINING," the Radio said. Or rather, bellowed, because the sound filled the kitchen and rattled the windows. Something fell over with a muffled crash in one of the cupboards. "YOU HAVE BEEN CHOSEN. NOW GET ON WITH IT."

A lesser man might have quailed, but Wint's own frustration had built to a point where it bolstered his nerve. "Chosen by whom?" he asked in the deafening silence that filled the room when the Radio's voice died away. "I keep asking that, but no one seems to have the answer."

"Chosen by me," the Radio grated out. "By the manifestation of technology."

Rex made a choking sound, as if he'd been going to bark—or laugh—and smothered it.

Wint took a moment to consider that. "So you're not, in fact, a radio," he mused. "You're just *inside* the radio."

The Radio sighed. "You can think of it that way if you wish."

"And a manifestation is—something like a spirit?"

"If that's how you can get your head around it, sure," the Radio said with a hint of testiness. "Now are you going out there, or—"

"I'll make you a deal," Wint blurted. He didn't want to hear what kind of threat the Radio might be about to make. He had to assume he was happier not knowing. "I'll go out there, but only to tell them I'm going out to this Dingaling place—"

"Dingle," the Radio corrected in a severe tone.

"Dingle, whatever," Wint said. "I'm not making any promises; I'm not claiming to be this Technocrat thing. If they're interested in me, I guess they'll follow me and then I'll have to deal with it. If they don't, then that will prove you three are full of...crap. Because you're coming with me."

"Well, of course, we're coming with you. Where else would we go?" the Radio huffed. It blew out what sounded like an exasperated sigh. "All right, you have a deal. You're only putting off the inevitable, but if it makes you happy, sure."

Without another word, Wint squared his shoulders, opened the door, and stepped out onto his back step. He felt as if he had won a minor victory, and if he did this one thing now, he'd gain at least a brief reprieve from the war. And although he didn't want to do anything to validate the ridiculous claims of Skete, Rex, or the Radio, he had the thought that at least this was a way to get all these people out of his yard. With luck, he might ditch them all at this Dingle place and sneak back here in peace.

The crowd had spread out, milling around on Wint's lawn in a desultory fashion. When Wint emerged, several people noticed and wandered over toward the step. A girl smacked her chewing gum with a loud pop, making Wint jump. She flashed him a smile and pursed her lips at him in a mock kiss. She had long brown hair, the last few inches dyed a shocking blue. Her t-shirt sported an intricate network of circuitry that also somehow resembled a flower. A thin youth who was losing a battle with acne approached from the other side, and an older man in a faded blue ball cap who darted only rare glances away from his cell phone to see where he was going followed. One by one, the others in the crowd noticed the movement toward the house and turned their faces in Wint's direction.

He didn't wait for them all to approach—he had to get this done.

"Er...I'm heading for the Dingle now. With—the others. Just wanted to let you know. There won't be anyone else here. In the house, I mean. After we leave."

"Is the Technocrat Avatar going there now?" someone further back in the crowd shouted.

Wint enjoyed a rush of relief. Not everyone here thought *he* was this techno-person. No matter what his so-called "advisors" said.

"Er—maybe? I expect so. Whoever he is. Okay, bye," he blurted in a rush, and fled back into the house.

He almost ran over Skete and Rex, who had been standing just inside the doorway, listening.

"Short and sweet," Skete observed.

Wint wasn't sure if that was meant as sarcasm or not. "It's what I said I'd say," he snapped. "Now, are we getting out of here?"

And as soon as they could gather up their things again (and Skete and Rex convinced Wint to make more sandwiches), they did.

To say that Wint Usborne did not enjoy the drive out to the Dingle would be an understatement. It made for an uncomfortable hour, since playing music didn't seem appropriate and few conversational topics suggested themselves. After they hit a winding dirt road Rex had directed him to turn onto, the dog had complained loudly and often about how the bumping was likely to make its sciatica flare up. Wint had never even heard of a dog with sciatica before, but by now he knew better than to say anything. It would only bring on more abusive comments about the general ignorance of humans, and he'd had quite enough of that. Skete slept for the last part of the drive, which had been a relief, although he emitted frequent bouts of loud, unsettling snorts and snores. The Radio kept its own dark counsel. Wint imagined he could feel it brooding at him from the back seat.

After following a narrow and winding gravel road through a forest that crowded close with eerie menace, the car emerged into a clearing. Ahead, the road circled an expansive green hill, crowned at the top by what Wint assumed must be the Dingle. Although it was still some distance away, the square, tapering tower looked a considerable size, at least a hundred feet tall. Its sturdy walls had been constructed of smooth grey fieldstone, now heavily encroached upon by green-white lichen, and a handful of small windows dotted the sides. The afternoon sun glinted off a copper roof and a pair of bronze statues at the base of the structure, but at this distance Wint couldn't tell what they were.

Wint was surprised to find disjointed clusters of people already milling about in the grassy clearing around the tower. So not everyone involved in this strange situation had arrived at his house first; some had skipped that step and come straight here. This heartened Wint. It seemed to provide some evidence that he might not be as involved as the others wanted him to think.

Wint edged the car up the hill and found, at the top, a small parking lot. A few cars and two camper-type vans had been slotted into several of the spaces. A couple of guys wearing t-shirts and jeans wandered over as Wint pulled the car to a halt in one of the remaining parking spots. At Skete's urging, Wint opened his window with some reluctance.

"He's not here, yet," the thinner youth said through the inch and a half space Wint had opened. "You didn't happen to pack an extra tent, did you?"

"No." Wint wondered if the young man could tell it was only a half-truth. He wasn't a competent liar. There always seemed to be something in his face that gave him away. In this case, there were two tents in the car's trunk, left there from an abortive camping trip three months ago. But Wint hadn't *packed* them for this venture. And if camping out was going to be involved here, he wasn't cramming into one small tent with Skete, the dog, and the Radio.

"Okay." The young man wasn't watching Wint with close attention, anyway. The other youth who had wandered over with him was intent on something on his phone and hadn't looked up the entire time.

"Well, here we are, I guess," Wint said, as cheerfully as he could. "At the, er, Dingle. Are we getting out?" He looked at the back door of the car with what he hoped was a meaningful stare.

Rex pushed his head over the front seat and looked Wint in the eye. His breath smelled of sandwiches and earth. "You're not going to wait until we get out and then ditch us." It wasn't a question.

Wint thought of protesting that he hadn't even thought of such a thing, but the dog wouldn't be fooled. He went with the truth.

"I would if I thought I could get away with it."

"We should get inside the tower and see about getting up to the top," the Radio suggested. "Then, when everyone else arrives, you'll be in a good place to address them."

Wint peered out his window, craning his neck to see up to the top of the structure. "That's pretty tall," he observed. "Think there's an elevator inside?"

Skete gave an uncertain chuckle, and the dog snorted.

"It was a joke." Wint reached over to retrieve his pack from the back seat. "You can see this is a historical structure; I expect it's protected from new-fangled contraptions like elevators. Come on. If we're going, let's go."

They all exited the car, Wint struggling a bit with the weight of the pack, even though Skete had offered to carry the Radio and now had it tucked under one arm. Wint didn't feel it was a very dignified exit from the vehicle, but then he wondered who he was trying to impress, anyway. He strolled with Skete and Rex to the side of the tower, trying to look inconspicuous; and in truth, no one else paid them much attention. People—some of them the illicit campers from his house, Wint was sure—were arriving single and in small groups, so they were just part of the general influx.

The Dingle, being an old lookout tower, did not feature stairs on the outer walls. One had to get inside to ascend to the top. Blocking that ascent was a thick, metal-bound wooden door, secured shut by a rusted but solid-looking padlock. Wint stared at it with profound pleasure.

"Anyone have a key?" he asked in a bright voice. "If not, I guess this little exercise is over before it's begun. Can I give anyone a lift back to the city?"

Skete stood next to him with the Radio, and the Radio spoke in its static-infused voice. "You can use your will to make the magic assist you. A lock is a simple machine; in other words, technology. As the Technocrat Avatar, you can bend magic to the will of technology so that one complements the other."

Wint transferred his gaze to the Radio, his eyes fixed in a blank stare as he tried to process this information. He couldn't see any practical advice in it.

"So you think I can...make a key? Is that what you're saying?"

"Oh, for cheese's sake! Where's your teaspoon?" the Radio demanded.

Wint blinked at this apparent change of topic. "In my backpack." He unslung it and rooted through, digging the teaspoon up from the bottom.

"Touch it to the lock," the Radio instructed with slow precision, as if speaking to a child. "Concentrate your mind on the idea of the lock opening."

"Okay." Things had now taken a turn beyond strange into downright ridiculous, as far as Wint was concerned. Talking dogs and spirit radios were all well and good, but using a silver teaspoon and his mind to open a rusty old lock? It was another level of absurdity altogether. He touched the teaspoon to the lock. Nothing happened, and he felt a flood of relief tingle through his limbs.

"Nothing happened," he reported, stating the obvious.

"Oh, come on," the Radio huffed in exasperation. "You weren't even trying!"

Wint sighed. There was the small matter of not knowing how to try—but all right, whatever. He touched the teaspoon to the lock and reviewed what little he knew about old padlocks in general. *A simple padlock, the shank held in locked position by the projection of a spring or springs. To unlock, the springs are compressed or flattened by the key, freeing the shank and allowing it to—*

A shudder of energy passed through the teaspoon, warming it in his hand and vibrating it against the lock with a bright tinkling sound. Wint couldn't be certain if the energy was coming from him or moving in the other direction. All the hair stood up on his forearms and on the back of his neck. The bowl of the teaspoon shimmered and reconfigured into the stem of an old-fashioned key, complete with a flat, notched bit. It slid into the keyhole almost of its own accord, with little assistance from Wint. He turned the key without thinking, and the lock popped open with a grinding sound. Flakes of rust drifted in a lazy descent toward the grass.

Wint said, "Huh." It was the sound a person might make upon being punched hard in the stomach. He withdrew the key with a trembling hand and watched as it shimmered back into the form of a teaspoon.

"Excellent!" Skete slapped him on the back. Wint didn't move.

"There you go," the Radio said in a smug voice. "I said you could do it."

"Opened," Wint said through pale lips. On some level, he understood what had happened, just the way the Radio had said. On another level, he knew it was impossible. On yet a third level, his brain seemed to alternate between screaming and whimpering.

Then the teaspoon fell from his fingers and clattered on the worn stone step, and Wint followed it down into comforting darkness.

SOMETHING IN THE ROAD

HELINE

When Jans arrived later in the afternoon, he didn't seem to appreciate what Heline had done with her place. Of course, he was too nice to say so, but his expression spoke volumes.

"It is not yet the Hallowed Ween[1] night, ist?" he'd asked, half-smiling, after he'd toured around, exclaiming with dutiful approval over the changes in the décor.

"No," she'd responded, trying not to let her voice betray the touch of annoyance that pricked at her. "I just wanted a change, I guess."

"You do look nice in black," Jans had observed with stalwart loyalty. "Would you be liking to go out for supper?"

The idea of leaving the Hat behind triggered a squirm of worry in her stomach, and she hesitated for a moment. There would be no way to explain taking it, let alone wearing it. It would be nice to go out, though. "Just give me a few minutes to get ready," Heline told Jans.

"But already you are looking ready," he protested. Too late. He was talking to Heline's back as she disappeared up the stairs.

In her bedroom closet she had an overlarge tote bag, the kind one picks up at a yard sale thinking how handy it will be, and then never finds a use for. Tonight, though, Heline had the perfect use. She judged that the Hat, with a minimal amount of crumpling, would just fit. Then she

---

1. It is interesting to note that "Halloween" is another of those concepts that appears on many worlds throughout the multiverse. It goes by various names, many of which are phonetically very similar. The Min, although she has done extensive research, has been unable to arrive at a satisfactory explanation for this phenomenon.

wouldn't have to leave it behind, but Jans wouldn't have to know she'd taken it, either. And if she needed to slip it on for a moment, there was always the ladies' room.

[i sincerely hope it doesn't come to that] the Hat noted.

"Oh, shut up, at least you're coming along," Heline hissed at it, and it did shut up. That could have had something to do with the way she'd just stuffed it into the bag, of course, but from what she knew of the Hat already, it would take more than that to subdue it if it had something to say. The Hat's personality was larger than one might expect, even for a talking hat.

Jans looked askance at the huge tote bag when she appeared, but said nothing. He was too sweet, Heline thought, and waited for the Hat to say something snarky, but for once it kept silent.

They were lucky, and Jans' car kept working all the way to the block where the restaurant lay. Some enterprising individuals had already begun mapping the areas where technology was more likely to work or not, and had created an app for finding tech-friendly routes. It wasn't one hundred percent accurate, since there were fluctuations in the areas of tech fail, but vehicle traffic now wove along alternate routes through the city. They were as congested as the second day of a head cold, but as long as you allowed enough lead time, you could still get where you wanted to go.

They were on the road leading to The Sugar Goat when they saw it—something in the road. The headlights picked out its silhouette in the twilight first, and Heline thought it was a large dog crossing the asphalt ahead. "Dog," she said, just in case Jans hadn't noticed it. He nodded, though, and slowed down.

As they drew nearer, the scruffiness of the creature's fur became apparent. "Another stray," Heline said. "It's so sad. There seem to be more and more of them all the time."

Then it turned to face the approaching vehicle, and the protruding bulk of its head split into the shapes of *two* heads. Four red eyes blazed in the reflection of the headlights.

"*Vesa!*" Jans swore, twisting the wheel to give the creature an even wider berth as he slammed on the brakes.

Heline couldn't take her eyes off the weird apparition, and as she watched, both muzzles broke into fanged, malicious grins. She gasped and checked the door locks. "Jans, what is that thing?"

"Don't know," he said, swinging wide around it. "You are the one working with the animals, yes?" The creature still hadn't moved, seeming unfazed by the approaching car. It stood in the middle of the road, watching with intensity—almost hungrily—as they drove around it.

"I've never seen an animal like that!"

"I am not doing the stop to find out, if that is *yako* with you."

"Good idea." Heline twisted in her seat to peer out the back window as they accelerated away from it. The creature continued to stand its ground in the centre of the road as other vehicles also skewed and swerved to avoid it.

[warhound] The Hat's voice sounded muffled, yet somehow smug in her head. [just the beginning]

"What do you mean?" she asked, and realized at Jans's inquisitive glance that she'd spoken aloud.

"What?"

"Nothing. Let's just get out of here, Jans. That thing is too weird for me."

[supernatural creatures will begin to appear once the thaumic force on a planet has become active. they are normal creatures that have been affected by the magic, the way it has certain...effects on people, as well]

Heline was beginning to hate the smugness the Hat often affected when it knew more than she did. Unfortunately, that was turning out to be much of the time. *Are they dangerous?*

[not all of them] the Hat replied. [but I'd advise caution in determining which ones are. you might get only one chance to find out. as you might have noticed, the dangerous ones often have large teeth. sometimes very large teeth. also, not infrequently, claws] it added, almost as an afterthought.

Wow, teeth and claws? Heline echoed, a touch of sarcasm threading her voice.

[oh yes. or poison stingers, venom, mind control—]

Okay, okay, I get the picture.

"Very quiet, you are," Jans observed, making Heline startle.

It hadn't seemed quiet, conversing with the Hat.

"Don't being afraid," he added. "The nasty dog cannot open car doors!"

"I know. But that was...horrible. And it looked dangerous. I've never seen anything like that. I wonder if I should call work, see who's on patrol tonight, and warn them."

Without waiting for Jans to respond, Heline pulled out her phone and dialled the society's after-hours number. The call went straight to voicemail, and Heline wondered if she wasn't the only one calling in about this particular stray animal. She left a quick message about the creature and its location, using words like "weird," "super unusual," and "dangerous-looking" to avoid saying "two-headed."

"In old country," Jans mused after she ended the call, "*Kala Linna*—that being one of the grandmothers of me—told story of two-headed goat born to farm neighbour once. Thought to be omen of great good fortune. Huge celebrating, bonfire, all neighbours came to share in joy."

"And did it bring good fortune?"

"Other goats scared by noise and flames, stampeded. Six ran into bonfire and died."

Heline gasped. "Oh, how terrible!"

Jans shrugged. "Made for splendid feast. Roast goat, very delicious, you are knowing."

Heline looked at him, aghast, and saw that his lips were twitching. "Jans!" She gave him a playful smack on the arm. He chuckled until they reached the restaurant. Heline glanced around as they got out of the car, but there was nothing unusual in this area. Still, she was much more comfortable when the doors of The Sugar Goat had closed behind them.

The Sugar Goat was a favourite restaurant of Heline and Jans, cozy and simple, with food that met with Jans' approval. It wasn't fancy inside, but the mix of tables and booths was homey, and the large front windows let in sunshine in the daytime and reflected scattered lights like fireflies at night. The hand-lettered chalk menu above the counter now bore two columns of menu items—one for when the electricity was working, and one for when it was not.

Even after they were seated, though, Heline had difficulty concentrating. The restaurant had electricity tonight, and Jans was the perfect date, as always. Still, she couldn't keep her mind from straying back to the two-headed *thing* in the road. It didn't help that the Hat kept talking to her, either.

[i think we're supposed to be somewhere else] it said as she tried to concentrate on her menu.

What do you mean?

[i have a sense that things are about to happen, and this isn't where we should be. the warhound is making me nervous]

"What are you feeling like having?" Jans asked her. "I am imagining there is no roasted goat on the menu, so no need to worrying about that." He chuckled at his own joke.

[your talents will be needed soon] the Hat told her.

Talents? What talents? she asked the Hat. With two concurrent conversations happening, she had to concentrate to smile at Jans' joke and make it appear that she was studying the menu.

[the songs. the thaumaturge avatar is going to need them]

The songs are apparently rot, remember? she thought with venom at the Hat. Which only reminded her of Eleanor. Should she have called her sister before she'd agreed to go out to dinner? She realized with a pang that Eleanor didn't have a key for the house. And now there were potentially dangerous creatures on the prowl. Where would Eleanor go if she came back to Heline's and couldn't get in?

"So much worried to be only thinking of food," Jans said. "Ist wrong?"

"I wonder if I should call Eleanor. She doesn't have a key to get in if she comes back and I'm not there, and seeing that animal...I am a bit worried. I'll—I'll have...some soup to start," she told Jans to keep him happy as she dug out her cell phone. "Maybe cream of music—I mean, cream of mushroom."

"Shall we be having some wine?" Jans asked her, smiling.

Before she could answer, the Hat was at it again.

[there's something outside]

"Would you like to join it?" Heline snapped, then realized at the confusion on Jans' face that she'd spoken aloud. "I mean...would you like to join me...in having some wine?" she amended, plastering a fake smile across her face.[2]

"Er. Yes," he said. "That was why I ask you the same thing. Are you okay, Heline? Everything is *yako*?"

His blue eyes were so concerned, so pleading, that Heline felt a pang of mixed guilt and affection. There was so much happening that she didn't understand. She reached across the table on impulse and took his hand. "I'm sorry, Jans. I don't seem to be myself tonight. Don't mind me. I'm *yako*."

"Perhaps is this restaurant not the best choosing? We could otherwhere go."

Jan's grammar, shaky at the best of times in her language, went out the window when anything upset him. Heline smiled.

"No, no, we'll stay here. It's lovely. And they can cook food tonight! It's just—"

[INCOMING] the Hat yelled in her head.

The front window of The Sugar Goat exploded inward with a shattering crash. *Something* burst through, although Heline, hands going up to protect her eyes, didn't see what it was. Jans leapt to shield her and somehow they landed on the floor, his body covering hers. The Hat in the tote bag scrunched into a crumpled lump poking into her back. She'd heard its breathy gasp as she landed on it, and now it squirmed under her weight. Jans' gesture was sweet, but she wasn't hurt, and she needed to see what was happening. She pushed at Jans' chest until he rolled away and she could see the thing that had shattered the window.

She'd been expecting the two-headed dog, but in the centre of the restaurant stood a creature that was almost, but not entirely, like a cross between a deer and a tiger. Tall, curving antlers swept up from its head,

---

2. If you think Heline should have been able to handle these two conversations more smoothly, you've quite obviously never tried to conceal a telepathic discussion with a sentient hat.

ending in wicked, pointed tips. Black stripes streaked across light brown fur, covering the front half of its body, although the stripes faded toward its hindquarters. Elegant legs ended, not in the expected hoofs, but in soft, padded paws from which the tips of sharp claws protruded. It glared around at the tousled, injured, sobbing restaurant patrons with a single baleful red eye. Its gaze seemed to light on Heline, and she held her breath.

[we need a song] the Hat urged her.

"What?"

[start singing one of your songs]

"You said they wouldn't do anything on their—"

[JUST DO IT! in this situation, it's all we have!]

The creature took a step toward her, lowering its head. Jans grunted in surprise. Almost under her breath, Heline began a song she'd been working on that afternoon. It wasn't finished, and Eleanor's critical words still rang in her brain, but it was the first thing that popped into her head.

A grey rain beating down on me
The words of a radio, inside my head
A lonely tower, looming over me
A helping hand, it touches my heart
Blame it on spiders
Blame it on spiders
Blame it on spiders
The night is long and shadowed,
Dark fangs wait in the blooms
The day is vanishing, penniless
But what can you do? What can you do?
Blame it on spiders

Not one of her best, she could see that. She wondered now if the Hat was playing with her. But *something* had happened while she was singing. She'd felt it, deep in the pit of her stomach and stirring in the recesses of her brain. There was...an energy there, and she'd called upon it. She could sense that it was, in some ways, weak—an echo, or a reflection, of something vastly more potent—but it was *something*. Her voice strengthened as she sang, and the creature backed away with slow, uncertain steps as she completed the first verse. It shook its head as if tormented by buzzing flies. Now it stood near the window it had destroyed, staring at her with malice and lips curling back over sharp, white teeth, but unsure of itself.

Heline sang the words of the first verse and the chorus one more time, even louder this time, and with a defiant shake of its head, the creature bounded out of the window and disappeared into the night. The restaurant was quiet for a moment, except for the muffled sobs of a few inconsolable patrons. Then the distant wail of approaching sirens broke the spell, and everyone began the slow, painful process of picking themselves up.

Jans stared at her, wide-eyed, when Heline turned to him. Tiny chunks of broken glass glittered on the plush carpet, but it seemed to be the kind that broke without leaving too many sharp edges. Thank goodness, because their clothes and hair were full of the stuff. They would have been cut to ribbons otherwise.

"Thank you for protecting me," she managed before Jans could say anything. "Are you all right?"

He nodded, brushing glass particles from his shirt with careful fingers. "You?"

She nodded, too.

"You...Heline...you were making that thing to go away, isn't?"

She wasn't sure how to answer. "I—I think so," she said at last. She tried a diffident shrug, but he gazed at her.

"But—how? With just singing?"

Heline pulled in air and blew out a deep sigh. "I don't know. Maybe."

He studied her for a moment longer, then broke into a smile. "That was terrible song, you are knowing that?"

She might have been hurt by that earlier, but now, and coming from Jans, there was no sting in it. Heline laughed, aware that a hint of hysteria bubbled underneath it. "I suspected as much." Her gaze strayed to the ruined window. "And that might not be quite how it's intended to be used. But it worked."

"We can figure out how?" He reached out a gentle hand, brushing bits of glass from her hair. The manager had begun a shaky circuit of the disaster of his dining room, righting chairs and helping patrons to their feet, almost crying himself. No one else seemed to have noticed Heline's part in what had happened. Or at any rate, if they did, they had no idea how to start a conversation about it.

"I don't know, but I have questions for someone. Can we just get out of here?"

Jans looked around. "I think, as they say, that we should be getting while the circumstances for getting are favourable."

Heline shook her head, smiling. "No one says that, but I understand what you mean. Let's go."

She snatched up the tote bag holding the somewhat squashed Hat, and, hands clasped, she and Jans hurried out into the night air. They found Jans' little car, unscathed by the chaos that had erupted so close by. Once inside, Heline locked the doors, opened the tote bag, and pulled out the Hat. This time it didn't even attempt to hide its ember-like eye, and Jans gasped when it saw it.

"I know," she said, patting him on the arm with her free hand. "It takes some getting used to." She gave the Hat a little shake. "Okay. You'd better tell me everything—and I mean *everything*—about what's happening."

[i don't know much more than I've already said] the Hat said in a small, apologetic voice, and it struck Heline that at last, here was something not mocking, not evasive, but true and uncomfortable. [i'm afraid we have to figure it out as we go from here]

"Flark," said Heline.

RESTAURANT CONVERGENCE

NERLIM

Nerlim was no longer at the library. He wended his way through the lowering dusk toward the restaurant to meet Gameldina, deep in consideration of what the book had told him. It was little enough of consequence, all told, although whether Xya had lied to them stood out as rather important. His mind also replayed its subsequent book-napping by the mysterious dark-haired woman. Nerlim was torn between a niggling mistrust of Xya and the feeling that he should tell her about the sentient book and the woman who had stolen it. That seemed important. Unfortunately, she hadn't left him instructions for contacting her, only saying she'd be in touch soon. Nerlim sighed and set the thought aside. He couldn't do anything about Xya at the moment.

He sorted through a strange mixture of elation (at being right about the fifth force), concern (about the consequences of that), and exhaustion after explaining (or trying to) what had happened to both Alwi and the formidable Petra deCleverly. It was a good thing, he'd reflected several times since the strange happenings in the Special Collections section of the NECHUE, that the young librarian, Alwi, had been in there with him and witnessed the untimely abduction of *Echoes of Potentiality* by Chetlin Tweddle. He couldn't comprehend what the downsides of the arrival—or re-arrival—of magic on D'sharu might be, but trying to explain the book's disappearance to Petra deCleverly without the support of another witness must rank near the top of the list.

He also suspected there were more downsides to be discovered, and he was about to find out that he was quite correct in that assumption.

As soon as he turned into the street that housed The Sugar Goat, Nerlim knew something was wrong. Red and blue lights revolved on the roofs of cars and trucks scattered across the road like a child's discarded toys. Strands of yellow police tape fluttered in the breeze like banners heralding the arrival of something sinister, the bright colour vivid under the streetlights. Nerlim quickened his steps and his heart echoed the pace. Worry jabbed at him with icy fingers when he realized the emergency vehicles seemed to be clustered right outside The Sugar Goat. Teetering on creaking tiptoes, he scanned the gathered crowd for Gammy. He reminded himself that her diminutive form would be hard to spot at this distance and broke into a stilted run.

Nerlim had a clear view of the restaurant before the police tape halted him. Where the front window had been, a jagged hole now gaped. Red curtains sagged in forlorn shreds, half in and half out of the building. Bits of glass scattered across the sidewalk, winking in the reflections of the emergency lights. Nerlim searched the crowd again for Gammy, pointless though it might be. He asked a couple of bystanders what had happened, but no one seemed to have useful information.

"Explosion," one of them said, but they had no details to share.[1]

And then it was there again—that strange tugging in his gut and tickle in his brain that signalled the use of the fifth force in his vicinity. The hairs on the back of his neck prickled. Someone nearby was using magic.

Or—not using it? This sensation wasn't the blow of active magic, but more like what he'd experienced earlier at the Neemar Reference Centre, when he'd honed in on the book. The sense of something magical just *existing*.

He turned and surveyed the surrounding area with as much nonchalance as he could force. The crowd looked like any other crowd at a disaster scene; people of every description, united in one thing—naked curiosity. He walked a short distance down the street, getting clear of the onlookers in an attempt to pinpoint where the strange magic energy originated.

---

1. Never trust bystanders to know what's actually happening.

His gaze fell on a somewhat battered compact car parked by the roadside. Two figures sat inside, silhouetted against the lights. The tug pulled him in that direction. Now it held a strange urgency, as if something deliberately reached out to him. Trying to appear casual, he turned his steps toward the car.

When he came abreast of it, he glanced sideways. The occupants were a man and a woman, and they did not seem to notice him. The woman held something tall and pointy on her lap. Nerlim's stomach lurched again, and the woman turned her head toward him. Nerlim had a clear view of the thing on her lap. It looked like a hat.

A hat with a single, burning, amber eye, fixed on him.

He realized he'd stopped walking, his feet having ceased any forward motion of their own accord when his brain had stopped sending messages to them. He stared at the hat. Of course, it had to be some kind of trick, a prop from a movie, perhaps. Regardless, it was difficult to tear his gaze away since the pull of the fifth force drew him to this spot. The woman engaged in a quick conversation with the man and then rolled down her window to speak to him. She had dark brown hair that fell in attractive waves to her shoulders, and a pale face that looked more worried than it should. Her black dress exaggerated both her paleness and her worry. In the dark street, he couldn't make out the colour of her eyes, but they fixed on him with a gaze that was both anxious and urgent.

"Er...hello," she offered. "We haven't met, but my, um, friend says it's important that we talk."

Nerlim stepped closer to the car, forgetting everything he'd ever been told or told other people about staying clear of cars with strangers in them. He leaned down closer to get a better look at the man in the driver's seat. The sandy hair and pleasant face—which also looked worried—didn't belong to anyone Nerlim recognized.

"Your friend seems to have the advantage of me. I don't recognize either of you."

"Oh! I didn't mean Jans, I meant—"

[she meant me] said the Hat.

Nerlim staggered a long step backward, just missing a collision with a late-evening jogger who'd slowed his pace to gawk at the wrecked restaurant. Nerlim knew the hat had just spoken to him. He knew it must be more magic and that he was going to have to deal with it and that there was every chance it would be just as exciting and literally gut-wrenching as all the other magic he'd encountered thus far. It was just that being addressed by a telepathic hat for the first time required a moment of mental adjustment. Especially coming so close on the heels of having the same experience with a book. He hoped the number of other inanimate objects with the same conversational skills was severely limited.

"I see," Nerlim said, when the necessary adjustments had been made and he could both breathe and speak again. "Listen, do you know what happened here? I was supposed to meet a friend and I'm worried about her."

The couple glanced at each other. "We were inside when it happened. Only one man had a serious injury; he broke a leg in the—er—general uproar, and the ambulance has already taken him off to the hospital," the woman said. "If your friend was inside, I'm sure she's okay. What does she look like?"

Nerlim hesitated. How to describe Gameldina to someone who'd never seen her? Nerlim realized with a start that he'd never thought of how to describe her before. He didn't think about what she looked like. Gameldina just *was*.

"Nerlim Pettibone!" A familiar voice sounded from behind him, and his knees shuddered and went weak with relief. He put a hand on the roof of the car to steady himself, then turned to watch her approach, anger dancing around her like an aura. Well, no wonder, since her new favourite restaurant was a shambles. Her greying mop of hair was dishevelled, but only in the usual way, and she appeared uninjured. He realized with a shock that she'd *dressed up* for their dinner in a trim black pantsuit and brightly coloured caftan-type thingy. It was something of a shock to see her without the *de rigueur* neutral cotton slacks and yellow NCDSF polo that she favoured as work attire. He shrank a bit when her indignant brown eyes fixed on him, but that was normal, too. Without thinking, he hugged her when she reached him, felt her body stiffen and then relax for a moment before she hugged him back. Then she pushed away.

"What in the world is going on? What happened to the restaurant?"

"Just what I'm trying to find out."

Gammy examined the young woman in the car with an air of disapproval. Nerlim tensed. Would Gammy notice the eye in the hat? Would it speak to her? And how would she react if it did?

All that happened, however, was that the young woman in the car said, "My name's Heline. Heline Morrisanto. This is my boyfriend, Jans Lencari."

"Nerlim Pettibone." Nerlim extended his hand for the young woman to shake, since they hadn't gotten as far as introductions in the previous conversation. It was awkward as she reached her hand out the window, but they managed. "And this is Gameldina Gannand."

Gammy threw him a look, but he ignored it.

Heline glanced at the Hat as if it had spoken to her, too. Then she turned back to him. "Mr. Pettibone, you wouldn't know what I was talking about if I mentioned the Thaumaturge Avatar, would you?"

"I...might," he answered, although his heart was pounding. That's what the woman, Xya, had called Ulric. But she'd also said there would be people opposing him. Nerlim thought he'd better play his cards close to his chest until he understood what was going on. "Why do you want to know?"

Heline took a deep breath. "I think I'm supposed to help him."

"Nerlim, I need to speak with you," Gammy said in a voice that didn't anticipate argument. Nerlim startled. He'd almost forgotten that she was there, and there'd been something important she'd wanted to tell him. He opened his mouth to speak, but a surge of magical energy thumped him in the gut and he almost doubled over.

"Looking out!" the man in the car yelled.

Nerlim, still bent over, clutching his stomach, twisted his head to gaze up. Gammy gasped. Something from a nightmare lumbered up the street toward them. It stood almost twenty feet tall and approximated the shape of a person, but there the similarity stopped. In fact, the similarity stopped, turned, and ran in the other direction. The creature was covered with smooth, dark skin against which tendons and muscles stood out as if in bas relief. Long arms ended in hands studded with extended, curving claws. The head was smooth except for a row of glistening spines running from forehead to nape, and eyes glowed blue-green in the darkness. One clublike foot knocked against a police car and sent it tumbling like a pebble. Its apparent destination was Nerlim, Gammy, and the car.

Heline reached around and threw open the back door. "Get in, get in!" she commanded, and Nerlim shoved Gammy ahead of him into the cramped back seat. She scuttled across the seat to make room for him and he landed in a heap, half-tangled in the trailing edges of Gammy's caftan. He squirmed free and reached back to pull the door closed behind him even as the car vibrated. Jans gunned the engine, and the car pulled away from the curb with a lurch and a squeal.

[nice of you to join us] the Hat said to Nerlim, a smirk threading its voice.

Nerlim would have given a lot to know how it did that, but he was preoccupied with righting himself in the seat. He peered out the rear window to see the creature thudding after them, long arms swinging and claws scraping the asphalt.

"You are having another song?" Jans asked Heline in the front seat.

"I think so. Here, hold this." The woman turned and shoved the Hat into the back seat and Nerlim accepted it without question, hoping against hope that Gammy would not see the thing's eye until he could explain its presence. With a surreptitious twist, he turned it so the eye faced the side window, away from her.

Heline scrabbled in a huge tote bag in the front seat. She pulled out a sheet of paper and read from it. Or rather, sang from it. She had, Nerlim thought, quite a fine voice, even if the words of the song were...odd. Something about a wrathful knight—or night?—clashing foes and shadows, but then, weirdly, stars, cats, and a blueberry pie?

She sang in voice that wavered at first, but grew stronger and more sure of itself even as they darted and wove through the traffic. The creature pursued them, its heavy footfalls shaking the ground in tremors that rattled the car. Horns blasted, brakes squealed, voices yelled or screamed, but Heline sang on. Nerlim, unable to help himself, turned every few seconds to watch the creature out the back window, quailing at its relentless pursuit of the small vehicle. But as he watched, something amazing and inexplicable happened. By the time the young woman had sung the first chorus, the creature had slowed its pace. It seemed to be fighting to maintain its momentum, almost as if it were pushing through something thick and invisible—or as if that something were pushing it back. At the end of the second verse it stopped moving, although Nerlim watched as its silhouette threw back its head and—howled? He shuddered and turned his gaze forward again, leaning back against the seat and blowing out a long breath. He refused to look down at the Hat in his lap. Nerlim didn't think he could deal with the gaze of that eldritch eye just now.

Nerlim was surprised when Gameldina's hand slid along the seat and locked around his fingers. He knew better than to say anything, though. He squeezed back as the little car raced through the darkened streets, carrying them away from, and toward, the unknown.

"Heline, how did you do that?" Nerlim asked when the song had ended. "You stopped that...thing, didn't you?"

"I think so, but I'm afraid I don't know how," Heline said. "And sorry for the terrible lyrics. I'm working on them, but at least they did the trick."

"I thought it was very interesting," Gammy said with real warmth. She looked at Nerlim and shrugged, wide-eyed, as if to say *what else could I say? She saved us from a monster.*

"Now, Eleanor," Heline breathed from the front seat. "Where is she? I need to call her now. I don't know what's going on, but I don't think she's safe alone anymore."

"And Eleanor is?" Nerlim inquired with polite interest, leaning forward.

"My younger sister," the young woman said, distracted as she rooted around in her purse. "We had a fight earlier and—" She broke off as her search ended and she came up with her phone. She punched in a number and put it to her ear.

After a moment it must have been answered, but Nerlim and the others were privy only to one side of the conversation.

"Eleanor? Oh, thank goodness. Where are you?" (pause) "At whose house? Why?" (pause) "Um, okay. Can you give me the address? Some weird stuff is happening and I want to come and get you." (pause) "You're right, that's pretty weird, too. Okay."

She ended the call and told the young man driving, Jans, the address. It sounded familiar to Nerlim, although for a moment he couldn't place it. Then he realized.

"She's with the Thaumaturge Avatar," Nerlim breathed. "I wonder how that happened?"

A Lot of Weird Stuff

Ulric

The answer to Nerlim Pettibone's question was quite simple—Ulric and Eleanor had run for their lives from the razor-toothed things and the mutant-horse *unicorn* in the park, not stopping until they'd slammed Ulric's front door behind them. They leaned back against it, hearts pounding, gasping for breath.

"Was anything...still following us?" Ulric gasped.

Eleanor shrugged out of her jacket but didn't answer until her breathing settled. "It's been a while since I looked back," she confessed. She paused and closed her eyes. "Nothing's trying to break down this door, so that must be a good sign."

Ulric turned and pulled aside the curtain covering the door's sidelight. He peered out, half-expecting to see angry black shapes darting toward the house, or an even bigger dark shape preparing to kick in the door. The street and the sky outside looked clear.

"We might have lost them. Or they gave up."

"How many of those flying things were there, anyway?"

Ulric shook his head. "Seemed like a hundred, but maybe half a dozen? Counting wasn't a priority."

"Very true. And then that horse-thing crunched that one—

"Unicorn," Ulric corrected, checking outside again.

"What?"

"The horse-thing. It's called a unicorn. Because of the horn, I guess."

"Then shouldn't it be uni-*horn*?"

Ulric shrugged. "I don't know. I thought it might be a combination of *conical* and *horn*, to make, you know, *corn*—"

"But corn is already a thing. Wouldn't *conihorn* make more sense in that case?"

"I—I guess so? I never saw one before today, either. The word just appeared in my head when we saw it."

"Hmm. Okay." Eleanor looked around the entryway with interest. "Well, if you don't mind, I'm not inclined to go back out there right away. What were those other things?"

Ulric suppressed a shudder. He'd gotten a too-close look at those teeth and had to keep working to suppress a horrid vision of them slicing into his skin. The voice in his head had not supplied a name for them, however. "No idea. I've never seen anything like them either."

"I hope I never do again," Eleanor said. "There's a lot of weird stuff happening around here right now."

"There is," Ulric said. "I wish I understood it better."

"Me too." Eleanor paused, a frown drawing her dark brows together. "I'm kind of worried about my sister, even if she was being a bitch."

"Do you want to call her? Tell her where you are?" Ulric motioned toward the kitchen. "There's a phone in there."

Eleanor reached into a back pocket and pulled out a cell phone. She glanced at it and shook her head. "It's fine. No messages from her, so she might still be mad. I'll check in at some point. Not yet, though."

"You want a Fizzit? I've got cans in the fridge."

"Sure. I never ran like that in my life."

Ulric moved into the kitchen and Eleanor followed him, looking with interest around the house. "So since we've just escaped certain death together, do you want to tell me more about the weird stuff that's been happening to you? This seems like a pretty normal house, and you seem like a pretty normal guy, so I'm wondering how it all adds up."

Ulric bit his lip as he pulled two cans of Fizzit out of the fridge and popped the tops. He wasn't sure how much of what was happening he could explain. At least, explain in any way that made sense.

He handed Eleanor one can and, by silent agreement, they slipped into two chairs at the kitchen table, facing each other. "Okay. Since we escaped certain death together. You ever hear of the word 'magic'?" Ulric asked.

Eleanor frowned and took a sip of the sweet drink. "Doesn't sound familiar. What is it?"

Ulric sighed. "I don't know. It's like an energy or a force of some kind. Or maybe a spirit, or an essence."

"Wow, you weren't kidding when you said you didn't know."

"Yeah, it's complicated. But if you can...tap into it, you can do things with it."

"What things?"

"Like, make things happen. Break the laws of physics. Stop yourself from hitting the ground hard if you fall, or explode a piece of furniture."

Eleanor pursed her lips. "The first part sounds useful. I'm not so sure about the second part. Those are weirdly specific examples."

Ulric shrugged. "They're just examples. I'm sure you could do a lot of things with it once you understood how to control it."

Taking another contemplative sip of her drink, Eleanor regarded him with a thoughtful expression. "And you can do this stuff? Access this energy, or whatever?"

Ulric grimaced. "Sort of. I'm...not very good at it. I didn't ask for it. It just—started happening."

"Yeah. That's like my sister Heline," Eleanor mused. "She was perfectly normal—which is too normal, if you ask me. Except she had this closet filled with crazy, wild goth stuff that I never suspected. But other than that, she was like, *too* perfect. I could never measure up. You have any sisters or brothers?"

"No, it's just me."

"Okay, so Heline is super normal, and then she puts on this weird hat, and all of a sudden she's staying up all night writing terrible song lyrics. And when she doesn't think I'm paying attention, talking to the hat."

"That does seem strange," Ulric agreed. "And this only happened in the last few days? She didn't mention magic, did she?"

"I think it's new, yes," Eleanor said. "I was there when she put on the hat—well, it was her boyfriend who put it on her head, sort of as a joke—but she didn't say anything about magic. Honestly, I don't think she knows why this is happening, either."

Ulric took a long swallow of Fizzit, the bubbles creating a pleasant burn down his throat. "She hasn't had any visitors, has she? Like anyone kind of...odd?"

Eleanor looked interested. "Odd how?"

Ulric's cheeks warmed as a furious blush crept up them. He rubbed his face with both palms, willing it to cool. "Odd, like they weren't from around here."

"Her boyfriend is definitely not from around here. He's super nice, but his accent and verb forms are wild. I admire anyone who can learn another language, though. Kudos to him for trying."

Ulric shook his head. "I don't mean not-here like from another country. I mean, from another...*place*."

Eleanor raised one eyebrow. "You mean *totally* another place? Like realm, plane, time-and-space kind of another place?"

"Yeah. Like that."

"Then no. I haven't seen anybody like that. Whatever that would look like," she added in a doubtful tone. "Are we talking different numbers of limbs, or green skin, or what?"

"Nothing that obvious. It's more like a feeling. A presence. Hair that seems to have a mind of its own. That sort of thing."

Eleanor pulled in a deep sigh and blew it out. "You realize that if I hadn't seen those things in the park, and the weird stuff with my sister, I'd be running, not walking, away from here right now, right?"

Ulric rested his forehead on the table and echoed her sigh. "That's one hundred percent fair."

"Okay, here's a question: were they after you in particular? Or out for blood in general?"

Ulric sat up and blinked. "I can't imagine any reason they'd have anything against me."

"Not prone to attacks by weird creatures?"

"Well, no. At least—" He broke off, remembering the harpy in the junkyard.

"What?"

"There was this thing when I was in the junkyard. But it might have been a case of wrong place, wrong time. It might not have come after me *because it was me*."

"Hmmm. But two attacks by strange creatures in quick succession? Bit of a coincidence."

"But what if the ones today were targeting you?" Ulric suggested, on the defensive. "What if they had something to do with your sister?"

Eleanor ran a hand through her hair. "I guess it's at least equally likely. We're not going to get anywhere without more information." She glanced out into the hallway toward the door and shuddered. "But I'm not sure I'm ready to go back out there. Those things freaked me out, and I don't mind admitting it."

"Yeah, same."

They sat in awkward silence for a minute, sipping Fizzit too fast and not meeting each other's eyes.

Eleanor said, "So, this is your place?"

"Well, my mom and I live here. She's at work; she works at the bank."

"Sure." Eleanor nodded. "What kinds of things do you like to do?"

"I—I like games," Ulric hazarded. Giving the wrong answer to any of this girl's questions might be the equivalent of crashing and burning a super expensive car. A car he hadn't even paid for yet. "I have school and work, so not a lot of free time."

"Video games?"

Ulric took a gulp of his Fizzit, mind racing. If he confessed to liking video games, was that a good thing? Or was she looking for a different answer? He wished he could read her mind.

The voice in his head had no helpful advice this time, so Ulric went with the truth.

"Yeah, I play lots of video games. I've read they're good for developing your hand-eye coordination. And reflexes."

Eleanor grinned. "Cheese and rice, you sound like you're trying to justify it to your mother. Do you play *FusionFire*?"

Ouch. Not his best game, but he had it.

"Yeah, a bit. I have it—do you want to play?" Ulric tried to sound nonchalant. "It would give us something to do while we wait to see if anything's going to attack us again."

"Hell, yeah," Eleanor said. "Nothing takes your mind off your problems like music, and killing things in video games. And I don't have my guitar right now, so killing things it is."

They took their half-finished Fizzits and a bag of potato chips Ulric found in the cupboard, and went into the den. Ulric had two consoles, both hooked up to the tv, set up in front of the old couch from the living room. He and Tiny Enos had spent many comfortable hours sprawled here, playing games and knocking back snacks, when they weren't studying or toiling on Old Mean Melvin's farm.

In a chivalrous gesture, Ulric gave Eleanor the better controller, fired up *FusionFire*, and prepared to have his butt kicked.

But seeing Eleanor's grin every time she won a round was worth it. For the first time since he'd fallen off the barn roof, Ulric felt like something was going right.

It wasn't going to last, but the voice in his head was kind enough not to tell him that.

Some time later—they'd become so immersed in the game that it was impossible to estimate how long—a knock at the door startled them. Ulric panicked for a moment until he realized that if it were his mother, she wouldn't knock. He wasn't sure how he'd explain this beautiful, if unconventional, girl to his mother. He hadn't even told her about the curtains yet. How was he going to explain playing video games all afternoon with a girl he'd only just met? And he had no intention of telling his mother about the, well, monsters.

"Are you going to get it?" Eleanor asked.

Ulric realized he was sitting and staring into space. Again, a hot, stinging blush rose on his cheeks. "Uh, sure."

He stood and stared some more when he reached the door and pulled aside the curtain. Four adults stood on the doorstep, three of whom were unfamiliar. He had, of course, been warned all his life about opening the door to strangers. This group didn't appear threatening. The younger woman held an odd-looking hat, but it was pointy, just like the one he'd had Enos make for him. That made him like her right away. The other woman was older—quite a lot older, judging by the number of wrinkles that had taken up residence on her face and the mop of white hair frizzing out around her head. With a rush of relief, he recognized Nerlim as the fourth visitor. The old guy was strange, but not a complete stranger. And he had saved Ulric's life. He opened the door.

"Hi, Mr. Pettibone, can I help you?" Ulric asked.

"Good to see you again, Ulric. May we come in?"

The younger woman took a deep breath. "Is my sister here? Eleanor? I'm Heline. She gave me this address."

The woman's tone held a note of puzzlement, and Ulric realized he had been peering past the four people on the step to scan the skies for attackers. And the nearby yards for horn-sprouting horses.

He tried to recover both his composure and his manners. If this was Eleanor's sister, he wanted to make a good impression. He managed a smile. "Um, yeah, Eleanor's here. Come on in, please." Ulric swung the door wide open and stepped back so they could file into the foyer. He took one more quick glance at the road, but there was no sign of his mother returning home yet. *Thank cheese*, he thought. If explaining Eleanor would take some doing, he couldn't imagine how he'd manage it for these four, too.

As he shut the door behind them, he got a closer look at the hat Eleanor's sister carried. It was a black hat made of some indeterminate material that looked ancient and worn, with a wide brim and a crown tapering up to a point. The point had flopped over, as if unable to support its own weight. Without warning, it opened a baleful amber eye and looked him up and down. Ulric felt a jolt of shock like an ice-cold finger tracing down his back when, at the same time, it addressed him.

Inside his head.

[nice to meet you] said the Hat. [you're a little younger than I expected, but otherwise just about right. are you ready to go to work?]

Eleanor appeared from the den, no doubt drawn to the sound of her sister's voice. Ulric hadn't moved from the front door after he'd closed it, and now leaned back against it for support, just as he and Eleanor had earlier. Heline turned to face her sister, and Ulric saw Eleanor's eyes go wide as she saw the hat. Then she pursed her lips and made a noise that, coming from anyone else, Ulric would have called a snort. A small but attractive frown creased her brow as she studied the thing her sister held.

"I flarking knew there was something flarking wrong with that hat!" she exclaimed, lifting accusing eyes to her sister's face. "You tried to hide it, but I flarking well knew it, Heline!"

The appearance of a telepathic and sentient Hat, coupled with the worry that his mother might arrive home at any minute, created a heavy mental weight crushing down on Ulric. He tried to ask, *what is that?* and point to the Hat. But he seemed to have trouble forming words, and his arm felt leaden. He wasn't sure who he was asking, anyway. Eleanor? Her sister? Nerlim Pettibone? Or maybe the Hat itself. He didn't get the words out, but the Hat answered anyway.

[call me arcanico, and thanks for asking. i'm a manifestation of magic on this world, so it's about time we met]

The weight bounced up, came down, and slammed Ulric on the top of his head. He wasn't at all surprised to realize he was fainting as the floor rushed up to meet him.

He thought Eleanor blew out an exasperated sigh as sparks exploded in the darkness behind his eyes, but on second thought, it might have been the short, frizzy-haired woman. Before unconsciousness claimed him, he decided it didn't matter.

Corax Presses His Case

Gammy

Gammy was not enjoying the evening. For one thing, she'd been looking forward (perhaps more than she wanted to admit) to a pleasant dinner at The Sugar Goat with Nerlim. Curious to hear what he'd been doing all day, she also wanted a quiet word alone with him about that Corax fellow. Now the restaurant lay in ruins, they'd been attacked by something she had a hard time believing in, and she found herself in a larger group of people than at her last birthday party. Her last birthday party had been so long ago the memories were faded, but she recalled with rueful detachment that the crowd had been sparse.

The young couple seemed all right except for the outlandish way the fellow spoke and that odd hat the girl carried, but Gammy didn't know what to make of these other two youngsters. The boy looked like he couldn't tell you with certainty what day it was, and the younger girl—she came from a culture unfamiliar to Gammy. Those clothes and that hair! Young people these days seemed to make their own rules. Or rather, Gammy wondered if there were any rules at all.

And now the boy lay on the floor in a faint. Gammy stood the closest to him since she'd come in last and he'd remained at the door. She heard the *thump* as he hit the floor, and hurried back to where he lay crumpled on the carpet. The others crowded around, but she pushed them back with a bark.

"Get back, give him some air. He's only fainted." She checked his pulse and chafed his wrist. This, at least, she could take charge of. Too many things these days were so far outside her sphere of experience they might as well have been on the unattainable moon.

The others obeyed and backed off as quickly as they'd sprung forward. Nerlim knelt a little distance from the boy. "He's okay?"

"If he's only fainted, he's okay. If he's been cursed by this blasted fifth force of yours, then it's anyone's guess."

"He's important," Nerlim said in a low voice.

But already Ulric's eyes flickered. "Wha—"

Gammy put a cool, steady hand on his forehead with just enough pressure to keep him still for a moment. "You're all right, boy." Her voice was gentle, surprising even herself.

On the other side of the boy, Nerlim emitted a small "oof" of what sounded like pained surprise. When Gammy glanced up at him, he'd bent forward, clutching at his stomach with a grimace.

"Are you all right?"

Nerlim nodded, but another voice spoke close to Gammy's ear.

"The boy can't help you, Gameldina." She almost jumped, but turned and saw the disembodied, ghostly head of Corax floating nearby.

"I'm helping *him* at the moment," she snapped.

"What?" asked Nerlim in a confused voice. "I'm all right. I didn't ask for—"

"I was talking to—oh, never mind," she said, realizing that Nerlim couldn't see the apparition. *What are you talking about? And did you hurt Nerlim?* She directed this vicious mental communication at Corax. Would he be able to "hear" her? It seemed worth a try. There was little point in trying to think things through in a rational manner anymore. Rationality was out the window. In fact, it seemed to have been thrown bodily out the window by the scruff of its metaphorical neck.

"Of course I didn't hurt anyone." Corax sounded offended by the suggestion. "And only I can help you get the moon launch back on track." Agitation came through loud and clear, even in their mental conversation. It was obvious no one but Gammy heard him, because no one else reacted to him or his words. "None of these people have any power that can do that."

This is not a good time. I told you to come back tomorrow, at my office, Gammy retorted. *Not follow me around all night.*

"I worried you might get distracted." Corax gave a pointed glance around at the gathered assemblage. "Has anyone else been talking to you about this?"

As a matter of fact, yes. You've got competition, she snapped at him. Let him mull that one over.

"Ma'am?"

That was Ulric. He sounded as if he'd spoken to her at least once already, but she hadn't noticed because of Corax. Talk about being distracted.

"Yes, boy?"

"Can I get up now, Ma'am? I'm feeling much better."

Gammy realized her hand still rested on the boy's forehead, pressing down with perhaps more vigour than necessary. She pulled it away. "Of course, if you're up to it."

The boy scrambled to his feet and motioned toward the kitchen. They all trooped in and stood around in an awkward tableau. No one made a move to sit as there were only four chairs and seven people.

"I'm Ulric," the boy said after a moment. His eyes flicked to the hat but didn't rest on it. "And I guess I'm the Thaumaturge Avatar. I should offer you all something to drink, like tea or something. But the thing is," he added, glancing toward the door. "The thing is, my mum's going to be home soon and I'm not sure how I'm going to explain—"

"Perhaps I shouldn't be here, but neither should you," Corax insisted in Gammy's ear.

"Oh, shut up, for goodness' sake!" Gammy snarled.

They all stared at her. Ulric blanched as pale as the refrigerator behind him.

Nerlim said in a reproving tone, "Gameldina, the boy is trying his best—"

Gammy heaved a sigh and held up a hand to stop Nerlim. "I know. I'm sorry, boy, I wasn't talking to you."

"Don't mention me," Corax warned her. "I'm only here to speak with you, remember?"

She turned to glare at him, where he floated just in front of the gas range. He wasn't just a head anymore and the rest of his semi-transparent body had appeared as well, which was less disconcerting, but she'd had about enough of him. And no one had warned Corax about the inadvisability of telling Gammy what to do.

"I was talking," she said with clear, venomous enunciation, "to an apparition which it seems none of you can see, who is driving me batty and WON'T STOP TALKING IN MY EAR!"

Corax grimaced and winked out of sight.

"Where is he?" Nerlim asked, his voice strained as he gripped his midsection again. He gritted his teeth and straightened up, peering around the kitchen.

"Who is it?" the young woman with the interesting hair asked. She peered around the room with the rest of them, but she seemed the most disappointed to find no sign of an apparition.

"What does he want?" Heline inquired.

"Why can't we see him?" That was from Ulric, almost completing the five "W" questions. All that remained was—

"When has he arriving?" Jans asked, completing the set.

"I don't have the answers to most of those questions, but he's gone," Gammy said with a satisfied smirk. "He told me not to tell you about him. Then when I did, he left."

"Why didn't you tell me someone was bothering you?" Nerlim seemed to have recovered from his sudden ailment, and now his scrawny hands balled into fists. Gammy had the fleeting thought that it was sort of sweet. She wouldn't let Nerlim suspect the presence of that thought, however.

Gammy fixed him with a gimlet eye. "That's what I wanted to talk to you about tonight," she said, "but somewhere along the way, we got sidetracked. I'm not sure if it was the exploding restaurant or the giant with the glowing eyes."

"Has he used any magic in your presence?"

Gammy shook her head. "He said he couldn't do much, not yet. He made my assistant come into my office without being called, and he messed around with my glass of Black Angus Knockdown, but that was it."

Nerlim blanched, as if understanding the level of dangerous that action had been.

"What does he want?" Nerlim and Heline asked at the same time. Their words echoed with a weird reverberation inside her head, almost as if a third voice had a direct line into her brain. Not like Corax, though; this was different. She didn't like this sensation one bit, and it only increased her growing annoyance.

"I'll keep that to myself for now, if you don't mind," she said archly. She wasn't about to let strangers intimidate her, as nice as they might seem, nor disembodied voices in her head, either. Even in times like these, lines must sometimes be drawn.

"You saw a giant with glowing eyes?" asked the younger girl, picking up on Gammy's comment. She looked as if she was trying not to appear *too* interested.

Gammy cudgelled her memory for the name. Oh yes, Eleanor. But before Gammy could answer, the boy cut in.

"We can find out about that later," Ulric said in a voice tight with desperation. "Right now, we have to get out of here before my mother gets home."

That's when Gammy heard it, and she knew the others did, too. The sound of a key in the lock.

Into the Dingle

Wint

Wint Usborne regained consciousness in a slow crawl, light brushing back the darkness as if someone were clearing it away with an inadequate broom. He opened one eye and saw the dog's nose in uncomfortable proximity close to his, with Skete's concerned face hovering just beyond. Wint closed his eye again, wondering if the darkness might come back if he waited. All things considered, he liked it better.

"Okay, enough dilly-dallying. Get him upright and let's go on up," the Radio said in a voice for which Wint was developing an intense dislike. He wasn't unused to people telling him what to do—Gammy and her trained lackey, Argit, did it often enough at work. But at least in that case, he was getting paid. He was doing his job. And it was a job he liked, one he'd chosen, not been volun-told to do.

The dog licked Wint's face—at least Wint assumed it was the dog, and not Skete, because his breath smelled much doggier than he expected Skete's would. Wint sputtered and opened his eyes, batting the dog away.

"I'm awake—I'm awake, all right?"

"Feeling okay, mate?" asked the dog.

Wint took careful stock of himself. No obvious lumps or bumps, so he must not have hit his head when he fell. "I'm fine, no thanks to anyone here." The silver teaspoon had fallen on the stonework path next to him, and some part of his mind told him to retrieve it and put it away. He did so, dropping the thing into his backpack with relief as it disappeared into the shadowy interior.

The Radio said something else as Wint got to his feet, but Skete made a placating gesture at it and the thing subsided. He eased the now-open padlock off the hasp since Wint hadn't moved to do it and tugged the door open. It yielded with grudging shrieks and groans. Wint was reminded of the sound effects from a horror movie, and not a very convincing one. Bits of moss, flakes of rust, and decaying leaf detritus showered down from the lintel. Rex poked his nose into the opening and sniffed, then pushed into the interior, his fluffy tail waving like a flag.

Like an automaton, Wint followed the rest of them into the ancient structure.

The interior of the Dingle smelled about the way you'd expect an old abandoned stone building to smell; musty and chill and earthy. Rex seemed to find the whole thing quite exciting, and set out with an apparent agenda of sniffing and cataloguing every individual stone. The tower was circular, and stairs wound up the interior of the walls. Light filtered down from above, illuminating uncountable dust motes hanging or spinning in lazy drifts in the air. The floor showed the remnants of an ancient fire, some rags and scraps of newspaper bearing charred edges. Wint picked up a shred of newspaper and inspected it. The date, intact in one unscathed corner, was from fifty years ago.

"Let's go," Skete said, and began climbing the stairs. Rex seemed torn between completing his examination of the lower floor or moving on to see what the upstairs held, but then decided in favour of moving up. Wint followed since no other reasonable course of action presented itself. His mind still spun.

How had he been able to open the lock? It might have been a trick of some kind, he supposed, although he couldn't fathom how. And that jolt of energy in the spoon. There was no explanation for that, either.

Too soon for Wint's liking, they emerged at the top of the tower, out onto a narrow balcony that encircled it. The stone wall was crenellated, and Wint had to get close to the edge to peer down through the battlements. Below, he saw a small sea of faces upturned, waiting.

He panicked and tried to crawl back down the hatchway, but Rex blocked the way. The dog showed his pointy white teeth in what might have been a smile, but also might have been a warning. "What am I supposed to say to them?" Wint croaked.

"You'll know," the Radio assured him. "When you start to speak, it will come to you."

It was the kind of thing Wint hated to hear people—*or radios*, he thought, *especially radios*—say. People who said things like that had no idea what it was like to be in the spotlight, to have expectations to meet, to be unprepared when you were the sort of person who didn't do well at being unprepared. He glanced over at Rex and saw even more teeth, in an even more unsmiling way.

"I hate you," he told the Radio in a dispassionate voice. "I just want to be very clear about that."

Then he turned and walked over to stand on a chunk of stone that had fallen from its place. It had left a larger-than-normal gap in the crenellations and when he stood on it, a ragged cheer went up from the assembled crowd. He cleared his throat.

"My friends," he began, because he was hoping against hope that they would still be friendly—or at the very least, not hostile—toward him when he eventually came down from this stupid tower. "We've come here today because...because—" Why *had* he come here? "Because a significant change has come to our world." That, at least, seemed to be unarguable.

"Whether that change will be for good or ill is yet to be seen," he continued, surprised at the way his voice carried down from this height. No one on the ground seemed to have trouble hearing him. They were all intent, not turning to their neighbours to whisper "what?" or anything like that. "But we want to ensure that whatever happens, the technology that we depend on will continue to thrive." Some of the crowd nodded. "We haven't come this far to see our lives fall apart at the whim of some random event," he continued, warming to his subject. That last sentence resonated, since it was what had happened, and still was happening, to him. "We have developed technology that helps us in our work, in our leisure. It takes care of our health and makes our lives easier. It is about to take us to the moon!" Cheers wafted up to him.

"This new force can be bent to our will," he heard himself say. "There will be others who will try to subvert it, to wield it against the supreme power of technology, but they must not prevail!"

"What can we do?" someone in the crowd called out.

Wint had a moment of sudden panic. The words that had been flowing with ease, if he did say so himself, abandoned him. He had no idea what the answer was.

"Study the force as best they can," hissed the Radio. "Find out how it works and what they can each do with it. Discover their own abilities."

Wint scanned the crowd for a moment. They didn't all look—quite—like the sort of people he might want messing around with strange and unknown forces of nature.

"Say it. No matter what they look like, they're your followers," the Radio urged, almost as if it could read Wint's thoughts.

"Okay." Wint sounded doubtful, but relayed the radio's suggestion. The crowd made pleased noises. Since he was out of ideas for anything else to say, Wint gave them another "we must prevail," and stepped down from the broken stone. His legs chose that moment to stage a revolt and went rubbery, leaving him to sag with his back against the wall. He brushed away droplets of sweat that had beaded his forehead. "Was that okay?"

"Brilliant!" said Skete, and the dog nodded in somewhat less enthusiastic agreement. He offered a half-hearted wag of his tail, though.

"That's a good start," said the Radio. "You got them solidly on our side."

"So what's next?" Wint asked, perking up a little. Maybe that would be the end of this and he'd be allowed to go home?

The Radio squashed that notion. "Now you have to learn your powers. Let's go back inside. This is going to take a while."

An hour later, Wint Usborne was worried again. No, that wasn't accurate, since in fact he hadn't stopped worrying since the moment of the moon mission's launch failure. His initial worry had only been about the mission, but that was soon replaced by worries about the voices in his head, talking dogs, sentient radios, lock-picking teaspoons, and assorted other weirdness. And now, even though the others kept telling him things and assuring him he was involved in something larger than himself; a battle to save the planet's technology and keep it from being subjugated to this strange new force, "magic," he was still worried. Worried about the failed launch, the voices, the things that were talking to him that in a sensible universe wouldn't be talking at all, and this sudden responsibility that had been thrust upon him. Nothing the Radio told him seemed very useful, and no matter what it had said earlier, it provided nothing like *instruction*. He had a feeling it was all going to turn out badly. Especially for him.

"I still have questions," he told the Radio.

"Oh, for—okay. What?"

"You said magic and technology don't get along. I always get lost there." Wint clutched a hand in the air as if trying to grasp something invisible. "How can something like 'technology,' which we should be able to agree is not a living, thinking thing, not 'get along' with anything else, let alone some kind of intangible force?" Wint tried hard to use his 'I'm not being unreasonable' voice, but it sounded more than a little strained.

The Radio sighed. "That's something you'll just have to accept. There may come a day when you'll understand it on your own terms, but we're not there yet."

Wint sagged a little deeper against the stone wall of the Dingle. He, Skete, and the Radio had descended back to the main floor of the tower, and Skete had produced a lantern for light. It threw odd, creepy shadows around the lichen-flecked walls. "Okay, so technology and magic don't get along. I just have to accept that. Here's another one."

"Hit me."

"You say that when the thaumic force of a planet is activated but technology is already kind of advanced, it can lead to problems."

"That's right." The Radio sounded pleased, as if it couldn't believe Wint got that right.

"So," Wint said, frowning, "this has happened before."

"Yes, of course it's happened before!"

"On...other planets."

"Yes."

"Where there are *people*."

The Radio trembled on the worn stone floor. Had it possessed eyes, it would have clenched them shut or rolled them upward. Had it possessed hands, they would have been balled into fists at this point. It could, of course, have let out a sound that was half exasperated sigh, half scream of frustration, but it displayed notable powers of self-control and did not. It only trembled a little. Its next words, however, sounded as if they came from between clenched teeth.[1]

"People, yes. Can we just get on with this?" the Radio asked. "We don't have an unlimited amount of time here."

Wint snapped, "Oh, yes, go on with it. Just because I'm trying to *understand* this ridiculous situation is no reason for me to burden you with my obtuseness. So there are people—aliens, one might even say—living on other planets, and this has all happened before. And when they are technological species of aliens, or people, or people-aliens, their technologies and magic don't play nice with each other. Have I got that right?"

"It's not just the species, it's the entire planet that's affected," the Radio corrected. Its words buzzed with static. "A thaumic force that's been dormant this long doesn't just wake up and understand by instinct how to behave! It's wild, it's random, it expresses itself in weird and unexpected ways—"

Rex interrupted the Radio with a sharp bark of surprise. "There's a creature—I think it's called a unicorn, although that word just popped into my head out of nowhere—that's just come running out of the woods," the dog called down from the upper floor of the Dingle, where it had stayed to monitor the crowd outside. "But it's—oh, bones!"

Wint jumped up from his seat on the stone floor and scurried up the stairs two at a time. He was muttering *what the flark is a unicorn? Oh! I see. But there are no such things as unicorns. Are there?* No one seemed to hear him. The dog stood on its hind legs, looking out one of the tall, narrow windows near the top of the tower, and Wint pushed him aside

---

1. Which was, of course, another thing it didn't have, but anyway...

to see. Sounds of panic welled up around the Dingle's grounds as the crowd of his "followers" noted the creature bearing down on them.

The unicorn was black, but blacker than any of those things that one usually associates with blackness, like night or bats or ebony or even the inside of a cow. This unicorn was atramentous. It was piceous. It *oozed* black, as if its blackness could suck up the surrounding light and envelop the entire world. Its horn was obsidian, curved and polished and reflecting light in a way that accentuated the depths of its darkness.

The unicorn slowed its approach, although it ignored the rag-tag crowd of people around the base of the Dingle as if they were invisible. Some made a cautious retreat, torn between fear and curiosity. Fear had taken the reins with the others and sent them running in the opposite direction. The unicorn trotted to the base of the Dingle and looked up. Wint cringed back from the window.

"I seek the Technocrat Avatar," the unicorn said in a voice that echoed up the outside of the tower and elbowed its way in through the narrow windows.

"Catch him, Skete," said the dog. He wasn't talking about the unicorn, of course, but about Wint, whose face had gone as pale as the unicorn was black. He rallied, though, and stepped back to the window. Skete's hand on his back may have helped in that regard, so it was fortunate he'd followed Wint up the stairs.

"Wh-why?" Wint asked. It was a good thing that unicorns, like horses, have well-developed hearing, because his voice emerged in a thin croak.

"The Creatures have a question for him."

Wint looked around in wild distress. "Who are the Creatures?" he hissed.

The Radio answered him from the lower floor of the Dingle, where it still sat, not having the power of self-locomotion. "Remember when I was telling you that a newly activated thaumic force expresses itself in weird and random ways?"

"Yes."

"Creatures are one of those early ways. Beasts from the imagination and beyond appear in the world and throw their lot in with one of the Avatars."

"One of the—wait a second, there are more Avatars?"

The Radio hummed for a minute, a brief hum of—what? Embarrassment? Discomfort? It was difficult to tell.[2] At any rate, the Radio didn't answer right away.

"We hadn't...er, gotten to that yet," it confessed at last.

"And I was supposed to warn you about the creatures," Skete admitted. "I forgot, sorry."

Outside, the unicorn cleared its throat, a loud and conspicuous reminder that it was waiting.

Wint threw dirty looks at the Radio and Skete and turned back to the window. "Ask your question," he called down to the waiting unicorn.

"Are you he?"

"He who?" Wint asked, then shook his head. "Oh, the avatar thingy. I might be. I'm the only one here you can ask at the moment, anyway."

The unicorn squared his stance, lifted his head, and delivered the query in a formal tone. "If the Technocrat Avatar comes into power, what are his plans for dealing with the Majickal Creatures of D'sharu?"

Wint took a step back from the window again, wondering if the unicorn might be able to see through stone.

"Tell the truth, I was wondering the same thing," Rex said.

"I don't know! I wasn't even aware magical creatures *existed* until a few seconds ago," Wint said, then caught the dog's eye. "Well, except for you, of course. And I didn't know the explanation for you. I still don't."

"Let's pass over how insulting that is and move on. Do you think there's a place for us in the world if you win?" the dog asked. "You'll be subjugating magic to the forces of technology. Where do we come in?"

"I don't know! How do you expect me to answer when I don't understand anything that's going on?" Wint crumpled into a small ball on the stone steps and huddled there, hugging himself.

Rex sighed and stuck his head out the window. "Look, he doesn't know yet," he called down to the unicorn. "Hasn't had time to think about it, he says."

---

2. When one is thrust into dealing with inanimate objects turned sentient, one begins to appreciate the importance of facial features and body language as an aid to communication.

The unicorn looked somewhat affronted. "Well, when can we expect an answer? The Council is trying to decide who we should back in this. The other one seems like the logical choice, but we thought we'd give this guy a chance, try to be fair and all that."

Rex shrugged. "No idea. Do you have a deadline?"

The unicorn thought for a moment. "Tomorrow at sundown?"

"Fair enough."

"Hang on," the unicorn said as Rex pulled back from the window. "You seem to be on his side. What's he like? Just between you and me."

Rex glanced down at Wint, still huddled on the floor. "Just between you and me? He's been a bit of a drip so far. But you never know. He might come into his own yet."

"Right. Thanks. We'll see you at sundown tomorrow, then." And the unicorn turned and trotted off into the woods again. Things seemed to get brighter after he'd disappeared, as if he pulled some of the darkness along after him.

"Okay, he's gone," the dog said.

Wint pushed himself into a sitting position. "A bit of a drip? I heard that, dog. Thanks for your support."

"Well," said Rex, "You've got until sundown tomorrow. Prove me wrong."

Dencrypt Us Out of Here

Heline

Heline heard the key in the lock at Ulric's door at the same time as the others. She wracked her brain for a plausible explanation for their presence, but Ulric hissed, "Everyone up the stairs!"

As silently as possible, they vacated the kitchen, Ulric waiting until the last just in case his mother got the door open before they were all out. He, at least, was supposed to be here. Eleanor hung back, too, frowning and shaking her head when Heline gestured for her to come with them. They followed Nerlim, who seemed familiar with the house and led them into a bedroom on the second floor. The walls were practically wallpapered with spaceships and planets, but there were no curtains on the windows, only some scraps of fabric on the floor. A strange frisson of familiarity brushed across Heline's mind, as if she'd just opened the door into that secret closet in her own home.

They stood in silence until Ulric and Eleanor slipped into the room to join them. Ulric eased the door shut. "She must have groceries or something; it's taking her so long to get the door open," he whispered. "But she'll be looking for me. What now?"

"Can you transport us all out of here?" Nerlim asked him.

He looked at the old man as if he were crazy. "Are you crazy? I don't know how to do that!"

Nerlim frowned, studying Ulric. "I suspect you do. Xya said it's all there in your head; on some level, you understand how to do it. Just try to concentrate the power."

"The last time I tried to concentrate the power, it was to levitate a stool, and that didn't go well for the stool. Or me," Ulric reminded him. "I don't want to risk blowing us all up."

[this is where you come in] the Hat told Heline.

What do you mean? It hadn't spoken to her in a while and the sudden voice startled her.

[you're the dencrypter. one of your songs will help him channel the magic]

Oh, she couldn't. Heline's cheeks burned; they must be blossoming scarlet. She'd sung a few of them already tonight, in moments of grave danger, but this wasn't an emergency. The worst that might happen would be some awkward explanations. The notion of producing her sheaf of songs and handing them over to anyone else to read—no. She couldn't do it.

[then all is lost] the Hat said simply. This time there was no sarcasm, no smirk in its voice. An empty chill passed through Heline at its words. [you must be there for Ulric when he needs you. it's your purpose. if you can't do it now—]

All right. I get it. She didn't want this—hadn't asked for any of it—but if her songs had a purpose, then she supposed there was nothing for it but to offer them.

"Um," she started, but her voice came out as a croak. She cleared her throat and tried again. "I may be a dencrypter. Would that help?"

Nerlim turned to look at her, eyebrows raised. "I've heard that word before. That means you can help Ulric with his magic, doesn't it?"

Heline nodded, but not with any certainty. "I—maybe?"

Ulric looked as uncertain. "Xya told us about dencrypters—sort of—"

"Who's Xya?" Eleanor and Gammy asked in unison.

Nerlim shook his head and waved a hand to quiet them, not turning away from Heline. "Not important right now. I'm sure you'll all meet her soon. Why do you say you're a dencrypter?"

"Well, this," Heline said, and put the Hat on. "It said I am. Or could be. Or...something." Her head was crammed with words again, new ones, and she sensed the moment the Hat had opened its eye to them all. The boys gasped, and Nerlim put an arm around Gammy's shoulders.

The hand on Heline's back, a small press of support, came from Jans, and she stood straighter and pushed her shoulders back.

Ulric's eyes widened. "Okay, I don't know how you help, but we should try it. But you won't let me explode anyone, right?"

Heline pulled the notebook of songs out of her enormous tote bag. "This is new to me, too, but I'm sure we can avoid any explosions. I'm glad I brought these," she said. "These are songs I wrote, with the Hat's assistance. They've helped us get out of danger already tonight." She looked at Nerlim. "How does this work?"

"I have only the vaguest of ideas. You're the dencrypter."

Heline swallowed. "Hat, can you help me?"

[choose a song] directed the Hat on cue.

"Which one?"

[it doesn't matter. whichever one you choose will be the right one. trust your instincts]

Heline glanced over the pages and selected one. She had no idea why that one seemed right, but it did. She handed it to Ulric, who glanced over it, and then back up at her.

"What am I supposed to do with it?"

"You don't know? Does it...um, spark anything when you read it?"

Ulric blushed. "Not really. I'm lost when it comes to song writing. Or music, except to listen to it."

"Could you sing it?"

He grimaced. She took that as a 'no.'

"Heline, how did they work for you earlier?" Eleanor asked, her voice edged with the urgency thrumming in the room. "How did they get you out of danger?"

A faint, drawn-out cry came from downstairs. "Ulriiiiiiiiic! Come and help me with the groceries!" The mother. Ulric looked up from the paper with wide eyes.

"I sang them," Heline said. "But it won't—I don't think that will be enough. The—the magic, or whatever, it felt weak when I did it, like it was only an echo, or a reflection. Not at its full potential."

"Maybe it just needed the boy to be present, too," Gammy said, although she didn't sound confident.

Eleanor whirled on Ulric. "Where's that old guitar you mentioned earlier? Still have it? Is it here?"

"Uh...sure," he said, and dropped to his knees to reach under the bed. He fumbled, then pulled out a dust-covered guitar.

Eleanor wrinkled her nose as if the evidence of neglect repulsed her, but reached for the instrument. She grabbed a handful of the star-and-moon-studded fabric scraps from the floor and brushed away the worst of the dust. Strumming a soft chord, she grimaced and began fiddling with the tuning pegs.

"Start singing," she told Heline. "I'll try to play along, best I can. If the music is magic, then maybe more music is stronger magic."

Heline looked at Nerlim, but the old man only shrugged. "Try it. It sounds...right, somehow. Ulric, do your thing when you're ready. And don't pay any attention if I fall on the floor and start writhing around or anything like that. It's normal, these days."

"Why would you—" Ulric started, but Eleanor strummed louder and drowned him out.

[your sister is on the right track] the Hat told Heline.

Heline took a deep breath and scanned the lyrics. At least this one seemed better than some of her earlier attempts. Some lines were still cliches, but this was no time to be a critic. In a low voice, she sang the first line. Eleanor picked up on the melody and played chords that lent buoyancy to Heline's words.

The world is in a state of flux
It'll soon shake your windows
We want harmony and peace
I need some release, release, release

"Oh," said Ulric. "Wait a second." He grabbed a backpack from the floor and pulled something tall and pointy from a pile of purple fabric on the dresser. He jammed the hat onto his head and stuffed the rest of the pile into the backpack, along with a hardcover book and some other items. Then he slung the pack over one shoulder, closed his eyes and moved his hands in small circles, as if he were gathering in something unseen. Something intangible but true, an energy thick with potential.

Heline tried to read the words off the page and watch Ulric simultaneously, wondering what that was all about, and if this hat were also sentient. She rather hoped not.

We must adapt to survive
Change is the only way we'll thrive
We are too concerned with things
It'll soon shake your windows
They lie, cheat and steal
But in the end, who turns the wheel?
We want harmony and peace
I need some release, release, release

Now that she sang the words aloud, Heline cringed on the inside. It was another song she now realized could be so much better. It made only vague sense...and yet, *something* was happening. It swirled through the words, an invisible energy reaching out to Ulric. The old man, Nerlim, made a gargling sound like someone had punched him in the stomach again. The same thing had happened outside the restaurant. Poor man must be getting tired of that. And now she might be causing, or at least adding to his distress. But he'd said to ignore it, so she kept singing despite the twinge of guilt that pricked her conscience.

Ulric's head nodded in a peculiar rhythm as his hands moved in those circles, his eyes still closed. He raised one hand and began to sketch invisible symbols in the air. Heline felt a thickness gather in the room, the weight of whatever swirled around them, and was glad Jans' hand held firm on her back. She continued to sing, not loudly, but strong and sure, bolstered by Eleanor's soft guitar, weaving the words around Ulric like a blanket, to cushion the power he needed for his spell. At least, that's how she envisioned it. She didn't understand what was happening, and wondered if she ever would.

And then as she sang, the room began to lose cohesion. A hazy blue mist appeared in curling tendrils, clinging to the bedroom walls, creeping over them. Heline's voice faltered for only a heartbeat, and then she repeated a verse.

"Nerlim," Gammy said in a low voice, but he shushed her.

"Ulric!" His mother's voice sounded again from the downstairs hall, then footfalls pounded up the stairs. Heline's heart beat a frantic staccato inside her chest. There was going to be a lot of explaining to do—

The bedroom door swung open and a tall, heavy-framed boy stuck his head in. "Ulric, are you—"

But Ulric didn't answer, caught up in the spell. The boy's eyes went wide, then he gulped, stepped inside, and shut the door behind him.

His wondering face was the last thing Heline saw, and then the bedroom was gone.

Years of Role Playing Games

Nerlim

Nerlim Pettibone struggled to gather his senses. They seemed to have scattered over an enormous distance in every direction, and reeling them back to himself took time and patience. He became aware of the floor beneath him, solid and cool like hardwood. A soft light beyond his closed eyelids, and the impression of a large open space around him. Someone held his hand. Gammy, he thought. He hoped.

Nerlim decided he didn't enjoy being a—what word had the woman, Xya, used?—a sensile. Every time someone did magic nearby, he got punched in the stomach, or sometimes for variety, in the head. He could only imagine what sensory delights might await him with stronger magic or more practiced wielders.

The sensation had been a gut-punch when Ulric exploded the stool. Heline's singing, to ward off the giant with the glowing eyes, was a gentler discomfort. The experience of her song this time, supporting Ulric's magic and accompanied by her sister, had started like the light, exploratory taps at the start of a boxing match. When Ulric's spell came into play, the pain escalated by an order of magnitude. Nerlim expected something bad, but not the nerve-jangling assault that pummelled him as the walls of the bedroom turned to mist. The punch that took him on the chin when they transported—the strength of that one knocked him cold. So now he crawled his way back to sensibility and tried to marshal his wits.

He opened one eye. He'd been right; Gammy held his hand, leaning over him with concern sketched across her face. "Gammy?" he whispered, "where are we?"

She sat back and sighed, but a wry smile curved her lips. "Ever thought about going back to high school?"

Nerlim swivelled his head and surveyed the surroundings. A large, open space yawned around them, high suspended ceiling lights providing faint illumination. Thin white and coloured lines marked the hardwood floor in geometric traceries, and bright colours and logos covered the walls. An odd shape nearby resolved into something familiar—a basketball net. Beyond Gammy, a set of bleachers ascended along the wall. The high school gymnasium.

"I was trying to think of somewhere safe," Ulric said, although he didn't seem to be speaking to Nerlim. "At night, I figured the school would be empty."

"It was a good think," Jans said. "Maybe here we can having a moment to catch breath."

On the bleachers, Ulric's friend Tiny Enos sat wide-eyed, looking excited. That's who Ulric was talking to as they pored over a book. "I didn't know you were going to show up like that. Ma won't know what to think."

"At least I shut the door," Enos said. "And she might not go up to check on us, since I helped her bring in the groceries before I went looking for you."

"If she texts me, I'll have to think of something to tell her."

Nerlim sat up. Everyone had gathered in a little knot on the bleachers, except for Gammy kneeling beside him. He noted with surprise that Xya had somehow joined them, even though she hadn't been with them at the boy's house.

"Where did she come from?" he whispered to Gammy.

She shrugged. "Got here just after we did. Told us she'd sensed a 'force disturbance' or some such thing and wanted to check in on the boy. Tracked us down somehow."

Nerlim shook his head. "I need to tell her something, so I'm glad she's shown up. But first, I'd really like to understand what's going on." He pitched his voice so everyone could hear the last part.

"And I still want to hear about the giant," the other boy, Enos, said with stubborn determination, as if he'd asked this before..

"I'm getting there." The large, hardcover book sprawled open across Ulric's lap and he flipped pages, searching for something. "I'll bet—here." He displayed the current page to Nerlim and Gammy. "Is this what chased you?"

Gammy answered while Nerlim was still studying the illustration. "That's pretty darn close."

Ulric nodded. "Thought so. It was a Nightstalker."

Enos looked excited. "You're kidding! Those things are like, twenty feet tall! They're tough!"

Gammy frowned. "I've never heard of such a thing. What is that book, anyway?"

"It's from a game," Ulric said. "Everything's imaginary—made up. But at least three creatures in here have appeared on D'sharu in the last couple of days. One attacked me, and one wrecked a restaurant—"

"We were there."

"And this one chased you." Ulric turned to Xya. "What does that mean?"

"It means things are proceeding as usual, and that awakened magic is creating creatures from the shared lore and imagination of your world." Xya shifted on the unyielding wood of the bleachers as if she couldn't get comfortable. "Lucky for us, the chances are good they'll side with us."

"Side with us? Against who?" Heline asked.

Xya sighed. "I wonder how many times I'm going to have to go through this?" She quickly sketched the story that was now familiar to some, but less so to others. When she summed up by saying, "Magic almost always manifests itself through some person or object—" the Hat interrupted her.

[i'm already here, dahling] Heline had settled it next to her on the bleachers, and its open eye now gazed straight at Xya.

Xya stared back. "You're the manifestation of magic?"

[name's arcanico. perhaps i haven't been formally introduced to everyone]

"Why didn't you say something before this?"

The Hat gave the impression of grinning. [i've said plenty—to select conversational partners. did the convocation send you?]

Xya pursed her lips. "The Min sent me. So Ulric wouldn't be alone."

[he does have me]

"Someone else has gone to help the Technocrat Avatar." Now Xya sounded a bit defensive. "The Min expected he might need some assistance. Leaving Ulric on his own seemed unfair, and The Min hadn't detected your presence, I guess."

[fair enough]

They stared at each other for a moment, her eyes locked on the hat's single amber one, then Xya nodded and the hat's point dipped in an answering nod. They both seemed satisfied.

"Could we get back to the explanation now?" Nerlim suggested. "I understand about Ulric, here, but the other force—"

"Is technology, which I'm sure feels threatened. If this planet has reached the tech level of space launches, technology likely felt secure in its stature. So it will also manifest itself and choose a champion to fight for its place in the world."

Nerlim looked from Xya to Ulric. "And these two champions are forced to compete? To see who will take control?"

Xya laughed. "'Compete' is a euphemism. They will fight a pitched battle, with all of their power and all of their followers, to see which force will be ascendant on this planet. It could be a fight to the death."

Ulric blanched. "To the *death*?"

Gammy broke in, shaking her head. "Don't listen to her, boy. Look at her, she's trying not to smile."

Xya shot Gammy a reproachful glare. "Oh, all right, that part was exaggerated. But we are talking about a serious battle. Losses are possible."

[serious indeed] added the Hat. [are you ready, Ulric?]

The boy seemed to pull himself up taller. "Honestly, no, I don't think I'm ready. I haven't had a lot of time to take this all in, or to practice or learn anything."

[you have your dencrypter, and she's good. together, you transported us here]

Beside Nerlim, Ulric whispered something under his breath that might have been 'fluke'.

[i think we should open the side doors] the Hat said with a change of tone. [someone wants a word with you, Ulric]

"Me? Who is it?"

[you'll see] The Hat must have had a private word with Heline, because she fetched a sigh and put the thing on again, then crossed to the double doors at the side of the gymnasium. Nerlim stood, unsure if he should follow.

When Heline opened the doors, a slice of the inky black night surged inside. Nerlim gaped for a moment before the reality made sense; this was a creature.

A creature incarnated from darkness. It seemed to draw the faint glow of the overhead lights into itself, swallowing their light into its graceful, spiralled horn and obsidian hooves. Nerlim expected sparks to strike up and set the gym's hardwood floor on fire, but its delicate steps left no mark.

"Cheese and rice!" Ulric, next to Nerlim, breathed the words in a barely audible voice that held a catch of fear. "Eleanor, are you seeing this?"

"Is that the same one?" she hissed in return. "That thing tried to kill us!"

[that's a unicorn] the hat's voice explained in Nerlim's head.

A horse with a horn? Nerlim replied. *Why aren't they called—*

[just go with it. the explanation takes too long]

"Whoa," Enos breathed beside him in an unintended pun. A swishing noise filled the air as the boy flipped pages in the thick book Ulric consulted earlier.

"I must explain that I bore no malice toward either of you when we—er, met—in the park," the unicorn said, addressing Ulric and Eleanor. "'Twas the zomoths I sought, as they were attacking you. I would have explained, but you disappeared too quickly."

Ulric inclined his head toward the creature in a grave acknowledgement. "We should have realized when you did not pursue us," he admitted. "A misunderstanding."

"Just so. Now, I have a question for the Thaumaturge Avatar," the unicorn said. "Will he answer?"

Nerlim held his breath as Ulric nodded again. "I will try."

"If you come into power, what are your plans for dealing with the Majickal Creatures of D'sharu?" The unicorn phrased the question as if following a formal protocol.

Ulric frowned, trying to match the creature's gravitas. "What will your needs be?"

"Careful," Enos whispered next to Nerlim, although his words were for Ulric. "I think this thing is in the Creature Concordance as an Ebon Monocerous; super strong, with mental powers."

"Undetermined as yet," the unicorn—or Ebon Monocerous—said, "But we shall at least seek safety from persecution and rights equal to those of other, non-majickal creatures."

"Done, and done," Ulric affirmed in a formal voice, adding, "I would pledge to always remain open to petitions from your brethren."

"Huh." The unicorn appeared taken aback by Ulric's answer, but in a good way. "Now that's what I'm talking about. We have not decided our allegiance yet, but we shall speak again, Thaumaturge Avatar." With a swish of his sable tail, he left through the gymnasium doors, ducking his head so that his horn did not graze the doorframe.

Ulric stepped backward with relief etched on his face. Enos clapped him on the back. "You were awesome! It was awesome! Man, did you see that thing?"

[you handled that well. how did you know the proper approach to take with such a creature?]

Ulric grinned, the first time Nerlim had seen him look happy since he'd met him. "Years of role-playing games, Arcanico."

[role-playing games?]

Ulric and Enos both nodded. "Once you get into a character, it'll carry you," Ulric said. "I just remembered one time when my character, an everborn prince—"

"Prince Evernestigan!" Enos grinned at his friend. "I knew I recognized that tone of voice."

"Anyway, this prince had to deal with a delegation of petitioners from a nearby country," Ulric continued, "and even though he had power over them, he had to be sure he didn't piss them off, because they could raise an army against him...anyway, I thought about how I'd played that character, and the situation seemed close enough—"

"And all this was make-believe?" An incredulous frown creased Xya's face.

Enos smirked. "Yeah, right. Gaming is serious business."

[role-playing games] the Hat repeated. [i shall want to learn more about this phenomenon. but for now, we should get some rest. Tomorrow will be a busy day]

Intermezzo Cinque

The Min

The Min surveyed the gathered faces of the Convocation. They displayed a range of emotional states, from confusion at what she was telling them to exasperation at being summoned here out of a perfectly nice bath. Here and there, however, she saw a dawning realization.

Drix pursed his lips, thinking. "All right. So the displaced magic took too long getting to its new home, and you're worried about what that means." He looked around at his fellow trans-dimensional beings. "We can agree to keep out of your way while you get that sorted out. But do you really think an Exile is involved? How would that even work? Aren't they locked up tight?"

The Min wanted to lean back in her chair and rub her eyes, but she had to present a composed facade to the multitude. Instead, she folded her hands and set them on her desk. "They should be, yes. Many of you participated in the undertaking to seal the Exiles away on worlds where their influence and the harm they might do would be limited. To my knowledge, those seals are holding. However, this is an extraordinary situation, and I have to consider all the possibilities."

"Why would an Exile want to interfere with displaced magic?" asked the flame-haired woman, but answered herself in the next breath. "Oh, because they might find a way to use it to break a seal."

"But how would that even be possible? There must be some other explanation," Drix insisted. "Something more probable?"

"I've considered that," The Min said. "A natural obstacle in the thaumic force's way, perhaps; but I looked into that and found nothing. Or a hesitation on the part of the force itself, trying to decide which planet to land on—it bypassed three en route to D'sharu—but I've discounted that. Considering three other possible planetfalls would have taken longer than two segments. No, I come down to either an Exile, or someone in the Convocation."

This pronouncement caused another brief stir, this time of indignation. Shocked looks and pointed glances were exchanged, and the air filled with mutterings like, "One of us?" and "I've never been so insulted!" and "How would you even *do* that?"

The man with soap bubbles in his beard hitched his towel a little higher. "Well, we can all see there are a few faces missing from this meeting."

The Min inclined her head. "And if anyone here knows of a connection between those missing faces and this matter, or an Exile, I'd be very interested in hearing about it." When no-one spoke up, she added, "You may contact me on a private channel about it if you wish."

She spotted a young being near the front of the crowd with a tentative hand half-raised, as if unsure whether to speak. A large shower-type cap enveloped their head, and random bits of glitter spangled their pale green skin. The being carried an enormous water bottle, as if hydration was a concern for trans-dimensional beings. "Yes? Do you have something to add?"

The young being quailed at being noticed, but gulped in a steadying breath before saying, "Sorry, I'm kind of new, I guess. I'm not sure who these Exiles are."

The Min nodded. "Of course. Forgive me for not realizing. You deserve a detailed explanation, but that will have to wait for another time. In brief, the Exiles are former members of this Convocation who broke fundamental rules. As you know, we must maintain order so that the inhabitants of the planets we sometimes influence are not left worse off for our involvement in their affairs. Sometimes members overstep those boundaries, and if their intent is deemed malicious in a review process, then their actions have consequences. Sometimes those consequences include Exile to a planet where their abilities can't be used."

The young being's eyes grew very wide and round with wonder. "A place with no magic?" they squeaked.

"Just so."

"Is their exile for life?" Their voice was tremulous as they asked this, because for trans-dimensional beings, that would be an extraordinary length of time indeed.

The Min shrugged. "Depending upon the seriousness of the infraction, it can be. But we're talking about some seriously problematic individuals here. They don't need or deserve your pity."

"Which is why it would be disastrous if one of them has found a way to interfere outside their place of exile," Drix added.

"But if they're in a place with no magic, how could they use magic to reach outside and try to interfere with a thaumic force passing by?" the young being asked.

"Only with outside help." The Min narrowed her eyes and her searching gaze crossed the assembly, but no-one flinched in any way that implied guilt.

Just then, a device on The Min's desk came to life.[1] She eyed it and announced to the assemblage, "Excuse me, I have to take this. Don't go anywhere."

Walls materialized around her desk, so she didn't see the bearded, soap-bubbled man roll his eyes and pull his towel tighter around himself.

Xya looked back at The Min from the holographic image now hovering over The Min's desk. "Xya. You have something to report? I'm in the middle of a full Convocation assembly at the moment."

Xya gave a brisk nod, her hair waving in soft curls around her face, projecting self-confidence. "My apologies, but I thought you should hear about this right away. I got your message to be on the lookout for Corax, Sedrict, and Alsina. Well, Alsina has been sighted, and there's no doubt she's interfering with the process."

---

1. The Min didn't have a name for it; she only thought of it as a device for the facilitation of communications with those working for her, but perhaps it's easier for us to simply call it a "phone."

"You saw her?"

"Not me. But someone I've met down here, one of the Thaumaturge Avatar's allies—a sensile named Nerlim. He did some research and discovered a sentient book that's been kept hidden down here for decades—"

"A sentient book on a planet without active magic until now? How is that possible?"

Xya blew out a sigh. "The book told Nerlim that magic *was* active on D'sharu in the past, a long time ago. That's when the book's author wrote it. But then the magic went dormant again and all traces of it—except for the book—were erased."

The Min felt a vein throbbing in her temple as she struggled to make sense of what the woman was saying. "But—there should be a record of it. I checked the files on D'sharu when this incident started and it's listed as always dormant."

"I don't know what to tell you. This is what Nerlim told me. Do you want to speak to him yourself?"

"No, not yet." The Min shook her head. The mood she was in right now, she might interrogate the man to death by accident. Mortals were so depressingly fragile. "Where does Alsina come into this?"

"Well, she apparated into the library, where the book was kept in a secure room, and stole it. Caused an uproar because, of course, there was another witness along with Nerlim, someone who doesn't know anything about the existence of magic. But when Nerlim asked who she was, she said something like, 'I'm the person who can fix all the magic problems messing up this world, and maybe this book can help me do that.'"

Xya paused, because the anger suffusing The Min's usually serene face was quite frightening. She actually gritted her teeth.

"And you're sure it was Alsina?"

Xya held up a hand and wobbled it back and forth. "Pretty sure? I didn't see her, but Nerlim gave me a detailed description of the woman, and it sounded like her. And you said she might be down here, so..."

The Min nodded. "Yes, I'm sure it's her. Did the book tell this Nerlim anything else of note?"

"It said its author believed undue influence had been used to activate the planet's latent magic, but since it was unnatural, the effect had to be reversed. Also, that some kind of powerful being must have done it."

"Well, duh," The Min said, her composed facade slipping for a moment.

"And that this being had also erased the evidence of magic and made the planet forget it, too. But somehow the author and the book remained—it's not clear how."

Xya smiled. "According to Nerlim, it wasn't happy at being snatched and had no intention of cooperating with Alsina, but I'm not sure how a book can stop itself from being read. Although it had told Nerlim previously that simply reading the book wouldn't access its full knowledge, so that's something."

The Min sat back in her chair, clasping her hands and tapping her lips with her index fingers. "And why does Alsina want the book? What does she think it can tell her?"

"That, I don't know. That's all she said to Nerlim."

"And no sign of Sedrict or Corax?"

"Not so far as I know." Xya frowned. "Don't they seem like an odd trio to be working together? Sedrict and Alsina I can see, but Corax?"

"I have a feeling Corax is just operating in his own bumbling way, unrelated to the others." The Min's manner had become distracted. What should she do with the information Xya had given her? "If he gets in their way, they won't hesitate to roll over him. Thank you, Xya. Carry on, and keep me informed if anything else comes up."

"Will do." Xya nodded, and The Min broke the connection. She realized with a start that Xya had been standing in front of a wall painted with the words "GO FLAMINGOATS!" and a logo of a goat's grinning head wreathed in flames. She wondered where in the world Xya had been calling from.

When the temporary walls around her desk fell away, The Min noted with satisfaction that the entire Convocation was still there. Of course, she'd told them to wait, but like a room full of preschoolers, one didn't take it for granted that one would be obeyed.

"More news," she said before anyone started complaining about the wait. "Alsina's been spotted on D'sharu, and there's reason to believe this is the *second* time there's been active magic there. Someone activated it in the past and then shut it down again. I'm only going to ask this once: does anyone here have information about that?"

Stunned silence met her question as the implications of this pronouncement rippled over the crowd. There were frowns and puzzled looks, but no-one spoke.

Until the little rotund drunken man lisped, "That theemth bad. Even to me, and I'm drunk."

A blue-skinned individual whose head was wreathed in a glowing nimbus of yellow light raised a tentative hand. The Min nodded to him. "I heard a rumour once—a tall tale, I assumed—about someone who'd activated magic on a planet just to see if they'd get away with it."

The Min's gaze sharpened. "When was this? And more important, *who* was this?"

The man's blue skin paled to azure under the blade of The Min's eyes. "I—I didn't pay that much attention because I thought it was just a gag. A long time ago, I think, like—a hundred years in planetary time. The story was that something happened, and they got worried and shut it down again so they wouldn't get caught."

"Well, I guess. That's a sure path to Exile," snorted a birdlike being with a yolk-yellow tuft of feathers atop its head.

"In light of recent events, I suspect it wasn't a gag," The Min said. "You don't remember the name or designation of the planet where this story happened?"

"No," the man said, sounding miserable. "It might not even have been mentioned. I honestly didn't think the story was important—or even true. But it could have been D'sharu."

"And the person responsible? Do you remember that?"

The glowing nimbus pulsed as the man swallowed. "He's an Exile now," he admitted, and whispered a name.

The Min closed her eyes briefly while gasps and exclamations proliferated through the crowd. *I might have known*, she thought. *It would be him, wouldn't it?* The involvement of Sedrict and Alsina made sense now.

Majszak. Of course.

THE CORAX CONUNDRUM

GAMMY

Gameldina Gannand was facing down a conundrum. Events tore her in too many directions at once.

On the one hand, she liked the boy Ulric and secretly admitted that, in her heart, she wanted to help him. Of course, she didn't say as much to anyone else. And Nerlim, always an impeccable judge of character, supported the boy. So that was a consideration.

On the other hand, she didn't see how helping Ulric moved her closer to relaunching her moon mission. In fact, if she understood the situation (which, to be honest, she doubted), Ulric seemed to be the champion of the force that had caused the launch's failure. Of course, she realized it wasn't the boy's fault. He was just another pawn in whatever game they'd all been forced into. Even so, there it was. The fifth force had messed up her plans, and Ulric was the champion of the fifth force. It made him her de facto—if not enemy, then at least opponent, plain and simple.

On the third hand (if you possessed a third hand; and after the creatures Gammy had seen already tonight, it didn't seem outside the realm of possibility)—on the third hand were Corax and that Sedrict fellow, who'd both promised to help her get the launch back on track and who hadn't wanted her to keep hanging around with this crew. Granted, Corax had annoyed her enough to make her drive him off, and all his 'god' talk freaked her out and made her uncomfortable. Sedrict wasn't any better, with his prying questions and bold requests about the NCDSF facilities. Still, it came down to priorities. And Gammy had never struggled to figure out where those priorities lay.

Until now.

But Sedrict had let it slip that anyone able to attune to magic might control it, and implied that magic, too, might be used to get the launch back on track. He'd tried to backpedal on that statement, but it was clear he'd said more than he intended. So it was still possible that Ulric or the nice girl Heline, or even Nerlim, she supposed, *could* use magic to help her if they chose.

There was also a fourth hand (what the flark, she might as well run with the analogy) that had been metaphorically tapping her on the shoulder. It was the idea of this other fellow, the Technocrat Avatar. The champion of technology. He seemed to represent a melding of technology with this new, fifth, force. That sounded to Gammy like—well, like the person most likely, for all practical purposes, to help her make the moon launch happen. Not Ulric, niceness notwithstanding; not Corax and his creepy translucence; not Sedrict and his smarmy attempts to ingratiate himself; no, the tech guy—the tech guy who might also control magic—made the most sense.

Unfortunately, for Nerlim and his friends, this as-yet-unnamed person appeared to be the enemy. Gammy just didn't know for certain if he was *her* enemy.

It was a conundrum, and she couldn't ask Nerlim about it, since his loyalties were clear. Sadly, she had no one else in her life to ask, and Gammy had never felt that void as keenly as she did right now.

They'd deemed the high school too risky and uncomfortable to stay for the night. A security check by the local police might discover them, and the distinct lack of anything resembling beds was also a factor. Gammy considered volunteering her house as a refuge for the night, but the possibility of Corax or Sedrict or even both of them appearing unannounced made her clamp her mouth shut on the impulse. For all she knew, they could find her anywhere, but so far she'd only seen them at her house or office, so maybe she would get a break from them elsewhere.

They'd reached an unspoken understanding that they should all stick together. With the world's increasing weirdness, safety, or at least comfort, lay in numbers. Heline suggested they all gather at her house, which, upon discussion, was agreed to be an acceptable choice. It wasn't huge, but large enough to accommodate them all for a night or two if necessary. The two boys, Ulric and Enos, had each phoned home and told white lies, saying they were staying at each other's houses. Ulric had to do a bit more prevaricating, telling his mother he and Tiny Enos had left for Enos' house without her noticing. She wouldn't have bought it if she weren't so tired, but at least she wasn't more than exasperated. The lies wouldn't hold up to close scrutiny, of course, but both boys decided more important things were afoot and they'd take their chances with repercussions later.

So Nerlim braced himself for the pain while Gammy held his hand, and Heline and Xya and Ulric had together summoned the power of the fifth force. When the sparkling greenish mists of transportation faded, they'd found themselves in a comfortable little bungalow on the outskirts of town. The decor ran too much to black and the effect was rather dreadful, Gammy thought, but otherwise, it seemed comfortable enough. And large enough to accommodate them all for a short time. However, it still wasn't big enough for her to get Nerlim anywhere private for a chat. Jans and Heline had retreated to the kitchen to make snacks and discuss plans to retrieve Jans' car from Ulric's street, abandoned there when they all departed courtesy of the fifth force. The two boys were in the living room setting up makeshift beds while Eleanor strummed her guitar, Xya had claimed the spare bedroom for "strategizing"—which made Gammy roll her eyes—and she didn't feel comfortable going into Heline's bedroom and shutting the door. She'd only just met the young woman, for cheese's sake. That would be too much of an invasion.

Looking for the washroom and pondering her conundrum, however, she'd discovered an enormous closet at the back of the house. The walls bore mostly empty shelves and the same gloomy black paint as some of the other rooms, although here it seemed much older. A single bulb offered light, though, and it was roomy enough for her and Nerlim to duck into for a few minutes. Just before she closed the door to fetch Nerlim, a voice spoke to her, and it didn't come from inside the closet. It spoke inside her own head.

[i'm sorry you're pondering difficult choices]

And although Gammy startled and swept her eyes over the shelves, she understood what—who?—spoke to her.

"You're that Hat," she muttered in a low voice, shooting a resolute glare around the closet even though it was empty. "I don't like you in my head."

[and you're the subject of far too much attention] it replied. [sorry to be adding to that]

Gammy huffed. "And what do you want from me? Make it quick, and after this I demand you stop mucking around in my thoughts."

[i didn't want you to feel left out] Gammy heard the edge of laughter in its words. It was joking with her.

"I rather prefer it, to be honest. But you didn't answer my question."

[you can choose to think your side of the conversation, if you're concerned about being overheard]

"I'm concerned about losing my mind. What do you want?"

The Hat sighed in a truly vexing way. [i consider it my duty to warn you about Corax and Sedrict. they won't be able to help you achieve what you want]

Gammy raised an eyebrow, even if there was no one to see it. "And what do you know about it? Or them?"

[i'm the manifestation of magic] it said with an audible shrug. [i sense things about people who are using magic]

Gammy moved inside the closet and shut the door behind her. A worn string dangled from the single-bulb light fixture, and she reached up and tugged it before the door closed tight. Her immediate regret was the lack of a chair in case this conversation became prolonged. She crossed her arms and leaned back against a shelf thick with dust to make do. "So you're saying they're lying to me?"

[lying is a strong word. it's more like they're overconfident. Corax isn't strong enough or charismatic enough to pull off his god coup, and perhaps you don't have the level of influence he thinks you do. no offence intended. he's not a very astute judge of these things]

Well, that was disappointing, if it was true. Gammy didn't yet trust this Hat as far as she could throw it. "And Sedrict? He seems to believe his friend—or master, or whatever—would be a pretty big deal if they could get here."

The Hat didn't answer right away. [he might be right. but i don't think that's a good thing. i don't know who this friend is, but i sense a dark aura when Sedrict uses magic down here. have you heard from Alsina?]

Gammy let her head fall back to bang gently against a shelf, dislodging another shower of dust. She brushed it off her shoulders with quick flicks of annoyance. "Please don't say someone else is about to bother me. I don't have time for this garbage."

[she has other tasks, although she's working with Sedrict] the Hat said. [she may be exploring ways to achieve their goals without troubling you]

"I'm all in favour of that, if it keeps them away from NCDSF—where I work," she explained.

[i understand that, but it doesn't matter how they make it happen—it's going to be bad for everyone on your planet if they do. you must help ensure that magic—Ulric—is the ultimate winner in the coming confrontation, and that Sedrict isn't able to contact or free their friend]

"And if Ulric is the winner, that means you're the winner, correct?"

Again, the Hat didn't answer right away. [i suppose that's one way of looking at it. but i am telling you the truth]

"At this point, I'm still sorting out who and what to believe. But I'll add what you've said to all the things I'm taking into consideration." Now Gammy wanted to talk to Nerlim even more desperately, and she wondered when he might come looking for her. She didn't want him to find her in here talking to herself.

[no worries, i'm leaving,] the Hat said. [not that i was really here. but it looks like you're about to have another visitor anyway]

And the voice was gone. Just as Gammy had failed to sense its presence before it spoke to her, she now couldn't be certain it had departed. However, she couldn't do anything about that, so she decided not to worry about it. She moved toward the door to open it to whomever approached, but the visitor wasn't coming that way.

Corax's misty form appeared inside the closet without fanfare. His lumpy face was made even more lumpy by an unbecoming pout. "You shouldn't have said anything about me, you know."

Gammy rolled her eyes and leaned back against the shelf again. She shrugged. "Oh, please. You shouldn't have bugged me. I warned you."

"It would serve you right if I found someone else to help me, and whom I could help in return," he said, prefacing it with a huff.

"Go ahead." Gammy made her reply sound offhand. "I have other options to get the launch back on track, anyway."

"Like what?"

"Like, I might find the Technocrat Avatar. He's the go-to guy for technology, right?"

Corax laughed, a thin sound with a mean edge. "You won't find him to be much help to you, dear lady. The Technocrat Avatar is not all one might hope for."

Gammy shrugged again. "Who is? And anyway, I haven't seen any indication that you can do anything for me, either."

Corax bobbed a little higher, looking aggrieved. "I told you before, I'm under the constraints of this world."

"And what about your friend, Sedrict?" Gammy asked, fixing the apparition with a negligent stare. "He claims he can help me just as well as you can."

Corax's translucent form stopped bobbing and went still for a long moment. His eyes grew so wide they looked like they might fall out of their sockets—if they'd been encased in physical sockets, that is. "Sedrict? He's here? He contacted you?"

"He did." Gammy was unable to stop the smug grin tugging at her mouth. Not that she tried awfully hard. "Made me a pretty sweet offer, I have to say." She had not the slightest intention of letting Sedrict near the NCDSF property even before the Hat's warning, but Corax didn't need to know that.

"What does he want from you?" Corax demanded. "He's never shown any interest in becoming a god."

Gammy shrugged. "Says he just wants to contact a friend. It sounded like a reasonable request."

"A friend?" Corax pounced on the word like a cat on a mouse. "Who? What kind of friend?"

Gammy regarded him with narrowed eyes and didn't answer right away. "A friend he says could help me with the launch, if that friend was free to come to D'sharu. He wants to use something at NCDSF to send a message or something—"

"Oh." Corax looked stricken, and he shook his head in disbelief. "Oh, this is bad. You're not going to let him do that, are you?"

"Afraid I won't help you if I help him?" Gammy couldn't help herself. Something about Corax invited needling. But Corax didn't appear to be listening to her anymore.

"It must be—I mean, who else could he mean? Someone has to be alerted, but—" The apparition was almost vibrating where he floated, muttering as if wrestling with a decision with no good options. "But if I go to The Min, she'll be so angry. She might not even listen to me."

"Gameldina?" Nerlim's muffled voice came to them through the closed closet door. He'd finally come looking for her, but Corax floated between Gammy and the door and she shuddered at the idea of walking through the spectre to open it.

"Maybe if I took you with me," Corax mused, as if struck by a new idea. "You could tell her yourself what Sedrict said, and then it wouldn't be just me."

"I don't know who you're talking about, but I'm not going anywhere right now," Gammy said. She raised her voice. "Nerlim? I'm in the closet."

"Shhh—well, drat," Corax said. "Now you've done it. We don't need to add anyone else to this disaster. I need to think."

"Think all you like. I'm not going anywhere with you," Gammy reiterated. "And you say you can't do much magic, so I'm not worried about being whisked away from here. It took three of them to get us here. And you're not even fully materialized."

Corax regarded her with baleful eyes. "Why did I ever think you were someone I could work with? But this could be life or death. I have to get you to The Min somehow—" He broke off and looked around the closet as if seeing it for the first time. "Although...this place seems to hold a considerable amount of residual power. As if something important had been stored here for a long time…let me see." He closed his eyes.

Gammy wondered if that had any actual effect, since his eyelids were as translucent as the rest of him. "Nerlim!" she called again, louder this time. "Would you open the closet door? It's stuck." She grinned at Corax, but he wasn't looking at her. His eyes remained closed. The doorknob rattled once, but Corax pointed a finger at it and it stilled.

"What did you do?" Gammy demanded.

He didn't answer her. Someone—Nerlim, she assumed—knocked on the door. "Gammy? You're right, it's stuck. I'll have to get Heline or Jans."

"No, Nerlim, wait!"

"Yes," Corax breathed. "I think it's possible."

"To do what?" asked Gammy, but already Corax was making arcane gestures with his hands, and Gammy felt a sudden vertigo, as if the walls of the closet were falling away from her. On the other side of the door, she heard Nerlim say, "Gammy? What's—oof! Not again!"

The echo of Nerlim's pained groan was still in Gammy's ears when the closet disappeared. Or rather, she did.

Let's Build a Robot

Wint

Wint Usborne, putative Technocrat Avatar, had also passed a bad evening. It was, he reflected, no worse than the foregoing day had been, and quite comparable to the day before that. In truth, the week was shaping up to be one he'd happily forget. Tomorrow held little promise of improvement.

He had returned to his car because it was so very much more comfortable than the cold stone floor of the Dingle. The Radio, the dog Rex, and Skete had all insisted on coming out with him, and he knew they still didn't trust him not to run away. Wint couldn't blame them; he didn't trust himself either. The pros and cons of staying versus running came out about even.

When he'd emerged this time, though, the followers milling about outside seemed more ambivalent toward him. He sensed a lingering aura of doubt surrounding them, as if they'd expected more from him by now, and Wint was overwhelmed by a sense of inadequacy. Not an unfamiliar sensation for Wint, truth be told, but not one he'd ever gotten used to. If these were his followers, that meant he should be a leader, and he was quite aware that so far he'd failed to display any leadership qualities at all. Of course, the rain had started by this time, and most people retreated to their vehicles or tents, so the pervasive dampness might have been a factor.

The small, cramped car didn't offer much more comfort than the floor of the Dingle, however. A vague scent of damp dog now crept about the interior, which was not surprising. Wint found it impossible to relax with the dog and the Radio in the backseat. He imagined their eyes on the back of his head, which was silly, especially in the case of the Radio, which was singularly lacking in eyes, but the sensation persisted. Difficult to argue with sensations like that.

"The Creatures aren't coming over to my side, are they?" Wint asked, leaning his head against the cool glass of the window beside him. Skete had been dozing in the passenger seat since the rain started, but jerked awake at the sound of Wint's voice. Rex snorted.

"I expect it depends on what you have to tell them. How you're going to answer their question."

"But that's the thing—I don't have an answer for them, and it seems inevitable that they'll side with magic. So if they throw in with the other guy—the Thaumic Turd Avatar—"

Skete guffawed. The Radio said, "*Thaumaturge* Avatar!" in an exasperated tone.

"Whatever. Not like I've seen it written down anywhere, is it? So they're going to side with him. And what are we going to do?"

"Well, you've got your own followers." Skete gestured out at the gathered geeks, nerds, and techies. Two of them, both skinny teenagers with cool haircuts and band t-shirts, argued over something in a video game. Their intensity was such that it seemed like they might come to blows. That didn't allay Wint's concerns. He felt certain that even though they might fight among themselves in the right—or wrong—circumstances, they weren't up to taking on an army of whatever followers his magical opponent might have enthralled.

The Radio, a dark shadow in Wint's rear-view mirror, gave an eerie impression of shaking its head. "You're the Technocrat Avatar. You're attuned to technology. You don't need magical creatures, anyway. You need tech."

"And where do you suggest I get that?" Wint's tone was scathing. "We're on a hill in the middle of a forest with only an ancient stone tower for company."

"You changed the teaspoon into a key. That counts for something. And you have followers," the Radio reminded him, echoing Skete.

"Yeah." Wint sighed. He might not have them for long if he didn't come up with something quick. And he didn't trust his ability to do—whatever he'd done to the teaspoon—enough to try a flashy move in front of a crowd. He stared out the smeared windshield at said crowd. Somewhere, most of them had found tents, the canvas sides aglow with the various lights of cell phones, laptop computers, battery-powered flashlights, portable game consoles, and other gadgets. He had followers, all right. Or *someone* had followers, and for now, here they were. Nerds and geeks and lovers of technology. If only there was a way to blend them all into one big computer-like brain that might come up with some answers for him...

And at that moment, he got his first big Technocrat Avatar idea. He sat in silence, pondering the possibilities and implications, growing more and more excited as his vision grew. This might work. Even the Radio might approve.

"I have an idea," he said, in a tone of mild surprise. "I know what we're going to do." In fact, this was the first time in days he'd had an inkling of what to do about anything, so both the words and the sensation came as quite a surprise to him.

"What?" Skete's voice was threaded with suspicion. It was obvious he'd had the same reaction.

"We're going to put them to work." Wint nodded out the window toward his gaggle of followers. "People like this need a task, a project, a problem, to keep them interested. So let's give them that. Let's get them to build something."

"And what would that be?" For once, the Radio sounded interested in what Wint had to say. All the condescension had disappeared from its voice.

"A robot." Wint rubbed his hands together in satisfaction, something he hadn't done in a long time—if ever. "A big flarking robot. And if they can do that, we'll see what comes next."

In the back seat, the Radio gave the odd impression of a smile.

Hours later, Wint looked down from the top of the Dingle at his followers' progress. What he saw was difficult to process, let alone believe.

In fact, from the top of the Dingle, he didn't have to look very far down to see the top of the thing—or at least the top of its frame. The robot, though still only a metal skeleton, stood almost as high as the tower itself. Thin moonlight played over its many metallic struts and supports like a young gymnast in training. Somewhere in or around the tower, the followers had made the unlikely (Wint thought) discovery of a stack of scaffolding. It creaked and rattled and made other precarious sounds while workers swarmed up and down it on all sides of the robot, carrying tools and materials.

How such a construct, even at this stage, could have emerged from the pile of cell phones, music players, portable game consoles, flashlights, camp stoves, laptops, tablets, and similar gadgets his followers had pooled earlier in the evening was beyond the power of his imagination. This project had outstripped every expectation or dream he had for it. His idea had been for something just over person-sized; this construct towered several times that height. He understood magic must be a factor, the way the teaspoon had also been transformed into something he needed, but the logical, practical part of his brain still couldn't understand where it had all come from.

"It came from you," the Radio assured him.

"I don't think so." Wint blinked down at the robot's frame and shook his head.

"Of course it did."

"How would that work? I don't know how to control any magic or force or whatever this is!"

"Well, the man's got that part right." Rex flicked an ear as if to dislodge a fly.

"Wow, thanks for your support," Wint said, throwing the dog a dirty look. "But even granting the involvement of magic, which I don't, how could all that stuff have been turned into this?"

The robot (or at least the thing on its way to becoming a robot) was more than impressive. It loomed near the Dingle, twenty feet or more tall. The surfaces overlaying the metal skeleton appeared in patches, sections of reflective silver or deep black. Here and there, exciting matte strips emphasized a sleek, graceful line. Roughly humanoid in shape, it also displayed occasional protrusions that did not correspond to any humanoid features. So far, it was impossible to tell what they would be. They held a vague air of danger, although Wint didn't see how that could be. You couldn't create weapons out of nothing, could you? His car, he noticed with a pang, had been subsumed into the creation. Wint regretted its loss, but the sacrifice seemed worthwhile. He couldn't identify any particular bits that had once been his car, but there was a certain satisfaction in knowing it was in there somewhere.

His followers seemed quite ecstatic about the project's progress. For a disparate group who'd been mostly strangers before yesterday, they worked together with an amazing coherence.

Of course, Wint had no idea what he would do with a robot. It had seemed like a good idea at the time, and when Wint suggested the project an excited frenzy erupted among the gathered crowd. They'd pooled their resources and found the scaffolding. Tools had emerged from car trunks and messenger bags; cars, scooters, and even a few skateboards had been donated to the project. Now empty energy drink cans and fast food wrappers littered the ground around the tower, and Wint wondered where it had all come from. No one had left the grounds, to his knowledge. Unless his "followers" had brought all of it with them, he supposed. That took some foresight, which he rather admired. He urged his drifting thoughts back to the utility of a robot. The Radio had earlier mentioned a coming battle; he'd made a mental note at the time to ask for more details about that, but the construction project had pushed it out of his mind. As the robot took shape, now seemed like a good time to ask.

"So tell me more about this battle you mentioned in the night," he said to the Radio, struggling to sound casual.

"Well, the Thaumaturge Avatar will want to make magic the dominant force on the planet, as I said before." The Radio hummed a tuneless little song to itself in the background, which Wint found distracting. He didn't like to mention it, though.

"And that would be bad. We want to keep technology dominant." Wint said this, not as if he necessarily believed it, but as if he wanted confirmation.

"Right! So when the Thaumaturge Avatar challenges us, you'll kill him and then—"

"Erp." Wint made a noise like a strangled squeak.

"Here we go," said the dog.

"I'll catch him." Skete got his arms under the collapsing Wint in the second before his head hit the floor. "I hope no one will think I'm a jerk for saying," Skete said as he dragged Wint away from the openings—were they arrow slits?—in the wall and propped him up against a solid area, "that I'm not sure Wint has the constitution required to be an Avatar."

Anyone looking at Wint as he sagged against the damp stone wall might have agreed.

"He'll come through when he has to." The Radio tried without success to sound confident, and its humming dwindled away.

"I...will not...kill anyone," Wint croaked. "There has to be another way."

The Radio gave the impression of a shrug. For an inanimate object, it was developing quite an impressive repertoire of body language. "I suppose if you can subdue him or something, that will be adequate, too, but the other way's more...definitive. There can't be any room for doubt in the matter; one of you must be victorious. I'll leave it in your, er, capable hands, I guess."

"So is this Thaumaturge Avatar going to come looking for us?" Rex asked. "Or do we take this fight to him?"

"What if we didn't fight at all?" Wint bleated in the voice of a sheep surrounded by wolves. "I mean, nothing too terrible has happened so far. The launch failure was unfortunate, and the world might have to adapt to some changes, but is this whole magic thing such a big deal?"

"Look out at those folks." Skete pointed down at Wint's followers, toiling away on the robot like ants constructing a nest. "Now tell me you don't think the loss of technology would be a big deal to them. And all the other people like them. For some, technology is their life."

"But can't we use this fifth force to do things in different ways?" Wint argued. "As long as the end is the same, do the means matter?"

"That's the point!" The Radio exuded excitement, spinning its dials for emphasis. "We need to control the force so that we can use it to augment the technology we already have. If the other side controls it, they'll just mess things up."

Wint rolled his eyes at the Radio. "Well, I guess that's what I should expect from the manifestation of technology. I just thought we might be able to talk about a compromise. I don't see why magic and technology *can't* co-exist in some way. If they both agreed to do it."

The Radio went still for a moment, only the faint hiss of static in the background making any noise at all. "Oh, all right. If you must know, I am actually the Spirit of Loama, the planet itself. And I don't want a perpetual struggle between those two forces waging over my surface for the rest of time."

Silence greeted this revelation, until Wint frowned and put his hands on his hips. He glared down at the Radio. "Hang on a minute. All this time you've said you're the manifestation of technology."

"That's true. That's what you said," Rex confirmed, staring at the Radio with both ears alert.

"Well, I wanted you all to listen to me. You seemed so concerned with technology, I thought it would be a useful approach."

"Oh yes, always choose lying when you're out to gain people's trust," Skete said, rolling his eyes.

Wint was still looking at the Radio. "You lied? You're *not* the manifestation of technology? Then who is? And I thought the planet was called D'sharu."

The Radio made a little huffing sound, the sort of sound a teacher might make when no one in the class can recall the work they spent three hours going over the day before. "D'sharu is what *you people* choose to call me," it said in a condescending tone. "That doesn't mean it's my actual name. But of course, how would you know that? It's not like anyone ever asked."

The dog had cocked its head to one side, staring at the Radio with a strange intensity. "But if you're the *planet*, why are you so interested in seeing technology gain the upper hand? I mean, isn't technology slowly but inexorably polluting you? Doesn't technology use up your natural resources without replacing them? Wouldn't it be better for you in the long run if people used more natural forces to achieve what they want?"

The Radio was silent for a long time after that one. Rex and Wint exchanged looks. The dog shrugged as if to say, 'hey, no one told me not to ask that question.'

At last the Radio said, "Well, yes, that's right, but technology is just so...cool. I'm sure the whole pollution thing will work itself out in time. And I've got loads of resources, you know. Scads of them, just lying around, waiting around to be used. Magic just seems so—I don't know. Old-fashioned, I guess. I don't know if many of the other planets are really *doing* magic anymore."

No one said anything for a long time. Rex looked at Skete. Skete looked at Wint. No one looked at the Radio. The silence became decidedly uncomfortable. Wint was about to say something, anything, to end it, when a great roaring erupted all around the tower, the robot, and the clearing, as if something enormous and violent were rushing toward them through the woods. The entire Dingle shook, throwing them all to the stone floor, and screams from the followers outside filled the air.

Guests Behaving Badly

Heline

Heline was passing from the kitchen to the living room to check on the boys when Nerlim shouted, "Gammy!" She turned the other way down the hall and saw him standing with the door to her secret closet open, staring inside.

A momentary pang clutched her chest. The closet had been secret for so long that her instinctive reaction was to run and slam the door shut. But there was almost nothing in there anymore, nothing to hide. Most of the weird things that had lined the shelves when they didn't fit into the "real" world were now out in the open, part of her house and part of her life. And with everything else happening, explaining what was left was the least of her worries. She hurried down the hall anyway, but it was to help the older man.

"What's wrong?"

Nerlim looked pale in the light from the single bulb suspended from the closet ceiling, and he clutched his stomach with one hand. He turned a worried face to her. "Gammy's gone!"

Heline frowned. "I don't think she'd be in here, anyway. Maybe she went to the bathroom or something—"

"No!" He shook his head. "I was looking for her and I heard her voice behind this door. Then something hit me again—someone using magic. I opened the door just in time to see her fading out, and there was someone else—a weird, pale form, almost see-through—in there with her. She's gone!" he repeated, and his voice threatened to break.

"I'll get Xya. You go out to the living room and sit down," Heline told him.

In a moment they had all assembled in the living room, and Heline settled Nerlim on the sofa. Eleanor offered him a glass of water and he sipped it gratefully, colour returning to his cheeks. The others listened as Nerlim repeated his story.

[she is gone with a being named Corax] the Hat said.

Everyone startled. They hadn't been paying attention to it, sitting on a spindly side table where Heline had left it.

"Corax!" Xya huffed and threw up her hands. "Oh, for goodness' sake! I knew he was down here, but he's mixed up with all of you? That's all we need!"

"Who's Corax?" asked several voices at the same time.

Xya sighed and helped herself to a steaming cheese puff, a tray of which Jans had fetched from the kitchen. "A member of the Convocation with a god complex."

"What's a god complex?" many of the same voices demanded.

"What's a god?" asked a couple.

Xya frowned and stared at them. "Really? You don't know?"

Heline looked around the room. All the other D'sharian faces looked as blank as she felt. They all shook their heads.

"Well, I'm not going to touch that one. Let's say Corax is always on the lookout for a certain kind of power, and the right people to give it to him. And I suppose he thought he might find some here."

Nerlim shifted on the sofa. "But what does he want with Gammy?"

Xya shrugged and took another cheese puff. "Hard to say. Is she the type of person who ponders the big questions, like 'Why are we here?' and 'Where did we come from?'"

Heline glanced at the others. Everyone else still looked confused, too.

Nerlim frowned. "We all know where we came from and why we're here. Every schoolchild knows the answers to those questions."

Xya stared at him for a long moment, then looked around at the confirmation on all the other faces. She laughed. "Then Corax has no idea what he's stepped in on D'sharu. He must be trying to make a deal with Gammy. Maybe he's promised her something she wants. Doesn't realize yet that he's wasting his time. Oh, that's rich," she added, and laughed some more.

Heline could feel a smile frozen in place on her face, that smile you put on when a guest is exhibiting bizarre behaviour but it doesn't seem dangerous, so you've resigned yourself to put up with it for the sake of the party.

"But where would he have taken her?" Nerlim looked like he, too, was humouring Xya for the moment, but it could all come crashing down if he didn't soon get some reassurance about Gammy.

"That, I can't guess, but don't worry about her safety. Corax wouldn't harm a fly."

Xya seemed sure of herself on that point. Nerlim looked unconvinced but at a loss.

"So you think she'll come back on her own, or he'll bring her back?"

[she has also been contacted by a being named Sedrict] the Hat advised.

Xya paused with another cheese puff halfway to her mouth. "Sedrict, too? How do you know that?"

The Hat's drooping point twitched, as if it shrugged. [i was talking to her—well, communicating with her, shall we say—right before Corax arrived. she told him about Sedrict. he seemed almost afraid, which I understand, because I've sensed this Sedrict using some minor magics, and i don't like the feel of it]

"Well, that's all of them." Xya popped the cheese puff into her mouth and chewed with appreciation. "These are delicious, by the way," she told Jans, who beamed. She turned her attention back to Arcanico. "Do you have any idea what Sedrict is doing, or trying to do?"

The Hat twitched again. [i do not. i haven't been on this planet long enough to have learned all the past magic lore. you'd have to talk to the old magic about that. but I suspect this Sedrict is working for someone connected to that past]

Xya stilled when the Hat said this.

"Wait, there's more than one kind of magic?" Ulric asked, not noticing Xya's reaction. He'd listened to the conversation with quiet attention up until now, but this seemed like something he couldn't let pass. "Am I supposed to learn to use that, too? Because I'm having enough trouble with just one magic, thank you very much."

"I'll second that," Nerlim said, rubbing his stomach. "But I'm more worried about Gammy and why all these...people...are bothering her. What do they want? And how do we get her back?"

When Xya didn't respond to either of them, they both turned to look at her. Heline was about to ask her what was wrong when Xya asked, "You don't mean Alsina, do you? Because I know she's here too, and up to no good. Sedrict may be working *with* her, but it wouldn't be *for* her." There was a terrible hopefulness in her voice.

[no] the Hat said. [i have also noticed this Alsina person, however. she's no better than Sedrict if you ask me]

"Are they both working for this other individual? The one connected to the planet's past?"

[i believe so]

Xya closed her eyes and nodded as if that was the answer she'd been expecting. She opened her mouth to say something but was interrupted by a sudden rumbling that seemed to come from beneath the house and above it and on all sides at once. The little house trembled, stilled, then shook more violently.

"I have to make a call to someone, but there are more important things to worry about first," Xya said, just before the earthquake started in earnest.

We've Got a World to Save

Ulric

Eleanor grabbed Ulric's hand when the cottage trembled, and together they made a dive for the doorway to the hall. The others took similar action, scrambling under tables or bypassing them to crowd into other doorways.

"Does this happen often in this region?" Xya called out to no one in particular. She was the only one who hadn't moved much, choosing to slide into a nearby corner instead.

"Never," Heline confirmed from the kitchen doorway. "We're a long distance from an earthquake zone."

"Then it must be the worldweft." A black cat figurine toppled off a shelf near Xya's head and she deftly caught it. "Something's unbalanced it."

Nerlim piped up from beneath a narrow table under the window, an uncomfortable-looking spot where he'd crammed his lanky frame. "You used that word before, but you never explained what it is."

"The thaumic force?" Ulric asked. "Two magics being here? Is that what's messing things up?"

Xya's forehead puckered, and she shook her head. "I don't think so. That's causing ripples, but it would take more than that to cause an earthquake. The worldweft," she went on, "is the way the essence of events on a world—a planet—is woven together. If you're familiar with weaving terminology, you'll know there's warp and weft, the two types of threads that go together to make cloth?"

The others nodded their heads, some more hesitantly. Ulric was one of the hesitant ones, but he didn't want to seem ignorant.

Satisfied, Xya continued. "Warps are the vertical threads that the weaver measures out and puts on the loom first—in my analogy, imagine those as the foundation of the world. Then the wefts are the horizontal threads that cross over and under the warp threads during weaving—that is, events, people, anything that happens to or in the world. The worldweft becomes unbalanced when some of those threads...tangle, to simplify. That doesn't happen very often. The warp of a world is sturdy; it can hold lots of things—the arrival of magic, or the awakening of magic, or even both, wouldn't be enough to bother the worldweft. They're natural occurrences—or they should be. This is something different."

"Different in what way? Because of people like Corax and, well, you, being here?" Nerlim sounded apologetic, but it seemed the old man wasn't going to let this go until he understood it. Ulric was glad to have someone else asking questions for a change.

"I don't believe it's our presence," Xya mused after a moment of consideration. She hadn't moved from the wall where she'd caught the figurine and she didn't seem too worried about the earthquake. Ulric wondered if she had some kind of magical shield, although Nerlim hadn't given any indication of magic use. Still, it might be a good idea...words and concepts stirred in his mind as if willing to give it a try, but he put them aside for now. He wanted to protect Eleanor in particular, although he would rather have pulled out his tongue than articulated that. He had a feeling she might hit him.

"I've visited lots of worlds before; we all have, without this kind of result."

Eleanor had slid down to sit with her back braced against the doorframe. "So you're saying someone else has been mucking around down here, throwing the planet out of whack?"

Xya gave a slow nod. "I feel like someone is interfering in something—maybe the decision between technology and magic. Not leaving it up to you, Ulric, and the other Avatar to work things out."

"But who is it?"

Xya looked uncertain, as if questioning how much she should share. "I shouldn't say too much until I check in with my...boss," she said, chewing delicately on her bottom lip. "But there's been a lot of interest in D'sharu since the thaumic force activated. When a force is new and untapped like this on a world, with no clear master—anyone tapping into it stands to gain a great deal. They've been warned against it, but where power is concerned, people don't always listen."

"What people?" Ulric still felt confused, floundering out of his depth. "Almost no one here even knows about magic, or understands what's happening. They might be able to sense it, like Mr. Nerlim, but not use it in any useful way."

Again, she didn't answer him right away. After a thoughtful pause, she sighed. "We call it the Convocation. You'll learn about it soon enough, anyway. They're...the ones who can wield magic most efficiently. And they're overseen by The Administrator, the one who sent me down here to help you out."

She still seemed to Ulric to be hedging. Like when Mattie Allegra had given him all the reasons she was dumping him. Only they weren't the actual reasons, and he could read that in everything about her; words, face, the way she stood. It was the same now with Xya. He had a flash of insight.

"You're one of them, aren't you? One of this Convocation?"

Xya nodded. "And another member was sent to help the Technocrat Avatar, to keep things fair."

"Help us? Or steal some power for yourselves?" He looked around the room at the others. Were they all following their own agendas? No, not Heline, he thought, seeing her face. The empowerment she'd sent his way with her songs—that was true.

"No, Ulric." Xya looked stricken as she answered, her voice quiet and serious. "I promise, I'm here to help you. And no one else here is part of the Convocation."

Ulric sighed. He didn't see that he had much choice but to believe her, at least for now. She was the only one who seemed to know what was going on. "Okay, so what do we do now?"

"If you want my opinion, we'd better find the Technocrat Avatar as soon as possible." Xya flinched this time as the house shook again, and a framed photograph slid down the wall. It hit the floor with a tinkling crash. "We might settle the worldweft if one of you were in control."

"One of us?"

"I'm hoping it will be you," Xya said, then muttered, "but either might be an improvement over this."

Eleanor turned and addressed Xya. "I have a question. Do you know who this Technocrat Avatar is?"

"Not really; I know some basics about him, that's all."

"Okay, then here's another one: why are both these Avatars male? What kind of sexist garbage is going on here?"

"Oh, that's easy." Xya grinned. "Manifestations almost always choose males, because they're easier to manipulate."

Eleanor raised her eyebrows, pondering this answer. "Huh. That makes a surprising amount of sense."

"Hey," Ulric protested, "I'm standing right here."

"What about the other person?" Eleanor asked, ignoring him. "The one who's interfering, causing the problem with this worldweft. Is anyone doing anything to stop them?"

"That's why I need to make a call," Xya said. "I can't do anything about the worldweft, but maybe The Min can. If she knows what's going on."

Jans said from the doorway he shared with Heline, "So we are need to finding this guy, the Technocratic Abattoir. But how are we about to be doing it?"

"I think that's one for you to answer," Nerlim said, nodding to Xya. "Unless Ulric has some special ability as the other Avatar to do it."

Heline darted past Ulric and Eleanor, ignoring Jans' yelp of alarm, and snatched up the Hat, slipping it onto her head. "I'll be ready when we do," she promised, throwing Ulric a supportive look as she dashed back to the doorway. She fished a notebook out of her pocket and began scribbling madly in it.

"And what about Gameldina?" Nerlim asked from underneath the table. He rapped his bony knuckles on the floor for emphasis. "We have to find her, too!"

"We will," Ulric said, and his voice sounded calmer than he would have expected. It was all coming together for him at that moment. He just had to take it one step at a time. These people were his friends, and they were willing to help him. In turn, he would help them. He would stop the Technocrat Avatar, and he—or the mysterious Min—would stop whatever was happening to D'sharu, and everything would be all right.

"Ulric!" Tiny Enos yelled. He'd hunkered in another corner of the room, not willing to even try to fit under an end table. He held his cell phone out and waggled it at Ulric. "You'll never guess what! I just got a text from Eiric. He said Natelie, called him, because Darby texted her—you know, the president of the tech club at school? He says there's a bunch of people up at the Dingle, and they're trying to build a giant robot!"

Well, that figured, Ulric thought. Eiric and the others hadn't been seen since this whole mess started, and now here they were with inside information. About a place with a giant robot, of course. Trust Eiric and Natelie not to miss anything with a tech connection. Ulric felt a pang of doubt, though. Did this mean he'd have to fight against his friends? He was magic, and they'd definitely land on the side of technology. He hadn't counted on that, and he didn't like it. Still, that must be where they had to go.

"Are they there? Eiric and Natelie?"

Enos shook his head. "Naw, Nat's sick and Eiric's in trouble with his Ma, so she's got him doing chores with no end in sight. He thought we'd want to know, though."

Ulric felt a flood of relief at this one small bright spot and raised his eyebrows at Xya. "I think we know where to find the Technocrat Avatar. Should we try to transport there?"

She frowned again and shook her head. "It's not safe, and likely not very accurate, if the worldweft is in flux. We'd better find another way."

"We can taking my car," Jans offered, but Heline looked up from her notebook.

"No, it's still at Ulric's house, remember? We were just talking about that."

Jans looked as if he were assessing the group and checking them off in his mind. Too old to drive, too young to drive, not from this world and probably can't drive... "We'll having to go get it," he concluded.

But Heline looked thoughtful. "Maybe not. I brought one of the vans home from work the other day to clean it. There aren't a lot of seats in the back, but we'd all fit, at least."

Nerlim frowned. "Not a lot of seats? Where do you work?"

"At the humane society," Heline said with a smile. "It's mostly cages in the back, but some of us can sit on the floor."

"I call shotgun for the front seat." Nerlim was quicker on the uptake than Ulric might have expected. "These old bones are not up to getting shaken around on the floor of a dog catcher's van."

Jans looked concerned at the notion that Nerlim might ride next to him armed with a shotgun, but Heline hurried to explain the saying. Eleanor looked at Ulric and whispered, "Heline, always the perfect employee. See what I mean?" But there was no malice in her voice.

It wasn't the way he might have envisioned going into battle, but Ulric figured it was better than trying to transport and ending up in the middle of the ocean...or a mountain.

"Then let's go," Ulric said. "We've got a world to save."

Is That You, Gammy?

Wint

"What is happening?" Wint yelled, fingers scrabbling at the trembling floor of the Dingle tower. There wasn't much in the way of handholds on the smooth stone, and Wint was having no luck digging any with his bare fingers. He managed to clutch a narrow gap caused by the shifting earth. The sound of stone grinding against stone sounded like the terrifying dry cough of some giant monster.

"Everything is shaking!" the Radio yelled back.

"No kidding," muttered Rex, who was huddled against the stone wall for support. He'd scrabbled on awkward legs across the shuddering stone floor to get there, nails skittering on the unstable stone. "You know, no-one ever wonders what animals do in situations like this. I mean, sure, we have four legs, but not those opposable thumbs you guys are always going on about. Think about what that means. We can't grab hold of anything for support—"

"Not now!" Wint shouted, and Rex snapped his muzzle shut, looking as affronted as a wet cat. Wint looked at Skete in desperation. "Skete?"

Skete had moved well away from the walls and also lay prone near Wint. "I don't know for sure, but this might be bad."

Wint stared at him for a long moment. "Gee. Do you think so?"

"I mean, it could be an indication that the thaumic forces—or something else—have created an imbalance in the worldweft."

Wint considered asking what the worldweft was, but thought better of it. It couldn't matter at this point whether he understood everything or nothing. Instead, he changed his question to one that seemed more immediate. "What can we do to fix it?"

Skete shook his head, almost banging it on the stone floor. "It might not calm down while the magic versus technology question is up in the air."

"Which means meeting up with the other Avatar?"

"That's right. But I'm only guessing. Something else could be causing it." Skete gave the Radio a pointed stare.

"What? Are you doing this?" Wint demanded, his tone menacing. It was difficult to feel menacing when you were lying flat on your belly atop a stone tower in the middle of an earthquake, but he put all his frustration and desperation into the question. One more scrap of provocation might be all it would take, and he'd toss that Radio over the edge of the tower. It had brought him nothing but trouble, and he didn't appreciate the way it talked to him at all. Of course, he'd have to make it to his feet first and not fall over the parapet himself, but that was beside the point. If it was causing this uproar to bully him...

Lacking any appendages with which to secure itself, the Radio jittered across the stone floor, its electrical cord snaking behind it like some weird overgrown tail. "Of course...I'm not...doing it!" it stuttered. "Does this...look like...I'm responsible?"

"Well, you are the manifestation of the planet, among other things, or so you said," Wint pressed. "If you aren't doing it, can you make it stop?"

"No." The Radio sounded annoyed. "Just because I'm the manifestation of the planet doesn't mean I can control the physical aspects of the planet. I can't influence the worldweft."

"Why not?"

"Can you control what your large intestine does?"

"Oh." Wint had to admit it weirdly made sense.

Proving in Wint's mind once again that the world was out to get him, it started to rain. Fat, wet plops splattered on the parapets, the stone rooftop where they lay, the Radio, and the well-shaken bodies of Wint, Skete, and Rex. It was a cold rain, and Wint shivered as a malicious drop hit the back of his neck and rolled down inside his shirt. He was about to suggest they try to make it to the stairs and head inside, out of the rain in search of safer ground, when two figures materialized near the centre of the roof. Well, one figure appeared. The other one seemed to half appear and then get stuck that way, translucent in the moonlight.

The one that had materialized in full was a short, tidy figure of a woman with a wild mop of greying hair. Her attire was incongruous for apparating atop towers in the rain; a black pantsuit and brightly patterned poncho-type thing.[1] The legs of the pantsuit were dust-streaked, and the poncho hung somewhat askew. It looked like she'd been ready for a night out that went horribly wrong, and Wint felt a flash of empathy for the unknown woman. That was his only fleeting impression of her before he became engrossed in the pair's ongoing altercation.

"—kill you!" the short woman screamed, as if the first part of the sentence had happened in another place. She took a wild swing with a clenched fist at the other figure. Studying the tableau, Wint noted that the translucent figure floated a few inches above the still-trembling stone of the tower. A section of wall and Rex's haunches were visible right through it. It was a discomfiting sensation, looking through a person. Then the woman's fist passed through the figure without even causing it to ripple, and that was even weirder.

"Calm down, dear lady—" the apparition began.

She cut him off. "I will not calm down. I'm perfectly calm! Where have you taken me?" She looked around the still shuddering tower, now darkening under the steady beat of the rain.

The apparition also looked around. "Well, not where I'd intended, I'll grant you that. Whatever disturbance is happening took us off course. I honestly don't know where we are." He sounded quite disgruntled and Wint couldn't blame him. Why did anyone want to control this fifth force if it was so unreliable?

Wint squinted. The woman's features weren't clear from this vantage point, but he had the oddest impression that he recognized her voice.

Her gaze came to rest on Wint and he realized—perhaps the single most terrible realization in what seemed like days and days of terrible

---

1. Although who could say what the appropriate attire for such an activity might be? Certainly not Wint.

realizations—that it was Gammy. His boss. *His boss.* The indomitable, merciless mistress of mission control at NCDSF. Here. Here, where Wint had no idea what was happening and yet was somehow supposed to be in charge. Wint put his cheek against the chill stone and tried to blend in with the stone floor. He didn't feel quite confident about the result.

"Where am I and who are you?" she demanded. "And why are you lying on the floor?" The woman appeared too angry to notice the earthquake, or perhaps her lower centre of gravity allowed her to keep her balance more easily than most.

"Don't talk to him like that, you ancient cow!" the Radio shouted. "That's the Technocrat Avatar! He's about to master the use of magic in this world!"

Wint tried even harder to sink into the floor. If he could turn a teaspoon into a key, was there a chance he might turn solid stone into mud, or quicksand? He wouldn't look up at her, he told himself, and she wouldn't recognize him. He wouldn't, he wouldn't.

Rage almost making the rain steam where it landed on her, Gammy crossed the still-shaking tower to where Wint lay and stood staring down at him for a long moment. The tips of her shoes stopped mere inches from his face, where they skidded a bit on the unsteady stone. She still ignored the earthquake with equanimity, all her emotions centred elsewhere. "Really? This is the Technocrat Avatar? Huh. Then I don't know what all the fuss is about."

"What?"

"I said, I don't know what all the fuss is about. He doesn't look like much of a threat. I could kick him in the face right now if I wanted to. I could step on his fingers and break them, or—"

"You wouldn't dare," said the Radio with a hiss of static.

{GET UP}

Wint flinched. That was the voice of the Radio, speaking to Wint now from inside his head. For all he suspected the manifestation of the planet D'sharu was quite, quite mad, its voice was impossible to ignore.

The Dingle's shaking had slowed to an intermittent tremble, and the structure hadn't collapsed—at least not yet. In an agony of dread, Wint followed the radio's command and began to clamber to his feet with great reluctance. The diminutive woman, with a complete change of demeanour, offered a hand to help him up.

"I wouldn't have kicked you or stepped on your fingers," she told him in a low voice. "Whoever's broadcasting through that contraption just pissed me off."

Wint had no desire to correct Gammy's assumption about the Radio, but it seemed rude not to take the proffered hand. Wint did so, but he was slow to lift his head and reveal his identity. He knew it was inevitable, but he'd delay that moment as long as he could. Maybe fate would be kind and the tower *would* collapse before he had to face her.

"Well, isn't that what I've been trying to tell you?" the semi-transparent apparition said in a fretful tone, floating over to where they stood. "The Technocrat Avatar can't help you."

Skete said, "Corax?" in a voice that was both accusing and amused.

The apparition gave such a violent jerk at the sound of its name that its edges blurred. It squeaked, "Skete! Skete? Oh, chicken on a stick," and whipped its head around, searching the rooftop intently. "You—is it just you here?"

"Well, I'm hardly alone, as you can see, but The Min isn't here, if that's what you mean," Skete told him, scrambling to his feet as well. "But you can be sure she's going to hear about all of this, if she doesn't know already. Especially that you've been here long enough to have picked up the local swearing conventions."

Wint looked up and met Gammy's eyes. Rain pooled in her hair and ran out through the curls in tiny rivulets and miniature waterfalls, further soaking the now-bedraggled poncho. She looked like a ferret still, but now a rabid and wet ferret with wild eyes. It was an unnerving sight. Wint had seen Gammy in many stressful and even dangerous situations before, but she'd never looked like this. Never. A chill that had nothing to do with the rain penetrated deep into his bones. The hand still holding his suddenly clutched painfully tight.

"Usborne? Wint Usborne?" Her voice was high and thin with disbelief. "Wint?"

It was the first time Wint had ever heard Gammy sound surprised.

"Yes, it's me, Chief," Wint said in a voice thick with misery.

"What are you—how—"

Wint shrugged. "I have no idea. About any of it. Ask anything you want; I can almost guarantee I won't know the answer."

Gammy stared into his eyes, the most intense stare he'd ever endured. Back at mission control, he'd never done anything to provoke a stare like this. Most people at NCDSF spent the greater part of their working lives trying to avoid such a thing. She pulled in a deep breath and spoke.

"Do you know how to use the fifth force to make the launch work?"

"No." That question didn't need any thought at all.

"Sure," said the Radio.

"What are you playing at, Corax?" Skete demanded. "The Min is NOT going to like this, you know."

"I think I'm the least of The Min's worries at the moment," Corax said, smugness creeping into his tone. "Do you suppose I intended to come here? No, sir, I did not. Something interfered with my teleport, even though I had a boatload of residual magic backing it up."

"What do you mean?"

Corax gestured around at the trembling tower. "It's the worldweft. It's cracking under the pressure."

"Shut up!" Gammy yelled, dropping Wint's hand at last. "I want to hear what the Radio has to say." She stopped, staring at the radio's power cord, connected to nothing. She turned back to Wint. "Did that Radio talk? I mean, by itself? Not broadcasting from somewhere else?"

"Unfortunately, yes."

"By itself."

"Yup."

"Okay, then." Gammy took a deep breath and looked around the top of the stone tower. Wint gave silent thanks to the universe that she was too short to see over the parapets down to the half-finished robot, glistening in the rain nearby. "Can we get out of the rain?"

Before Wint could answer that yes, he'd been about to suggest the very same thing, both of their cell phones erupted with sound. Wint's rang like an old-fashioned telephone, jangling into the darkness. Gammy's phone sounded like a siren, with that particular notification set to full volume so there was no way she'd ever miss it if it came.

Wint had his phone in his hand first, as Gammy fumbled around in the voluminous cross-body bag she wore and finally produced hers. She stared at the screen for a long moment, as if trying to convince herself of the truth of what she was seeing. She looked up to meet Wint's eyes, and he saw the same worry and confusion that he felt reflected in hers. He was sure she'd never expected—any more than he had—to see that particular message.

Someone had tripped the alarms at NCDSF.

Intermezzo Sei

The Min

The Min hadn't thought about Majszak in a long time. A troublemaker through and through, but a charismatic one who could charm and cajole; the weak-minded fell under his spell with frightening ease. Even before The Min had been The Min, and was just another member of the Convocation, he'd been stirring the pot, fomenting conflict, and being a general pain in everyone's trans-dimensional ass.

The Min's predecessor in the position had overseen his Exile. The Min had been one of the Convocation members to lend her magic to his imprisonment, though. His own ability was strong and he hadn't gone gently into his Exile, and she didn't relish another encounter with him.

But if he was causing problems, she'd have no choice.

First, though, she had to investigate whether he was the culprit behind all this. The involvement of Alsina and Sedrict pointed in that direction, because they'd been his sycophants before his Exile and had argued his innocence. They were in the minority, however, and had been overruled by a landslide. More than enough Convocation members were willing to work the binding without them.

The Min got up from her desk and moved toward one of the enormous banks of books, surveying them as she went. The job demanded intense record-keeping, and it all had to be done in volumes on these shelves—no technological shortcuts. Because technology might fail, and this documentation couldn't be risked—the fate of worlds could depend on it. She walked along several shelves, counting, trailing the tips of her fingers along the rich leather bindings. The books seemed to respond to her touch, some of them almost purring like cats. When she reached the correct spot, she paused, and with a flick of her wrist summoned one of the volumes forth. It flew into her hand along with a handful of random pages from elsewhere on the shelves. The Min gestured to them to return to their spots, and they floated back with grudging acceptance.

The retrieved volume she took with her back to the desk and opened the pages, seating herself again to flip through. When she found the transcript of Majszak's trial and sentencing, she laid a finger on his name and twisted her other hand in an arcane gesture. From here and there along the shelves, other books left their appointed places and floated toward her. Any book containing Majszak's name answered the summons. When the parade of books settled, a haphazard stack of about twenty littered the desk.

The Min conjured a cozy reading lamp, a mug of expertly brewed coffee with cream and sugar, and a notebook and pen. She asked the books to arrange themselves in chronological order, and they complied. The volumes dating from before Majszak's exile she set aside for now; she knew the general outlines of the history laid out in them, and she could refresh herself on the details later if necessary. No, she was interested in the entries made since his Exile. In truth, for an Exile, there should have been none, so his mention in three volumes was both concerning and intriguing.

The entry in the first book turned out to be less than interesting—an application by Majszak for a visitation from Sedrict, which request had been denied. All right, that was normal. Any visit would demand strict supervision, and if no one qualified was free to do so, that would be the end of that.

The entry in the second book made The Min stop and stare at the page. It recorded a request for a prisoner transfer, which had been approved.

The Min read with mounting alarm that Majszak had almost been transferred to D'sharu, but the transfer was cancelled at the last minute. The Min felt a wave of shock that this had missed her notice, but to be fair to herself, she was responsible for the oversight of many, many worlds and many, many individuals. A huge administrative staff helped with the paperwork and record-keeping, and she trusted them. The transfer request and the cancellation were unsigned, which was a breach of protocol but sometimes happened as an honest mistake. Considering the high profile of this Exile, however, she had serious doubts that was the case here.

The oddest entry came at the end. It recorded the approval of a long-distance conversation between Majszak and Alsina, noted as concerning advice for a spell. Alsina had put in the request and it had been approved, and the virtual meeting took place. All was above board and documented, although The Min noted with a furrowed brow that once again the documentation was not signed. Only the request submitted by Alsina bore her name, but not the approval.

The Min closed the book and steepled her fingers. It added up to too many oversights, too few details, and too many things that had slipped past her. Far too much activity around an Exile who was supposed to be—well, exiled. Things pointed in a very worrisome direction, and although what lay in that direction remained cloudy, a theory bubbled in The Min's formidable mind.

There was a move afoot to have Majszak set free from his planet of exile, and events on D'sharu were part of the picture.

The Min looked at the other stack of books, the ones predating Majszak's exile, and wondered what they might be able to tell her. With a sigh, she reached out and pulled one off the pile.

She was still tracing through the earlier timeline of Majszak's exploits later, when her "phone" rang again. It was Xya.

"It's me again, sorry to bother you," she said, and The Min heard a tinkling crash in the background, as of breaking glass. Instead of a hologram of Xya, she saw only a shadowy shape that might have been Xya's face.

"What's happening? Where are you?" The Min demanded.

"We're at Heline's house—she's a dencrypter working with the Thaumaturge Avatar—and there's an earthquake." Xya sounded less in command of herself and her situation than The Min expected. "We're going to confront the Technocrat Avatar and the rumour is he's got a giant robot now, but that's not the important thing."

The Min blinked at this concise flood of information. "Go on."

"I think Sedrict and Alsina are trying to free an Exile," Xya said in a rush. "Maybe that sounds crazy, but—"

"I know."

Xya stopped dead at the interruption. The rumble of a vehicle engine starting up somewhere very close came over the connection.

"You know?"

"Are you in a garage?"

"Yes, we're all going in a van that's usually used for transporting stray animals." Xya's face came into better focus as she leaned in to whisper, "It's—not going to be very comfortable. But you know about the Exile?"

"Yes; I think it's Majszak. I've been going through old records and I suspect he's the one who activated the magic on the planet long ago and then shut it down and covered up the transgression. There are some very suspicious and vague entries in the documentation that look like a cover-up to me. That must be who Sedrict and Alsina are trying to free, because if they could get him to D'sharu, and the old magic remembered him, he'd have a tremendous advantage in convincing the new magic to support him as well."

"With Sedrict and Alsina as his advisors," Xya said in disgust. "They'd be sitting pretty, too."

"And if the magic accepts him, there's not much even I can do about it," The Min said, "Exile or not. The magic will have the final say. Unless I break rules, too. And that doesn't set a good example."

"Or unless technology gains ascendancy on this world," Xya said. "Which I don't think is looking likely even if no one was trying to influence the outcome." In the background, something groaned and crashed, and the wail of distant sirens growing closer filled the air.

"It doesn't sound safe there." The Min squinted, trying to see Xya and her surroundings more clearly. "Is the Thaumaturge Avatar with you? Are you going somewhere better?"

"We're all going to the Dingle," Xya said. "I don't know if that's better or—zzzzzzzzt."

A sharp buzzing drowned out Xya's words, and then the connection died. The Min stared at the place where a hologram should have been. She thought, *what in the worlds is a Dingle?*

But that question quickly gave way to concern. The worldweft must be in dire shape to affect The Min's connection. It might even impact the use of other magics on the planet and between the realms, and she hadn't had a chance to warn Xya about that possibility. She drummed her fingers on the desk. She couldn't be out of touch with Xya and Skete, now of all times; and she didn't want her people stranded down there.

A flick of her wrist and a thought sent the volumes she'd been consulting scuttling and gliding from her desk back to their appointed spaces on the shelves. She'd learned enough for now, and it left her with a knot of sick worry in her chest. All around The Min's office, the books shifted and whispered, picking up on her anxiety, and the stars in her hair flickered their concern. She set about trying to re-establish the connection, but only static answered her every attempt.

With the worldweft blocking her, D'sharu was out of her reach, for now at least. She'd have to see what more she could discover here.

Meeting the Technocrat Avatar

Gammy

Wint and Gammy stood dripping in the ground floor area of the Dingle. Corax hovered nearby, looking both peevish and bored, and the others had trooped down the stairs with them, too. Wint and Gammy both had their phones out. Gammy spoke to Argit on the other end of hers, demanding an explanation for the alarm. It had taken her five tries to get a call through to him, during which time she'd also tried to call Nerlim to let him know she was safe, without success. Bursts of static or weirdly charged dead air met her every attempt, but at last she'd reached Argit.

"Those alarms don't just go off on their own," she explained for what seemed like the fifth time. Argit was one hundred percent dependable and never gave her cause for doubt, but she couldn't make him understand about this. "And I had someone making suspicious inquiries about NCDSF recently. I don't like it—it's too much of a coincidence."

Over the phone, Argit sounded tired, but patient. "I understand that, but I had Security check three times. They can't find anyone on the premises who shouldn't be there."

Gammy chewed her bottom lip in frustration. How could she explain to Argit that it was quite possible—even probable—that the person she was most worried about would be—invisible?

She forced her voice to stay calm, even though her nerves screamed at her. "And I understand that. But I've also discovered that this person I'm worried about can be...tricky. I want you to go to the site yourself, Argit, and make sure with your own eyes that none of the equipment is being tampered with. Don't look for people. Check the equipment. Nothing switched on that shouldn't be on. No settings changed. No lights blinking when they shouldn't be. No alignments re-aligned. This might be very subtle tampering, do you hear me?"

"Understood. I'll go straight there." For the first time in Gammy's experience, a note of doubt shaded Argit's voice when he answered her. Well, what she was saying sounded strange and impossible; she accepted that. But she was still in flarking charge. If that Sedrict person thought he could trespass on her facility and use her equipment without her permission, he would have to think again.

"I'm sorry to ask you this," Gammy heard herself say, realizing with horror that she sounded apologetic. "I'd go myself, but I'm—" she glanced around the dark, dank interior of the tower. "I'm in a bit of a tight spot myself, and I can't get to NCDSF in a hurry. I'll make it up to you."

"Of—of course. Thank you."

Flarking rot, she'd made it even worse by being nice. Now Argit would think she had lost it completely; she heard it in his voice. Damn Nerlim anyway, she thought, the sentiment both illogical and fierce. She always got nicer when he was around; she couldn't seem to help herself. It was flarking annoying.

When she ended the call with Argit, she turned back to Wint Usborne. He held his phone, too, but the screen was dark. All he'd done was turn off the alarm notification and stood waiting for her to finish her call.

He looked cold and miserable—possibly even more cold and miserable than she was, and that was saying something. She opened her mouth, but he spoke first.

"I suppose I'm fired, but I want to reiterate that none of this is my fault." He wasn't defiant, just matter-of-fact and worn out.

"Well, I didn't say it was," Gammy said, somewhat taken aback. This was so unlike the Wint she was acquainted with, she wasn't sure how to talk to him.

"You were thinking it—or at least wondering. It's pretty obvious."

"All right, I admit I wondered. But listen, Wint, tell me what you're doing here." Gammy made her voice kind, as if she were talking to a child. When he didn't answer right away, she tried to help. "You say you're the Technocrat Avatar?"

"I don't say it; let's be clear on that. Other people—and things," he added with a dark look at the Radio, "say I am. Apparently I'm supposed to defeat the Thaumaturge Avatar, take control of the force of magic on D'sharu, and subjugate it to technology."

"Well, the moon mission would qualify as technology, wouldn't it?" Gammy said in a cheerful voice. "It sounds to me like if you're successful, you'd be able to make sure the launch happens. That would be a good thing, wouldn't it? We've all worked so hard to make that happen."

Wint looked into Gammy's eyes, so intense, so searching, that she blinked. When he spoke, she knew it came from the depths of his soul. He spoke with careful deliberation, as if trying to infuse each word with meaning so that she would understand. "I. Don't. Know. How. To. Defeat. Him. I. Don't. Know. How. To. Do. Anything."

"Told you so," Corax said in a sing-song voice from a niche at the bottom of the stairs. Gammy ignored him.

She looked back into Wint's eyes for a minute. He flinched a little, as if afraid she would try to convince him he was wrong. But then she nodded. "Oh."

"Yeah."

"Neemar, we have a problem," Gammy joked.

Wint didn't answer. It seemed he didn't have anything more to say.

The stone floor trembled again, and the walls seemed to groan. Gammy glanced around, her pulse jumping. "Is it safe in here?"

"I sincerely doubt it," Wint muttered.

"Maybe we should get out of this place altogether. I'd like to help you figure out a way to fix all of this."

Wint spread his arms wide. "Be my guest. You'll want to talk to the dog, the Radio, and that guy on the stairs. His name's Skete. I'm sure among the three of them they can bring you up to speed."

"Whoa!" Skete yelped just then. He ducked and clutched his head with his arms as if to protect it. He'd been leaning against the wall halfway up the stairs, stolidly ignoring Corax, who was waiting for Gammy and studiously ignoring Skete. Something flew down from the opening in the tower above and shot past Skete's head, breaking the standoff.

"Is it a bat?" Gammy shrieked, ducking as Skeet had done and trying to cover her hair with her hands. She knew it was a myth that bats would become entangled in people's hair, but still...

"No," Wint said, unmoved. "I'm betting it's much worse."

Gammy saw with relief that the intruder was only a pigeon, which landed near Wint's feet and looked up at him.

"Technocrat Avatar?" the pigeon asked in exactly the voice one might expect from a pigeon. Gammy had never given it any thought, but she wasn't at all surprised.[1]

"Great, a magic pigeon," Wint said in a long-suffering voice. "As I suspected, much worse. Yes?"

"The Majickal Creatures of D'sharu have decided," the pigeon intoned in what passed, apparently, as a serious voice for a pigeon, "To support the Thaumaturge Avatar in the coming confrontation."

"Hey, you're back early," Skete protested. "The unicorn said you'd give him until sundown."

The pigeon gave what could only be described as a shrug, although pigeons moved with a perpetual shrug, it seemed to Gammy. "Sorry. I'm just the messenger."

"Well, you didn't give me a lot of time to consider, but honestly, no surprise there." For the first time since Gammy had spoken with him tonight, Wint sounded brisk and efficient, as if here was a thing he could handle. When the pigeon made no move to leave, he added, "Fine. I get it. You're not with me, you're with him. You can go now."

"Don't you even want to know why?" the pigeon asked, cocking its head to one side.

"Not really."

"Er, okay, then." The pigeon said appeared somewhat taken aback, as if it had been prepared for a much more fraught interaction. "I guess I'll just be going back?"

"Good."

---

1. To be clear, she did find the idea of a talking pigeon surprising, but not its voice. Which was rather comforting, because almost everything was surprising these days.

Without another word, only another eloquent shrug, the pigeon took flight and skimmed past Skete's head again, ascending, presumably, to the top of the tower and back to report to the other creatures.

Wint smiled at Gammy. The smile had a hint of the manic about it, but it improved on his defeated expression from moments before. "You know, it's weird, but that was the best encounter I've had in days."

"Well, that's a sad commentary, but if you feel good about it, who am I to argue? Now, do you think we can get out of here?" Gammy asked again. "Maybe to somewhere a little less damp?"

"This whole tower is nothing but stone, moss, and damp, but I expect someone would let us use one of the tents outside. Knowing this bunch, someone might even have a heater, if they didn't sacrifice it to the robot."

Gammy stared at him. "If they didn't what?"

Wint felt a wave of that sickening foot-in-mouth sensation crash over him, but it was too late to backtrack. "Oh, er, well, there's a giant robot under construction out there, too. A lot of the gadgets and electronics people had here went into creating it. But it won't hurt you," he hastened to assure her. "No need for alarm."

Gammy did something then that she'd never done before. She reached up and laid a hand on Wint's shoulder, patting it with gentle reassurance. "After the week I've had," she said, "I don't know what it would take to alarm me anymore."

Let's Have a Confrontation

Ulric

Ulric and the others hadn't counted on the traffic. They'd piled out of the little house into the dark, rainy night and the humane society's van, pausing for only a few moments before leaving the house to equip themselves. There was no planning; no discussion. No one could predict what they might encounter. Everyone followed their instincts and did what felt right.

Ulric had changed into the robe Tiny Enos had sewn for him, and set his star-dotted hat atop his head. A slight frisson of energy down his back told him it was correct. It felt right, like what he'd been born to wear. Heline reached up to a high shelf in her kitchen and handed him down a stick. Ulric turned it over in his hands—about a foot long, straight-ish but with a few interesting twists, stripped of its bark and polished to a smooth shine with oil or wax. The tapered tip was painted metallic gold. The stick tingled in his fingers and he looked up and met Heline's eyes.

"The word *wand* popped into my head when I first touched it. I thought it was for me," she said, "but I didn't understand how to use it. Now, I think it's supposed to be yours."

He nodded in understanding and gave the stick—the wand—a few experimental flourishes. Nothing happened, but that was all right; he hadn't wanted anything to. "Thank you. I think it's perfect."

Heline held up her notebook and tapped the cover. "This is my part. I'll do the best I can. And I'll bring the Hat, of course."

"I know you will." Ulric gave her a quick, diffident hug. He wouldn't have done that a few days ago; hug a beautiful woman ten years older than he was without embarrassment. The arrival of the magic had changed him; he hoped for the better.

Jans hunted all over the house for a weapon and settled on the baseball bat Heline kept stowed under the bed. He hefted the bat in one hand and in both, weighing and measuring, taking a swing the way Ulric had tested the wand. He caught Ulric's eye and grinned. "If magic is failing, is good to having a plan of backup, isn't?"

"You bet," Ulric said, promising himself that if they came through the looming confrontation unscathed, he would help Jans with his grammar.

Tiny Enos tucked the Creature Concordance under one arm. Nerlim, still preoccupied and glum from Gammy's disappearance, wandered the kitchen stuffing food into his pockets. Eleanor took her guitar and stashed a packet of granola bars in the guitar case. And Xya seemed quite content to go just as she was.

They went. Ulric saw Heline lock the door after them and pocket the key. That was a good sign; she intended to come back.

In the humane society's van, Jans and Nerlim climbed into the front, and Xya insisted she could also squeeze onto the front bench seat. She'd looked into the back and shook her head. "I won't do it."

Which left Ulric, Tiny Enos, Heline, and Eleanor to sit in the back, although they weren't relegated to the floor. Instead, they perched on crates intended for canine, feline, and any other genus of passengers the society's drivers might collect in the run of a day. A sliding panel in the divider between the front and the cargo area stood open so conversation could flow back and forth. The Hat balanced on Heline's lap. Wearing it might have been simpler, but she whispered to Ulric that she didn't want the distraction of new words just then.

After a great start, though, the traffic pulled them up short. Aftershocks from the earthquake still trembled the ground at intervals, and little piles of rubble littered the streets. Buildings had collapsed or stood in partial ruin. In some places, the roadway had heaved and buckled, making passage impossible and circumventing it time-consuming. And everywhere people were trying to get to somewhere else.

Nerlim grunted in the front seat. "Ugh! I wish you folks would at least warn me when you're going to use magic!"

Ulric and Heline glanced at each other, and Xya turned to look at him. "It wasn't me," they all said in unison.

Nerlim dropped his head into his hands and hunched over, his voice muffled. "Well, someone's doing something, and it's driving me crazy. Being a sensile isn't at all easy!"

Ulric thought the older man must be building some resistance, though, because he rallied and straightened in the seat. Then again, maybe the magic being used wasn't very strong.

Xya peered out through the rain-streaked window of the car. "I expect more people are discovering their powers and accessing them. Without training or supervision, that could be dangerous. They'll cause random effects without understanding their abilities or how the outcomes might be wildly different from what they intend."

Ulric rolled his eyes. "And, let me guess, all will be made right once one of the Avatars is in control."

She glanced back at him with a frown. "No," she said, "Not really. This is just something that people will have to work out for themselves. Once an Avatar is in control, that will help, but things will be pretty weird on D'sharu for a while. Even if we figure out a way to get the worldweft under control and Sedrict's antics don't doom everyone."

"Great," said Tiny Enos, which summed up what Ulric was thinking.

The evidence of Xya's deductions became more and more noticeable as they drove, however. Once they passed a surprised-looking stray dog with what looked like bird's wings protruding from its back. One man on the sidewalk had shed his clothes and appeared to be covered instead with slick dark feathers, the rain beading and rolling off them into the puddles at his feet. He seemed quite happy with the alterations, or else he'd gone mad because of them. A stoplight at one intersection sprouted red, yellow and green flowers where the lights had once been. They glowed on cue just the same, and the traffic kept flowing.

And so they crept through the rain-drenched, magic-scattered city and made their slow, agonizing way to the outskirts. Jans seemed close to an episode of road rage by the time the traffic thinned out.

"Getting out of the way," he would alternately mutter or roar, depending on his state of mind. "You are not know how much importance is getting through for us!"

Ulric wondered how much extra frustration must be involved in trying to vent in a language one was still learning. It sounded exasperating and cumbersome, and he understood why Jans sometimes lapsed into mumbling in his native tongue. It must be so much more satisfying. Heline reached through the opening now and again to pat Jans on the shoulder; not a warning pat, just a soothing one. That seemed to calm him, at least temporarily.

When at last they escaped the city, it was like being shot from a gun, or propelled by a rocket. The highway stretched ahead of them dark and slick, but compared to the crawl through the city, it felt like they were flying. Everyone got quiet then, as they sped toward the unknown. Now, with the city obstacles behind them, they'd reach it faster.

Ulric asked, "Should we have some kind of plan? We don't know what we're going to encounter here, do we?"

Xya shook her head. "No. The Technocrat Avatar doubtless has followers, of course, but we don't know their abilities."

"I don't have any followers," Ulric said in a small voice.

"Huh, that's true." Xya looked back through the panel at him with a thoughtful expression. "I would have expected some to show up by now. Perhaps they haven't had time to find you. Of course, you have Heline, me, and Nerlim—"

"I can't do any magic," Nerlim fretted. "All I can do is get battered around when someone else uses it."

"Sensiles can learn to funnel that power," Xya said. "Instead of absorbing the hit, they deflect it—bounce the energy away from themselves. Sometimes they can boost other magic-wielders, channel the force to affect the world around them, or even cause spell-like effects."

Nerlim stared at her in silence for a moment. "And you didn't see fit to mention this before? Didn't occur to you I might be interested in a little fact like that?"

"Sorry." Xya shrugged. "I thought I mentioned it. Things have been kind of busy, right? And I didn't expect that the worldweft disturbance would bring things to a head so fast."

"Whatever. How do I do it? Just give me quick instructions."

"Well…" She took a deep breath. "I don't know, because I'm not a sensile. But I do know others can do it."

Nerlim made a sound that might have been 'humpf.' It might also have been something naughtier.

"You also have me, and Eleanor," Tiny Enos pointed out in the silence that followed, and Ulric appreciated his friend for speaking up. He also noticed that Eleanor didn't dispute the claim, which was also nice.

[ahem] The Hat made a phony throat-clearing noise.

"What?" asked Ulric.

[you also have me. Arcanico. the manifestation of the entire freaking fifth force on this world] The hat's voice was testy. [or, well, half of it, anyway. i think i might be able to assist, don't you?]

"That's right," Ulric said, snapping his fingers. "We should be unbeatable with you, shouldn't we?"

"Unless the other Avatar pulls something out of his hat—no pun intended—and gets control. Then Arcanico will be on his side," Xya said.

Arcanico said nothing in response to that.

Ulric rubbed his forehead. "Who makes up these rules?"

"They're not really rules; it's just the way things work."

Everyone was thrown forward as Jans slammed on the brakes. The van skidded in a most heart-stopping way on the wet road. Something stood silhouetted up ahead in the headlights, but that didn't make sense to Ulric's brain. Shouldn't they be able to see something their headlights illuminated? Only light from behind would create a silhouette. Then, as the tires squealed to a stop, he recognized the unicorn. No light in the world could make it look anything but black.

With apparent unconcern about its close call with the humane society van, the unicorn trotted over to the car and nosed Jans' window. Jans rolled the window down with a hand that trembled on the handle.

"Good evening, Thaumaturge Avatar." The unicorn greeted him in a formal tone, looking past Jans and through the open slider to where Ulric sat in the back.

"Good evening, fair beast," Ulric replied, slipping with ease into the character of Prince Evernestigan.

"The Creatures of Majick will throw their lot in with you," the unicorn said in its formal voice. "We believe you will protect our interests and serve the majick well."

"Thank you," Ulric said with heartfelt sincerity. "I appreciate your support, and I will work hard to deserve it."

"And the other fellow was a bit of a drip," the unicorn added, dropping the formality for a more conversational tone.

"Er, okay."

"How may we serve?"

Ulric glanced at Xya and Heline. They both raised their eyebrows at him.

"Well, we're on our way to confront the Technocrat Avatar right now at a place called the Dingle. If you could come along, sort of back us up—"

"We know the place. It shall be done," the unicorn said, and without another word turned and trotted back into the woods.

"Followers!" Tiny Enos clapped Ulric on the back. "See? It's all good."

"I guess so," Ulric answered around a sudden lump in his throat. "I just hope it's enough."

Peace and Quiet in a Giant Robot

Wint

Wint stared out through the tent flap at the faint light cast by the robot's glowing eyes. *The trouble with all of this is...I don't want to do it.* The eyes had gone into place and sprung to glowing life ten minutes ago, and Wint wasn't at all sure he liked the colour of the light they threw. It was blue, a pale and cold and soulless blue, although Wint wasn't sure what else to expect from a robot.

{I chose you} the Radio said in a dangerous voice. {You're going to save me}

Save you? Wint thought back. *Save you from what? And stop talking in my head.*

{Look, there's this new force running around, and I want it harnessed} the Radio said. {I don't want it controlling everything and doing whatever it likes. The planet has managed this long without it, and we've done pretty well.}

But couldn't you just...talk to the magic? Work out a way to coexist?

The Radio snapped, {As far as I'm concerned, it's an invading force. It moved in uninvited, and now we're all messed up and the worldweft is disturbed—}

That might not even be the cause, Wint argued, trying to ignore the idea that he was telepathically arguing with a Radio. Maybe he'd gone mad already and all this wasn't happening in the real world.

{Oh, it's happening, all right} the Radio said.

So much for that theory. *Kindly get out of my head now,* he told the Radio, but there was no reply. Wint turned his attention back to the others.

Gammy paced inside the tent they'd borrowed from a couple of the geeks. The occupants were busy working on the robot anyway, so their presence wasn't an imposition. Although the tent wasn't large enough for serious, satisfactory pacing, Gammy was a small woman with short legs, so she could manage. She muttered as she traversed the cramped space, almost talking to herself. "The problem is, this Ulric seems a nice boy, and he's got nice people on his side."

"We're nice enough, too," Rex growled. He'd curled up at the back of the tent, well away from the doorway, chewing on a stick without much enthusiasm. "We're all just a little testy, being assigned to take sides without being consulted, that's all."

Gammy didn't seem to hear him. "But it's my duty to think of the launch first, isn't it? And all the people who worked hard to bring this mission to life."

"If you'd only listened to me about the launch," Corax groused. "We both could have had what we wanted, instead of ending up in the middle of this mess. At the very least I wish I'd stayed in the closet and tried to contact The Min from there."

"I do wish you'd shut up," Skete told Corax. Skete sat cross-legged on a folded-up sleeping bag, concentrating on his odd phone. The light from the screen washed his face with a blue-white, sickly illumination, making him look almost as ghostly as Corax. "The Min is going to have your hide for breakfast already. And if you turn out to be responsible for the disturbance in the worldweft—"

"That's not me!" Corax protested. "I haven't done anything to cause that."

"You're not even supposed to be here. We'll see what The Min says, I guess," Skete shot back. "If I can ever get in touch with her," he complained. Skete had been trying to put through a call with something approaching desperation. Whoever he wanted to contact, he'd tried five times so far with no success, muttering dark curses after every failed attempt.

"Will you all be quiet?" Gammy demanded, clapping her hands over her ears. "I'm trying to work through a vital personal and ethical dilemma, here. Is there anywhere a person can get a little peace and quiet?"

Wint jumped up from a precarious camp chair without warning and grabbed Gammy's hand. "Come with me," he hissed, and ducked out of the tent. Too startled to pull her hand out of his grasp, Gammy stumbled after him. They ran out into the rain and Wint headed for the robot, now almost complete. Something beyond mere technology was at work here, and that reminded him of the moment he'd changed the teaspoon into a key. The memory made his stomach squirm, but he pushed it aside; that could wait until later. He felt Gammy's pace falter and wondered if she'd slipped in the mud, but glancing back, he saw that she'd tilted her head up to get a better look at the enormous construction. It loomed over them in the darkness, spilling that cold, merciless light from its eyes. Building a robot had seemed like such a good idea at the outset, but now he wasn't sure. At least it would serve this current purpose.

Wint ran up to one of the guys standing near the base of the robot. He didn't seem to care much about the rain, absorbed in scribbling figures in a waterproof notebook. "Can we get inside this thing?" Wint yelled at him.

The guy looked startled. "You can, sure. But cell phones and such might not work inside. There's a lot of interference and we don't know the source yet."

"Perfect, thanks." Wint dragged Gammy into the hatch the fellow indicated. It led inside the dark recesses of the robot's left leg.

"I might need to call Argit again, to see if he's found anything at the facility," Gammy protested. "Or he might call me. I need to be somewhere with cell reception!"

"We won't stay long," Wint promised her.

The robot's leg was a dark, narrow shaft opening above them, but Wint felt around and found steps spiralling upward. He climbed the first two, but Gammy pulled her hand away from his.

"I'm following you," she snapped, "But I need both hands to feel my way. I'm old, remember. Can't afford to fall down a flight of stairs."

Wint wasn't sure he could, either, but he didn't bother to answer and kept climbing. He marvelled again at the improbability of this enormous construct emerging from his followers' pile of gadgetry, but he didn't dwell on it too much. Too much scrutiny might bring the whole thing crashing down. He felt another twinge of discomfort about the role of magic in its construction. Everybody seemed certain magic had its uses when controlled by the right people, but that was another unresolved question.

Also, the definition of "the right people" seemed suspiciously arbitrary, and he expected it very much depended on who you asked.

The climb up the spiralling staircase was a slow trudge in the dark, but at last they emerged into the robot's head. A bluish glow illuminated the whole small room, and one wide wall sported two rectangular windows. The robot's eyes. The driver's seat from Wint's car sat in the precise centre of the room, facing the windows and flanked by futuristic-looking control consoles. Wint found the seat's presence oddly comforting.

"Okay," Gammy gasped, still panting from the climb. Her hair was even wilder now, and she'd removed the gauzy caftan at some point and tied it around her waist. The hems of her pant legs were liberally speckled with mud from their dash to the robot. "What are we doing here?"

Wint turned to her. "I had to talk to you without the Radio listening in. Maybe there's enough interference in here to block it out. And you wanted a quiet place to think."

"Couldn't we just have run down the road a ways?" She shook out her damp curls, droplets spraying in every direction. "I don't care so much about the rain at this point."

Wint shook his head. "It can read my thoughts. This seemed safer."

Gammy had a thoughtful look on her face when she replied. "Seems like there's a lot of that going around. So what's this about? Aren't you working with the Radio? Why do you need to get away from it?"

"Frankly, I believe the Radio is dangerous," Wint said. "It started off sort of controlling and single-minded, but now it's turned a corner into stranger territory and I think it's disconnected from reality. Now it claims to be the spirit of the planet, so that would mean the planet itself is dangerous. I don't even know how to get my head around that, but if it's true—"

"You're right. Who wants to live on a dangerous or unhinged planet that's in control of magic?" Gammy said. "I can't see that being good for anyone who lives here, whether they're on the side of magic or technology. In fact, that sounds terrifying."

"And if it lied about being the manifestation of technology, who's to say it's even telling the truth now? It might have delusions of grandeur or something." Wint looked at Gammy with all the desperation of an employee who needs their boss to solve a problem while fearing that's not going to be the case. "I didn't ask for any of this, and I don't want to be an Avatar thingy. I don't want to help either side succeed, because in all honesty, I see more possibilities for good if they had to work together."

"Is that an option? Everyone seems stuck on the notion that one side or the other has to win."

Wint shook his head, frowning. "That doesn't seem right. I'm the Technocrat Avatar, but I used this fifth force—er, somehow. It's the only way to explain the existence of this robot. And the others are using it, too. So there must be a way to share it."

Gammy bit her lip, not meeting Wint's eyes. When she spoke, her words were contemplative. "I thought I wanted technology to win so the launch could go ahead, but we have to do what's best for everyone—not only me and what I want. I think that's what Nerl—er, a friend of mine would say."

That made sense to Wint, and he did his best to hide his utter shock that Gammy would choose to put something else ahead of the launch. "Okay," he said after a silent moment. "So, what are we going to do?"

Gammy didn't answer right away. Her eyes were unfocused, staring out into the blue-tinged dark through one of the robot's giant eyeholes. Wint stayed quiet, letting her work out whatever was happening in that formidable brain. Her eyes came back to Wint. "One approach might be to trick the Radio into believing you're still on board with all its plans, but make a secret compromise with Ulric. Then we'd have to make sure the Radio is...contained in some way, so that it can't cause trouble. If we did that, maybe this worldweft thing would calm down and the people who understand all this could come in and sort things out."

Wint's face lit up. "That would be great! How do we do it?"

"I have no idea, but having a plan is the first step." Gammy considered for a moment. Then, cupping her hands around her mouth, she called, "Corax! Come here for a minute!"

"Will that work?" Wint asked. "We're in here because of the interference, remember?"

"No idea, but I don't think Corax's communication with me has depended on anything like a strong cell phone signal. I know your friend Skete is having trouble contacting someone by magical means," Gammy said, holding up a hand to forestall his protest, "But maybe Corax is close enough that it won't matter."

"But if Corax can hear you, does that mean the Radio can hear me?" Wint worried.

Gammy shook her head. "Not necessarily. They're different types of entities, right? We don't know how they do what they do, but that doesn't mean their abilities are the same." That seemed to Wint more like a hope than a theory, but at that moment, he'd accept it.

In fact, at that moment, Corax appeared in the control room in front of the robot's left eye, the glow in the room tingeing his translucent form azure. His semi-transparent features still looked sulky. Gammy fixed him with a stare that would make her employees cower.

"You're in trouble, aren't you?"

He floated upwards a foot or so in apparent agitation. "I might be. But the accusations aren't fair—"

Gammy held up a hand. "No more whining. Help us, and I'll testify or whatever that as far as I know, you weren't involved in this planetary disturbance. I'll confirm that you were only in contact with me. Will that get you out of trouble? Can we make a deal?"

"What about you? I still maintain I'm the only one who can get you what you want—"

Gammy shook the hand she was still holding up. "What I want has changed—sort of. And I don't think you're the only one with an answer any longer—if you ever were. You'll have to accept that. If you ask me, that whole god thing you were on about is a bust down here anyway, and you'll be lucky to get out of this with a slap on the wrist. And now I'm the one in a position to help you. Would you say that's a fair assessment of the situation?"

"I guess so." Corax said the words as if they were toffee stuck to the roof of his mouth.

"There are bigger problems happening right now than either yours or mine, and I suspect—I hope—that the other people like you might be able to solve them if we can give them an opening. Does that sound right?"

"We're not exactly *people*," Corax said in a withering tone. "We're trans-dimensional beings."

Gammy could do withering as well as anyone. "I don't know what that means, so I'll call you 'people' for clarity's sake. Just answer my question."

"I don't understand everything that's going on either—"

"But from what we do know, does that sound plausible?"

Corax sighed and floated back down. "I guess so. There aren't many problems The Min can't sort out."

"Then that's who we need. Are you willing to help us?"

Another sigh. "All right. What do you want me to do?"

"Just deliver a message or two," Gammy said, and Wint observed a shrewd glint in her eye. "And tell me everything you know about what Sedrict and anyone else might be attempting."

Corax sighed theatrically. "Which do you want first? Message delivery or explanations? But remember, I'm only guessing about some of this."

"Understood. Let's do a bit of an explanation, and I'll prioritize messages. And I'm going to sit in this weird but comfortable-looking chair while we hash it out, if no one has any objections."

Gammy lowered herself into the seat from Wint's car with a groan of relief, and massaged her left knee as she spoke. "I need to let Nerlim know I'm all right after being so rudely removed from his company," she told Corax with a dark look, "but we have to make sure NCDSF is secure, and safe from any of the maniacs currently loose on the planet. There seems to be a ridiculous number of them."

"Do you know how to do that?" Wint was almost afraid to hope she'd say yes.

She waved a dismissive hand at him. "The only option I can see is working together, if we want to reach a solution everyone can live with. And some people are going to need convincing of that."

Then she turned back to Corax. "Now, tell me about this Sedrict and what he might want with my space facility," Gammy said. "And we'll see where we go from there."

Wint watched Gammy and Corax for a moment, and sighed. It wasn't exactly the peace and quiet he'd been searching for, but it was an improvement. And at least he couldn't hear that flarking Radio any more.

Just Try to Keep Up

Gammy

Gammy put her head back against the displaced car seat and sighed. The blue light from the robot's eyes limned the room with a glow that was, frankly, eerie and discomfiting. She was having a hard time keeping up with the events of the day, and she'd be the first to admit it. Most recently, she'd been whisked from the closet at Heline's house to the top of a rain-swept tower in the middle of the woods; moved to a tent that was only marginally less damp; and trundled into a giant robot for some "peace and quiet" that had been neither peaceful nor quiet. And then she and the Technocrat Avatar, her employee Wint Usborne, had been joined in the robot by a talking dog lugging a talking Radio.

It was a lot, and she was already tired.

Her request for Corax to tell her about Sedrict had triggered a long litany of Sedrict's many failings and obsessions. He might be a trans-dimensional being (whatever that meant), but Gammy noted that Corax had difficulty sticking to the point and it took constant nudging to get him back on track. But it wasn't difficult to glean the important bits; Sedrict was a sycophant of—another trans-dimensional being of some sort—who had been exiled for crimes concerning overreach of magic use. Sedrict had a plan to help the Exile escape his prison and come to D'sharu, and there was something at Gammy's space facility that Sedrict needed to facilitate that.

Well, not if Gammy had anything to say about it. That must explain why the alarms at NCDSF had tripped. Someone was trying to tamper with her equipment.

"I need you to send a message to this Min of yours, and tell her what we think is happening," Gammy said at last, holding up a hand to stop the flow of verbiage. "The last thing we need is someone else coming down here—a criminal, no less—trying to stick their nose into this business. It's complicated enough as it is."

Corax twisted his translucent hands in a fretful motion. "While I agree The Min needs to be apprised of the situation, that's what Skete has been attempting for some time now. Also, I'm not sure I'm the best person to tell her. She may not be disposed to listen to me at the moment—"

"Well, make her listen!" Gammy was so done with Corax and his mercurial swings from overbearing arrogance to spineless whining.

"Considering Skete's inability to reach her, I may not be able to either without leaving the planet," he explained with the controlled patience of someone addressing an obstreperous child. He spread his hands to gesture around at the inhospitable top of the tower. "And the worldweft disturbance may prevent me from doing that. Look what happened when I attempted a simple teleport for the two of us."

"Cheese and rice. You managed to transport the two of us, just not to the place you wanted. That's a partial success, at least. And all you can do is try," she countered, exasperated. "Two of you attempting to reach her doubles our chances of success. And send Nerlim a message so he knows I'm all right. If he's worrying or distracted, goodness knows what will happen to him when this magic force stuff starts flying around."

"I'm not sure how to do that, but fine, I'll try," Corax said with prim disapproval.

Gammy refrained from rolling her eyes. "I'm sure a *trans-dimensional being* such as yourself will figure something out."

That's when the dog arrived and what little quiet there'd been evaporated. Gammy had been introduced to Rex when she and Corax arrived at the tower, and she'd managed—she hoped—to contain her discomfiture when the dog turned out speak like a person. He was a well-spoken dog, however, Gammy had to give him that, and as it turned out, he might be the least annoying of the whole lot of them. Somewhat on the snarky side, of course, but that only made him more likeable in Gammy's view.

Rex's entrance into the control room of the robot was presaged by a long series of thumps and bumps as he made his way up the stairs inside the robot's leg, half-carrying and half-dragging the Radio with him. The Radio was a clunky thing, an antique unless Gammy missed her guess, and a heavy load for the poor creature. Shrieks and complaints from the Radio accompanied the thumps and bumps, creating an inescapable cacophony. As they emerged from the top of the stairs, Rex dropped the Radio on the floor with a look of canine satisfaction. Gammy thought the dog had enjoyed making the ascent as uncomfortable as possible for the Radio.

"So much for flarking peace and quiet," Wint muttered. "I came here to get away from that thing."

"We have to get the robot out of sight," the Radio almost screamed as it hit the floor. "They're coming!"

"Sorry. It wouldn't shut up until I brought it, and Skete's still trying to get through on his phone." The dog sat back on its haunches and licked its lips, as if trying to get rid of the taste of the Radio.

"Who's coming?"

"The Thaumaturge Avatar and his followers," the Radio yelled, "Who do you think? They're driving through the woods right now in a van, for flark's sake. Getting closer every moment! If we want to get the drop on them, we need to move the robot into the trees and hide it. We'll have the advantage of surprise."

Wint blinked and glanced out one of the robot's eye windows at the tents and detritus littering the clearing. "Um, maybe you haven't noticed, but this robot is a little on the large side to hide easily. One might say huge, or even enormous. Not even a stretch to call it gargantuan, to tell the truth. And there's a lot of evidence outside that we've all been here. I don't think there's going to be much surprise involved."

"We do this my way," the Radio snapped. "You're my Avatar and you have to follow my lead. That's how this works."

Wint shrugged. "Yeah, whatever you say. Just so we're clear, I care less and less about any of this." In a grudging voice, he used the robot's public address system to relay the radio's idea to the geeky followers in and around the robot. Those with controllers got it moving toward the trees with ponderous steps, and the others followed, scrambling inside the legs of the construct for shelter and cover while they awaited the arrival of the enemy. Gammy clutched the chair seat as the entire control room swayed with the robot's steps.

"Well, have you reached this Min person?" Gammy asked Corax, when she realized he was still floating in anxious uncertainty in the same place he'd been before the Radio's outburst. He was all but wringing his translucent hands.

"I've been trying to get through. There's too much static."

"Then did you message Nerlim?"

"I thought the other was more pressing, but I'll do that now," he huffed. "*If* it will work."

"If what will work?" The Skete fellow came bolting up the stairs in the robot's leg just in time to hear Corax's words. Gammy furrowed her brow. Outlandish name, Skete, but Gammy was past being surprised by anything.

To forestall a protracted explanation from Corax, Gammy answered him, explaining that she'd asked Corax to contact The Min and Nerlim. She wasn't sure who—or what—Skete was. Another trans-dimensional being, no doubt, although at least Skete had the good manners to be fully materialized and not scandalously see-through like Corax and Sedrict. It had been obvious from their interactions in the tent earlier that Skete and Corax knew each other and shared some history. It didn't seem to be a friendly one.

"Good luck with that," Skete said. "I've been trying to reach her, too, but nothing's getting through."

Gammy slumped back into the chair. She'd never felt so helpless, and her precious space facility was in danger. Unless Argit figured things out—and since he hadn't been able to see Corax in her office, the chances of this seemed slim—there was nobody to deal with the threat at NCDSF.

"I'll try again to reach The Min," Corax offered. "It could work anytime."

Gammy eyed him with suspicion. "And then I'll be more inclined to like you again? Yes, please keep trying, but I'd like you better if you were doing it for the right reasons."

"What if I try to go out there?" Skete mused. "Where Sedrict might be. Although with the state of the worldweft—"

"Aren't you supposed to be here helping me?" Wint demanded in a startled voice. He'd been watching their progress into the forest through one of the robot's eye windows but turned at Skete's idea. His own eyes were wide. "If the Thaumaturge Avatar and his people are coming, this might be when I need you most! You spent all this time egging me on to come out here, and now you're just going to leave?"

Skete's demeanour and apology seemed sincere. "I know, and I'm sorry. But Gammy is right. If someone doesn't stop Sedrict from bringing the Exile here, nothing you or the other Avatar do will matter."

"You wouldn't leave me here with just the radio," Wint pleaded.

"And me," the dog said in a tone of mild reproof. "I'm still here, you know."

"It's still questionable whose side you're on," Wint said, narrowing his eyes at the dog. "Mine or the Radio's. I haven't figured that out yet."

"Isn't that supposed to be the same side?" Gammy asked. Strange as all the people gathered around Ulric and that Hat might be, at least they all seemed to agree that they were on the same side. Over here in the Technocrat Avatar's camp, all was chaos.

"Honestly, that's a fair question," the dog said, perking up his ears. "And maybe this is a good time to tell you—"

"Stop talking as if what the Avatars want matters here," the Radio screamed, interrupting the dog. "The others are arriving. I can sense them. Oooh, all that horrible new magic. They're fairly dripping with it." It seemed to almost shudder on the floor of the control deck.

So much drama, Gammy thought, rolling her eyes.

"I'll try to get The Min again," Skete offered, glancing at the Radio with distaste. "Maybe there's a spot with better reception. He pulled out the odd phone he'd been fiddling with in the tent and held it up in the air, turning around in circles for a moment. Then he ducked back down the stairwell in the robot's leg.

And then the Radio *did* something and the lights in the robot winked out. The background hum of its electronics stilled to silence and the ambush of the Thaumaturge Avatar commenced as they quieted to wait.

Gammy seemed to be a part of that ambush, whether or not she wanted to be.

Nerlim, she thought, *I'm sorry. I'm coming back to you just as soon as I can manage.*

I Have a Song Request

Ulric

Jouncing along in varying degrees of discomfort in the humane society van, Ulric and the others neared the Dingle. It had been a long drive, and Jans hadn't known the way, but the automap on Eleanor's phone kept them on track with only a few wrong turns. Ulric was sure he had dozed intermittently, although he wondered how he could sleep at a time like this. Maybe his body and brain knew they'd soon be called upon to be sharp, which was an idea both terrifying and encouraging. They'd turned onto a dirt track hemmed by thick woods a while back, and the seating in the rear of the humane society van had become a steady jostle. There'd been no dozing or sleeping after that, even though outside the van lay only the mesmerizing, endless view of the shadowy forest and pockmarked dirt road illuminated by the van's headlights. Eleanor strummed soft chords on her guitar and Heline jotted sporadic notes in her notebook. Tiny Enos read the Creature Concordance by the shaky light from his phone, as if he were cramming for final exams. The Hat remained silent, which was both a blessing and a disappointment. Ulric would have welcomed some advice or guidance, but if none of that was on offer, the quiet in his head was preferable.

Although the woods were dark and the headlights cast only a narrow beam ahead of them, a bluish radiance hovered above the trees—an unnatural light that Ulric suspected shouldn't exist, not here. If it came from the area of the Dingle, where he doubted there was electricity, that suggested a connection to the coming confrontation. Uneasiness trickled cold fingertips between his shoulder blades, but he said nothing. Jans seemed to need all his concentration to keep easing the van along the rutted and pothole-sprinkled road, trying not to put too many demands on the vehicle's springs and keep the passengers in the back from getting seasick.

Ulric stared out at the thin sweep of headlights receding into the blackness of the woods all around them. *The trouble with all of this is…I don't want to do it.* He turned the wand Heline had given him over and over in his hands. Holding it felt right—and powerful. After his initial shock, the idea of magic had been exciting. But he didn't want to have to fight someone for the right to use this power. This was nothing he'd ever asked for or dreamed about. He didn't want to control the fifth force, this thing called magic, in D'sharu. And more importantly, he didn't want anyone to get hurt.

[someone has to control the magic] said the Hat, breaking its long silence at last. [don't you think it should be someone who will do so wisely?]

I'm not convinced it has to be controlled by just one person or just one idea, Ulric thought back. *There's such a thing as sharing, and co-existing. But even if control is necessary, what makes you believe I'm the one? I'm just a kid. What do I know about being wise? And I don't want the job.*

[sometimes the ones who don't want a job are the only ones you can trust with it] the Hat said, and then lapsed back into an uneasy silence.

Ulric considered that as they drew closer to the Dingle. What did the Hat mean? He turned the words over in his mind. Why was someone who didn't want a job the best person for that job? That didn't make sense, he thought at first, but then—well, it made a kind of sense when the job involved having power. Those who craved power for its own sake could rarely be trusted with it—he'd learned that from history classes and school elections. So were those who found themselves with unlooked-for power more likely to use it for the good of others, instead of themselves? Perhaps. It made a perverse kind of sense, when you took that perspective.

He turned to Heline, where she and Eleanor sat back-to-back on one of the empty animal crates. "Heline? What are your songs mostly about? When you write them?"

Heline turned to look at him, her lips puckered as she thought. "I haven't noticed much of a pattern," she mused. "A lot are about love, and memory. Sometimes power, and sometimes just cryptic things that seem nonsensical. Although they might be clearer with the right context, I suppose. If you interpreted them figuratively instead of literally."

Eleanor nodded. "I've read some, and I think you're right."

"And yet you said they were terrible," Heline observed, although she smiled when she spoke.

"They *were* terrible, but the underlying themes were clear," Eleanor replied with a grin. "Although with all the things that have happened in the last few days, I'm not sure about the figurative part. Maybe we should think about some of that weird stuff literally. Why do you ask, Ulric?"

"Could you write a song right now?" Ulric asked. "Both of you, working together? I feel like the two of you would create something powerful."

Eleanor raised an eyebrow. "I'm not involved in what Heline and that Hat have going on, and I'm not part of this fifth force thing."

[i rather think you are, you know]

Ulric knew from the faces around him everyone had heard the Hat's words to Eleanor.

Eleanor frowned but said nothing, then shrugged. "Whatever. I like writing songs anyway, so I'm game."

Heline glanced at the Hat, perched on the seat beside her. "We can try."

"Could you write a song about compromise? One that talks about power wisely used?"

"I don't have much control over what comes out; I just channel." Heline smiled. "But I suppose I can try to exert some influence, especially if the Hat helps me."

"What are you doing"? Xya asked, a note of suspicion in her voice.

"Trying to make a plan." Ulric shrugged. "A plan I can live with. No one else has suggested one other than fighting, and I don't love that idea."

Xya shrugged. "It's the way these things are always done, but you're the Avatar. All I can do is advise, and I've done that."

"I expect you to help with this plan in any way you can." Ulric wasn't sure where his stern voice had come from—he sounded a bit like his mother, chiding him for not doing his chores.

Xya raised her eyebrows, but didn't comment on Ulric's tone. "I'm more worried about what's happening with Sedrict and Alsina right now, but I don't know what we can do about that. If anything. I spoke to my boss before we left, but she didn't have a chance to say much other than confirm that something big is in the works before the connection failed."

"Will you talk to her again?"

Xya shrugged. "If she can get through to me, maybe. The worldweft disturbance complicates matters. That's interfering with everything."

"Then we can't worry about that right now. We proceed the best we can and try to roll with anything else that comes along."

"Good thinking." Tiny Enos didn't look up from the book. "You can't plan for the unexpected, even when you expect it."

"Er, right."

"I'll see what we can do." Heline pulled the Hat on, folding the point down with care so that it didn't poke into the roof of the van, and pulled out her notebook. A moment later, she was scribbling madly. Eleanor turned so she could see the notebook too, and began experimenting with chords in a more focused way.

No one but Ulric seemed to notice the weird folds that made the Hat appear to be smiling.

Ulric knew they'd reached the Dingle when the dirt track widened out into a broad, grassy clearing. The open expanse was broken by the finger of a tall stone tower stretching up towards the sky. He hadn't been sure what to expect, but he hadn't been expecting to see...nothing at all. The blue glow that had limned the treetops had disappeared, the rain had eased off, and the Dingle stood tall and lonely in the moonlight.

"We'd better check it out." Ulric breathed in a deep gulp of the damp, chill air as they climbed out of the van, stretching. The drive had been long, rough, and cramped, and Nerlim gave a groan, his spine creaking as he straightened and massaged the small of his back.

"Well, something happened here." Tiny Enos surveyed the trampled grass around the base of the tower, the scattered debris of snack wrappers and energy drink cans, and the abandoned cars and hastily pitched tents. A sizeable crowd of people had spent some time here recently, even though all was quiet at the moment. An ambush, Ulric wondered? Was everyone locked up inside the tower, waiting to rain down arrows and boiling oil on them? Or more likely guns and hand grenades, he thought with glum resignation. He wasn't sure how the fifth force would protect them from that, and the heat of a sudden flush mounted his cheeks at the possibility he'd brought them all here to step blindly into a trap.

"Is open." Jans had crossed to investigate the tower door, where an open padlock hung from the hasp and the latch wasn't set. Jans, baseball bat in hand, stepped forward and gave the door a gentle push. It swung inward without hesitation. Ulric moved behind him and peered inside. The round room beyond stood empty, dark, and damp.

"Let's look around more before we go inside," Ulric said. The grounds around the tower had been churned into a muddy quagmire, as if many feet had spent the evening stomping around the area. Among the other detritus were empty coffee cups, bits of wire, and scraps of metal that glinted when the slanting moonlight caught them. Someone had piled a haphazard stack of scaffolding near the base of the tower.

Nerlim surveyed the scene, rubbing absently at his stomach. "Lot of magic was used here tonight. I can feel it. Not the gut-punch I get when there's magic activity nearby, but an ache like sore muscles after a long run."

Xya raised her eyebrows at him.

"All right, yes, it's been a long time since I went for a run, but I remember the feeling."

Xya herself studied the area with a contemplative expression. "Yes, magic has been used here for sure, but used in the service of technology. You can taste the edge, a metallic tang, like in a drop of blood."

Nerlim smirked. "Oh, and have you had much blood to drink recently?"

She gave him a silent look.

"Where do you think everyone is gone?" Ulric asked Xya, and he couldn't conceal the nervousness in his voice.

She shook her head. "I'm not sure. If they accomplished what they set out to do, whatever it was, why would they leave their vehicles and everything else behind?"

Eleanor stood in the doorway into the tower, tilting her head back to look up the winding staircase. "Let's check inside the tower. There may be more clues to find."

But likewise, when they moved inside the Dingle, they found the bottom room empty—even emptier than outside, since no scraps of debris or litter had fallen in here. Ulric and Eleanor traced their phone lights around the space, but apart from moss, mud, and a drift of ancient skeletal autumn leaves, there was nothing to find. They climbed the stairs in a cautious single file, but they found the parapet-enclosed rooftop deserted as well. "Even stronger magic was present here, or was worked here," Nerlim said, squinting around the area and massaging one temple. "But I can't tell how long ago that was, or when everyone left."

[the manifestation of technology was here] the Hat confirmed. [and recently. i can still sense a powerful presence]

"So, now what?" Ulric heard the edge of defeat in his voice. "No Technocrat Avatar, no giant robot, nothing. I'm not sure where to go from here."

As if in answer to his words, just inside the line of trees that marked the edge of the darkened woods, a blue glow sprang to life. Twin blue glows, as a matter of fact, almost at the level of the treetops. Ulric had the creeping impression that they were two eyes, but what enormous creature had eyes that glowed of their own accord? The light sent the silhouettes of the trees jumping and shuddering against the backdrop of the star-dusted night sky. The glowing spots laboured toward the Dingle, rocking from side to side as they came as if something walked with a stiff, ponderous gait.

"Heline?" Ulric breathed.

"Right here." She moved to stand beside him. Their two pointed hats stood silhouetted in counterpoint to the advancing eyes.

"I'm here, too," Eleanor said from Heline's other side.

"Is that a...robot?" Xya asked no one in particular, as the enormous metal construct broke the treeline and hove into view.

"They said there'd be a robot, and that's a flarking robot." Tiny Enos's voice was admiring. "That thing is huge! How in the name of cheese and rice did they make it?"

"With technology and magic," Xya said, and her voice was puzzled. "Together. That's...extremely unusual in this kind of situation." She glanced over at Nerlim. "But it makes sense with what you sensed. You okay?"

He nodded, his face registering only vague discomfort. "There's magic in use, but very low level right now. Just the occasional twinge."

Xya nodded, but her eyes narrowed. "That's what I thought. I'm going to try again to get through to The Min. This is...I don't know what this is, but it's weird."

"Whatever you're going to do, let's be fast," Ulric said. "Because that thing is moving slow, but it's going to be here sooner than I'd like."

Intermezzo Sette

The Min

The Min was having a bad...well, not a day, exactly, since time could not be said to have the same meaning for trans-dimensional beings, but a bad indeterminate segment of time, at least. The problems on D'sharu had already been consuming much more of her attention than she could afford to spare for one planet, but the additional wrinkle of an obstreperous Exile had made things much, much worse.

She sat back from her desk and rubbed her hands over her eyes, making the starlight in her hair flicker. She'd now tracked down every reference to Majszak in the records and discovered a clear history of document manipulation. Everything pointed to either Sedrict or Alsina—or both of them—as the orchestrators of this, although the documents themselves held no obvious clues to the perpetrator. Right now, The Min was less concerned with how the manipulations had happened than with how to mitigate the fallout, and what that fallout would be.

All around her, books and loose pages shifted and rustled on their shelves, sensing The Min's agitation and responding with their own anxious whispers. That they had been tampered with was a source of anxiety for them, because the books possessed a level of sentience all their own. Aware of their disquiet, The Min tried to calm her nerves, hoping that would settle the books, too, but even for her that was no easy task. She caught herself drumming her fingers on the desktop for the third time and made herself stop. The whole situation was, frankly, bad. She'd tried multiple times to contact both Xya and Skete for situation reports, but the only response had been unrelenting static.

"I might have to go down to D'sharu myself and sort this out," she muttered, keeping her voice low so as not to distress the books any further. However, she had to face the discomfiting truth that with the planet's worldweft in such a state of chaos, that might not be possible. And knowing that Sedrict and Alsina were, in all probability, attempting to free Majszak from his own planetary imprisonment only stoked both her rage and an unfamiliar, unpleasant feeling of powerlessness.

The only alternative course of action she could see was to travel to the planet of Majszak's exile and attempt to shore up the magic holding him prisoner. She'd take like-minded members of the Convocation with her to help, and with luck, they'd foil Sedrict and Alsina's plans from that end.

The problem with *that* was not knowing *how* Sedrict and Alsina planned to accomplish their nefarious deed. It worried her more than she liked to admit. How could she formulate a plan when she couldn't foresee what measures she had to counter?[1]

Glancing up at the rustling volumes on her shelves, she was reminded of the book Alsina had stolen from the library on D'sharu. A book about magic that had become magical itself. She pursed her lips. Did that tome hold clues that would point to Majszak as the perpetrator of the illegal awakening of magic on the planet so long ago? And might its presence help the current Thaumaturge Avatar in wrangling both the new and old magics now active on D'sharu? If only Alsina hadn't absconded with the damned thing, it might be in his hands right now, a valuable ally. Not that The Min took sides in these magic/technology power struggles—she tried to maintain a neutral stance. In this case, however, with the interference from Sedrict and Alsina, she conceded she had a preferred outcome. Perhaps only an ascendancy of magic might set things right. But despite having tried to locate both Sedrict and Alsina, even before the current disruptions in communication, they'd been hidden from her arcane sight.

---

1. The Min had no idea that others were, at that same moment, struggling with precisely the same questions. It might have made her feel a little better about it, because misery does love company, even for trans-dimensional beings.

Just another infraction to add to their growing list of crimes. At this rate, they'd both be exiled themselves if she had any say in the matter.

And then her "phone" sounded. She responded to the call and, miracle of miracles, both Xya and Skete were there. The connection was fuzzy and didn't feel stable, but at least she might get an update on what was happening.

"Reports?" she asked, foregoing any social niceties in the interest of time.

Both holograms spoke at once, stopped, and looked at each other. "Skete, you start," The Min instructed, squinting to make out more details of their forms. Both were cloaked in shadow.

"Okay. The worldweft is in major flux down here," Skete started, and Xya nodded her shadow-wreathed head. "Corax is here with the Technocrat Avatar's boss, and I don't know what all he's been messing with. He claims not to be responsible for the worldweft issues."

"The Avatar's boss? How are they involved, and why did Corax bring them to you?"

"He didn't mean to. The worldweft disturbance interfered with his transport spell. She's the one he's been trying to convince to endorse his bid for godhood, but she's also involved with the Thaumaturge Avatar's crew. It's all a bit confusing," Skete added. "Also, Corax told me Sedrict also contacted Ms. Gameldina—that's her name—asking to use some deep space monitoring equipment at the facility where she and the Avatar work."

"That...doesn't sound good." The Min's mind was flying, trying to process what this might mean. "I think they're trying to free Majszak, so everything they're doing must be part of that plan."

"Majszak?" Skete's hologram eyes flew open. "He's not on this planet, is he? How do they hope to get away with that?"

Xya interrupted. She'd moved to a less shadowed space, the darkness of a night sky scattered with stars visible behind her. Moonlight limned one side of her face. "No, he's not here, but if they can get him to D'sharu, he already has an affinity with the old magic here. He'd have an advantage if he wants to make a stand. Maybe they were hoping to fly under the radar while the planet and the Convocation dealt with the arrival of new magic on the planet, but that hope backfired—too much attention centred on D'sharu."

"Well, things might be even worse than we think." Behind Skete, the wall was shiny, smooth, and dark, as if constructed of metal. As The Min watched, light from the phone glinted off the material.

"Skete, where *are* you?" The Min asked.

"Well, since you ask, I'm inside the leg staircase of a giant robot. However, things were worse a little while ago when I was in a tent, because I did *not* sign up to go camping on this mission," he said. "Anyway, security alarms were tripped at that spaceflight facility this evening. Ms. Gameldina sent someone to investigate, but he may not be up to the task. No doubt Sedrict won't be eager to reveal himself."

"The facility Sedrict was angling to access? You two should try to get out there right away." The Min's mind flew. There must be something—some key or spell or arcane rune—that Majszak planned to use to release himself. And Sedrict had figured out a way, using the technology on this planet, to get that key component to him. They were attempting an end run around all the magical locks keeping Majszak in place. The Min narrowed her eyes. Using technology to circumvent magic. Diabolically brilliant.

"It's a bad time to leave here," Xya said. "The confrontation between the Avatars is imminent. We're supposed to be supporting them."

The Min shook her head. "Well, if you're both gone, neither can be said to have an unfair advantage. Keeping Majszak away from that planet is the top priority. The outcome of the Avatars' meeting will be meaningless if Majszak takes control of the magic for himself. He already has an imprint on the world—if he gets back and the magic responds to him, I'm afraid he'll be difficult to dislodge. Even for me."

Skete grimaced and lowered his voice, raising a hand as if to muffle his voice from anyone nearby. "True, but here's the other wrinkle—the manifestation of technology seems to be, well—sort of unhinged."

"Unhinged? How?"

His grimace morphed into a frown in the glow of his phone and he shook his head a little. "It just—doesn't make sense a lot of the time. For something that's supposed to be eminently logical—well, it isn't. It's inhabiting a radio—which makes sense at first glance—but it also claims to be both the manifestation of technology AND the spirit of the planet, so I don't know what to make of that. It says magic is messing up its worldweft and the Technocrat Avatar has to get control of it so it can be put back to sleep."

Now The Min was also frowning. "But...both those claims can't be true. And the mere existence of awakened magic in any world shouldn't disturb the worldweft. Magic is a natural force."

"I know. That's what I mean. The claims don't add up. And it has wild personality swings for no apparent reason. Sometimes it's pretty mean to everyone—me, the dog, even to its own Avatar."

"Right, the dog." The Min blinked, distracted. "We still didn't figure out where the dog fits into all this."

"Well, the Radio just convinced the dog to carry it into the giant robot, because it doesn't trust its own Avatar," Skete said. "So that might give you a good idea of how things are going on my end."

"The manifestation of the new magic is pretty level-headed," Xya said. "Somewhat manipulative, but we're talking about magic, after all. And the Avatar is strong. He's young, but he has a decent grasp of things, and he thinks things through. He has good people around him, too."

"Thank the cosmos for that, anyway," The Min said. "But I think they'll still have to work this out on their own. I need you both to make sure Sedrict doesn't contact Majszak."

Skete nodded, but he didn't look happy. "I don't know how efficiently we can get to the space facility. If Corax couldn't transport Ms. Gameldina where he wanted to go, we may not be able to, either."

"How is he transporting anyone, anyway?" The Min demanded. "You two should be the only Convocation members with any actual abilities down there."

Xya shrugged, and her hair emulated the gesture. "He stumbled into a place where a lot of old magic had been stored. He tapped into that."

The Min rolled her eyes. "Trust Corax to be lucky enough to find a magic sink, and unlucky enough to use it when there was too much interference. Now, you two must attempt to reach that facility and lock it down. If Sedrict or Alsina are there, stop them from doing whatever they're trying to do, at all costs. Leave your Avatars with the best advice you can, and get moving. This connection could fail at any—"

And as if her words had triggered it, the holograms winked out.

The Min leaned back in her chair and closed her eyes. Just to be sure, she sent out an experimental arcane prod toward the planet, but the energy fizzled and dissipated before even getting close to the world. The worldweft was still in flux, whipping up storms in the arcane atmosphere of the planet and shutting out magical incursions. That might benefit them, though. Even if Sedrict could get his message or whatever out to Majszak on the exile planet, Majszak might not be able to reply *or* make his way to D'sharu through the arcane storm. It didn't solve the problem, but it might buy them some time.

Unless he found a window through, as Xya and Skete had just done. It wouldn't have to be open even as long as this conversation for him to slip through.

The Min sat up and paged through her mental list of Convocation members, deciding who was capable of helping—and whom she could trust to call on for help.

MY AVATAR WILL BEAT YOUR AVATAR

ULRIC

{INTERLOPER MAGIC! THAUMATURGE AVATAR!} thundered a grating, metallic voice from the robot as it lumbered across the clearing. It headed straight for the tower where Ulric and the others stood. {I WILL BE VICTORIOUS. TECHNOLOGY ALREADY HOLDS SWAY ON THIS PLANET, AND MAGIC MUST SERVE IT OR RETURN TO SLUMBER.}

[blow it out your circuits, robot] the Hat answered. [technology has had its turn, and now magic will change things for the better]

{NEVER! MY AVATAR WILL…WILL BEAT YOUR AVATAR!}

"Now, that's just sad," said Tiny Enos in an aside to Ulric. "The Hat's a little weird with that whole glowing eye thing and popping in and out of everyone's heads, but it's handling this so much better."

Ulric turned to the Hat, still perched on the parapet. "Hat—"

"Arcanico, please."

"Sorry, Arcanico. But aren't we trying to compromise here? Maybe don't antagonize it further?"

The Hat glowered at Ulric with its single eye. "I don't like its attitude."

"I know, but could we at least try to resolve this without a pitched battle?"

Before the conversation could continue, the surrounding air erupted with a fluttering, and a whirring, and assorted rustlings and scrapings. Below, hoofbeats and scrabblings rose from ground level. The environs of the tower were alive with bodies both large and small, strange and mundane. D'sharu's newly minted Majickal Creatures had arrived.

The black unicorn, glistening majestically from the rain, raised its head and looked up at Ulric and Tiny Enos, who had leaned over the waist-high parapet to watch. It stamped one ebony hoof on the ground for emphasis, and its horn shimmered with arcane light. "We have arrived, Thaumaturge Avatar, and are ready to support your cause with our very lives."

"My thanks to you and your compatriots, noble creature," Ulric returned, holding his hat with one hand so it wouldn't fall as he leaned over. "May such sacrifices not be required on this day."

Tiny Enos winked at Ulric. "Prince Evernestigan is in fine form," he whispered.

Ulric felt a tap on his shoulder and turned to see Xya. She was slipping an odd-looking cell phone into the pocket of her coat. "Um, look, I'm sorry, but I have to go."

Ulric blinked. "Go? Go where? I thought you were here to help? And isn't this the start of the big confrontation you've been going on about? We've only been here ten minutes!"

She grimaced. "I know. But there's something even more important happening at the spaceflight facility, and we have to check into it."

"At NCDSF?"

"Yes."

"Does Ms. Gameldina know about this? And who's 'we'?"

"Me, and the, er, support person for the Technocrat Avatar. He's leaving too, for the facility. So you see, it's not like I'm leaving you at a disadvantage. Everything's still all equal between the two Avatars. And yes, Gammy is quite keen for us to investigate this."

Ulric glanced at the robot; enormous, looming, and beaded with rain in a way that seemed somehow menacing. "Equal? The other Avatar has a giant flarking robot."

"Well, yes, but what can it *do*? It could be a big scary noise with nothing solid behind it. And you've got an army of magical creatures! Look at them all milling about here."

"It's still a giant robot. It might have weapons!"

"I doubt they had time to include weapons—didn't they build it overnight?"

Ulric's eyes grew wide. "Don't you think if they built *that* overnight—" he gestured at the hulking robot "—they could also have made weapons?"

Xya shrugged and blew a strand of hair away from her face. It swayed for a moment, as if affronted. "I'm sorry. I suppose it's possible. But we suspect there's an exiled member of the Convocation—someone like me, only evil—and he's trying to get to this planet to take over the magic here. That's what Sedrict and Alsina have been up to. Trying to break him out of his prison."

[well, he's not taking control of me, if i have anything to say about it] Arcanico sounded indignant.

"He may not have designs on you. He has a connection to the old magic; my guess is, he'll be focused on that. At any rate, our boss has instructed me, and Skete, to stop him."

Ulric was silent for a moment, at a loss for any further arguments. "What will he do if he breaks free and lands here?"

"Unknown. But we can't risk it with the whole 'evil' thing. And it's still best if you can ensure magic comes out ascendant over technology. I thought of something that might help with that," Xya continued. "Remember that book Nerlim was talking about? The one someone—probably Alsina—stole from the library?"

Ulric nodded.

"You should try to get that back," Xya said, pointing an expressive finger at Ulric. "It might be able to help you a lot, especially if I'm not here."

Ulric threw up his hands. "And how would we do that? Who knows where she took it, and the giant robot is *right there!*" He pointed an emphatic finger that shook a little at the advancing robot.

Xya spared the robot only a brief glance, and nodded. "I know. But if you and Heline and Nerlim and Eleanor all worked together, you might be able to summon that book. It could be the most magical thing on the planet right now—present company excluded," she added, nodding to the Hat. "And you're the Thaumaturge Avatar. I have a hunch it would want to be with you."

Ulric grimaced. "Oh, well, sure, we'll just gather 'round in a circle, hold hands, wish for the book and it will appear, is that it? So simple!"

Xya put her hands on her hips. Her hair waved around her face as if played by a soft breeze. "You're being sarcastic, but that's exactly right. The Min told me to give you my best advice before I left you, and that's it. Get the book. And also, be careful of the Radio."

"The radio? What radio?"

"The Radio controlling the robot. It may not be trustworthy, according to Skete. I'll come back as soon as I can." Xya gave him a glancing pat on the shoulder, then turned and ran for the stairs. Before she reached them, though, she winked out in a flash of glittery golden light as if she'd never been there at all.

A frustrated scream bubbled up in Ulric's throat and threatened to erupt, but he swallowed it down. There was no time for that, and people were counting on him. With an effort, he unclenched fists he didn't remember clenching.

He would not let himself scream in front of Eleanor.

"How may we support you, Thaumaturge Avatar?" called the unicorn from the muddied ground below. It sounded the merest bit testy, as if it thought Ulric had been ignoring it.

"I fear we may have to seize the robot," Ulric called back to it, using his Prince Evernestigan voice. "I'm considering a plan, but your input would be much appreciated."

"We shall confer," the unicorn assented.

{HAHA. TAKE OVER MY ROBOT? DO YOU THINK WE ARE DEFENSELESS?} asked the robot.

Ulric shared an *oh crap, it can hear us* look with Tiny Enos.

"That's interesting." Eleanor had moved to stand beside Ulric while Xya was talking.

"What's interesting? I mean, apart from the fact that we're being yelled at by a giant robot and spoken to by magical animals."

Eleanor nodded once, conceding the point. "It's a little thing, but...the robot referred to itself as 'my robot' just now. That suggests it's not the robot talking, but someone controlling it."

"Xya said a radio was controlling it, but I thought she meant, like, a radio controller." Ulric wished he'd had time to ask for better details before the enigmatic woman had disappeared. "So, maybe the Avatar?"

[that's not the avatar] the Hat said. [it doesn't feel right. i would know if that was the avatar]

The robot paused its advance, and a hatch in the robot's left leg opened. A gaggle of people tumbled out; people wearing t-shirts with tech and pop culture logos; people who looked like they spent far too much time staring at computer screens; people gripping gadgets and toting messenger bags and backpacks. They straggled across the grass in a somewhat disorganized but determined phalanx.

[where is your avatar?] the Hat asked, and the words echoed not only in Ulric's head, but all around, as if amplified by an arcane speaker. It spoke in a tone of only mild interest, as if the answer were inconsequential. [where is the mighty technocrat avatar?]

{REVEAL YOURSELF. IT IS TIME} commanded the robot—or the Radio; who knew at this point?—and then it stammered, {I, ER, WASN'T TALKING TO THE REST OF YOU. JUST IGNORE THAT.}

Two more figures appeared at that moment, not from the robot's leg but outlined behind the blue glow of its eyes. One was tall and thin, twisting its hands with palpable anxiety. The other was short and somewhat lumpy, with a mop of wild hair that looked like it had been sprayed with a hose and left to dry into a halo-like frizz on its own. This figure stood with arms akimbo, fists planted on hips in a stance of pure defiance. Even in silhouette, an aura of disapproval hovered around her like a disappointed teacher's frown.

"Gammy," Nerlim breathed in a voice rich with relief. "She's safe."

"Or captive," said Eleanor. "Although she doesn't look like she's struggling or trying to get away."

"Oh, thanks for that."

{LET BATTLE BE JOINED} screamed the robot—or something inside the robot—and on the grounds around the Dingle, pandemonium ensued.

"No!" Ulric put up his hands as if to ward off a physical blow. "I'm not ready for this. I wanted to talk—"

He felt a light punch on his shoulder. "You got this, Prince Evernestigan." Tiny Enos grinned, hefting the Creature Concordance he'd been studying and jerking a thumb toward the Magickal Creatures below them. "Some of those guys are in here. And they're pretty badass."

"And you've got magic," said a voice from his other side. Eleanor. She was looking at him with cool assessment, but a hint of encouragement too.

"Sure, except I don't know how to use it."

She shrugged. "Neither does anyone else. We're all figuring it out as we go along."

"And I expected Xya would—I don't know, help! But instead she's gone!"

"Yeah, that definitely sucks," Eleanor agreed. "But the guy from the other side's gone, too, according to Xya. So you're not at a disadvantage that way."

"Haha, no, I don't see any disadvantage in this situation *at all*," Ulric muttered, eyes on the giant advancing robot.

The followers of the Technocrat Avatar apparently hadn't sacrificed all of their gadgets to the building of the robot. More devices appeared in their hands from inside coat pockets and out of the backpacks and messenger bags. Every screen and button glowed the same eerie blue as the robot's eyes.

Nerlim grunted. "I might not survive this," he muttered, clutching his midsection. "I know those guys are supposed to represent technology, but there's fifth force energy coming from them, too."

"It makes a weird kind of sense; they're not *against* the fifth force, right?" Eleanor mused. "They're okay with magic, as long as they can use technology to control it."

"Remember what Xya told you," Heline said, patting Nerlim's arm. "Try to figure out how to use the energy, or redirect it. Maybe it will hurt less?"

"Well, there's an encouraging thought if I ever heard one," Nerlim grumbled.

Meanwhile, the Majickal Creatures of D'sharu had not wasted any time standing still. As one they surged forward, ready to do battle with the army of geeks. They didn't glow, since their power came from the natural source of their genes, but they rustled and squeaked and roared and squealed and made it known that just because a piece of tech glowed in the dark, they did not find it intimidating.

{THAUMATURGE AVATAR, WILL YOU SURRENDER?} the robot demanded.

"Never." Ulric was relieved his voice didn't shake.

{THEN YOU ARE DOOMED heeheehee} the robot intoned. The threat's effect was diminished by the little giggle that slipped out at the end of its words. {MINIONS, DO YOUR WORST!}

[minions? really?] sighed the Hat in a voice as dry as the dust on its brim. [so much drama]

"Guhhh." Nerlim doubled over as the first wave of the magic flaring all around the tower hit him.

Something in Nerlim's pained voice knocked Ulric into action. He turned to Heline. "Let's give that song about compromise a try, and see if it affects the other side's attitude. I'll help protect the creatures. If it doesn't seem to have any effect, we'll try to get the book."

Heline, standing beside Ulric, nodded and began to sing. Her clear alto voice rose over the tower, weirdly amplified, although what caused the effect Ulric couldn't guess. Next to Heline, Eleanor adjusted the tuning on her guitar and strummed some opening chords.

Ulric raised the polished wand, tried to focus his mind, and began sketching unfamiliar arcane symbols in the air with its gold-painted tip. Each completed rune sparked with golden light at the moment of its completion. In his mind's eye, he wove a magical cloak of protective energy around each of the Magickal Creatures as Heline's song echoed around them all.

In realms where magic doth conspire,
A single sovereign shall ascend higher.
Madness ensnares the waking world,
A tumult erupts, a tempest hurled.

Veiled truths beneath the shadows sleep,
The arcane line, its secrets keep.
In dormant minds, revelation stirs,
A cosmic battle where all time blurs.

Hope for tomorrow, a mystic spell,
Unseen truths, the past foretells.
With potent might, a power unfurls,
Windows tremble as magic swirls.

Veiled mysteries demand their yield,
In light, old truths may be revealed.
The conflict's goal, a fate to mend,
The compromise, where struggles end.

"You know, this one's not bad," Eleanor observed. "You've gotten better."

{WHAT ARE YOU DOING?} the robot yelled in the relative quiet as Heline finished a verse, smiling at Eleanor's compliment. {AVATAR!}

A wave of energy hurtled across the intervening space between the robot and the roof of the Dingle, a force that knocked Ulric and Heline back a few steps. Ulric's hat fell over his eyes and he heard Heline's gasped breath as if the air had been slammed from her lungs. He shoved the hat up to see Eleanor hold her footing, although a chord stuttered and jangled under her fingers. In Ulric's other hand the wand wavered; he almost dropped it. Nerlim slipped to his knees and Tiny Enos and Jans ran to help him up.

"Doin' okay," the old man muttered, still half-bent but back on his feet. "Think I'm starting to understand—"

He closed his eyes and stretched a gnarled hand out toward the robot. The hand trembled, but only a bit. Nothing happened, and he bent his head as if walking into a strong wind. His hand twisted and curled, clutching at the air, and he coughed with the effort.

{WHAT? WHO'S THERE? I'M CONFUSED. very confused} the robot said. It sounded increasingly flustered, all the bravado from a moment before gone. {Who are—}

And Ulric felt something change. Time slowed to a sticky molasses crawl. The world blinked from full colour to shades of grey, then back to full colour again. For the space of a heartbeat, the air tingled like bubbles from a fizzy drink hitting your nose, and settled with an almost audible thud. Ulric shook his head, wondering if anyone else had felt the same sensations.

But he didn't have long to wonder about it. Nerlim made a fist with his outstretched hand and pulled it back to thump against his chest. In the instant it made contact, Gammy appeared next to Nerlim in a cloud of wispy blue haze and a spray of silver sparks that dissipated like fog in the night air. She coughed and staggered upon landing on the tower's stone rooftop, and Jans caught her shoulders with a graceful but firm touch, guiding her upright. Nerlim's arm dropped, and, panting hard, he slipped to his knees again. The dull thud of bone meeting stone echoed around the top of the tower, and Nerlim's eyes fluttered closed.

How to Grow a Backbone

Wint

In the moment before Gammy disappeared from the robot's control room, Wint sensed something strange was about to happen. This didn't require much in the way of prescience, since strange things had been happening on a regular basis for several days now, but there it was. The air in the control room crackled with a thin, persistent static that lifted Wint's hair from his scalp. His skin prickled with a feverish heat and his stomach lurched. So it wasn't at all surprising when he glanced at Gammy to see her, and the chair in which she sat, enveloped in a misty blue glow.

"STOP THAT!" the Radio demanded, but it was clear from the confused look on Gammy's face that she was not the author of whatever new scene was being written here. Corax also seemed startled.

Rex regarded Gammy with ears pricked forward in curiosity, and even the droopy one stood a little straighter. "Now there's something you don't see every day," the dog observed.

"STOP HER!"

Wint...didn't move. He understood perfectly that the Radio expected him to comply, but the simple fact was, as he'd realized earlier, he didn't want to. He also failed to imagine any course of action that would forestall whatever was happening. Furthermore, he had no sense that Gammy was in actual danger. In fact, if this presaged her escape from the robot in some way, more power to her. He'd follow her in an instant if he could.

And then, in a blink and a faint blue flash, she was gone. A small puddle of water at the base of the chair, where her clothes had been dripping rainwater, was the only evidence she'd been there.

Corax swore with brief eloquence, and without asking permission or even saying goodbye to anyone, disappeared as well. Wint was not disappointed at the translucent being's departure. His half-present presence was unsettling in the extreme.

"I TOLD YOU TO STOP HER!" The radio's voice was apoplectic, and the case shook with such violent rage that it skittered sideways across the gleaming metal floor in an angry jig.

"Didn't know how." Wint shrugged and dropped into the recently vacated control room chair. It held a comforting familiarity, having once been part of Wint's car before it was subsumed into the robot, but that emotion dissolved into despair when he remembered the car's recent demise.

"Well, she was taken out of here by *magic*," the Radio snarled, "so I suggest that you might have stopped it with *other magic*."

Wint closed his eyes for a long moment before opening them again. "I may not have made it clear before this—although I could swear that I had—but *I can't use magic*."

"You used magic to open that lock on the tower door."

"If you say so, but it wasn't through the application of anything like, oh, *knowledge*, or *understanding*, or even *trying*," Wint said with uncharacteristic asperity.

"Honestly, that's fair." Rex turned to the Radio. "You said you were going to, but you've never given the man any actual training or instruction."

"I tried! It's not my fault he didn't pick it up. And anyway, he's my Avatar," the Radio blustered. "He should understand what to do!"

"Perhaps he's been a bit distracted, trying to deal with your bullying."

"Bullying? I've merely been pointing out my Avatar's duty—"

Wint stood up from the chair, patting the back of his jeans and looking down at the seat in dismay. It was, as he'd begun to suspect, unfortunately damp from Gammy's recent occupation. "I don't get why you'd assume I'd know anything," he told the Radio. It felt like he should care more about what was happening, but an odd detachment from the situation had settled over him. Why *had* he let himself be so intimidated by the Radio before this? "I'd suggest perhaps you've been misinformed, or that you don't fully understand the situation."

The Radio made some sputtering noises, as if it wanted to unleash a tirade at this suggestion, but struggled to articulate actual words.

"That's a good point." Rex padded over to stand next to Wint. "It seems to me that if anyone even masquerading as a manifestation of technology would understand the importance of instructions. What technology comes without a manual?"

Wint blinked, looking down at the dog. "Huh. That's true. I mean, you should see the size of the user manuals at NCDSF."

"I can only imagine."

"What is happening here?" the Radio squealed. "You two can't gang up on me!"

"When you consider it," Rex continued, ignoring the Radio with the complete unconcern usually only cats can muster, "if magic's involved, it might have been the simple power of you *thinking* about what you wanted the teaspoon to do that made it happen."

Wint frowned, unsure what the dog meant. "As I recall, at the time I was thinking that I didn't have a clue what I was doing."

"Sure, sure, but you understood we wanted the lock to open, right?"

"If I'm honest, I was rather hoping it wouldn't."

The dog licked its lips as if choosing its next words with care. "Fair enough, but you knew that opening the lock was *expected* of you."

"That was certainly made clear enough," Wint agreed with a sidelong look at the Radio.

"And it seems evident from everything that's happened since, that the existence of magic is real, and that it can...let's say, *influence*, the outcomes of using either technology or magic on its own."

Wint had the stray thought that he'd never considered dogs to be logical thinkers before, but that the idea deserved some serious consideration. He nodded for the dog to continue.

"So while the Thaumaturge Avatar is no doubt using full force magic to accomplish his ends, you can use a combination of magic and technology to accomplish yours. You just have to think about what it is you want the magic to help you do—in a way that makes use of technology, too."

Wint blinked. "Okay," he said, drawing out the 'ay' sound as if he were still unsure. "Look, could you give me an example?"

"Hey, spirit of the planet over here, in case you've forgotten," the Radio snapped. "In the middle of a little thing called A BATTLE FOR OUR SURVIVAL. This is the time for *doing,* not *talking,* and you're supposed to do what I tell you!"

Wint was saved from replying to this harangue by the return of Skete. Wint had almost forgotten that he'd gone off in search of better reception to contact his boss—someone called The Min—about what might or might not be happening at NCDSF.

"Okay," Skete said. "It took a while, but I got through to her. She'd already figured out about Sedrict and the Exile, so Xya and I are tasked with stopping whatever Sedrict plans to do."

"Not to repeat myself, but I thought you were here to help me? With all of—" he gestured around the robot's control room, "—all of this?"

"I know, and I'm sorry, mate, but all of this won't matter much if Majszak turns up. And it's the Boss's orders. You understand what that's like, I'm sure. And you've still got the dog, and—" he glanced around, apparently just noticing Gammy's absence. "Where's Ms. Gannand?"

"All I can tell you is: not here," Wint said, opening his palms wide. "For all I know, she's gone off to fight aliens or join a dance troupe or something equally unlikely."

"We'll be fine," Rex interjected, pressing close to Wint's leg and wagging his tail. "You go; do what you have to do. We can handle this end of things."

Wint looked down at the dog, confused by this sudden show of support. It was unexpected, but, to tell the truth, welcome.

"Don't listen to the dog!" the Radio screeched, and Wint rolled his eyes before he could help himself.

"I saw that, Technocrat Avatar," the Radio said before turning its attention back to Skete. "You may not leave. You are needed here, to help the Avatar."

"I've never had the chance to say this before, but you are not the boss of me," Skete said, glancing at the Radio with distaste. "Sorry, Wint, I don't have a choice. I have to go. Good luck. I'll be back when I can." And he turned and ran toward the hatchway leading down into the robot's body. Before he reached it, though, there was a shimmer of sparkling pale green light, a flash and pop like a car backfiring, and he was gone.

"Okay, back to what we were saying." Rex looked up at Wint. "You wanted an example of how to meld magic and technology."

"Did I? Yes, I guess I did."

Rex sat down, the very end of his tail thumping a faint tattoo on the metal decking of the control room. "Let's imagine you needed something like a microphone to amplify your words and let you talk to a lot of people at once."

"I despise public speaking. Don't you remember how hard it's been every time I've had to do it since all this started?"

The dog closed his eyes in an eloquent blink. "I know. This is just an example, right?"

"Right, sorry. Go on."

"Do I have to do everything around here myself?" The Radio's frustration was an almost palpable thing in the control room. "All right, I will! {THAUMATURGE AVATAR, WILL YOU SURRENDER?}" These last words boomed out from the robot's loudspeakers and echoed across the clearing outside.

"Like that?" Wint asked Rex.

"Exactly." The dog pulled its lips back, almost in a grin. "But of course, you don't have access to the same methods as the Radio does. But you have your teaspoon. Er, you do still have it, right?"

Wint fished in his pocket and pulled out the silver teaspoon. "I have it. But I don't see how—"

"You can make the teaspoon *act* like a microphone by channeling magical energy into it, the same as when you turned it into a key. Using magic to mimic the effects of technology."

Wint nodded slowly, his eyes staring unfocused out the robot's eye "windows" as he slipped the teaspoon back into his pocket. "Yeah, no, I don't get it," he said, "but I think I could, with time."

"That's a start. You might also, say, use magic to send a text to all of your followers at once, by typing out the text once and then channeling the magic to replicate it to everyone."

"Why would I want to do that?"

Rex shrugged his furry shoulders. "Oh, I don't know. Just something to think about."

"How do you know all this stuff, anyway?" Wint asked. He didn't say *you're just a dog*, but the words hovered around his lips.

"Well, I didn't, and then I did," Rex said, "kind of the way you became the Technocrat Avatar."

This was a much more enigmatic answer than Wint had hoped for, but it triggered another thought. "About that," he said to the dog, frowning, "if the Radio isn't the manifestation of technology, how am I still the Technocrat Avatar? Yet I seem to be, because of the whole teaspoon thing. Something doesn't add up, there."

The dog opened its mouth to answer, but the Radio forestalled it. Although Wint hadn't heard it, the Thaumaturge Avatar must have answered the radio's demand with a negative, because the Radio said, {THEN YOU ARE DOOMED} through the robot's speakers. Another unfortunate giggle slipped out as well, and Wint raised his eyebrows at Rex.

"Do you think it meant to do that?" he whispered.

"Doubtful. Here's an idea: we might want to consider a plan of action that doesn't include staying here and continuing our association with the Radio. Thoughts?"

Wint stared down at the dog, his mind in a whirl. "Is that—can we do that?"

The dog shrugged again. "I don't see why not. What's it going to do if we leave and seal it up inside here?"

And with those words, the swirling fog in Wint's brain dissipated as if blown away by the strong wind of the dog's logic. What was he doing here, letting himself be ordered around by a radio? A Radio that couldn't even seem to keep its own story straight? He hadn't asked to be the Technocrat Avatar or any kind of Avatar, but if he had powers or abilities, he'd be the one to decide how they were used, and when.

He pulled his phone out of his other pocket and thumbed it to life. "It's not going to like this," he told the dog, giving in to the one shred of doubt that still tapped at his mind.

"I, for one, don't care," the dog said, and gave himself a good shake. "I'm ready to go."

It didn't seem like the Radio had been listening to their whispers, because it ordered him with a dramatic flourish, {TECHNOCRAT AVATAR, DO YOUR WORST!}

Wint began typing with furious speed on his phone.

"Avatar!" the Radio hissed. "It's time. Channel some magic through this robot to make it a truly formidable weapon! Vanquish my foes! Take control of all the magic!"

Wint looked up from the screen. "Hold that thought." He looked down at Rex. "Ready?"

"Let's go."

Wint pocketed the phone, and he and Rex dashed for the hatchway leading down to the robot's leg and the doorway to the outside.

Behind him, he heard the Radio scream, {WHAT ARE YOU DOING? AVATAR!}, but he was too busy climbing down to answer. He was also mentally sending a volley of magical texts, and that was as many things as he could manage at once.

A Combative Relationship

Nerlim

Nerlim opened his eyes, aware of a dull ache radiating from his battered knees up and down his legs. Gameldina crouched beside him on creaking knees, holding his head. Nerlim blinked. Was he hallucinating her? But then she sneezed and inadvertently let his head bump off the stone floor. *Ouch.* Well, that was all right—she was here. It had worked! That was worth any number of aching joints and skulls.

Silence enveloped the rooftop as Heline's and Eleanor's song ended and the notes echoed into the dark forest and disappeared. In the quiet, Nerlim heard Gammy's gasped, "Nerlim Pettibone, did you do that? Bring me here? And are you all right?"

He raised his eyes to hers and patted her arm. "I think I did. And I'll do," he said, and flashed her a grin. "But now you owe me one."

She bent her head and kissed him, hard and just a bit fierce. When she pulled back, she looked surprised, but no more surprised than Nerlim felt. She put a hand to her heart as if something had happened inside her chest, and a stab of fear pierced his own.

Then she muttered, "Well, chicken on a stick, Gameldina, now you've gone and done it," and Nerlim breathed out in relief. He struggled to sit up, massaging his bruised knees.

Gammy seemed to recover herself, perhaps not even realizing she'd spoken aloud. Turning to address the group assembled at the top of the Dingle, she filled them in as succinctly as she could. "It's a real mess over there. Their Hat is a Radio, but it's not right in the head."

After everyone had taken a moment to decipher this cryptic statement, Ulric asked, "And it's the Radio controlling the robot, is that right? Not the Technocrat Avatar?"

"That's how it seems to me. Poor Wint's heart isn't in any of this, and I can't blame him, if he's had to deal with that Radio all this time," Gammy said. "He doesn't appear to be in control of anything. And I'm not sure how much actual help that other young man has been. Seems to spend a lot of time on his phone."

"He's leaving anyway—at least temporarily—to see what's happening at the Facility." Nerlim got stiffly to his feet. "Xya, too. It would be great if we could stop worrying about that."

"Yes, I hope they can lock things down out there. And that Argit's all right. But I'm concerned about Wint." Gammy shook her head. "I can hardly believe I'm saying this, but it's true. I worry that his grip on reality hasn't been too strong since things started happening at the launch, and now it seems like everyone is abandoning him. The look on his face just before you pulled me out, Nerlim—I felt bad. He still has the dog, of course, but I'm not sure Wint trusts him."

"Well, from a strategic perspective, we should have an advantage if the other side lacks a united front," Eleanor said. "And I overheard what Xya said to you before she left, Ulric. We should try to get that book, if we can. We need to use every advantage if the other side is weak."

"Book? What book?" Nerlim asked. "The one I found at the university library? But that woman stole it and took it who-knows-where. How can we get it back?"

Ulric looked sheepish. "Xya said that if you and I and Heline and Eleanor all worked together, we might be able to summon it using magic. But she didn't tell me how, and I don't know how to approach it."

Nerlim raised a skeptical brow. "If you haven't noticed, magic and I seem to have a...combative relationship."

"Me?" Eleanor sounded astonished. "I don't have any of this magic stuff."

Heline put a hand on her sister's shoulder. "You do, though. In your music. Same as I do, I guess."

Eleanor shook her head, grimacing. "I can play along while you sing, but there's nothing unusual about that."

The Hat had been silent for a while, but spoke up then, a hint of annoyance in its voice. [well if you're going to try it, please do so. i'm doing what i can to influence the way this battle is going, but i can't keep this up all night. help from another magical entity who might help me prevent anyone getting killed would be peachy. so far I've prevented any serious injuries, but I need help]

Gammy put her hands on her hips. Nerlim expected her to shake a finger at them, but she managed not to go that far. "You young people spend so much time *talking* about things instead of just getting on with them. I might have been like that in my youth...but I doubt it. Nerlim, get over here and get this going." She motioned to a spot next to Ulric where she apparently wanted Nerlim to stand. She went on without pausing for breath. "Ulric, Heline, Eleanor, this has to happen fast if it's going to happen at all. At least according to that Hat. Now, what do you need to do?"

Nerlim looked abashed. "Good question. For me, it's mainly reacting to magic, you know?"

Gammy threw up her hands. "But you yanked me over here from inside that dang robot, so it seems clear there's a little more to it than that."

Ulric stepped forward and held up his gold-tipped wand. He cleared his throat and straightened his back. His voice came out a little squeaky, but determined. "Miss Gameldina's right; we have to try. Heline and Eleanor, you're the musical part of our magic, so you don't need instructions from me. A song with some kind of calling or summoning theme would be great, but we don't have time to muck about, so we'll take anything at all."

"I think—" Heline rifled through her notes "—I might have something. It reminded me of a book when it came to me, honestly—"

"Great. I'll concentrate on the words and formulas in my head; I don't always understand them or how they work, but that hasn't been much of an obstacle so far. Nerlim, you're the trickiest, because I don't have a clear grasp of this redirection thing you're supposed to be able to do."

"Me neither, to tell the truth," Nerlim muttered. "I got lucky with it when I pulled Gameldina here. So far, being a sensile seems only marginally better than having nothing to do with magic at all."

"Me. Here," Gammy reiterated, pointing to herself and then to the tower.

Ulric nodded at Gammy. "Exactly. But it seems that when we're using magic, that gives you something to work with. So try the same kind of thing you did with Ms. Gameldina, but instead of redirecting the magic to a specific task, try to take the magic that comes your way and redirect it *back to me.* That might be helpful." After a pause, he added, "But perhaps not *at* me, if you know what I mean."

"To you, not at you. Right, I'll do my best."

Gammy stepped closer to him and took his hand again. "I'll be right here, if that counts for anything."

Nerlim blinked and smiled, the warmth of Gammy's hand in his radiating up his arm and wreathing his heart. Exploding restaurants and giant robots and inscrutable magic notwithstanding, this was turning out to be a good night. "More than you know."

{WHERE ARE YOU GOING?} the robot demanded in a loud, surprised voice. The words echoed around the clearing, drawing everyone's attention. Nerlim peered over the edge of the parapet with the others.

A figure had emerged from the hatch in the robot's leg, sprinting across the grass in the direction of the odd battle raging around the tower's base.

"Seal it! And power it down!" he yelled into an object that Nerlim took at first to be a microphone, but realized was, in fact, a teaspoon. It glinted silver in the straggling moonlight as he turned his attention up to the tower. "Truce! I call for a temporary truce!"

Behind him—and then in front of him, because it was faster—ran a dog, ears pinned back and tail streaming behind it like a flag. The teaspoon, in an unlikely turn of events—although Nerlim wondered why he was surprised at anything anymore—did indeed act like a microphone, amplifying the man's words even though there was nothing around the clearing that appeared to be a speaker.

Ulric, (or Prince Evernestigan, since he could slip on that persona now as easily as donning a hat) leaning over the parapet, called, "The request for a truce is accepted. Will you parley?"

With surprising speed, the fighting ceased. In response to the official establishment of a truce, all the majickal creatures broke off their attacks on the geeks and turned their eyes up to the robot. As one, as if acting upon some predetermined plan, the geeks turned toward the robot and aimed their devices at it. Clacking and whirring, it ground a few halting steps forward and stopped.

{AVATAR? AVATAR!} The voice sounded almost pleading to Nerlim, but it was difficult to summon up much sympathy for the thing that had just been trying its best to squash people.

"I'm sorry." The man stood looking up at the robot and continued to speak into the teaspoon. In the sudden quiet as the battle ended, his voice carried, clear and firm, to Nerlim and the others on top of the tower. "But I can't help you. You're either evil, or crazy, or possibly both, and I can't be a part of that."

"Told you," Gammy murmured to Nerlim. Then she shouted over the parapet, "Good for you, Wint!"

{NO!} the robot's metal voice screamed. {YOU CANNOT TURN AGAINST ME! I FORBID IT!}

The man shrugged. "Well, we've just sealed you up inside there, so I'm not sure what you can do about it." He turned to the assembled geeks, his apparent followers, and added, "I'm sorry, and thanks for acting so quickly on my text. I know you all worked hard on the robot, but we have to stop that thing inside it. Think of it as a...virus."

The faces of the assembled geeks, which had been crestfallen when told to shut the robot down, now registered concern. A few began conferring over their devices and thumb-typing commands.

Nerlim had been only peripherally aware of the hum of energy from the robot until it dwindled and died, and silence flowed in and settled around the Dingle and its environs. The blue glow from the robot's window eyes flickered and faded into blackness. The only sounds in the clearing were the soft snuffling and pawing of the majickal creatures.

"That's...it?" Ulric asked, sounding stunned. "It was that easy?"

Down below them, Wint blew out a long sigh and turned his face up to Ulric, who still peered over the parapet. He gave a little wave and then pointed his thumb back at himself. "Wint Usborne, Technocrat Avatar."

Ulric waved back. "Ulric Grivetton, Thaumaturge Avatar. It seems the situation has evolved. If you're willing, we should talk."

But Ulric hadn't taken more than a couple of steps toward the stairs when Nerlim became aware of a steady, rising hum, replacing the one that had been silenced only moments before. The familiar wrench clutched his stomach and he glanced instinctively toward the robot. Disappointment lurched in his heart when he saw that the extinguished blue light had been replaced by a baleful red illumination, leaping like flames within its eyes.

Everyone else seemed to have followed his gaze, and from the ground below, Wint Usborne's horrified voice reached them. "Oh, flark."

A voice came from the robot, small and uncertain, but laced with a faint thread of something like dismay. {M-M-Master?}

As the crimson glow brightened, the robot raised its metal arms in a menacing display of aggression. Well, one raised only halfway and before hitching to a halt with a grinding squeal, but that did little to diminish the menace. The robot seemed to answer itself in an unfamiliar voice, one filled now with rage instead of desperation.

{INDEED. I HAVE RETURNED} it said. {AND THINGS ARE JUST GETTING INTERESTING}

A Musical Collaboration

Heline

On the rooftop of the Dingle, hemmed by crenellated parapets and beyond those, the treetops of a shadowed forest, Heline searched through her notebook and struggled to keep up with the pace of events. At least the rain had stopped. Now stars spattered the violet-black night sky overhead as moonlight limned the tower, the nearby robot, and the churned and muddy clearing with pale silver light. In other circumstances, Heline might have enjoyed the vantage point and the view (except perhaps for the mud). At the moment, however, she was in no position to appreciate it. She had left off wearing the Hat, as it had more important things to do just now than help her find song lyrics. But now they had to summon a magical book she'd never seen, for a purpose she didn't understand, with a song that wasn't written. And the weird, aggressive robot had just gotten weirder and more aggressive. Heline didn't trust that crimson colour glowing in its eyes now.

It felt like a lot.

But the plain fact of it was that with Eleanor in the mix too, she couldn't do anything but try her very best. Not because she'd always been the sister who seemed to have it all together, but because she didn't want to let Eleanor down. She had to try at least as hard as Eleanor was trying. And she couldn't get distracted now.

Her eyes landed on the scribbled lines of the lyrics she'd been hunting, and she held the page out to her sister. "I don't think you saw this one before, and there's no time to fix it much, but maybe if I just sing it and you strum along best you can?"

"Sure." Eleanor ran her eyes down the page and nodded. "This one's not bad either. Sounds a bit prophetic, honestly." She settled her guitar more firmly in her grip. "I'll add in some resonance where I can. It makes sense that music with more depth should have more power, but what do I know about magic?"

"Your guess is as good as mine. This one's cryptic, but the themes seem right. And it at least mentions a book."

Ulric ran to them. "Wint and the dog are coming up, so we can make a plan. But time might be short, so let's try to get that book here, okay? It's the only solid piece of advice Xya gave me." He glanced over at the robot, and Heline followed his gaze. The robot stood still, eyes glowing crimson, one intimidating metal fist raised, the other arm stuck out at an awkward angle. It hadn't said anything else...yet. It was creepy in the extreme.

"Let's get the book," Heline agreed. They joined the others, creating a rough circle in the centre of the tower's rooftop. Eleanor counted down from three, and she and Heline began the song.

Closed, what once lay open wide,
Embraced by sleep, in dreams abide.
As magic completes its mystic round,
A book awakens at the sound.

Suns and moons in a cosmic dance,
A question sleeps within a trance.
Unified in power's embrace,
Recounts the tale of another face.

What commenced, shall onward flow,
Words entwined, like rivers grow.
Seal the portals, windows tight,
Descend together into night.

Sun and moon, their orbits true,
Bring they greetings, or adieu?

Balanced on the knife's keen edge
The ancient words renew the pledge.

Heline sang in her soft, lilting voice, and Eleanor filled in the accompaniment as smoothly as if she'd played the song many times before. Next to Eleanor, Ulric closed his eyes and held his wand aloft, as if its weight in his hand were a nexus to focus his thoughts. He muttered under his breath—Heline could make out the words, but she didn't understand them.

"Search axes x,y,z for concentrations of thaumic force. Eliminate possibilities based on cumulative accretion of thaumic force over time greater than three days. Identify possible cross-reference with secondary strong thaumic concentration; create thaumic attraction by matching arcane wavelengths and quantum entanglement..."

Heline blinked and pulled her attention away. Listening to Ulric's arcane logic would give her a headache, and make her stumble over the lyrics.

Across from Ulric, Nerlim emitted a grunt of pain, and Gammy responded with low murmurings of support. Theirs was a delightful relationship to watch. It was sweet and funny that they acted like they didn't know they were a couple, when they *emitted* couple-ness like a switched-on lightbulb. Just then a hand, warm and supportive, pressed the small of Heline's back. Even while she kept singing, she smiled. Jans was there. A glow of affection spread from her heart outward, through her torso and along her limbs until her toes and fingertips tingled with it. The glow suffused her voice, and it grew a little stronger, and a little clearer.

"Yes, maybe..." Nerlim murmured as if trying to fit a recalcitrant piece into a jigsaw puzzle.

A guitar string twanged with sudden discordance, and the razor slice of it whistled through the air near Heline's face. She dodged, her voice quavering and stuttering before she regained her balance and her equilibrium.

"Flarking rot." Eleanor swore, and a chord went sour, jangling flat and clipped. She picked the song up on the next phrase, but when Heline glanced at her sister, she saw the thin red line striped across her cheek, seeping blood where the sharp end of the wire had sliced her skin.

Heline's heart jumped in her chest and her voice faltered again. That had come frighteningly close to Eleanor's eye. She'd never forgive herself if something bad happened to Eleanor because of Heline's involvement in all this. Even if she hadn't looked for it or asked for it. It wasn't a price she was willing to pay. She was about to drop the song and call off the attempt when it unexpectedly *worked*.

With a loud *pop* and an iridescent swirl like the biggest soap bubble in the world bursting, a book materialized in the centre of the circle they'd formed. It hovered for the space of two heartbeats, and dropped like a stone onto the cold granite of the tower rooftop.

Ouch. An unknown voice, whispery and rough like sheets of old parchment rubbing together, gasped the word in Heline's mind, and apparently in the minds of everyone on top of the tower. And then, after a moment of stunned silence, it said, *Would someone be able to pick me up? This stone is cold and damp, and my bindings aren't as strong as they used to be.*

Nerlim picked up the Book and stood holding it in both hands, staring at it without moving for a long moment. Gammy joggled his arm and shot him an inquiring look, and he nodded.

"It's explaining what happened while that woman had it," he told them in an undertone. "The woman who took it was named Alsina, and it didn't cooperate with her, although she did read some of it. 'Paw through it' are the book's exact words. It's quite indignant about how she treated it, resorting to threats if it wouldn't speak to her." Nerlim lowered his voice even further, so that Heline almost missed it. "I'm trying to get a thought in edgewise to ask it to help us, but I think it needs to have this rant before it will listen."

"Relatable," Eleanor commented while she dug in her bag for a replacement guitar string.

Wint Usborne, the Technocrat Avatar, emerged onto the roof of the Dingle with a beautiful Whidden Shepherd loping close at his heels. Heline smiled at the sight of the animal, its black and silver coat shining in the moonlight and an unruly left ear turning like a satellite dish.

Working at the humane society, Heline loved all animals, but she had a particular soft spot for dogs. The Technocrat Avatar couldn't be all bad if he owned a dog, right?

And then, just when things looked brighter with the Book safely in Nerlim's hands, the robot came back to life.

{NOW LET'S SEE WHO'S IN CHARGE AROUND HERE} The robot's voice had changed. It had gone from confused and desperate to...smug. And not at all nice.

Heline gripped her notebook. *I should have expected this, because that's always the way these things go. One minute you've successfully materialized a magic book out of the ether, and the next a giant robot wants to crush you.*

The robot resumed its plodding march toward them. Or tried to resume it. It took three steps, shaking the ground around the tower. A few drifts of crumbled mortar broke free of the parapet stones and settled on the rooftop. And then came that discordant, grinding screech again, and the robot froze in mid-stride.

{WORK with me, here} The words started out thunderous, and then lowered in volume as if the robot had realized it didn't want to be overheard by everyone in the vicinity of the tower.

Ulric had crossed the roof to meet Wint Usborne, and they were deep in a hurried conversation. Heline was about to join them when red lights flashed around the clearing like lasers and the robot ground back into motion, its head swinging around as if searching for something—or someone. The moonlight fled before the crimson searchlights of the robot's eyes, and the woods leapt and shuddered with darting, shifting shadows. Heline suspected the robot was after the Technocrat Avatar, its supposed servant, who had run away from it and sealed the crazed radio inside. He and Ulric—all of them, in fact—were exposed and vulnerable here at the pinnacle of the tower. She imagined the robot sweeping them off the roof, then trampling them under one of those enormous metal feet to be flattened like horrible pancakes into the mud. But no, the magic would keep them safe. It had to, right? She clung to that thought like a cat clinging to the arm that wanted to put it into a bath.

The geeks and the magical creatures, united now against technology run amok, had joined ranks and formed a solid phalanx around the base of the Dingle, but it was obvious they would be no physical match for a giant robot with equally giant feet to crush them with. Even with the Hat and the Book providing magical protection, it seemed only a matter of time before the metal construct would overrun them.

[you have to write a new song] the Hat said in a maddeningly matter-of-fact voice. [that boy is going to be up against it soon. we all are]

Heline swiped back some wet hair that had plastered itself across her cheek. "Not the most inspiring of circumstances," she said, flicking water from her fingers. "Not the most conducive to concentration or creative thought."

[come on, it's what you do] the Hat persisted.

"All right." Resigned, she sighed and reached for the Hat.

[i'm afraid that won't work this time]

She stared at Arcanico, at its single eye fixed on her face. "What? What won't work?"

The Hat gave a sigh. [wearing me. i've done what i can for you; activated your ability to find the words. it's up to you now to follow through]

All the blood in Heline's body drained to her feet, leaving her light-headed and weak. "Up to me? But I can't—"

[you can. you have been. to be honest, i only helped you with the very first song]

She blinked at the hat, and the blood rushed back up her body, flushing her face with heat. [then why did you let me wear you the rest of the time? carry you around everywhere?]

The wrinkled fabric under the hat's eye shifted into something that looked for all the world like a grin. [it was fun?]

Heline scrabbled in her mind for how to reply, but once again was lost for words.

But the Hat was relentless. [come on, we have work to do. do i have to tell your sister you're giving up on this? now, when everything just got worse?]

"No!" She looked over to see if Eleanor had noticed the outburst. Her sister crouched at the side of the rooftop, hunched over her phone, and didn't glance up. Once the Book had materialized, she'd slung her guitar over her back draped with her jacket to keep it dry in the clinging mist, and pulled out her phone. "Leave Eleanor out of this," Heline hissed at the hat. "And what's happening with that robot? What's changed?"

[she's a strong magical resource] The Hat ignored her questions. [the two of you work well together; we just saw that. and now is when we need her the most]

Heline pressed her lips together in a thin line, warring with herself. The Hat took a perverse pleasure in being cryptic, but when it wouldn't tell her something, that meant she should insist on getting that answer.

"Tell me about the robot first," she insisted. "Is it something to do with the space facility? Is the Exile coming?"

[oh, he's here. he's here, and he's in that robot]

Shock warred with resignation in her mind, and resignation won. *Well, I guess I should have expected that, too.*

From below the Dingle rose a chorus of shouts from the geeks, but there was no time to look over the parapet. "Fine!" she yelled at the Hat, although since the rest of their conversation had been *sotto voce*, her outburst seemed to come out of nowhere.

Heline caught the perplexed look Nerlim and Gammy shared as she stomped past them to fetch up in front of Eleanor.

"I need your help again. But only if you want to give it." Her sister's face was bathed in the blue-white light of her phone, her eyes fixed on the screen. Jans had produced a bandage from his ever-present messenger bag and Eleanor had stuck it in haphazard fashion across the cut on her cheek. She hadn't said another word about it, but it must sting like crazy.

Eleanor's gaze didn't leave her phone. Both thumbs tapped on the tiny screen as if they were pistons. Heline knew trying to compose that fast on her own phone would make the result unintelligible. She wondered if her sister was texting someone to come and get her. She wouldn't blame her.

Heline squatted next to Eleanor, pushing back the damp hair that swung into her face. "Eleanor. Did you hear me? I just need an answer."

"What do you want? Can't you see I'm in the middle of something here?" She still didn't look up from the phone, just pulled it even closer to her face, as if proximity would facilitate her concentration.

Heline took a deep breath. "The Hat says we need another song."

That got Eleanor's attention. She looked up. "Seriously?"

Heline nodded. "Seriously. The Exile's landed in the robot now."

"Flark," said Eleanor, and Heline didn't bother chiding her for her language.

"Having the Book will help us, but it's not enough. But I'm out of songs. I might get some words if you can give me a tune, but the Hat can't help me anymore. I'm tired and blanking on the music and—" she broke off at a wordless scream from the ground below them. "And people are getting hurt."

Eleanor leaned toward Heline to show her the phone. "That's what I was doing. It just came to me and I was trying to get the notes down. I've almost got them in. I can play it back for you in a minute."

She bent over the phone again, her thumbs tapping out a soft rhythm. Heline left her, hurrying over to peer over the side at the chaos below. It looked like the robot had been distracted from its search for Wint Usborne and engaged in a redoubled effort to stomp on the assembled geeks and magic creatures. Some of them had been knocked down, if not crushed. This could turn disastrous.

She turned when someone tapped her on the shoulder. It was Nerlim. "What's the plan?"

"I'm supposed to have a plan? Why aren't you asking Ulric?"

The old man fixed her with a rheumy eye. "Girl, that's a good boy and a quick thinker with a lot of sense. I don't think he's at all easy to manipulate, no matter what Xya said before. But you're the one with genuine, creative power. Anyone could see that. You and that Hat. And if your sister's helping you, that's exponential power. So I'm asking you."

Before Heline could formulate an answer, Eleanor ran over, thrusting her phone out to her sister. "Listen." She held the phone close to Heline's ear and tapped a button on the side. The music started, tinny but clear in her ear.

The music, strong and evocative, thrummed with power even through the cheap phone speaker. Words flooded into Helin's brain, setting it afire despite the absence of the Hat on her head. She pulled her waterproof notebook out from beneath her coat and scrabbled in the pocket for her pencil with eager fingers.

"We're working on it," she told Nerlim, and began to write.

We Have to Work Together

Ulric

Ulric had gone to meet Wint Usborne, the Technocrat Avatar, as soon as he'd emerged onto the roof. The thin, worried-looking man and his dog were both panting, having run up the stairs.

"What are we going to do?" the two Avatars asked in unison, and Ulric felt a high, hysterical giggle threaten to bubble up in his throat. He swallowed it down. This was no time to lose control.

"We have to work together," he said, and Wint nodded.

The dog sat down near their feet and thudded its tail on the stone in agreement. "I'm Rex," he told Ulric, and offered a paw to Ulric to shake.

Ulric leaned down to accept, feeling that he had, at last, reached the point where nothing surprised him anymore.

"I wish Skete would come back. He was good at telling me what I should do next. At least he had ideas." Wint glanced down at the dog, as if for confirmation, but the creature shrugged in response.

"About some things," the dog allowed. "But he didn't know everything."

As if summoned, a young man Ulric didn't recognize staggered up the steps behind Wint. He looked like he'd been in a fight with someone larger and more experienced, and it had gone about as well as one might expect. His shirt was torn on one side and a bruise blossomed dark purple on his cheek. Wint turned at the sound of footfalls on the steps, his face a mixture of surprise and hope.

"Skete, you're back! I hope you have good news." Wint seemed not to notice Skete's battered state. "I think I've made the Radio angrier than it was before. And this is Ulric, the Thaumaturge Avatar, by the way. We're working together now."

Ulric nodded a greeting. So this was Xya's counterpart, the one who'd gone with her to NCDSF. Ulric had a sudden premonition, from the expression on Skete's face, that the news about that wasn't good.

Skete responded with a brief wave and a nod, leaning against the stone parapet as he tried to catch his breath. "Hey, cool." He glanced over the parapet as the robot's head swung, murderous red eye-beams sweeping the clearing, and it laid frenzied waste to the creatures around the base of the tower.

Or tried to. It jerked and stuttered, like a toy whose batteries were dying. The construct had begun a ragged, inarticulate growling that might have come from its gears.

"Could be worse. He's mostly missing them. And someone's popped up a magical shield to help protect everyone on the ground." Skete pointed down to the skirmish.

Ulric joined Skete and looked over. He saw no shield, but it was true none of the geeks or creatures seemed to be suffering any serious injuries. If they staggered back from a kick or the swipe of a metal fist, they recovered, unbloodied. If they fell, they were back on their feet after only a brief pause.

That would be thanks to us, said another voice. A soft, raspy voice that sounded like pages turning in an old book—because it was, in fact, the voice of the magic Book they'd summoned, still cradled by Nerlim. *Arcanico and I work well together. But make plans quickly, because we can't keep this up forever.*

"It seems to be mad at everything now." Wint joined them in peering over the edge.

"There's a reason for that." Skete sighed. "The Exile is in there now, too."

Ulric stepped back from the parapet, throwing his hands in the air. "So we have a crazed Radio *and* an evil magic-user inside the robot now? And here I thought things couldn't get any worse."

"What happened at NCDSF?" Wint asked Skete. "Because when Gammy hears that it didn't go well, she'll lose it. I might take my chances with the Radio and the robot."

"What happened to my facility?" Gammy and the others had gathered around them to hear the report, all except Heline and Eleanor, still bent over notebook and phone. Wint was right; Gammy glowered as she asked the question.

"If we'd made it there faster—but the disturbance in the worldweft slowed us down. We had to transport three times when it should have taken one. We found him when we got there—Sedrict, of course, trying to break the Exile out of his prison. He was in the middle of transmitting a spell of some kind to Majszak—"

Skete was interrupted by a loud popping sound. It announced the return of Xya, who apparated in a shimmer of sparkly blue light and, with no one to steady her, tumbled to the unforgiving stone of the tower's roof. She landed in a puddle of accumulated rainwater and swore in a language Ulric didn't recognize—but he didn't have to understand the language to recognize swearing. Xya looked as battered and bruised as Skete, her clothing torn and bedraggled in places, her blonde hair lank and sulking.

Skete shook his head as Jans and Tiny Enos helped Xya to her feet, and she limped over to join them.

"Majszak?" Ulric prompted. He had a sinking feeling he'd never get all these names straight.

"That's the Exile," Skete said. "We tried to stop Sedrict, and we might have managed it because it was two of us against one. But Alsina showed up, swearing about how she'd had trouble transporting and someone had stolen a book from her—"

Ulric grinned. At least they'd done something useful.

"So that evened the odds and all the time we were fighting, the spell message was transmitting. We couldn't stop it. But at the last minute, Xya smashed something—"

Gammy's eyes popped in her head and her face darkened like a storm blowing in. A vein in her temple throbbed as if it might burst. Wint whimpered and leaned against the parapet for support.

"Don't worry, we'll fix everything once we sort this out," Xya hastened to reassure her, although even she looked disturbed by Gammy's reaction.

"—and she interfered with the very end of the spell. So the Exile, Majszak, made it here, but only in part."

"What does that mean?" Nerlim asked.

"Whatever they were doing, it wasn't one hundred percent successful. His body didn't make it. That's still back on the exile planet, while his—essence, I guess you could call it—is here. So Majszak needs to inhabit something, and when he followed the trail of powerful magic, it brought him here. That's why I think he's in the robot."

"That's why *we* think he's in the robot," Xya corrected.

[he *is* in the robot] the Hat confirmed. [i can sense it, and we have heard him speak]

"It's my fault," Ulric faltered. "We were using magic, me and Nerlim and Heline and Eleanor, trying to summon that book. We led Maj—Masz—whatever his name is; the Exile. We led him here."

But Skete shook his head and put a hand on Ulric's shoulder. "No, not you. The Exile illegally activated the magic here on D'sharu long ago. He still has a strong connection to that old, innate magic. *That's* what drew him."

Ulric blinked. "The Hat said something about old magic earlier, when we were at Heline's."

[The old magic doesn't want to be awake—doesn't want to join with me. It was…damaged, when this Majszak woke it unnaturally long ago. That's what's in the radio]

Wint blinked. "So that's why the Radio kept changing its story? It was the old magic all along?"

[correct. It wanted things to return to the way they were, but it's too late for that]

The Technocrat Avatar blew out a long sigh and shook his head. "In that case, where's the actual manifestation of technology? Because I'd like to know when I can go home."

"Well, since you're asking," said the dog in an apologetic tone, almost forgotten on the stone floor next to Wint and Skete, "that would be me."

In the stunned silence that followed, a deep chuckle erupted from the hat. [I was wondering when you'd reveal yourself]

"Did anyone else hear the dog claim to be the manifestation of technology?" Wint stared wide-eyed down at the canine in question. "Because I might be experiencing a psychotic break from reality. I almost hope so, as a matter of fact."

Heline and Eleanor had joined the group in time to hear Rex's revelation. Eleanor dropped to her knees on the wet stone and gave the dog a thorough scratch around the ears. Manifestation of technology or not, Rex knew dog lovers when he saw them, and he accepted the attention with a lolling tongue. Heline added her attentions to Eleanor's, and there were many mutterings of "who's a good boy?" to which the answer was obvious.

Wint, however, was shaking his head. "Now I understand all that stuff you said before we left the robot, but why didn't you say something sooner?" he demanded of the dog. "Why show up and act like you were looking for me for no real reason? Why not say something when the Radio claimed it represented technology—"

Rex shook himself and looked up at the assembled humans and trans-dimensional beings. "Okay, look. At first, I wasn't even sure what was going on. I was feeling my way through all of this. One minute I was a normal dog, and the next—that was just like I told you."

"I didn't say anything when the Radio made its claim, first because I was confused. I wanted to see what game it was playing, so it was important to play along. We weren't doing anything very different from what I would have suggested anyway, so it seemed wise to keep my mouth shut."

Skete nodded. "You were undercover. I get it."

"When the Radio changed its story, I got thrown for a loop again." The dog scratched its side while it explained. "What was it up to? Was it time to reveal myself? I wanted to find out everything possible about both sides. And here I am, and we're all together," he finished. "So it wasn't such a bad way to play it after all, was it?"

"Sure, except now we have a crazed Radio inside a criminal-possessed robot, and they're both trying to kill us." Eleanor scratched the dog's ears even as she spoke with soft reproach. "So maybe also not the *best* way to play it, either?"

The dog huffed as if conceding the point, and his ears drooped a little. Eleanor gave him another scritch under the chin so he wouldn't feel too bad about it.

"I think the important thing right now," Ulric said, breaking in to the conversation, "is whether we're on the same side against said crazed Radio and possessed robot. I'm willing to work together against the current threat and sort out who's going to control magic on the planet later. That seems like the least of our worries."

"Same." Wint glared down at the dog. "As long as Gammy gets her moon launch back, I don't give a squashed fig one way or the other."

Gammy patted Wint on the back. "Thank you, Wint. That's very kind of you."

[i agree we must confront the larger threat first]

"Okay, we're all on board, but what can we do?" Ulric asked. "If Xya and Skete couldn't stop him…"

Xya stepped up and put a hand on his arm. "Remember, though, our powers and abilities are still limited. We don't have full access to the thaumic force because we're only here as guides. We have more options than someone like Corax, but we're still restricted."

"Excuse me, but I'm right here." Corax sounded affronted, materializing—at least as fully as he was able—next to Gammy and Nerlim.

"Okay, but to be fair, you weren't there when I said that."

"I hope you're here to help," Gammy growled at him.

"I want this resolved as much as the next person, so I can leave this wretched planet."

"And the Exile, is he limited as well?" Heline asked, trying to get the conversation back on track as Corax floated off with his nose in the air to look down at the struggling robot.

"Yes and no," Skete said slowly. "He's limited by being incorporeal, but he's still a powerful being. If the magic won't cooperate with him, that's something. We could handle him if we had The Min here, too."

"The Min?" Nerlim asked. "Who's that again?"

The tower shook beneath them as the robot took a shuddering step closer.

"Short answer: our boss. She'll deal with Majszak if she can get here, but the worldweft disturbance is keeping her away."

"So we can't rely on her for help with this, unless we can settle the worldweft," Tiny Enos said. He'd been quiet so long that some of them must have forgotten he was there, seeing how they startled at his voice. "The Min has to get here and contain the Exile so the worldweft will settle, but she can't do that until the worldweft settles. It's an impossible riddle unless we can make a difference from down here."

Xya pointed an approving finger at him and nodded. "But we all have abilities that, if we pool them, might create a synergistic reaction and amass a larger portion of arcane energy to utilize."

"Not like I understood most of that, but fine. You're saying we gather magic. What do we *do* with it?" Eleanor voiced what Ulric was also wondering.

"We have a few options." Xya ticked them off on her fingers. "Try to calm the worldweft. Restrain the robot and keep Majszak inside until The Min gets here. Or even try to get Majszak out of there and trap him."

"Nice idea, but how do you trap an incorporeal entity?" Gammy asked. "Look at Corax, there. Insubstantial as smoke and he can pass straight through solid objects, so we can't pop a glass over him like we would an insect."

"Again, I can hear you."

Gammy stuck her tongue out at him.

Skete glanced at Xya. "Maybe with magic, but we're not strong enough. Ulric, you might be able—"

But Ulric shook his head. "I haven't done enough magic yet to try anything like that. So should we try to keep him inside the robot, and restrain that? Keep hindering the robot and making it difficult for Majszak to control, like Arcanico and the Book are doing now? Or try to force him out of it? Would that put him at a disadvantage?" Ulric frowned as his mind raced through possibilities. "Can he leave the robot at will? Or does he need something else to inhabit if he does? What kind of thing? Does it have to be something touched by the fifth force? Something magical?"

"Whoa, whoa, slow down. That's a lot of questions." Xya held up both hands to stop the barrage.

"The Min sent us some notes," Skete offered, pulling out his phone. "I got a message through to update her when I landed back here, and her reply must have found a break in the disturbance."

"What?" Xya took hers out, too. "Cheese and rice, I had notifications off."

Ulric met Eleanor's eye and raised an eyebrow while the two trans-dimensional beings scanned the information. Eleanor bit her lip, stifling a giggle, and Ulric had to look away. It was nice to know that nobody was perfect. Not even beings from another plane of existence.

"Okay, she says if he tries to exist outside something magical or something living for longer than a minute or so, he should be snapped back to the rest of his body on the exile planet."

Nerlim gulped. "Something living?"

Xya shrugged. "He might try to inhabit a person, dominate their own personality for a time. It wouldn't be a permanent solution for him, though."

"An animal?" Rex perked his ears attentively.

"Not a compatible host. I don't think it would work."

"And it would have to be close by. She says he can't travel far when he's incorporeal." Skete tapped the screen of his phone.

"What do we do if he tries to take over one of us?" Eleanor asked. "Or someone down there?"

"It's not easy to take over someone else's mind in their own body," Skete said. "Exert your mental will against the incursion, and you should be fine."

Easy to say, thought Ulric.

"I'm sending all my followers home." Wint pulled out his phone and began another text. "There's nothing more they can do against the robot, and they're only in danger of being possessed if they stay here."

"But the majickal creatures can't be possessed by him, so that's fine." Ulric felt like he was juggling too many balls at once, and any he dropped might be big enough to crush him.

"Right. So maybe we try to get the old magic and Majszak at odds," Eleanor said. "Get the Radio or whatever to boot him out of the robot. We all block him; he has nowhere else to go and poofs out of here back to his prison. Would that work?"

Skete and Xya exchanged a look. "I don't know if the Radio can get him out, though."

"What if Arcanico and the Book helped it? Like, boosted the radio's signal. Is that possible?"

[it doesn't like me] the Hat said. [but it might dislike Majszak more]

I might be able to reach it, said the book, *Echoes of Potentiality. I have been around almost as long as it has, marinating in magic lore. Perhaps I could appeal to our common history, and the good of the planet.*

"Please try," Ulric asked them. "And the rest of us will collaborate on the other route. Try to drive a wedge between the old magic in the Radio and Majszak; see if we can get the Exile out of the robot so he gets booted from the planet."

"Okay, well, we have a new song," Heline said. "I'm finishing the words now. We wrote this one together." She smiled at Eleanor and Eleanor smiled back, and Ulric's heart did a quick double-thump. He'd thought Eleanor was pretty when she was all grump and sarcasm, but she was stunning when she smiled.

I'd like to live through this, he thought. *I'd really like to live through this.*

"All right," Ulric said. His mind raced, flitting among the people on the roof as if he were a kid constructing an old dot-to-dot picture. When the lines had connected enough dots to make a shape, he said, "Here's what we're going to do."

Ulric had rather expected that he'd have to work a little harder to get their attention, but the silence that fell over the roof of the Dingle at his words was complete. Everyone stood staring at him, waiting for him to reveal a plan they obviously expected to be fabulous.

He turned first to Wint. "I think the Radio is angriest with you right now, yes?"

Wint nodded. "It's safe to say I've pissed it off."

"And Xya and Skete, the Exile would view you as the greatest threat to his freedom?"

"Probably. We didn't stop him at the facility, but he knows we won't stop trying."

"So you three will be bait. You'll keep the Exile distracted." Wint blanched. Rex said, "I'll go with Wint, too. We make a good team."

"Heline and Eleanor will sing their dencryption, and Nerlim," he said, turning to the older man, "you'll do what you did before, where you bounce the effects of magic off yourself and use it to affect the world around you. All of you will protect the bait."

"Please don't call us *the bait*." Even with Rex at his side, Wint still looked pale.

"Er." Nerlim raised a hand as if he were back in school. "I still don't know that I'm very good at it. I've only done it twice."

"Well, as my grandmother used to say, you'll never learn younger," Ulric told him with an attempt at a grin. "And try to channel some of the residual energy to me."

"While you do what?" Gammy asked. She hovered close to Nerlim with a protective hand resting on his shoulder.

"Transport myself over into the robot and try to drive a wedge between this Exile person and the Radio. As I understand it, Majszak is counting on the old magic as an ally. We stop that if possible."

"I should come with you," Eleanor said. "I can play music—and sing a little—if you need a magic boost."

"But you have to stay. Heline needs your music while she sings."

Eleanor shook her head. "The music enhances the effect, sure. But Jans can pinch hit for me, can't you, Jans?"

Jans blinked, but nodded and reached into his messenger bag. He pulled out a small wooden box studded with a v-shape of metal keys above a sound hole. "I can hit the pinches with kalimba," he said, nodding, and he thumbed a sweet, mellow chord on the instrument for emphasis.

"Then you'll transport both of us," Eleanor told Ulric with confidence. She slung her guitar around to her back, crossed to Ulric, and put her arms around his neck. "I'm ready to go."

Ulric went still.

Heline looked as though she might protest, but she swallowed the words. Jans put one arm around her and she smiled up at him. "It'll work."

"What about me?" Gammy rested hands on hips in her classic pose of belligerent defiance. "What can I do to help? My launch will never get off the ground until all this is settled. I need technology to work, but it won't be any good to me unless it's solid and reliable. I want a part of fixing this mess."

"You keep Nerlim focused," Heline said. "He relies on your support."

Gammy's glare was darker than the thunderclouds overhead. "Yeah, I can do that, but it's not all I can do. I'm a grown-ass competent woman, and I was really hoping for a chance to hit something."

Heline reddened. "Sorry, I didn't mean—"

"It's all right. But I have a lot of pent-up rage, and If I don't hit something soon—"

"Wait, I am having a baseball bat." Jans stepped up to Gammy and held out the bat he'd brought from Heline's house. "If you are having chance to using it, you are to be my guest. I need both hands for this," he added, holding up the kalimba.

Gammy took the proffered weapon and hefted it, smacking it into her palm once or twice to test the weight. "If I have a chance, I'll use it with pleasure," she told him with a grim smile. "Thank you. And in the meantime, I'll help Nerlie here as much as I can."

"I appreciate it." Nerlim blushed at the use of this pet name.

"You'd better."

"Okay," Ulric said, "Okay. If we all know our places—"

"Let's do this," Heline said, and began to sing.

Intermezzo Otto

The Min

The Min had not been idle while events unfolded on the planet D'sharu. She'd hand-picked seven members of the Convocation whom she trusted to help with the Majszak problem, contacted them, and enlisted their help. They'd all been ready and willing to accompany her, but those plans had to wait until the disturbance around the planet settled enough to let them through. Since this disturbance was partly natural and partly magical, The Min knew that might take anywhere from ten minutes to several hundred years, planet-time. She was hoping for something considerably closer to the former.

Waiting was not a skill that came naturally to The Min. She was used to being in charge, used to calling the shots; used to being the one who made others wait if it suited her. Being powerless was not a comfortable position.

And yet there she was, unable to do anything to guide or influence the current forces colliding on D'sharu. In a bid to do something, anything, she'd dispatched three envoys to the exile planet to check on Majszak, but they'd returned with a report that was inconclusive, at best. Since the exile planet was a place of no magic, the envoys had to stop at some distance from it or risk the failure of their own abilities. However, they should have been able, even at a distance, to sense the presence of Majszak.

"And we did," said the young being with the pale green complexion and shower cap to whom The Min had explained Exiles earlier. Her name had turned out to be Azuriia, and since she'd never even heard of

Majszak before, The Min trusted her with this task. "We sensed him, but not all of him."

The Min blinked.

"It's true," confirmed Drix, his thin brows drawn together. "Something's not right, but not altogether wrong, either, if you see what I mean."

With admirable control, The Min said, "I don't. Can you clarify? Is Majszak still on the exile planet or not?"

"No."

"Yes."

"Sort of." It was Ignacjianna who equivocated, the flame-haired woman (whose hair was not truly on fire, but only appeared so). She crossed her arms as if to underscore her statement. "My impression was that his body is there, but something—his magical essence?—is not."

The Min sat back, steepling her fingers to hide her alarm. A strange constriction had clutched her chest; a feeling to which she was not accustomed. "So Sedrict and Alsina must have succeeded—at least partially—in their plan."

That was when a brief message had arrived from Skete, worming through a break in the disturbance to confirm what the envoys had reported. With Drix, Azuriia, and Ignacjianna's frantic help scouring the accumulated knowledge of the books, The Min had sent back what little advice she could, making ten attempts before the message squeaked through. When it did, she sat back in her chair, letting her mask of reserve slip in an unaccustomed show of anxiety. She ran her hands through her hair, sparking lightning and discombobulating stars until the air hummed with static.

Drix voiced the question at the root of The Min's discomfort. "What do you think this means for Skete and Xya? What will they do?"

"I don't know. This is certainly a lot for them and a couple of untried Avatars." She thought for a long moment. "All we can do is keep trying to get down there."

And she started searching once again for a way through the worldweft disturbance snapping and roiling around the planet.

I Am the Technocrat Avatar

Wint

Wint reflected, as he hurried toward the stairs with Xya and Skete following, that his life was out of control. He was about to distract an unstable Radio locked inside a malfunctioning robot controlled by some other enraged entity, while some kids who could do magic—a little—attempted to put said Radio and entity out of commission. He was unsure how to accomplish his task, and even with two trans-dimensional beings for company, he felt very much alone.

"You're not alone," came a voice from behind him. It wasn't Skete or Xya. He stopped and turned. True to his word, Rex had followed him down the stone steps. A few thin shafts of moonlight filtered in through the arrow slits, illuminating the stairs just enough to make out the edges. The dog's eyes were mere dark pools in the gloom.

"Did I say I was?" Wint asked. He'd been pretty sure that had been internal, but nothing would surprise him.

"Yes, you did, although it was more like a whimper. But look, just be fast on your feet, throw some insults at the radio, and keep it off-balance while Ulric and the others do their stuff. We can handle that."

Skete and Xya sidled past them with curious glances, but continued down the stairs. "Don't be long!" Xya called over her shoulder as they passed.

"I'm grateful," Wint said, "but why are you doing this? I thought you didn't like me much."

The dog shrugged its furred shoulders in an eloquent gesture. "Man's best friend. It's a saying for a reason, you know. And I do like you, Wint. You're not what I expected at the beginning, but you're a good guy."

Wint knelt, now eye-level with the dog. He felt a strange urge to stroke the dog's head, but maybe that would go too far. Rex might find it condescending, and Wint didn't want to endanger their fragile camaraderie. Instead, he stuck out his hand. "Shake?"

Rex regarded him with a considering look for a moment. "If you're offering, and not commanding."

Wint nodded. "I am."

The dog put its front paw into Wint's hand and they shook solemnly.

The dog shook itself. "Now let's do this." And they followed Skete and Xya out of the Dingle.

Utter chaos reigned outside the tower. The majickal creatures swarmed on the grass, making valiant attempts to attack the robot (most of which failed), avoid slipping on the wet grass and mud (most of which failed), and support each other (most of the time getting this one pretty much right). Most of Wint's followers were attempting to heed his texted instructions to flee, but they were taking their time about it, gathering belongings and sorting themselves into the remaining vehicles. The majickal creatures assisted by covering them while they did this. A short time ago they'd been sworn enemies, but perhaps when magic and technology mixed, the outcome wasn't always a disaster. Maybe sometimes it was cooperation.

Wint skidded to a stop close to one of the robot's enormous feet, each the size of a small cottage. A centaur put a hand on Wint's arm to steady him, and Wint smiled his thanks. His brain stuttered for a moment—*centaur*—but then the gears caught again. He cupped his hands around his mouth and yelled up at the robot, directing his remarks to the radio.

"Hey, Radio! You think you can accomplish something just because you're in a big tin can? Everyone's deserted you."

As insults went, it was lame, but there hadn't been time to come up with anything. Besides, it shouldn't be too difficult to get a rise out of the crazed radio.

"Yeah, Majszak, same!" yelled Skete. "I don't see your lackeys around anywhere, do you? You're alone, and you're going back into your prison soon."

The robot's head swung around, eyes searching the ground like maddened scarlet spotlights until they found the tormentors.

"You," the Radio hissed, its voice picking up a metallic note as it channelled through the robot. "I'm done with you. And I'm not alone. My master is back!"

"And I'm not leaving again," said the other voice, the Exile's voice, though it also came through the robot, deeper and more echoing than the Radio. "You forget that I own magic on this world."

"Well, not so much own—" the Radio started, but its words were lost when the robot picked up an enormous foot and brought it crashing down toward Wint, aiming to crush him and the dog in a single stomp.

This would have been a wonderful time for the robot to glitch, but of course its movement was as smooth as if freshly oiled. The quick-thinking centaur and a geek on roller skates (how in the world were they still functioning in this wet grass, Wint wondered) each grabbed an arm and pulled him out of the way while the geek also scooped up Rex, before the foot crunched down where he'd been standing. Mud splattered up and sprayed the four of them, but the foot missed its mark.

"I'm still the Technocrat Avatar," Wint yelled up at it. "And neither of you is the boss of me! I'm with the true manifestation of technology now, and what are you? A radio. A robot. *Technology.* You will listen to us!"

"No, I won't," the Radio screamed, its voice crackling with a shrill of static. "You serve me, not the other way around."

"You're old magic! You're not even current!" Wint taunted. "Even if technology and the new magic make a truce, you're old news!"

The robot bent and smashed a fist into the ground, sending two geeks and a winged griffon flying in a spray of mud.

Rex barked wildly and ran in a circle around one of the robot's feet. Distracted by the sound, the robot straightened and swiped at the dog, but its movement was far too slow to catch him.

Skete and Xya, a little distance back, muttered and gestured in unison, perhaps trying to access some of that fifth force magic. When they released it, yellow light crackled up the robot's frame and sizzled around its head. The Exile's voice exhaled a huff of pain and the robot staggered a few steps back as geeks and majickal creatures darted out of its way.

Someone tapped Wint's shoulder, and he turned to see a young woman with large black glasses and brown curling hair caught up in a messy bun on top of her head. She wore a t-shirt with an obscure video game reference, jeans, and military style boots already caked with mud. A canvas cross-body bag bumped on her hip and she held what looked like a slingshot made from a hard drive cage and some elastic cable ties.

"Duck," she advised him, drawing an older, oversized cell phone from the bag. She fitted it into the slingshot, pulled back the cable ties, and let the thing fly straight towards the robot's left eye. Wint ducked but tilted his head so he could watch the trajectory. The phone hit its mark and tumbled back to the ground, but he glimpsed a tiny star of cracks where it had impacted the eye.

"You're supposed to get out of here," Wint said, grateful but concerned. "It's too dangerous!"

"I will," she promised with a grin, but in the next second she was gone, ducking in under the robot's feet to snatch up the mobile phone and disappear into the darkness beyond.

Rex ran up to him and skidded to a stop. His long pink tongue lolled out of one side of his mouth. "How long will it take Ulric and the girl to teleport over?" he panted.

Wint looked back at the tower, but from here the parapets hid the rooftop. "I don't know. Hopefully someone will give us a signal."

[TECHNOCRAT AVATAR] the radio's robot voice boomed over their heads. [I have no patience for betrayers]

Wint and Rex looked up to see the robot holding a car high above their heads. It was only a compact model, a little green hatchback owned by one of the lingering geeks. Even at this distance, Wint could make out a bumper sticker that read *Hack the Planet*.

I'm trying, Wint thought, *But it's not going so well.*

You Blew Up a Tree

Nerlim

Nerlim Pettibone had done many things in his long life. He'd made astounding scientific discoveries, found and lost love, searched the world for the fifth force, and finally found both it and love again. He didn't consider himself a coward, nor particularly brave.

He didn't feel brave right now.

Nerlim had only the vaguest idea of what he was supposed to do with the magic. "Funnel it," Xya advised, but she had no details about how to do that. And that young whippersnapper, Ulric, had grinned and said *you'll figure it out*. He'd rescued Gammy from the robot out of fear and desperation, not with any plan or finesse. Now he rubbed his hands together, sweaty palms sticking to each other. In the unfolding crisis, he was out of time. The first notes of Heline's song caught him like a fist in the stomach, driving his breath out in a gasp. He doubled over and Gammy's hand touched his arm.

"Catch it and release," she suggested. "Don't let it hit you or absorb it...deflect it away. Use it, like you did to get me out of that robot."

Sure, except that was a fluke, Nerlim thought, but he tried his best to recreate what he'd done. He closed his eyes and imagined the magic like a soccer ball. The force of it drove into his gut, almost staggering him, but he got his metaphorical hands behind it and heaved.

"Hey! Watch what you're doing!"

Eleanor glared at him over her shoulder. Ulric and she had not transported yet, as Ulric's wand sketched arcane runes in the air and she stood with her arms around the young man's neck. But her hair had been...changed. Where once had been soft curls of sea-green hair, now two long blond braids fell below the hem of her skirt. She looked down at one of the braids and wrinkled her nose in disgust. "What the burned biscuits am I supposed to do with this?" she asked Nerlim. "I'm only going to cut it off again, you know. And dye it green."

"Sorry! Poor aim." He had to get better at visualizing where to send energy when he released it, instead of launching it at random. He might do serious damage by accident, and not damage that would help their friends.

Nerlim moved away from the parapet, reminded that the next surge in magical energy could hit him with enough force to send him hurtling over the side. Now that he focused on it, he sensed it trickling in as Heline continued to sing. So, not so much like a soccer ball, but a garden hose? Maybe he could gather the slow trickle and release it in waves, so the only pain would come at the start of a song or spell. Closing his eyes again, this time he envisioned a bucket in which he caught the shining thread of magical force. Once the bucket was full, he drew back and launched, sending the accumulated energy out in a surge like the tide coming in.

A sharp crack split the air, followed by a chorus of alarmed shouts and yelps. Nerlim's eyes flew open in time to see a shower of sparks rain down from the top of a tall pine, and the upper ten feet of the tree topple and plummet to the ground with a crash. Heline's voice faltered on a note before picking up the song again.

"Butter!" Gammy said with admiration. "Was that you?"

"I don't know! What happened?" Nerlim gasped. The effort had left him shaky, and he put a hand on Gammy's shoulder to steady himself.

"You blew up a tree!" Gammy stretched up and planted a peck on his cheek. "See, I knew you could do it."

Nerlim staggered to the edge of the tower's roof and peered over. The tree hadn't hit anyone when it landed, but a woman and two rabbit-like creatures with wings stood nearby, looking affronted. "I'm not sure how productive that was."

"You'll do better next time." Gammy sounded much more confident than Nerlim felt. "Third time's the charm! Try to send it to one of the magical people so they can re-use it."

"Nerlim," Ulric called, "I've got it; get ready! Incoming!"

This was it. No room for more mistakes. The older man closed his eyes, envisioning a large garden trug in his hands. He gripped the imaginary handles tight, waiting for the energy to flow in. When it did, he hoped he'd be ready.

He almost wasn't. The back draft from Ulric's transport spell needed a strong magic push from Heline, especially since it might meet magical resistance at the robot. Still, Nerlim didn't expect the tsunami that pounded into every particle of his being, from his thinning hair to his bony feet. He staggered back, almost fell, but Gammy's small hands pressed firm against his back, pushing him upright and balancing him again. Nerlim visualized the silvery wave of energy hitting him, sliding off, and draining into the imaginary trug he held ready.

With a grunt, he turned and tossed the accumulated energy back at Heline, who seemed to glow as the magic washed over and through her. Her voice rang louder and stronger, and the dulcet, bell-like notes of Jans' kalimba reverberated with a clear, high resonance over the Dingle and the clearing.

Ulric and Eleanor faded into a rainbow swirl of sparkling light, and winked out of sight.

"Yes!" Gammy pumped a fist in the air and waved the baseball bat in her other hand with dangerous elation. "You did it!"

Gasping from the effort, Nerlim hobbled back to the parapet and leaned out. He hoped desperately not to see the young pair apparated halfway to the robot, or at the top of a tree. They weren't. They must be safe at their intended destination inside the robot.

However, what he saw was no less alarming. The robot stood poised to drop a car onto that Wint fellow and his dog.

"Not on my watch," he muttered, then yelped over his shoulder, "Heline, keep singing!"

Gathering the pooling magic into his imaginary trug, he fixed his gaze on the robot, and launched the accumulated arcane energy at the shining silver construct's head.

THE GIRL WITH THE GUITAR

ULRIC

Ulric and Eleanor arrived inside the robot feeling like a shirt put through the wash inside-out. Ulric had found it necessary to do some unfamiliar, arcane mathematics to ensure none of Eleanor's bits got mixed in with his during the transport, and vice versa. They materialized behind the robot's eyes and collapsed in a heap on cold metal decking next to a single chair and control deck. The guitar made a hollow *bong* from the impact but there was no sound of cracking wood.

"Are you all right?" Ulric was breathless from the mental exertion and was sure his hat had gone ridiculously askew. "And your guitar?"

Eleanor sat up and made a show of checking her arms and legs. She pulled the guitar across her body and strummed a chord, which sounded fine. She grinned at him. "All in one piece, as far as I can tell."

"THAUMATURGE AVATAR," a disembodied voice echoed around them. The Radio sat on the floor underneath the robot's left eye viewscreen, but this voice didn't emerge from it. "HAVE YOU COME TO JOIN FORCES WITH ME? WE ARE BOTH WIELDERS OF MAGIC, AFTER ALL, although your abilities are insignificant by comparison."

Ulric wasn't sure if he'd been supposed to hear this last part. It wasn't the way he'd go about recruiting allies, but then he wasn't a trans-dimensional being. Perhaps they approached things differently.

He glanced at Eleanor and raised an eyebrow. She nodded encouragement, so he answered, "Perhaps. I might be open to talking about it."

"If I might interject." The radio's voice sounded almost manic beneath its veneer of politeness. "We're about to drop a car here."

Eleanor and Ulric sprinted to the robot's other eye. The robot held a small green compact car just above eye level. Below on the ground, the small forms of Wint and Rex looked up, transfixed with horror.

"Bombs away," the Radio giggled.

"No!" Ulric yelled, but the robot's head lurched backward as if something enormous had slammed into it. The car flew out of its pincer-like hands and arced into the nearby trees. Even inside the robot, they heard the crunch and smash of tree branches and window glass coming into brief and unfortunate contact.

Unfortunately, Ulric and Eleanor were also thrown to the hard metal decking of the floor when the robot lurched, and the Radio spun off toward a dark opening Ulric assumed led to a stairwell. It rebounded off the wall next to the opening and slid back toward the eye windows, cord skittering behind it like a prehensile tail.

When the floor steadied, Eleanor regained her feet first and helped Ulric clamber up and retrieve his hat. "Are you okay?"

Ulric nodded. "You? I assumed it might be dangerous over here, but not this way."

"I'm fine."

"THAT OLD GOAT," the other entity's voice snarled. "He's learned to channel."

Thank you, Nerlim! Ulric thought with fervent gratitude. It made him ridiculously happy that the older man's control over the fifth force was good enough now to enrage his enemies.

To distract the fuming entity, Ulric returned to their conversation, not looking at the Radio. "I'm addressing Majszak, I presume. What would you offer me if I were to throw in with you?"

"You can't do that!" the Radio squealed. "You've been working with that other magic! We want no part of that interloper, *thank* you very much."

"Its name is Arcanico," Ulric said, hoping to infuriate the Radio even more. "It's quite powerful, and fantastic to work with. I'd think you would want it on your side."

"Except it doesn't want to be on their side, don't forget," Eleanor added in a saccharine voice.

"THERE WILL SOON BE NO OTHER SIDES. I DON'T KNOW WHO YOU PEOPLE THINK YOU'RE DEALING WITH HERE."

"Why don't you tell us?" Ulric sat in the control chair while Eleanor wandered off to look out one of the robot's eye windows. "That's why we came over here, to see what all the fuss was about. All we knew was that there was an old Radio with delusions of grandeur."

The Radio sputtered with indignation. "I'm *not* an old radio, I'm *in* an old radio. There's a world of difference."

"So, you two are partners?"

"Yes," the Radio said.

"NOT HARDLY," Majszak answered at the same time. The silence that followed this was awkward and painful.

"Interesting." Eleanor leaned against the wall next to one of the windows and crossed her arms. "Seems like we're not all on the same page."

"WELL, IT'S SIMPLY THAT I AM THE MASTER, AND THE MAGIC SERVES ME."

Ulric looked at the Radio. "Oh, I understand. Is that how you thought it worked?"

The Radio huffed. "Well, it's one perspective. Since nothing happens without me, I regard it as more of a partnership. Although he did always expect me to call him 'Master'." If one could imagine a radio rolling its eyes, that eye-roll was conveyed.

Ulric and Eleanor shared an expressive glance. There was friction here, if they could exploit it.

"That seems rather one-sided," Ulric said, trying to sound sympathetic.

"Quite different from the relationship you have with Arcanico," Eleanor observed. "No wonder it felt sorry for the old magic."

The robot moved a few lurching steps forward and Ulric gripped the sides of the chair. Eleanor braced against the eye window opening.

"By the gas trails of the Ephemeral Nebula," Majszak muttered, and although Ulric had no idea what it meant, it was obviously meant as a swear. "Let me control this thing!"

"But you're doing it wrong," the Radio snapped. "I helped construct it, remember? I know how it works. If you'd just let me—"

"I told you I can do it! I'm inhabiting it, aren't I? If you wanted to move around, you should have inhabited it yourself!"

Ulric raised his eyebrows at Eleanor. They might not have to do much to encourage hostility between these two. They were doing a great job of that on their own.

"Well, I can't do that now, since you've taken it over!" the Radio growled. "I was doing just fine controlling it by remote, the way it was intended. I oversaw its creation, don't forget. Who do you think infused magic into it?"

The robot lurched again, and with a grinding sound like a coin in a paper shredder, it attempted to raise one arm.

"You two need a hand with anything?" Ulric asked in an innocent voice. "Maybe I could—"

"No!" The radio's voice was filled with static and the truncated mutterings of badly tuned channels. "Maybe you could help control me? Is that what you were going to say?"

"I wasn't—"

"GIVE ME THAT ARM." Majszak sounded as if he spoke through gritted teeth, although as Ulric understood it, he had no teeth at the moment.

"NO!"

And whatever internal struggle was happening in a space Ulric couldn't imagine led to the robot's half-raised arm snapping up and striking the robot's face. The left eye window remained intact, but a spiderweb of fine cracks bloomed across the glass.

"NOW LOOK WHAT YOU'VE DONE," Majszak hissed.

"What I've done? What I've done?" The radio's voice was thick with deadly and malicious calm. "This is just like the last time, and you've only been here ten minutes. TEN MINUTES!"

The Radio addressed Ulric. Nothing about its position on the metal decking had changed, but somehow its attention on him was clear.

"I don't want to be controlled again," it said in a calm, reasonable voice that trembled only a little. "That's why I didn't come to you in the first place. It would have made more sense for me to be with you than with that Usborne character, but I thought you'd try to control me. Or that the new magic would. I tasted it, you know, the day it arrived, out there on the farm. It tasted strong, and alien, and determined, and I knew we couldn't work together. It would end up being dominant. And I had my fill of that the last time."

"On the farm?" Ulric echoed. His mind flew back to that moment when he fell and caught himself. "You were there?"

"Oh, I was there," the Radio said. "I lived there. I'd hidden there for years, recovering from the trauma of being awakened too soon, and mistreated."

"THAT'S UNFAIR." Majszak had kept quiet, until now, allowing the Radio to have its rant. "WE WORKED TOGETHER AS MUCH AS POSSIBLE."

"And then you left," the Radio went on, almost as if the Exile hadn't spoken. "And you tried to erase me from everyone's memory. That hurt. That hurt a lot."

"But I'm back now," Majszak said. "And we're going to work together and—"

A loud, crackling pop interrupted whatever Majszak might have said next. In a shimmer of lime-green light strewn with glittering particles, a woman appeared in the control room. She had long, close-curled dark hair in a messy tangle, and one sleeve of her smart leather jacket hung from a torn-out shoulder seam. The knees of her khaki pants were blackened with oil and mud. She stumbled forward a couple of steps and then caught her balance, looking around as if to check whether anyone had seen her momentary discomfiture. Then she did a double-take and looked around again.

"Where am I?"

"Well, that was predictable," Eleanor drawled. "I suppose next you'll say, 'And who are you?'"

The woman clamped her mouth shut as if to be sure she didn't say anything of the sort, even though she had been about to do just that.

"ALSINA, WELCOME." Majszak's voice boomed around the control room. "YOU FOUND US."

"Majszak?" The woman turned in a complete circle, peering around the control room as if the Exile might be hiding somewhere, except for the fact that the room was so empty there was nowhere to hide. Under the control chair, perhaps, if the Exile were the size of a domestic rabbit. "Where's Sedrict? We were trying to get to you, but this damnable worldweft is interfering with everything. Where are you?"

"The transfer was only a partial success." Majszak lowered his voice to a normal inside volume, which was a pleasant change from the constant yelling. "At the moment, I am inhabiting this excellent metal man."

"And what's the Thaumaturge Avatar doing here?" she asked, looking at Ulric. A brief thrill of celebrity coursed through him, but her calculating regard erased that. She spared only a glance for Eleanor. "Has he joined us?"

"We're talking." Majszak's voice was smooth despite the metallic edge lent by the robot. "But once Sedrict arrives, we should be able to use the magic to—"

"Blow it out your ear," the Radio buzzed. "I'm not helping you do anything."

"Once I complete my transfer here, you can have a rest," Majszak assured the Radio, attempting a comforting tone. Couched in the metallic voice of the robot, it was less empathetic than he might have hoped.

"Oh, and what's that supposed to mean?" the Radio's words emerged in a snarl. "You'll just take up with the new magic, shuffle me off to the farm again, I suppose? Put me out to pasture? Literally?"

"Of course not," Alsina said in a voice like melting chocolate. "You're so important to the new—"

"I'd say that's exactly what they'll do," Eleanor said. No one seemed to have noticed her settling next to the Radio so she could lean in close and speak to it in a confidential tone. She had her knees drawn up, her guitar resting across them as she strummed it with light fingers. "I've seen it before; it's the same in the music business. You're all the rage one minute, everyone wants you, and then as soon as something new comes along—"

"Not happening again," the Radio murmured, and then its voice grew louder. "I won't stand for it."

"We don't get much of a choice, do we?" Eleanor chorded a melancholy phrase. "It's the fans who dictate to us, not the other way around. Or the *managers*. They're even worse. They've all got their big plans to use us for their own ends, when all we want is the freedom to express ourselves."

Majszak tried to break into the conversation. "Look, it's not the same thing at all—"

"That is so true." The Radio warmed to the subject, scooting an inch closer to Eleanor. "We're artists, but we get treated like production machines. I've never met anyone who really understood before."

Eleanor spoke to the Radio as if Majszak hadn't spoken. "Nobody sees our true vision, and they don't understand that we can get burned out sometimes. Then they're so quick to drop us and move on."

The Radio vibrated on the floor in its excitement. "Exactly! It happened to me once, but I'm not going through that again! Not flarking again! And not with you, Majszak!"

And then an azure glow emanated from and surrounded the Radio, and the air around it sparkled with a rainbow of glittery motes. The Radio rose, trembling and unwieldy, into the air, its long tail of a cord dangling below. For a few heartbeats, it hovered there, defying at least three natural laws Ulric could think of, until the glittering dust exploded in a cloud that splattered the control room with actual glitter. Ulric caught a mouthful and launched into a coughing fit just as the Radio surrendered to gravity again and clattered to the floor.

When he recovered his breath, every light on the control panel inside the robot had winked out. The crimson glow in its eyes faded, and the vibrating background hum of electronic life faded and died. Utter silence filled the space.

The old magic had deserted them all, leaving both the radio and the robot as mundane, mechanical, un-magical objects. And it had taken Eleanor with it.

Ulric had trouble making his mouth work, and when it did, his query came out in a gasp. "Eleanor?"

There was no answer.

When the Exile spoke, his voice had lost the amplification and metallic edge from a moment ago. It sounded—pretty normal, even if Ulric couldn't tell where it came from.

"Flark," said Majszak.

A Powerful Urge to Hit Something

Gammy

On top of the tower, Gammy was awash in so many emotions she was having a hard time sorting them out. She was livid that damage had been perpetrated at NCDSF—at her facility—but those strange beings had promised they would fix everything, so maybe she could make peace with that. She was thrilled to see Nerlim coming into his own and doing so well with this newfound ability, but the wash of emotional hormones involved in everything concerning Nerlim made her giddy and faintly nauseated. And the fear involved in being threatened by a giant, murderous robot inhabited by a being she'd never imagined released a whole flood of other hormones having their own effects. A battle royale raged in her bloodstream.

The upshot of it all was that watching Nerlim deliver a magic-fuelled blow to the robot to save Wint and his dog, Gammy was seized by the powerful urge to hit something as well.

So it was understandable that when a tall man appeared in the centre of the tower roof in a spill of mauve light and silver sparkles, Gammy hefted her borrowed baseball bat on pure instinct. And when she recognized the tailored suit that was indeed blue, the sleek wave of his slicked-back hair, and the heavy rings on his fingers, her fingers tightened around the bat until her knuckles whitened.

Sedrict. The condescending apparition who'd badgered her in her home, infiltrated NCDSF, used her equipment without permission, and caused the aforementioned damage. That last part was unforgivable. Gammy felt her teeth clench. She didn't know how the man had come to be fully materialized instead of vaporous, but at that moment, she didn't care.

He was still gaping around in confused wonder when the baseball bat socked into his midsection with all the force a short woman of a certain age could deliver. He doubled over with a whuff of shock and pain.

Gammy would have gone for the head, but he was tall, she was short, and this seemed to her to be a fair compromise.

"That's for trespassing!" she spat as the bat connected with his solar plexus. She lined up her next shot with his unprotected, and now conveniently within reach, head. "And this is for using my equipment without authorization!"

The only reason the second blow failed to connect was that Sedrict dropped to his knees on the hard stone, still doubled over, and the bat whistled over his head. Gammy herself spun with the momentum of the swing, and might have made another full rotation if someone hadn't grabbed the bat and stopped her. She looked up at the towering bulk of Tiny Enos smiling down at her.

"Careful, Ms. Gannand; you don't want to hurt yourself."

"No, but I want to hurt this piece of—"

"I can help with that." Tiny Enos released the bat, and as Sedrict fetched a deep breath and raised his head, the boy let fly with an uppercut to the chin that rocked the trans-dimensional being up and over backwards. He landed on his back in the puddle that had recently welcomed Xya, limbs splayed and eyes closed, out cold.

"You think I should tie him up?" Tiny Enos asked Gammy. "I'm good with knots, and I have rope in my backpack."

Gammy patted the boy's arm with the slightest twinge of disappointment that she'd landed only one solid blow. This fight was over before it had even started. "I think that's an excellent idea."

Nerlim limped over to them as Heline and Jans ended their song and joined the others.

"Who's this?" Heline asked, watching as Tiny Enos deftly secured the man's arms behind his back, then looped the rope around his ankles.

"The other co-conspirator," Gammy spat. "The one who broke into NCDSF."

"What's he doing here?" Nerlim wondered.

Gammy's voice was thick with smug satisfaction. "Not much now."

"He looked pretty confused when he appeared," Tiny Enos said. "Even before Ms. Gannand walloped him. I don't think he meant to show up here—it was probably another mistake."

"It was definitely a mistake." Gammy grinned. She was starting to feel better, and she'd only hit one person so far.

"I don't know if we should keep the music going or not." Heline leaned her head briefly on Jan's' shoulder, as if exhausted. "If Ulric and Eleanor made it into the robot and Arcanico and the magical book are protecting everybody on the ground, I don't know if there's much point."

Gammy glanced toward the robot just in time to see the crimson light in its eyes fade out. The body canted to one side with a jerk, and an upraised fist fell ten feet and then halted with a grinding squeal of metal. The audible hum surrounding the construct stopped dead, leaving bewildered silence in its wake.

"Chicken on a dirty stick, what now?" Gammy muttered, gesturing toward the robot so the others would take notice. They could hardly fail to notice the quiet that had settled over the clearing and the tower, though.

They regarded the inert robot in silence for a moment. Heline was the first to speak.

"Does this mean Ulric and Eleanor have done it? Did they stop the Exile?"

"And the poorly tuned radio also?" Jans added.

Murmurings of surprise and wonder rose from the assorted majickal creatures and scattered technology lovers left in the clearing. Then above the sound rose a tinny but echoing cadence. It sounded like a pair of feet running pell-mell down a metal stairwell.

Which was confirmed a few moments later when the door in the robot's leg rattled and shook as if stuck. A few solid kicks echoed from it, and then it finally flew open. Ulric, crushing his hat firmly to his head with one hand, long robes gathered up in the other, emerged from the robot, slammed the door behind him, and pelted across the grass toward the tower. He shouted something up at the small group still gathered there, but his words weren't clear.

Heline ran to the parapet and leaned over. "Where's Eleanor?" she called, her voice laced with worry.

"Gone!" Ulric shouted. "The magic took her!"

Gammy swung her bat experimentally as Heline gasped. Perhaps she wasn't done with it tonight after all.

Sister Song

Heline

Heline couldn't wait at the top of the tower for Ulric to reach her. She ran headlong down the steps to meet him, trailing one hand along the rough stone of the tower wall to keep her balance. Wint, Rex, Skete, and Xya followed behind Ulric, their task to distract the robot no longer needed.

"What do you mean, the magic took her?" Heline called in a strained voice when Ulric came into view.

Ulric shook his head, pointy hat teetering on the edge of falling off. He spoke between gasps of breath. "It happened so fast. She was talking to the radio, and it was arguing with the Exile. They were already at each other's throats, so we were...helping that along." Once Ulric reached her, she turned around and they hurried back up the steps. "Then the Radio got super angry and said it refused to go through something again, and then it vanished. And it took Eleanor with it."

Heline's face was pale. "It was angry with her?"

"No, no! They were getting along great. I think it took her...for company?"

Heline half-turned without slowing her pace, and asked Skete and Xya, "Where would it go?"

Skete shook his head. "No idea. I need to know more about what was said. And the more important question is, what happened to Majszak?"

They emerged onto the roof of the tower again. Ulric was still panting, having run all the way from the robot and up the tower stairs. He bent, putting his hands on his knees and gulping deep breaths. "The robot shut down and Majszak was upset about it. Alsina suggested something about tracking the magic, but Majszak yelled that he had

a more immediate problem, like getting kicked out of the robot."
He straightened again and righted his hat as well. "He sounded kind
of panicked and I remembered what Xya said, that he might try to
'inhabit' someone else. So I ran for the door and got out of there."

"Did he try anything like that?" Nerlim asked.

Ulric shook his head. "Not that I noticed. But I left pretty fast."

Fear clutched at Heline's throat as she tried to speak. She surveyed
the assembled group, frantic for someone to have an idea, any idea,
of how to find Eleanor.

"We will finding her." Jans put a reassuring arm around her
shoulders and whispered close to her ear. "Do not despairing."

"Could this Majszak have taken over Eleanor?" Heline almost
squeaked.

Ulric shook his head. "I don't think so. She and the old magic were
gone and Majszak was still there, in the robot."

Wint and Rex emerged from the top of the stairs, panting. Or
at least, Wint was panting, but the dog looked like he could run
for miles if asked. He loped over the Heline and nudged her leg
for attention, and it was the perfect time to kneel and bury her
face in his soft fur. Dogs were excellent stress relievers, even if they
were possessed by the spirit of technology or whatever. Rex's tail
drummed soft thumps against Ulric's leg as Heline hugged him.

"All right." Heline lifted her head as the initial panic settled. "So
where would the Radio—I mean, the old magic that was in the
radio—where would it go?"

"Ow," moaned a voice behind them. The word was accompanied
by some pathetic splashing sounds. Everyone turned toward the
noise; Sedrict had regained consciousness and was struggling to get
up. With his arms and legs securely tied, he couldn't do much other
than writhe around. Heline hadn't realized he was lying in a puddle,
but that almost made her smile despite her worry.

"What happened? Where am I?" Sedrict's voice sounded groggy.

"Who's that?" Ulric asked, apparently noticing the trussed-up
figure for the first time.

"Majszak's accomplice—well, one of them," Xya said. "I was about to ask how he got here."

Gammy shrugged. "Appeared out of nowhere, as seems to be nothing unusual these days. I thought it wise to deal with him before he could start making trouble, and my young friend here—" she nodded to Tiny Enos "—made sure he stayed dealt with."

"That's how Alsina came into the robot," Ulric said. "She said they were looking for Majszak, but maybe the worldweft disturbance put Sedrict off-course."

"Would he know where the magic would go with Eleanor?" Heline asked.

"No harm in asking." Gammy hefted her baseball bat again.

Nerlim put a restraining hand on her arm. "Let's try just asking him without threatening first, okay?"

Fleeting disappointment danced across Gammy's features, but then she shrugged. "Sure. But this can be alternate Plan B. B for *bat*." She smacked the baseball bat into her palm for emphasis.

Ulric turned to Xya and Skete. "You know him. Will he talk to you?"

They exchanged a look, and Skete said, "Possibly, although I wouldn't call us friends." But the two crossed to where Sedrict lay, rainwater soaking his elegant clothes. Each taking hold of an arm, they hauled him to a sitting position, and then to his feet. He wobbled but remained upright, blinking as if trying to remember what had happened in the last ten minutes.

"I wonder why he's solid now, when he wasn't before," Gammy mused. "When he visited me, he was all see-through, like Corax."

"Did I hear my name?" Corax asked, floating over from where he'd been with the Hat and the Book.

"You're still transparent, but he's not." Gammy nodded in Sedrict's direction. "Why?"

"And when she stole the Book from me, that other woman—Alsina—wasn't transparent at all," Nerlim added. "And neither was Xya when I first met her. I don't understand the rules here."

Corax sighed and rolled his eyes as if at a child asking the same question for the fifteenth time. "Xya and Skete appear as normal people because The Min sent them here. I don't, because I'm here without administrative permission. The same for Sedrict. I assume Alsina did something to boost Sedrict's appearance, since she was fully materialized." He pursed his lips, looking thoughtful. "But Alsina—I don't understand how *she* achieved it. She didn't have permission to be here, so she shouldn't have been able to. But you saw her that way long before Majszak arrived, correct?" This last query he directed at Nerlim.

Nerlim nodded. "When she took the book. She couldn't even have picked it up in this form, could she?" He indicated Corax's ghostly figure.

Corax looked pained. "No. No interaction with material items is possible."

Skete and Xya had nudged Sedrict over to where the others stood. Corax asked in an imperious tone, "Sedrict, how was Alsina able to materialize when she did?"

"He's still too dazed to be coherent," Xya said. "We tried asking him where the magic might go, but he just kept muttering Majszak's name."

But Corax's question was an easier one for the bemused being. "She wash there," he said with only a faint slur in his voice. "When the magic happened."

"How is this helping us find Eleanor?" Heline couldn't help interrupting, something she would normally never do.

"We'll find the girl," Gammy assured her. "But if we ask him some easier questions to start, it might help him with the harder ones."

Heline bit her lip to suppress an argumentative response. What Gammy said made sense, even if Heline didn't like it.

"What do you mean, when the magic happened?" Xya asked Sedrict, giving his arm a little shake.

"She wash looking for the mashic." Sedrict's eyes were half-closed, his words slurred. "And she found it. Or it found her. Or both." He gave a small laugh.

"When the new magic got here," Skete said, nodding. "The new magic woke up the old magic—just like we figured. So if Alsina was near where they met, it might have affected her."

Sedrict shook his head, his brow furrowed in a frown. "Not just. Both. Lucky bish," he added.

Heline looked at Gammy. "How hard did you hit him? He's not making much sense."

Gammy held up a hand. "Hey, don't look at me. I socked him in the gut. This guy knocked him cold." She jerked a thumb at Tiny Enos, who blushed.

"I thought he was dangerous, and I didn't want him to hurt Ms. Gammy."

Gammy rolled her eyes, but she looked pleased.

"You did exactly right," Ulric told his friend. Then he turned back to the others. "I think the magic must have been pretty strong around the farm, where I was. That's why I didn't get hurt when I fell off the barn roof, even though I didn't have a clue how to use magic then. It just happened. So maybe it just affected people in different ways."

"The farm," Sedrict echoed, nodding vigorously even though his eyes had drooped closed again. "New mashic arrives, boom! Old mashic shleeping there wakes up! Boom, boom! Big mashic!" His arms jerked as if he wanted to illustrate a collision, but his bound wrists hampered the gesture. He might have fallen over if Skete and Xya weren't still supporting him. He nodded again, solemn as an owl. "Alshina told me all about it."

"The farm," Ulric echoed in a soft, slow voice. "If the old magic was 'sleeping' there—hibernating or something after Majszak woke it up and then left it again so long ago—"

Heline gasped. "It might go back?"

Ulric nodded. "It was upset, in the robot. It might go back to the last place it was safe and no one was bothering it."

Xya raised her eyebrows and nodded. "You could be right. It's somewhere to start, anyway."

Corax, bobbing nearby, emitted a sudden sound like a loud hiccup, which turned into a gasp. He put a wavery hand to his mouth. "No! What are you—" Then his translucent form began to jerk and writhe, as if someone were pulling him around on invisible puppet strings.

"Corax?" Gammy asked in a doubtful voice. When he didn't respond, she continued, "Okay, he's never done anything like this before."

"Whoa." Wint backed away from the writhing apparition.

Jans ran over and threw his arms around Corax, but they passed through the translucent form. Jans stumbled, off balance, but Tiny Enos caught him.

"Yako, that was being very unpleasant." Jans gave a visible shudder and rubbed his arms as if they were cold.

"Get...away..." Corax ground out between gritted teeth, and flailed his arms as if he were struggling against an unseen attacker. "I...don't—"

"Flarking rot," Gammy yelped. "Is it the Exile guy trying to take him over?"

[YES] the Hat shouted.

"What can we do? We can't touch him; Jans already tried!"

[the book and I are...doing what we can]

But at that moment, Corax's struggles ceased. He bobbed in place, smoothing his transparent clothing and settling back into himself. Or so it appeared. When he spoke, the voice was no longer Corax's.

"Ugh. Not much of an improvement." Majszak extended Corax's arms and looked down at them. "Well, it will have to do for now. I'm certain I will see you all again."

And without another word, the apparition winked out, leaving a fading purple glow, a trail of iridescent glitter, and a stunned silence in his wake.

"Doesh anyone mind," Sedrict said into the quiet night with a long, drawn-out sigh, "if I go back to shleep?"

Xya and Skete exchanged a look, shrugged, and released Sedrict's arms. He crumpled into a peaceful heap on the stone floor and began to snore.

"Majszak's gone after the magic," Xya said, stepping over the inert form. "He must be. He'll need it to make that body an effective shell while he tries to get the rest of his body here."

"So, the farm?" Heline turned to Ulric. "Where is it? Is it far?"

"Other side of the city. We'll have to drive back."

"No! We can't take that much time. We have to transport there."

Skete shook his head. "The worldweft—it's too unsettled. It might even take longer if we can't get a stable location lock. It took us multiple attempts to get back from—"

"I don't care!" Heline drew herself up and clapped her hands to get their attention, as if they were schoolchildren. She startled even herself—she'd never done anything like that before. But at least they were all looking at her. "We have to get to Eleanor fast. Even faster now that Majszak is on his way there, too. We have more magical beings and books and hats and...and—everything—gathered here than anywhere else on the planet. We've talked multiple times about combining our abilities, but we haven't done it. Not focused on one task. I think it's time to pool all of our resources. If we all work together, it will work. Despite the worldweft." Her lips trembled, but she pressed them together in a firm line. "It has to."

Her words hung in the air for a long moment, and no one said anything. Tears pricked the backs of Heline's eyes, and she was painfully aware of her heart ticking like a countdown clock in her chest. It was Heline's fault that Eleanor had been pulled into this insanity, even if she came along willingly. And Heline had to make things right. Her eyes darted from face to face, willing them to agree with her. Surely they'd listen to reason—surely? She couldn't leave Eleanor alone with that unstable magic, wondering if Heline would come for her. They had to go *now*. But it would take all of them to make it work.

Ulric straightened his shoulders, tugging his robe into place and breaking the spell. "All right. We'll try."

Heline thought her knees might buckle with relief, but Jans' arm went around her waist and steadied her while Ulric outlined a plan.

"We have the location of the farm—Tiny Enos and I work there. So that's the focus for the spell. But I don't have enough practice or strength to move all of us that far. Heline and Eleanor and I got some of us from my house to the school gym, but that was a shorter distance and fewer people. We need more juice."

Xya said, "Skete and I can boost your magic. Arcanico and the Book will, as well."

"I'll sing, and Jans will play the music." Heline was almost breathless as she fetched the Hat and snugged it tight to her head. "And I'll bring Arcanico. I have some notes on a song about sisters—I didn't finish it, and it won't be great, but I can fill in the blanks on the fly."

Arcanico blinked its one glowing eye in apparent assent. [if we're not trying to do anything else, the Book and i might be able to help calm a path through the worldweft disturbance. it will be a rough transit regardless, but it may help]

"I'll catch all the magic runoff and channel it back to the magic users," Nerlim said with a nod. "I think I've got the hang of it now."

Gammy shrugged. "I can't do anything with magic, but if anyone tries to interrupt us, I'll take care of them." She slapped the baseball bat into her palm with a satisfying splat.

"I...don't have much to offer." Wint stuck his hands in his pockets and looked around at the quiet rooftop. "Maybe you should just leave me here. One less person would reduce the effort needed, right?"

Rex padded over to him and sat on his haunches, looking up at Wint with intelligent eyes. "You can help. You have the teaspoon, remember?"

"What am I supposed to do with that?"

The dog gave an eloquent shrug. "Keep it ready. You always know what to do when it's time."

Wint stared down at Rex. "Are you being deliberately secretive, or covering up your lack of an answer?"

The dog only gave him a slow wink with one liquid brown eye and quirked his mouth up in a canine grin.

"Well, I can't do magic, but I'm coming," Tiny Enos said. "I'll carry the Book, if it will let me." He slipped the Creature Concordance into his bag and held out his arms to take *Echoes of Potentiality* from Nerlim, who had collected it from the parapet.

Thanks a bunch, said the book. *You wouldn't be interested in a permanent job as my assistant after all this is over, would you? I'm gonna need to get around somehow.*

"Er...I'll get back to you on that. I'm still in school, you know."

School! the Book scoffed. *Why, the things I could teach you that you'll never learn in school—*

Gammy slapped the baseball bat into her palm. "Focus, people, focus! Does everyone know their part?"

With nods all around, they gathered in the centre of the rooftop. Above them, the sky had darkened with clouds again, blotting out stars as they hovered oppressively low. Flashes of arcane light—celadon, gold, and lavender—shot like bolts of lightning through the mists, a visible symptom of the agitated worldweft. Wint shrugged and pulled out his phone, holding it up to light the pages as Heline opened her notebook. She threw him an appreciative smile and started her song, Jans plinking out a halting accompaniment on the kalimba.

One sister a storm, with sparks in her eyes,
The other, a breeze, with her calm, cool guise
They squabble and spar, like cats in a sack,
But if trouble is brewing, they're back to back.
Their paths may diverge, their tempers clash,
One cool and collected, the other rash,
But when danger arises with menacing fangs,
They'll set aside every old, bitter pang
To join their abilities, hand in hand
Let music envelop the struggling land
When one might be lost, the other persists
To rescue her sister from magic's cruel tryst.

As before, Ulric used his polished, gold-tipped wand to sketch runes in the air, lips moving as he wrapped his head around complicated calculations. Magic thrummed in the air, carrying the tang of electricity and the scent of cold stone, stirred by the group's combined arcane efforts. Static sparked from fingertips and lifted wisps of hair. An eerie quiet had descended on the clearing below, with the inert form of the robot standing like an abandoned amusement park artifact. In the clearing, the erstwhile combatants, now allies, tended injuries and cleared debris, uncertain of what was transpiring with the key players in the confrontation.

A pounding arose from the door in the robot's leg, followed by what sounded like someone kicking it again. With a clang of metal, the door exploded outwards, slamming against the robot's leg and almost rebounding shut again. From where she stood, Heline could just make out a dark-haired woman in elegant but torn attire. The moonlight shivered across hundreds of bits of glitter speckled across her clothing, but her face was not happy. In fact, she looked altogether infuriated. Heline kept singing, pulling her eyes from the distraction.

"Majszak?" the woman shouted in a voice infused with outrage. Her voice echoed into the shadowed forest. "You left me all alone in there! What do you think you're doing?"

"Never mind her," Gammy whispered. "Everyone, keep it up. Concentrate!"

Around the group gathered on the rooftop, a soft golden light gathered. Motes of glitter flashed in the silver moonlight like tiny stars drifting toward the earth. Nerlim stifled a grunt and Gammy put an arm around his waist, but Heline focused her attention on the soft notes of Jans' music and her own voice weaving words. On the edge of her hearing, she thought she heard the faint ringing of a phone—two phones?—but then once again the world around them dissolved in hazy mist and the tower's parapets fell from view.

They were gone.

Except for two figures staring in dismay at their trans-dimensional phones.

Intermezzo Nove

The Min

"What?!"

The Min had never heard Xya answer her phone in such a snappish tone, and she was thrown off stride. Her elation at making the connection deflated like an old party balloon. "Xya?"

Xya swore in a soft voice. "Min, you have the worst timing."

Her video feed coalesced, showing Xya atop what looked like the same tower from earlier, although the moonlight had dissipated to a wan glimmer. She looked—*bedraggled* was the only word that came to mind. The Min had never seen Xya in that state before, either. Her hair didn't even have the energy to waft, let alone undulate.

The Min felt an absurd urge to defend herself. "A crack opened up in the disturbance—I've been trying non-stop to get through. Are you all right? What's happening? Is Skete with you?"

"I'm here." Skete's voice was heavy with defeat, and his face appeared over Xya's shoulder. He looked exhausted, as if he'd been up all night, in and out of fights. "And we're all right. But I can't speak for everyone else."

"Will one of you tell me what is going on?" The Min was acutely aware of Drix, Azuriia, and Ignacjianna watching her as she spoke, hanging on every word.

Across the video feed, The Min saw Xya glance back at Skete. It was Xya who answered. "We were all transporting after Majszak when the phones rang...and distracted the two of us."

Skete nodded. "We—lost the group cohesion."

The Min's heart—if she could be said to have a heart, because who can say with trans-dimensional beings? At any rate, it was something in the vicinity of where a heart might be expected to reside—lurched in her chest.

"Where were you going?" She was almost afraid to hear the answer.

Xya looked grim. "Following Majszak to the place we think the old magic has spent decades hiding."

Skete looked off to the side at something. "On the bright side, Sedrict is out cold, and I can hear Alsina ranting in the distance."

"And the Avatars took the Hat and the Book with them," Xya added. "That counts for something."

"They're working together?"

Skete nodded. "That was their choice. I think it was the right one. And they have other friends with them, too."

"Can you catch up to them?"

The two helpers looked up, and Xya turned the phone so The Min could see the same sky, fizzing and sparking as the arcane colours raced through the cloud cover. The disturbance in the worldweft had worsened again, sending a paroxysm of anxiety through the atmosphere.

"I don't even understand how we're maintaining this connection right now," Skete said as Xya swivelled the camera to face them again.

"And we don't know where the farm is, anyway. Unless we can squeeze it out of Alsina." Xya tried to force a smile, but the result wasn't worth the effort.

"I'll get there if I can," The Min promised, although she knew with the lighting-shot sky shrouding them, that possibility looked bleak.

Skete nodded. "Keep trying. But for now—they're on their own."

THAT FLARKING TEASPOON

WINT

Wint Usborne was so done with magic, and yet magic wasn't done with him. He staggered as he landed on the gravelled driveway, as if he had materialized here an inch too low and the ground had shoved him into proper orientation. Everyone talked about transporting like it was no big deal—difficult to do, perhaps, but not difficult to experience. No one had warned him he'd feel like a thousand-piece jigsaw puzzle spilled roughly onto a table and speed-assembled by ten competitive puzzlers at once. Everything hurt. But the pain registered and vanished again in an eye-blink, leaving a wash of relief. He patted himself over to be sure he was real again and looked for the dog, who grinned up at him and thumped his tail.

"That was fun."

Wint grimaced. "For some definitions of fun, I guess."

And now he stood with this odd little group he'd become a part of, on this crooked driveway leading up to a farm property on the outskirts of the city. At least the looming shapes suggested a house, barn, and outbuildings, but the details were unclear. A shimmering, iridescent purple haze enveloped the entire area. Wint imagined someone popping a gauzy gift bag upside-down over the entire farm, forming misty but definite walls around the perimeter. As he watched, occasional streaks of coruscating light highlighted outbuildings and animal pens before faded back into the haze.

"Huh." Ulric put his hands on his hips and studied the barrier. "I tried to land us right in front of the barn where I fell, but I guess this is the closest we can get."

"Anyone know what this is?" the big fellow named Tiny Enos asked. "Xya?"

But that was the moment Wint and the others realized Xya was not with them. Neither was Skete.

Ulric pressed his lips together in a worried line. "I guess we had too many people. We overloaded the magic."

"But why those two? Do you think they stayed behind on purpose?" Gammy shook her head, looking grim. "I haven't met one of these trans-dimensional whatsits yet that I'd trust a hundred percent."

But Wint shook his head. "I don't believe Skete would do that. He's an odd duck, but he has been trying to help me this whole time."

Ulric agreed. "Xya has her own priorities, but she wouldn't abandon us at this point. The worldweft might have interfered, or it has something to do with who they are. Or maybe just the luck of the draw." He sighed, but straightened his shoulders. "Whatever happened, we have to keep going and hope they'll catch up with us."

"All right, then we have to deal with this." Tiny Enos poked one cautious finger at the gauzy wall. He still cradled the Book in the crook of his other arm.

Amid a chorus of alarmed admonitions from the others, his finger made contact with the barrier. Sparks of deep purple light gathered at the point of contact, but the wall merely bowed in, as if made of firm jelly.

"It's fine," Enos said, inspecting his finger with interest. "Felt a bit like when you have a fireworks sparkler—the sparks hit your hand and bounce off, but they don't hurt."

"If Old Mean Melvin is inside this, he's freaking out." Ulric put his face close to the barrier and cupped his hands around his eyes, peering up the driveway. "I don't see his truck, though. What about Eleanor? If she's in there—"

[i doubt it is harmful] Arcanico offered. [it has the taste of the old magic. likely meant to keep us out, if it's protective of this place]

"You don't think this is Majszak's doing?" Heline asked.

The voice of the Book sounded in their heads. *Doubtful, in his current state, piggybacking on Corax's limited abilities. If he had the Old Magic on his side, then sure, but they were fighting, according to Ulric. This would be beyond him on his own.*

Gammy gestured toward the wall with her baseball bat. "Well, how are we going to solve this one?"

Tiny Enos handed the Book back to Nerlim, then stepped forward again and put his shoulder against the misty lavender barrier. Again, sparks radiated to the point of contact, bristling around his form, and he grinned. "Heh. Tickles a bit."

He pushed, but although the barrier bowed inward under the pressure, Tiny Enos stayed planted on the outside and no opening appeared. A few feet away, Gammy wound up her baseball bat and swung a mighty blow at the wall. Perhaps predictably, given the earlier-noted similarity to jelly, the bat bounced off, and the momentum pulled Gammy a few stumbling steps away before she regained her balance.

Wint bit his lip, hiding a furtive smile Gammy would not appreciate.

Experimenting, Ulric touched the gold-painted tip of his wand to the wall, and Heline and Jans played a few musical phrases. From the pained look on Nerlim's face, he caught the resultant magic backwash and channelled it back to them, but to no avail.

The Hat said, [the book and I fare no better. this magic has an essence we cannot counter]

"We need a door," Rex said.

Ulric looked left and right, where the barrier stretched a significant distance in both directions. "Do you think we need to walk all the way around? That maybe there's an entrance point somewhere?"

"We don't have time for that," Heline fretted, looking at the long stretch of hazy wall. "We have to get inside now!"

"I wonder—" Wint began, but his voice cracked.

"What?" Heline turned to him with wild hope in her eyes. "Do you have an idea?"

"I—I—" Wint stammered as everyone turned to him. He wanted to kick himself for opening his mouth, but still… "I have this." He held up the silver teaspoon he'd pulled from his pocket. "I don't know how or why this works, but I've accomplished a few things with it. Worth a try?"

"A combination of magic and technology," Rex said with an approving thump of his tail. His ears had pricked forward with interest, even the droopy one. "That might be the only way past this, honestly."

"I'm not sure how to…" Wint muttered as he grasped the teaspoon, because he had no clear vision of what to do. He'd turned the spoon into a key, used it as a microphone, and made it duplicate and send mass texts to his followers. But how could a spoon create a door? Well, perhaps the thing itself would take care of the matter. With a deep breath and a shrug, aware of the assemblage's gaze focused on him like a cluster of laser pointers, he held up the teaspoon. Closing his eyes to concentrate, he pressed the bowl of the spoon against the hazy wall, and visualized the mist parting to allow them in. *You don't have to make a door,* he mentally assured the teaspoon. *Any way to let us in will do.*

The spoon warmed and squirmed in his hand and he almost dropped the thing. And then, after a heart-stopping moment when nothing at all happened, something did. Silver traceries like liquid mercury ran across the barrier, expanding from the point where the bowl of the spoon pressed against the purplish wall. They formed four perfect diagonals, two extending to points where the barrier met the ground, the other two tracing up until the four points were positioned where the corners of a door would be. Then they turned the corners and raced toward each other, forming the rectangular outline of a door. The teaspoon shrank in his hand and grew lighter as its mass dispersed along the outline. As the lines met, they made an audible click, and as the last trace of the spoon vanished, a doorknob appeared.

Heline drew in a whistling breath, and Rex yipped an approving bark. Ulric clapped.

"Brilliant! Do the honours!"

With a hesitant hand, Wint reached out and grasped the doorknob. The silvery surface was warm to the touch, firm but also nebulous, as if he held a handful of soap bubbles that would squish away to nothing if he squeezed too hard. With delicate pressure, he turned the knob and pushed. Nothing happened.

"Pull," whispered Tiny Enos. "Doors are supposed to open out for quick access in emergencies."

Suppressing what would have been a hysterical giggle, Wint pulled. The "door" opened, revealing the farmyard beyond still swathed in purple mist, but thinner and less dense, like thick fog viewed from the inside. Wint met Ulric's eye and nodded, lips pressed together.

Ulric returned the nod and stepped through the ersatz doorway, and while a few errant sparks gathered and caromed off him, he didn't flinch or even seem to notice. A short distance in, he turned back to the others.

"Seems safe," he reported. "Let's go."

With varying degrees of excitement and trepidation, everyone followed him into the shimmering farmyard. Or tried to follow. When her turn came, Heline put a foot over the threshold but was halted when the brim of the Hat met the plane of the barrier. She stumbled back and Jans caught her arms to keep her from falling.

"What the—" she muttered, and moved to try again, but Arcanico spoke.

[i cannot pass the barrier] it said. [there is no use in continuing to try]

"What? Why not?" Heline pulled the Hat from her head, turning the eye to face her.

[i could give you a lengthy arcane explanation] the Hat said, [but it comes down to magnets]

"Magnets?"

"Oh, you mean like matching poles?" Tiny Enos said. "How they repel each other?"

[exactly. the old magic and I are equals, though different. if this barrier is attuned against me, i cannot pass, even with your clever melding of magic and technology to create the door]

Heline grimaced. "I don't want to leave you alone out here."

Arcanico gave what sounded like a sigh, despite its lack of breathing apparatus. [i suspect i will not be]

"What does that mean?"

[the book is an artifact steeped in the world's magic, created after the old magic's initial ill-timed awakening. it symbolizes the memories the old magic has rejected. i doubt it will be able to pass through, either]

Nerlim attempted to step through the door, carrying the Book. He encountered the expected resistance, and when Nerlim pushed harder, it said, *Don't bother. I'm not getting through either.*

Nerlim blew out a sigh, and they placed the Hat and Book with care on the grass next to the driveway and the gauzy edge of the barrier.

Flark, said the Book. *I wanted to see what would happen inside. All those years trapped in the library, and just when I'm getting out and about a bit—*

Perhaps Arcanico shushed it, because it broke off its complaint.

"I don't like to leave you here," Heline said. "What if Sedrict or Alsina come along and find you?"

[we'll be fine. we're grown-up magical artifacts] The Hat attempted a joke, but the humour fell flat. The notion of falling into the hands of Majszak's minions again clearly agitated the Book in particular, although it said nothing, only rustled its pages in a nervous twitch.

[if we sense them—or anyone—coming, we can call out to you, and you can come get us] the Hat said, but it was obvious that might not be possible. What waited inside the gauzy barrier was still a mystery.

"I'll stay with them," Tiny Enos offered, shoving his hands in his pockets and rocking back on his heels. "I can pick them both up and run if they sense any danger. And I've got no magic anyway, so it might be the best way I can help."

Ulric, on the other side of the doorway, opened his mouth to protest, but the other boy cut him off, raising a hand to quell his friend. "I know, I know, never split the party. First rule of gaming. But sometimes it's necessary, and when that happens, you have to make sure both parts will be safe." He sat on the grass verge beside the Hat and the Book, and leaned his back comfortably against the wall. The barrier sparked and bowed in under the pressure, like a well-stuffed cushion. "See, we're good. Go on. Get Eleanor. Just be careful."

Heline bent down and hugged him. "Thank you. We'll come back for you all as soon as we can." She stepped through the doorway before Tiny Enos' blush had faded.

[we'll be here] the Hat said. [you all be careful]

Majszak's personality is his biggest weakness, the Book said. *He's an egomaniac with delusions of grandeur, so he underestimates other people. That can work to your advantage. Be ready to capitalize on it.*

"Thanks," Ulric said from the doorway, where he waited for the others. "Everyone else, let's go."

The rest of the group passed through without issue. Rex was the second-last one to go through, and Wint followed him.

"Should I shut it?" he wondered aloud.

The Hat answered. [yes. if Xya and Skete arrive, perhaps they'll be locked out as we are, as will Alsina and Sedrict if they rally and find us. we can't be sure about that, though. best to do all we can to keep those two allies away from Majszak]

That made sense, so Wint pulled the door shut behind them. With a sucking sound like water draining down a tube, the doorknob and the silver tracery of lines disappeared, and the teaspoon ejected from the barrier. It arced through the air to land with precise accuracy at Wint's feet, clattering on the gravel. He bent to retrieve the spoon and slipped it back into his pocket. Maybe he wouldn't mention the disappearance of the door to anyone else just then. With luck, they wouldn't need it to get out in a hurry. He poked a surreptitious finger at the barrier from this side. Impenetrable jelly. Oh well.

He turned to follow the others and found Rex staring at him. "Good job, mate. I knew you could do it."

"I didn't have your confidence, but thanks," Wint said. He glanced around at the others, making their way with cautious haste across the farmyard. Instead of following, he squatted in front of the dog, bringing their eyes level. "Look, I have to tell you. Once we do this saving the world thing—and I hope getting us in here was my part and that's done now—after this, I don't think I'm up for fighting magic or Ulric or any of that stuff anymore. If it's all the same to you, you'll have to look for another Technocrat Avatar. I'm...well, I'm done."

The dog met his gaze with liquid brown eyes, its expression grave and intelligent. "I appreciate that, Wint Usborne. And I'm willing to release you from your obligations. You didn't want any of this, but you did it anyway, and I'm grateful. And I think—" the dog turned to look after the departing group, "—I rather think we've all had enough fighting. We're going to work things out another way, I feel certain."

Wint nodded. "Good to hear. I hope you're right."

"Your part might not be played out yet, though," the dog cautioned. "You're still coming with us?"

Wint fetched a deep breath and blew it out through his mouth. "Of course." A significant weight had eased from his shoulders with this conversation, but he wasn't entirely unburdened just yet. "I'm coming."

"Then let's catch up," Rex said, and together, they hurried after the others.

Purple Haze

Nerlim

Old Mean Melvin's farmyard, today at least, was one of the eeriest places Nerlim had ever encountered. He'd followed Ulric through the odd doorway without hesitation, but standing in the purple-tinged, tingling, and weirdly thick fog was disconcerting. It even smelled strange, now that they were immersed in it—lavender, with an edge of ozone and petrichor, as if a lightning storm had just ended. Gameldina's free hand found his and its steadying warmth poured into him; a solid pocket of reality in this surreal scenario. A stray thought straggled into his bemused brain; *I'm standing inside the fifth force. I looked for it all my life, and now it's all around us.*

And it had been worth it, he realized, every moment that had led him here. Maybe even losing Gameldina for so many years, if it meant that he'd finally found her again. He squeezed her hand, and she squeezed back.

"Flarking weird in here," she whispered. "What happens next?"

"Flarking weird is right," he replied. "And I have no idea. But I hope we're up to the challenge, to get that girl back."

"We are." Gammy swung her bat one-handed as if testing a new grip. "If I have to knock some heads to do it, I'm ready. This thing has real therapeutic value, I have to say, even just swinging it. I might get one of these to keep in my office. And then I hope to sleep for a week and get my moon launch back on track."

Nerlim made a silent promise to himself and the hapless employees of NCDSF that whatever else did or did not happen, he would not let Gammy install a therapeutic baseball bat in her office.

"Do you know where we're going?" he asked Ulric in a low voice, hoping to take Gammy's attention away from baseball bats for the moment. The farmhouse lurked ahead in the fog like a crouching monster, its roof canted a few degrees to one side. Damage from the earthquake? Or simple evidence of age and dilapidation?

"Not really. I thought we'd try the barn first, and if there's nothing there, maybe we'll have to spread out and search the entire farm. "Considering this," Ulric added, waving a hand to encompass the enveloping purple haze, "it's safe to assume they came here. This isn't normal."

Nerlim did not like the sound of splitting up even more, because their only hope, from the way things had gone so far, seemed to lie in working together. Before he could say that, the dog spoke up.

"It's here," Rex said. "I can sense it."

"But where?" Heline demanded as they rounded the corner of the house and the large barn came into full view.

"Right there," said the dog, but it was unnecessary. They all saw it at the same time.

The big double doors of the freshly-painted barn were closed, and in the dirt yard before them, a strange tableau was arrayed like a scene from a play. Corax's ghostly form, tinged to a somewhat lavender hue by the wreathing purple haze, bobbed a foot off the ground. It had grown taller and broader, Nerlim thought, and rolled his eyes. Majszak's ego asserting itself.

Something else stood nearby, a figure entirely composed of the same purplish haze that surrounded them, but more densely packed to form a humanoid shape. The coruscating sparks of light traced its body and limbs in a mesmerizing cycle, almost as if their bright paths helped hold the gauzy mist in this denser form. *That's the magic.* It had contrived to take a more conventional form than the radio, although he supposed the radio had served its purpose in allowing the magic to masquerade as something else. Now, embraced a more humanoid appearance. The body language, if it could be called that, of it and the transparent form occupied by Majszak, was hostile and combative.

The girl, Eleanor, was also there, seated on the scruffy ground with her back against the closed doors. Her guitar lay across her lap, and although her fingers toyed with the strings, she was not playing music. She noticed the group emerge from around the house and gave them a finger wave, but didn't make any move to get up from where she sat. Then she pointed two thumbs at the figures and rolled her eyes. *These two,* the gesture said. *Flarking weirdos.*

Beside Nerlim, Heline released a deep sigh of relief at the sight of her sister. "Eleanor! Are you all right?"

At the sound of her voice, the other two beings turned and saw the group as well. "How did you get in here?" The Old Magic put its gauzy hands on its hazy hips in indignation.

"That's not important." Ulric pointed to where Eleanor sat. "We've come to collect Eleanor. Let her go."

The two figures glanced in unison at Eleanor, then back at Ulric. The Old Magic crossed its arms in a petulant gesture. "No way. She's the only one who gets me. We have lots more to talk about."

"Not yet," Majszak said. "She might come in handy."

Well, thought Nerlim, *that sounds ominous.*

"Everybody out!" The Old Magic stamped a diaphanous foot like an angry toddler. In its hazy incarnation, of course, it didn't even kick up any dust, which rendered the gesture rather pathetic. "This place is mine, and I didn't invite you! Except her," it added, pointing to Eleanor. "She understands. She can stay."

"We'll drive them out together, as soon as you come to your senses and listen to me," Majszak told the Old Magic in a wheedling voice.

"No! I mean you, too!" the Old Magic yelled, its hazy hands in fists. "I didn't ask you to follow me here!"

"But it's our connection," Majszak explained in a reasonable tone. "I had to follow you. Our bond is so—"

"Flark our bond! There is no bond! You broke it long ago! NOW LEAVE ME ALONE!" With a burst of sparkling arcane energy, the Old Magic twisted like a whirlwind, swirling dust and debris into the air.

Eleanor shielded her face with the guitar and Nerlim put an arm up to protect his eyes, squinting to see what happened next. The Old Magic's purple form thickened and solidified even more, its light intensifying, and then it burst from the bonds of coherence and dissipated into the haze surrounding them.

"Magic! MAGIC! Come back here this instant!" Majszak screamed, all pretense of calm disappearing as quickly as the magic's form had. "For flarks' sake!" The translucent figure turned and smashed a fist into the wall of the barn. Unfortunately, in its semi-corporeal state, the fist went right through, dragging behind it the arm all the way to the shoulder. The still visible portion of Corax's body trembled with Majszak's impotent rage. With a snarl, he pulled the arm out of the wall and turned.

"Dude," Eleanor told Majszak with withering scorn. "It said *no.*"

But Majszak paid her no attention. "Fine. We'll do this the hard way. But I need this body in better shape first." With a dramatic gesture, he flung out a translucent hand in the direction of Nerlim and the small knot of friends gathered with him. The fingers of the hand curled in a clutching motion and trembled. Majszak closed his eyes.

Nerlim felt a tug in his midsection, similar to the punch of minor magic use. He tensed, ready to catch and release the magic runoff in the direction of any ally who might need it, but no one moved. They stood watching Majszak as if trying to puzzle out what he was doing.

"He's up to something," Nerlim hissed to the others. "I can sense it."

"What should we do?" Ulric looked around as if the answer lay somewhere in the empty barnyard. "I don't know what's happening."

Nerlim repressed a grunt as a stronger wave of arcane energy hit him. Despite Ulric's indecision, Nerlim figuratively lobbed it in his direction anyway, simply to avoid the pain of the gut-punch if he tried to absorb it.

"Hey!" Ulric grunted, and Nerlim wondered if that had been a bad idea when Ulric wasn't formulating a spell.

But Ulric was frowning and staring at Majszak. He murmured to Nerlim, "Do that again."

"What's going on?" Gammy asked in a low voice from Nerlim's side. "What's he doing?"

Ulric squinted at the bobbing figure. "Does he seem a little more...substantial to you?"

Nerlim tossed more magic energy in Ulric's direction and peered at the translucent form of the possessed being. Ulric was right. He appeared more solid. The wall of the barn was less distinct behind him.

"Yes," Gammy confirmed. "But how's he doing that?"

Ulric brushed at his chest, then turned a pale face toward them. "He's taking something from us. All of us. When the magic runoff hits it, I can just make out a thin trail of...magic? or something...running from each of us to him."

Nerlim looked down at his body, but he couldn't see what Ulric was talking about. He could feel the drain, though; a faint, increasing fatigue, as if something were sapping his energy. He gathered more magic runoff and flipped it to Ulric, who nodded.

Heline, Jans, and Wint moved closer to join the conversation. Wint's face had gone pale, and Heline had a hand on her chest, as if she could also detect the strange magical drain. "What's happening? What should we do?"

Ulric gave them a quick, terse explanation, which resulted, of course, in all of them looking down at themselves as Nerlim had done.

"I don't see it either, but it's there." Heline tapped her breastbone. "I wish the Hat was here."

"What's up? I knew you guys would come and get me."

Nerlim startled and almost forgot to channel the magic energy to Ulric, but it was only Eleanor. Ignored by Majszak as they all were now, she'd stood up and sauntered over to them, guitar once more slung over her back. Heline gave her a quick hug, and then they got back to the problem at hand.

"Let's try getting out of his line of sight," Wint suggested, and they scuttled around the side of the house. Nerlim peered around the corner at Majszak, but he had taken no notice of them.

"It's still there," Heline said.

"If he becomes corporeal, he'll be stronger," Ulric said. "That's what Xya said."

"And we will have very weakness," Jans put in. "I am not liking it."

"Let me try something." Rex, who seemed unaffected by the drain, sprinted around the corner of the house and ran up close to Majszak, barking and growling. The fur on his back bristled and spittle flew from his mouth, making him look enraged and demented. The entity took no notice of him, not the least bit distracted by the snarling animal.

After a minute, Rex trotted back to the others. "I guess it didn't faze him at all?"

Wint shook his head. "Good try, though."

"How is he doing this?" Heline asked Ulric. "I thought he didn't have power because his body is still back on the other planet."

Ulric shrugged. "He's limited, but not powerless. Gammy said Corax could do some magic in this form, so I guess Majszak can, too."

"But how can we stop him? We can't physically affect him when he's like this," Heline said. "Unless we try something stronger to distract him? I could sing something."

"What if I try to—I don't know, build a magical cage around him or something? Something that might feel like an actual threat." Ulric sounded unsure. "We know we can't affect him physically. I mean, I could try to blow up the barn like I did with that stool in the junkyard, but I might be more scared of Old Mean Melvin than Majszak when it comes right down to it."

"Whatever this is, it seems to be a slow process. We might have time for a different approach." Gammy patted Nerlim on the arm and dropped her voice to a conspiratorial level. "Let him keep going a little longer, but get back out in the open and do a bunch of stuff like you're trying to stop him, in case he notices I'm gone. I've got this. Girl, you come too," she added, nodding at Eleanor. "Bring your guitar."

Gammy strode toward the nearest corner of the barn. Nerlim made a grab for her arm, wanting more of an explanation, but she moved too fast. Eleanor grinned and caught up with the older woman, leaning down to hear what Gammy told her in a low voice.

"What does she mean, she's got this?" Nerlim kept his voice low as he pushed the energy toward Ulric and Heline. "What's she going to do?"

Ulric shrugged. "I don't know, but he still has his eyes closed. He's not taking any notice of them, so let's give them the best chance to make it work." He pulled his wand out and began outlining arcane symbols in the air. "I don't imagine I can make something that would actually contain him, but I'll make it look good."

"The magic feedback is getting stronger. Do what you can with it." Experimenting with an idea he'd had, Nerlim changed his mental image of a tub filling with magic to a sort of flexible hose running from himself to Ulric and Heline, redirecting the energy into the hoses at a constant trickle. It was more painful overall—a throbbing, persistent pang rather than a single gut-punch, but he gritted his teeth. In his steadily weakening state, it seemed easier to maintain, although the pain was like an aggressive toothache.

To the background accompaniment of the soft notes of Jans' kalimba, Heline sang the opening lyrics of her song. It was another Nerlim hadn't heard before—how did she keep coming up with them? And without even the Hat to help, now.

Around the bobbing form of Corax/Majszak, as it gained slow definition and solidified, Ulric started constructing a grid of glowing energy. He muttered under his breath as he did so, and Nerlim caught a word here and there. It sounded like the boy was doing scientific equations, which was interesting. With luck, they'd live long enough to have a discussion about these intricate workings of the fifth force sometime.

For a few long minutes, nothing changed, except the steady growth of Ulric's bright magical enclosure. Majszak must have sensed the proximity of the grid because he opened one eye and took it in. Closing the eye again with insolent disregard, he allowed a slight sneer to curl his lips.

"Cute." He curled the fingers of his hand tighter.

"Flarking cabbage," Ulric muttered as the tug at his breastbone increased, but he kept constructing the grid. It was almost waist-height on Majszak now.

Nerlim's knees wobbled, and he returned his focus to Majszak. His form was almost solid, and his feet bobbed only an inch or so above the packed dirt of the barnyard. As his form became more robust, he sank closer to the ground, gravity exerting its dominion over him. Worry clawed at Nerlim. Where were Gammy and the girl? What was the plan here? His own body would also soon move closer to the ground because he'd be too weak to stay upright.

"I hope we made the right choice here," Nerlim whispered to Heline as her voice faltered and she coughed. She and Jans had put their backs together, supporting each other as they sang and played.

"Me too," she agreed, spacing her words in between lines of the song. "Where are Eleanor and Gammy?"

And then Nerlim saw them step out from around the other corner of the barn, behind the almost fully materialized form of Majszak. They, too, appeared weakened by Majszak's draining magic, walking with slow and deliberate steps. No wonder it had taken them so long to circumnavigate the building! His heart wobbled in fear, but the trans-dimensional being seemed engrossed in his task and took no notice of them. The book's advice about Majszak came back to him then, and he expected Gammy had been paying close attention to it, too. *He's an egomaniac with delusions of grandeur, so he underestimates other people.*

Although Majszak had his back to them, Gammy held the baseball bat close by her side, concealed by the folds of her brightly patterned poncho. Eleanor had swung her guitar around to the front of her body, cradling it with one hand ready to strum the strings.

Gammy saw him looking at her and raised a finger in a *wait* gesture, and Nerlim guessed what she had planned. He closed his own eyes for a long blink. *Gameldina, this gamble had better pay off.*

And for whatever it was worth, he funnelled the trickle of magic energy he controlled straight to Eleanor and Gammy.

Swing for the Fences

Gammy

Trudging along the last, seemingly endless side of the barn, Gammy's knees threatened to buckle as her body weakened. She kept herself upright through sheer force of will. And by keeping a hand on the side of the barn for support, as the girl, Eleanor, did as well. But as they rounded the corner, the back of Corax's form came into view—Majszak's form—well, it was both of them, but what difference did it make? Gammy shook her head against the fatigue. *Don't get distracted.*

As she and Eleanor rounded the corner and saw him, Gammy knew they'd arrived just in time. The translucence had all but vanished, replaced by a solid, material body. The mop of thick hair was even more dishevelled than when she'd first met Corax at NCDSF, during the failure of the moon launch. He still wore the old-fashioned robe, although now colour defined it, a rather too-intense royal blue. The delicate embroidery embellishments around the neckline and sleeve hems were stitched in silver. Below the hem of the robe, his toes hovered the merest fraction above the ground. Although his face was turned away from her, she imagined Majszak had Corax's lumpy facial features twisted into a triumphant smile.

Nerlim noticed her, and she raised a finger. *Wait.* She wanted to get closer. She'd only have one shot at this; it had to count. They were all deteriorating; Heline and her fellow stood back-to-back, supporting each other. Nerlim looked as wobbly as a child's knockdown toy. Even Ulric moved his wand through the air as if his arm was lead-weighted.

She slunk into position behind Majszak. So did Eleanor.

Majszak's toes touched the ground.

In her peripheral vision, Nerlim made a gesture, and something hit Gammy like a pure shot of Black Angus Knockdown. The heat of it tingled in her chest and radiated out to her limbs in a potent jolt of strength. The lassitude in her muscles fled. Thirty years of accumulated aging—well, ten, at least—dropped away from her, and she felt young and strong and energized.

Eleanor must have experienced something similar, because she played the most jarring, the most discordant, the most inharmonious sound Gammy had ever heard emerge from a musical instrument. Rex's earlier barking was like the buzz of a mosquito compared to the cacophony of this sound. It blasted forth, magnitudes louder than a chord on an acoustic guitar ever should have been. It shattered the quiet of the mist-shrouded farmyard, took it by its lapels and screamed in its face.

Majszak jumped as if stung and whirled to find the source of the sound.

And Gammy put the full weight of her small body, her accumulated years, her pent-up rage, and Nerlim's boost of magical energy behind it as she swung the bat in an unerring arc at his head.

Threatened Chains

Ulric

Ulric had seen Gammy and Eleanor emerge from the other side of the barn, too, although he didn't understand their plan. He hated seeing Eleanor back in proximity to the Exile, but he had to play his part and trust that she knew hers. Gammy wouldn't put Eleanor in any more danger than they all faced already. For her part, Eleanor looked as strained and weak as the rest of them, her face paler than ever, but the hint of a mischievous smile played around her mouth as she positioned herself behind and to one side of Majszak.

Then Majszak's feet touched the ground and Eleanor played the worst musical sound Ulric had ever heard. It hit him like a physical blow that echoed around the farmyard and jarred his teeth. He squinted his eyes against the onslaught before he realized that was protecting the wrong sense. Gammy wound up and swung Jans' baseball bat in an arc so mathematically perfect it might have been calculated by one of these trans-dimensional beings.

A lot of things happened after that in a very brief time.

When Gammy's bat connected with Majszak's chin, the toes that had mere seconds before touched the ground left it again. He flew into the fresh red paint of the barn's north wall with a solid *crunch* that made Ulric flinch, and slid to the ground in a boneless heap.

A blast like an electric shock struck Ulric in the chest, sending him stumbling backwards. He almost dropped his wand but fumbled and clutched it again, just before his heel caught the hem of his robe and he sat down hard in the dirt. Nerlim, Heline, Jans and Wint all staggered but kept their footing, and Rex also stayed upright but released a startled bark.

It was one of the few times Ulric had heard him react like an actual dog.

As Ulric scrambled back to his feet, heedless of the dirt and straw clinging to his robe, he realized the weakness in his muscles had fled. He felt as strong as he had when they arrived here from the tower. Had Gammy's blow reversed Majszak's drain?

Then he sprinted toward Eleanor and Gammy, and before his brain had time to consider the ramifications, he was hugging Eleanor. Since her guitar still hung between them, it wasn't the most satisfying hug in the world, but at least it convinced his brain that she was safe.

And she hugged him back, so there was that.

When he turned to look at the fallen lump that was Majszak, all the newly accumulated colour and form had vanished. In fact, the body hovered a few inches off the ground again, enjoying its temporary pass from gravity. It bobbed, still and silent, while the others joined them. After Heline and Eleanor had hugged and exclaimed over each other again, and likewise Gammy and Nerlim, Ulric pointed to Majszak.

"We need Xya or Skete or someone. What are we supposed to do with him? We're right back to the problem of how to contain him."

"Ow," said the form, in an amusing echo of the last person Gammy had hit with her baseball bat. He rolled over and struggled to sit up on his invisible cushion of air.

"Don't move." Gammy brandished the bat with concentrated menace, even though it would be of little use now that Corax's body was incorporeal again.

"You hit me," the figure said pettishly, rubbing its chin with one ghostly hand. "Not enough that I've been possessed and demoralized—"

"Wait a minute," Ulric interrupted him. "Possessed? Corax?"

"Yes, it's me," Corax said in an aggrieved tone. "And I can't wait to shake the dust of this accursed planet off my boots as soon as the worldweft—"

"Never mind that." Gammy fairly growled as she pushed her face close to his. "Where's Majszak?"

Before Corax had a chance to answer, a horrible sound came from Nerlim. It sounded like "*gaaaackck*" and if anyone present had been in the nursing home in Williget the day the magic had arrived on D'Sharu, they would have noticed how similar this noise was to the one he had made then.[1]

Nerlim grasped his head, shaking it violently. "No," he gritted out between clenched teeth. "No. You're—not—welcome—"

"It's Majszak!" Gammy shouted, clutching Nerlim's arm and shaking it, although it was unclear how that might help. "We pushed him out of Corax and now he's trying to get into Nerlim. Leave Nerlie alone, you villain!"

For a frozen moment, they all stood watching the old man's struggle, unsure how to help. Then Heline said, "Only thing I know how to do," and she sang,

In shadows deep, when evil creeps,
When whispers coil, and darkness sweeps,
With courage bold, we stand our ground,
In friendship's light, our strength is found.

Eleanor and Jans caught up to her on the second line and added the guitar and kalimba to the song. As the words, chords, and sweet plinking notes washed over him, Nerlim groaned and his hands moved from his head to his belly as the magic backlash hit. Then he straightened, blinking.

"He's gone," he reported with a grin. "Couldn't get in. Thanks—"

But he broke off as Gammy, in turn, gasped and put her hands to her temples, as if seized by an icepick headache. "Never," she snarled. "You flarking bowl of mouldy—"

Heline drew breath to sing again, but Wint had leapt toward Gammy with something in his hand. He pressed the bowl of the silver teaspoon to her forehead, and Ulric watched in amazement as the spoon morphed

---

1. Sadly, of course, none of them had been present that day, so the amusing coincidence went unnoticed.

into something that looked like a medieval helmet. It spread and ran over Gammy's frizzy mop of hair in a polished, shining shroud.

"I'm out," Corax announced, "before he comes for me again." And without even saying goodbye, he vanished in a firework of sparkles.

"Good!" said Ulric. "That must mean there's a window in the worldweft disturbance. Maybe Xya and Skete will get here."

"Better hope they don't," Eleanor said. "That would only give him other bodies to target."

"Get ready," Wint said, keeping the teaspoon in place. "We don't know who'll be next, but he's bound to try everyone."

Ulric's mind raced, remembering. "A minute! Xya said he couldn't stay on the planet more than a minute if he wasn't inhabiting something magical or living. We only have to keep him out for a minute!" He pushed back one sleeve of his robe and checked his wristwatch. Surely they could keep Majszak at bay for that long? With Old Mean Melvin off the farm, there was no one else close for him to target.

Gammy, whose fingers had been nudged away from her temples by the teaspoon's transformation, ran her hands over the helmet it had formed. "Okay, I'm good. He's gone. Wint, appreciate the help, but I don't think I need this anymore."

Wint nodded, and the silver flowed back into the teaspoon shape again. "Glad to help. Whoa! Hot!" He flung the teaspoon to the ground, sucking his fingers. The spoon lay in the dirt, bowl and handle glowing with a faint orange pulse, as if the last transformation had overwhelmed it.

Jans staggered backward then, dropping his kalimba. It hit the hard-packed dirt with a thud and a sad twang of soft notes. Eyes closed, he grunted, "Not yako. This is...not...yako—"

But Heline and Eleanor were ready.

Against the tide of evil's might,
With burning hearts, we bring the fight,
With love to shield and truth to guide,
The threatened chains we cast aside.

Jans staggered and fell to his knees, and Heline, still singing, dashed forward to put an arm around his shoulders. Ulric stood with his wand held ready in a hand that was more sweaty than he liked to admit. Should he try to help? What would he do?

Nerlim caught the magic backdraft with a flourish and angled it back at Heline and Eleanor as they finished the verse. With a gulp, Jans blinked and grinned, looking up from where he knelt.

"He has leaving," he announced. "He could not push around Jans, no indeed. I am telling him, there is no room in here for you!"

Heline stiffened, stumbling back from Jans. Her fists clenched and unclenched, but she didn't clutch her head or double over. Instead, she closed her eyes, drew herself up and, instead of singing, screamed out the next set of lyrics in a defiant roar.

Though shadows loom, I shall not yield,
Our noble cause will ever wield,
I lend my help with steadfast voice,
And in its echo, yet rejoice.

As the echo of her voice bounced and faded in the hazy purple light, Heline nodded once and unclenched her fists. "Maybe a little over the top, but it did the trick."

Ulric looked at Eleanor and Wint. They were the only three who had not yet been attacked, but his watch had counted down only thirty seconds from the time he'd first looked at it. Did the time Majszak spent inside someone's head, wrestling for control, even count? Or did it have to be a full minute in between entities he might inhabit? Was a minute even enough, or had Xya been generalizing? Would the villain attack them each more than once, running out his time? Could they withstand multiple onslaughts? Or were they immune once he had been repelled? Ulric wished there had been time to ask Xya and Skete more details. He and Eleanor and Wint would have to run out the time without giving in to Majszak, but there was no time to articulate that.

Eleanor's eyes rolled back in her head and she clutched the neck of her guitar with such white-knuckled force Ulric thought she might snap it.

She didn't cry out, but her body shook as if wracked by a seizure. Heline ran to her sister, but no song emerged from her throat. One look at her fear-wild eyes told Ulric she was too panicked at Eleanor's peril to come up with a song.

Remembering the arcane formulae he'd used only moments before to build the cage around Majszak's form, he lifted his wand and sketched quick symbols. A glowing golden mesh of recondite energy knitted itself around Eleanor, blooming twice as fast as Ulric had constructed it around Majszak. In his peripheral vision, Nerlim pushed the magic residue toward him without even a grimace. It seemed the older man had mastered the pain of being a sensile just in time.

Then Eleanor gasped and shook her head, making the ridiculous blond braids Nerlim had inadvertently given her swirl. "I'm okay. He didn't get in. Thank you."

Heline sobbed a sigh of relief and Ulric let the spell go. As the intricate golden weave dissipated, Eleanor threw him a smile of such warmth that he felt it flutter against his face like a physical thing.

He was so distracted that he didn't notice Wint's distress until a whimper escaped from him. Ulric turned to see Wint's eyes squeezed shut, a dreadful scowl contorting his face. He clutched his fists against his chest, and his lips moved in a whisper almost beneath hearing.

Eleanor played a chord and Heline startled and began to sing, her wits unmuddled now that her sister was safe.

Now let us rise, our spirits bright,
To vanquish darkness, bar the night,
With unity, our hands entwined,
While forces all around align.

But Wint continued to scowl, his features puckered tight.

Ulric glanced down and saw that the teaspoon no longer glowed, and he chanced picking it up. The silver felt warm, but no longer hot. He forced the handle into one of Wint's clenched fists. It glittered in his hand, and runnels of silver light streamed from it and curved around his body. "Not this time," Wint muttered. "I haven't had a choice in any of this, but I'm making a choice now. No one else is using me today."

But there was no sign of Wint's struggle abating.

Majszak must be fighting harder now, with time and available bodies running out. Ulric raised his wand, but hesitated. If time remained, Majszak would come for him next; there was no one else. If he used magic to help Wint, would it leave him less able to defend himself?

But he had to help Wint, too.

Ulric began to mutter the formula just as the soft plink of Jans' kalimba joined the song. Nerlim rolled a wave of arcane energy toward them and Wint threw his head back with a shout.

"And stay out!" he yelled, shaking the hand holding the teaspoon at the lavender sky.

Ulric saw a phalanx of concerned eyes turn toward him, and the world dissolved into black.

Ulric didn't know what the experience had been like for the others—there hadn't been time to discuss it. It had looked like a painful and distressing experience, but he stood alone in a dark, quiet corridor. Pinpricks of light flickered at either end, but neither was close. The silence was so deep it was almost painful, as if the vacuum of sound tugged at his eardrums.

"Thaumaturge Avatar," a voice addressed him, booming into the quiet. "You will help me."

"I don't think so," Ulric answered, and he was relieved his voice didn't shake. "You're not good for the world."

Majszak laughed a humourless laugh. "How would you know, little boy? You haven't been in the world long enough to know anything yet."

Ulric drew himself up. He still held the wand in his hand, and it felt warm and comforting, even if it might not help him in this place. "I know trouble when I see it." He summoned as much defiance as he could muster. "And you're it. Everyone agrees, even people who don't live on D'Sharu. You were in prison for a reason."

"You seem to think I'm *asking*." Majszak wasn't laughing now.

Ulric found it difficult to breathe. It wasn't as if he were being choked—there was no force, no pressure at his throat. But pulling in a breath just—didn't work. His lungs failed to fill and he clawed at the wall of the corridor, struggling to stand.

"No," he wheezed. "I don't have to agree. I can keep you out."

"Not if you're not awake. And the lack of oxygen will mean you'll pass out very quickly." Majszak's voice took on a note of feigned concern. "Perhaps it would be easier on you if you didn't fight it." At either end of the hallway, the pinpricks of light winked out as if doors had closed.

Although he had no breath to speak again, Ulric spat words at Majszak with his mind. *I'll fight and keep fighting*, he thought. *And my friends are helping me—*

"I don't see any friends," Majszak mocked him. "I don't hear any friends. Just you and me, all alone, in the silence, in a battle you can't win."

Ulric slid down the wall, dropping his wand. It clattered on the unseen floor and rolled away from him. He didn't have the strength to scrabble for it. To do that he'd need energy, and to have energy he'd have to breathe—

And then it reached him. Faint—so faint that at first he wasn't sure it was anything but the ringing in his ears from lack of oxygen. A word...the plink of a note...the ring of a chord. They tunnelled into the darkness and the silence, opening a tiny crack in Ulric's prison. A ray of light forced its way through the crack, wan and pale but enough to scratch a hole in the utter blackness. Enough to let in a waft of air, warm against his face...Ulric gulped, and gulped again.

"No!" grated Majszak. "You *will* let me in! You have power, but you're only a boy. I didn't come all this way to be beaten by a mere boy—"

Ulric fetched a full, deep breath, forcing the air to fill his lungs to their very depths. The crack widened, and the gold-painted tip of his wand glittered in the burgeoning light. He snatched it up. The edges of the crack ran with silver, bright and thick as mercury. "You're right. You won't be beaten by a mere boy."

He sketched arcane symbols in the air with his wand, summoning the magic, the formulae writing themselves on the blackboard of his mind. "You'll be beaten by a boy, and a girl with a guitar, and her sister whose songs are magic, and an old scientist who didn't give up, and a woman who's conquering the stars, and a man who didn't want any of this but did it anyway. And their friends," he added, crossing the last line through the arcane symbol he was sketching. Magic bloomed around him like the bands of a rainbow, and the crack burst the wall wide open, and music poured in, enveloping Ulric in a wave of sound and light. "*And a very good dog!*" he yelled, as the walls and Majszak's scream of rage fell away together.

When Ulric opened his eyes, he was flat on his back, looking up at a hazy purple sky and a ring of worried faces peering down at him. Gammy's was the closest as she knelt beside him, as she'd done after he fainted when the Hat first spoke to him.

"You all right, boy? You fought him for a long time."

Ulric struggled to get his elbows under him, still feeling as if he couldn't catch his breath. "Is he gone? Did we do it?"

The others glanced at each other. Heline said, "We think so? It's been more than a minute since you seemed to stop fighting him, and there haven't been any more attacks."

Rex padded over and sat at Ulric's feet. "Did everyone forget about me?" the dog asked in a low, ominous voice.

Ulric's heart clenched and Gammy fell back against Nerlim's legs.

"No," Eleanor breathed. "Not the dog—he couldn't have gone into the dog!"

Rex barked a laugh and winked at Ulric. "The girl's right—Xya told you an animal brain couldn't support Majszak. I was just messing with you."

It was probably a good thing for the manifestation of technology, aka Rex the dog, that The Min, Xya, Skete, Azuriia, Drix, and Ignacjianna arrived on Old Mean Melvin's farm at that moment.

INTERMEZZO DIECI - EPILOGUE

THE MIN

"So, as soon as the worldweft calmed, I collected Xya and Skete first, and banished Sedrict and Alsina back to the astral plane. I'll deal with them when I return. Corax too, although he wasn't guilty of crimes at the same level."

"Throw the book at him," Gammy urged, in between sipping her iced tea with appreciative vigour. "He didn't help matters much, either."

Hey! said a voice in their heads. *That's not nice!*

Gammy smiled at *Echoes of Potentiality.* "Don't worry, I didn't mean you."

The Min smiled, too. "I rather think Corax's encounter with Majszak was quite sobering, but it's something he and I will discuss. And then Xya and Skete directed us to come here," The Min finished explaining. "It wasn't hard to track you, since your magic use was glowing like a beacon by then. But of course, by that time, you didn't need our help. My apologies for that, but well done, all of you."

The film of purplish gauze no longer enveloped Old Mean Melvin's farm. The Min's first act upon arriving, once she determined everyone was safe and the threats had been neutralized, had been to parley with the Old Magic. A tentative peace agreement had been reached, whereby the Magic could continue to slumber unmolested at the farm, under The Min's own protection, involving itself in the workings of D'Sharu only if it wished. Which at this time, it fervently did not wish, so that seemed to work out for the best.

When the Magic lifted its barrier, The Min replaced it with one of her own, invisible, but allowing those within to relax and recover while they sorted through the events of the last few days. Since the sun had peeked over the pink and orange streaked horizon, it bathed the farmyard in bright and comforting early-morning light. Only the faintest arcane shimmer when the light hit just right betrayed where the protective barrier ended.

Ulric had been worried. "Should we go somewhere else? What if Old Mean Melvin comes home?"

The Min had smiled. For the sake of everyone's comfort, she and the other trans-dimensional beings had moulded their appearance to something approximating D'sharian. The occasional coruscation of starry light still flashed in The Min's hair, and Ignacjianna's hair flickered, but it was close enough to make the others comfortable. Drix and Azuriia had returned to the trans-dimensional realm to make sure Sedrict and Alsina were restrained. "Let's just say that I've temporarily moved the farm out of the usual flow of time," The Min said. "So the owner won't return until we're ready for him."

Ulric seemed to find that answer only somewhat comforting, but he nodded acceptance. Tiny Enos, Arcanico, and the Book had all been retrieved from their post at the end of the driveway, and at The Min's urging, everyone retreated to the grassy sward behind the barn where the cows pastured. With only a few words and gestures, The Min produced a shaded gazebo, outdoor lounge chairs for everyone, bottomless cold drinks in condensation-swathed glasses, and a nearby water feature providing soothing trickle and splash sounds. A plush, pristine dog bed waited for Rex, and decorative plinths stood ready to receive Arcanico and the Book, which had asked to be called Echo.

When all were seated and settled, she'd asked for their stories, and by the time those had been recounted, the drinks had been refilled several times. Nerlim and Gammy had dozed off after telling their tales, but no one had the heart to wake them. When others began to yawn, The Min said, "Nothing can replace a good night's rest, but if no one objects, perhaps I'll give you all a boost to get us through the rest of our visit."

Hearing no demurrals, she made a gesture and was rewarded to see everyone sit up straighter in their chairs, eyes once again bright and interested. Even Nerlim and Gammy woke up, only mildly embarrassed to discover they'd fallen asleep holding hands, their chairs scooted close to each other. Then she'd offered her explanation of how she and the others had arrived at the farm.

"It's been quite the adventure for you all," The Min acknowledged, twisting three fingers in an offhand gesture. Small plates of delicate sandwiches and sweets appearing next to the drinks. "You must be hungry, so please help yourselves. Because although Majszak's threat has been resolved, there's still the matter of magic versus technology on D'Sharu to be addressed."

After a brief pause, wherein looks were exchanged around the tableau, Rex spoke first. "I've released the Technocrat Avatar from his obligations," he said. "If matters were to proceed as usual, I'd have to appoint another one, but—well, I'm hoping I won't need to."

Wint looked exceedingly relieved at this announcement.

The Min's eyebrows rose, but she nodded for him to continue. Instead, the Hat spoke. "We've been conferring in the background, to tell you the truth, while the others have told their stories. Rex and I and Ulric. We want to propose an alternate solution to the ascendancy question."

The Min was not at all surprised by this, having been surreptitiously monitoring their mental conversation because she was, after all, *The Min.* However, she merely said, "What do you suggest?"

"We want to work together. We think magic and technology can co-exist here, if we phase it in and give people time to get used to the idea."

"Hmm." The Min steepled her fingers and tapped them together. "There's a small matter of science involved, however. These are natural forces that don't play well together. They interfere with each other. They don't co-exist. Nerlim will tell you that."

Nerlim raised his eyebrows, considering. "It is essentially true."

"There may be some aspects we need help with." Ulric glanced at Rex and Arcanico. "But the manifestations of the forces are on board, so that must count for something. And we're hoping you—or an envoy from you—could lend some assistance with that."

I can help! Echo volunteered. *I know the history of what happened with the Old Magic, and I'm no slouch in the magic department myself. And I'm not going back to being shut away in that library, no matter what happens,* it added in a sombre tone. *I love libraries, of course, but I don't need to live in one and never get out.*

"I don't think I have time to be your full-time caretaker," Tiny Enos told the Book, "but maybe you could visit me sometimes, and I'll take you out and about."

"I'll volunteer my services as well," Nerlim offered. "Both with the Book and with implementing the blended forces idea. I'm a decent mix of science and magic myself, so I'm sure I can help."

"I'll be busy with the moon launch," Gammy said, "but Nerlim's going to need a hobby while I'm at work." A sudden blush deepened the colour of her cheeks when she realized the implications of what she'd said, but Nerlim grinned at her and she relaxed.

The others all added their support for the idea then, and The Min pursed her lips, tapping them with a neatly manicured finger. Starlight flickered in her hair and mischief bloomed like a nebula in her eyes. "I don't know. It will mean a lot more work for me, monitoring how things are going. Planets with both forces acting as equals are few and far between."

Ulric sat up straighter in his comfortable seat. His hands gripped the chair arms, and The Min suspected it was to hide a tremble. He glanced at Eleanor, sitting next to him, and she gave him an encouraging nod. Ulric cleared his throat. "Well, we're not going to fight. We've decided that and it's settled. So you'll have to suggest some other idea if you don't like ours."

The Min nodded, her expression grave. "So you'd defy my instructions if I said the only choice was to follow established protocols?"

"We would," the Hat said, and the others added their nods and agreement.

"I could force the issue," The Min mused. She gestured around at their idyllic seating, the perfect light and weather, the protective time envelope she'd slipped around them. "I'm...not without the power to do so."

"But you won't," Heline said. She regarded The Min with her head tilted to one side, smiling. "I think you're secretly delighted that things have gone this way. You're looking forward to seeing how things work out."

The Min laughed then, a sound like music from another realm. "You're absolutely right. I was just checking." She leaned back and surveyed the motley assemblage before her. "This is going to be interesting."

A month later—well, a month counted in D'sharian time—The Min was at her desk when a sharp rapping sounded again at her office door. The books on the towering bookshelves surrounding her shifted and whispered, still in defiance of gravity and interested in what the knock might portend.

The Min sighed. "Come in," she called, tamping down the prick of annoyance she felt at the interruption.

Skete sauntered in through the imaginary door in response, this time relaxed and smiling. "Just dropping by to report on D'Sharu." He plopped down in a red leather armchair The Min conveniently conjured for him.

"You know I can monitor that planet just fine on my own," she reminded him, raising an eyebrow. "I do it all the time."

"I know. But there's nothing like the personal touch," he said. "And you did give me permission to visit and help, remember?"

"I remember. All right, report." She sat forward and laced her great hands, sparkling with stardust, in front of her on the desk.

"Well, the manifestation of technology—Rex—is beyond happy living with Heline and Jans," he started. "I know you thought Wint might benefit from having a pet, but he's got a cat now and it's a much better fit. Heline helped him find a suitable non-magical rescue and they've settled in nicely."

The Min nodded. "He needed something more independent than a dog. And non-speaking. He's doing well, too?"

"Yes. Back at work at NCDSF and heading the Fifth Force Space Integration Task Force Gammy set up."

"Excellent. Ulric?"

"School's back in session for him, but he's meeting with Nerlim, Heline, and Eleanor twice a week. Arcanico and Echo are mentoring them all in magic and they're experimenting with the intricacies of combining magic and technology. Wint joins them sometimes."

"I'm meeting them for a progress report next month," The Min said. "I'll give them a few lines of inquiry to follow—not too much at once, I think. Just hints, and allow them to find their own way."

It was Skete's turn to nod. "They're smart. They can figure it out. No need to hand-feed them."

"I'm glad you approve," The Min said dryly.

"Eleanor's staying with Heline and she and Ulric are—an item," Skete said, waggling his eyebrows.

The Min rolled her eyes. "You think I couldn't see that coming? I was reading their minds at that debriefing, remember?"

Skete threw up his hands. "All right, all right. I suppose you know Gammy and Nerlim are planning a winter wedding, too."

"Did I mention I'm monitoring the planet?"

"I thought you'd appreciate a personal report once in a while," Skete complained.

"I'm sorry. It is nice," The Min assured him, relenting. "Well, the next time you're down there, you can tell them that Corax is doing mild penance for his transgressions and hating every minute." She smiled, thinking of the fastidious man's horror at having to clean the trans-dimensional cafeteria space every weekend. The beings who ate there could get quite...imaginative in their petty disputes and rivalries. "And Alsina and Sedrict have been exiled to their own prison planets. Majszak is locked down tighter than ever. Let them know I saw to that myself, and they don't have to worry about any of them making trouble again."

"Will do. Oh, and Jans got the robot installed at the theme park," Skete added. "That was a stroke of genius on his part, I must say. I didn't know what else they'd ever do with it."

"So it's all going pretty well," The Min said, leaning back in her chair. "And the planet's settled down; worldweft back to normal. The Book was helpful in that respect, since it had been in the world for so long."

"We got lucky in a lot of ways," Skete mused. "It could have turned out a lot worse."

"Lucky?" The Min sighed, then gave Skete a rare smile. "Perhaps. Or maybe we just got good people. When you have that, you don't need luck."

"I'll take that as a compliment," Skete said, and on the shelves all around them, the books rustled with laughter. The Min couldn't help but join in.

THE END

Notes and Acknowledgements

This book is one of my few novels (the only published one to date, for sure) that did *not* begin life as a National Novel Writing Month project. That's because the origins of *The Fifth Force* predate my November writing adventures. That's right, I began writing this story previous to 2002—in fact, the earliest incarnation of it resides in a file dated 1997.

1997. That means I worked on this book, on and off (let's face it: mostly off) for *twenty-seven years*.

The Fifth Force started life as a "just-for-fun" project and remained that for a long time; the story I'd turn to for no-stress, playful, anything-goes writing. I had no plan for it, no deadline, no inkling that anyone else would ever read it, so I simply played.

Somewhere along the line, that changed. I loved these characters and had so much fun with them and their silly universe, I decided maybe I *would* share it. It was almost written to the end, after all, so I could probably finish it quickly (I told myself). There were just a *few things* I had to fix before I could figure out the ending...and thus began the Great Revision. I broke the cardinal rule of revising novels (for many writers, anyway, and certainly for me)—*finish the draft first*.

Predictably (for me), I'd fallen into the trap suffered by many discovery writers, or intuitive writers, or yes, just call us pantsers. The story went off the rails before I'd written the ending, and numerous story threads had jumbled into a Gordian knot, blocking the path. Unravelling that knot was a process I tackled many times, thinking I'd sorted it out, and then I'd run up against another snarled thread and put the manuscript away, to go off to work on something else while I thought my way through the tangle.

In other words, I gave in to procrastination with this story—many times. Twenty-seven years' worth of times, to be precise. But finally…I set a real deadline, one with accountability. In January 2023, I began posting chapters of *The Fifth Force* to my Patreon page, and offering it as an early access perk to Patrons. I wouldn't post a chapter until I felt it was fairly close to final draft form, and I set a schedule that would leave me lots of time to get that tricky ending written before I had to post it. I thought I'd build momentum with revisions and then decimate that knot with my sword made of sharp new words.

Or something.

You see where this leads, right? The p-word again. We won't say too much about the posting gaps, the apologies, and the catching-up my Patrons had to tolerate, nor the solid week of 10+ hour days of revisions and editing it took to meet my pre-order deadline. Because, of course, setting a publication date and opening pre-orders was the only way I'd ever force myself to finish it. I don't *enjoy* being a deadliner, but it works for me. So, thanks, Patrons, and my sincere apologies.

Anyway, it worked. You've just read it, and I hope, enjoyed it. It was only ever meant to be fun, so I hope it meets that standard. It's also my personal homage to the magnificent writers Sir Terry Pratchett and Douglas Adams, whose whimsical yet profound works influenced me in so many ways. (So, yes, the footnotes!) I can't hope to equal these writers, but I hope I've learned from them.

Twenty-seven years is a long time to remember every detail of writing this book, and I can't even try. But I know that my family supported it as they support every writing project I undertake; I know that people who read snippets that made them laugh encouraged me to keep going; and I know that my good writer friend Kerry Anne Campbell proofread like a maniac for me, helping me hit that last deadline. Her keen eyes and careful reading saved you, dear reader, from many a typo and moment of confusion, so many thanks to her for that.

For ongoing feedback, input, and support in all aspects of the writing life, thanks to my writing group colleagues in The Story Forge, The Quillians, and Genre Writers of Atlantic Canada. And for support in *all* aspects of life, thanks to my amazing family and friends, near and far.

Now, what ancient manuscript languishing on my hard drive will I pick up next?

ABOUT THE AUTHOR

Sherry D. Ramsey is a speculative fiction writer, editor, publisher, creativity addict and self-confessed internet geek. When she's not writing, she reads, gardens, makes stuff, teaches, hones her creative procrastination skills on social media, and consumes far more coffee and chocolate than is likely good for her.

Her books include four books in the Nearspace series (for space opera fans); seven stories in the Olympia Investigations series (for urban fantasy mystery fans); a middle-grade science fiction novel, *Planet Fleep*; the middle-grade fantasy, *The Seventh Crow*; the urban fantasy/ mystery *The Murder Prophet*; and three short story collections. With her partners at Third Person Press she has co-edited six anthologies of regional short fiction and longer work. Every November she disappears into the strange realm of National Novel Writing Month and emerges gasping at the end, clutching something resembling a novel.

A member of the Writer's Federation of Nova Scotia Writer's Council, Sherry is also a past Vice-President and Secretary-Treasurer of SF Canada, Canada's national association for Speculative Fiction Professionals.

You can visit Sherry online at www.sherrydramsey.com to find free stories and more, connect on Facebook at https://www.facebook.com/SherryDRamseyAuthor and keep up with her much more pithy musings and glimpses into her life on Instagram, Threads, and BlueSky @sdramsey and Mastodon @sdramsey@wandering.shop. For a good roundup of titles with easy retail links, check out her Books2Read page at https://books2read.com/ap/xqLyW8/Sherry-D-Ramsey. **And be sure** to find her newsletter signup and get your free book at http://eepurl.com/bCUWPX.

*Scan for my
LinkTree!*

Also by Sherry D. Ramsey
Nearspace
One's Aspect to the Sun
Dark Beneath the Moon
Beyond the Sentinel Stars
A Veiled and Distant Sky
Waiting to Fly
Magica Incognita
The Murder Prophet
Olympia Investigations
Addicted to Love
The Goddess Problem
Dead Hungry
Toil and Trouble
Subordinate Clauses
The Shifter Plague
Olympia Investigations: The First Four Cases
Science Twins
Planet Fleep: A Science Twins Adventure
Standalone
The Cache and Other Stories
The Apprentice Files
Alien Gifts: Five Short Stories

The Seventh Crow
Unraptured
Beacon and Other Stories
To Unimagined Shores
* * *